'A captivating and g
nostalgia and renewa

Sophie Han

author of *The Couple at the Table*

'An evocative and mesmerising tale of three generations of women, *Letters from Elena* sweeps you into the heart of Cyprus with its breathtaking descriptions and deeply human storytelling. The rich landscapes, culture, and intricate history come alive on the page.'

Lucy O'Callaghan, author of *The Lies Beneath*

'Anne Hamilton beautifully transports the reader to the stunning island of Cyprus, where the writer's vivid descriptions bring its landscapes, culture, and difficult history to life. A truly immersive read!'

Ruth O'Leary bestselling author of
The Weekend Break

'A warm and heartfelt examination of what attracts us to others and what keeps us connected over the years.'

Catherine Simpson, author of *Truestory*

'A gorgeous, haunting novel. Amid the precarity of our small lives in the sweep of history, love may be our greatest strength. April's story, like the stories of those around her, is captivating and deeply moving.'

Zoë Strachan, author of
Catch the Moments as They Fly

'Beautifully written, *Letters from Elena* is at times funny, heart-wrenching and surprising. It's also full of love, acceptance and ultimately, hope. It is a perfect read.'

Sharon Black, author of
The Life Daisy Devlin Designed

'With a deft hand and a stunning eye for detail, Anne Hamilton has woven together themes of friendship, music, and art, and wrapped them around a childhood mystery that is set against the turbulent backdrop of Cyprus... A masterful, melodic symphony of words that will enthral readers from start to finish. This one is a keep-forever novel.'

Clo Carey

'Since reading her first manuscript, *A Blonde Bengali Wife*, I have loved Anne's writing – that book inspired us to start the charity, Bhola's Children. In *Letters From Elena*, she retains her brilliant ability to conjure up people and places.'

Dinah Wiener

'A perfectly woven story of past and present friendships. Full of emotion, this will stay with you long after you've read it... Totally absorbing.'

Valerie Griffin

Letters
from
Elena

Anne Hamilton

Legend Press Ltd, 51 Gower Street, London, WC1E 6HJ
info@legendtimesgroup.co.uk | www.legendpress.co.uk

Contents © Anne Hamilton 2025

The right of the above author to be identified as the author of this work has been asserted in accordance with the Copyright, Designs and Patents Act 1988. British Library Cataloguing in Publication Data available.

Print ISBN 9781915643339
Ebook ISBN 9781915643346
Set in Times.
Cover by Ditte Løkkegaard

The quote on page 9 is reproduced with permission of Curtis Brown Group Ltd, London on behalf of The Estate of Lawrence Durrell. Copyright © Lawrence Durrell.

All characters, other than those clearly in the public domain, and place names, other than those well-established such as towns and cities, are fictitious and any resemblance is purely coincidental.

All rights reserved. No part of this publication may be reproduced, stored in or introduced into a retrieval system, or transmitted, in any form, or by any means electronic, mechanical, photocopying, recording or otherwise, without the prior permission of the publisher. Any person who commits any unauthorised act in relation to this publication may be liable to criminal prosecution and civil claims for damages.

Anne Hamilton is an author, editor and creative writing tutor who lives between Edinburgh, Suffolk and Co. Mayo, with her teenage son. Her first book, a travel memoir titled *A Blonde Bengali Wife* (2010) was based on her experiences in Bangladesh, which inspired and still supports the charity, Bhola's Children. Her debut novel *The Almost Truth* (Legend Press 2024) was the winner of the Irish Novel Fair, arising from a short story in the Edinburgh Charity anthology, *The People's City* (Birlinn 2022). *Letters from Elena* is Anne's second novel.

Anne has a PhD in Creative Writing from the University of Glasgow, and currently works with The Open University, The University of Cambridge and Edinburgh Council Adult Education. She is also one-fifth of the collaborative author group that received National Lottery Funding to write and edit the novel *Entitled* (KDP 2022). Her work has been listed in several competitions, including the Lucy Cavendish Prize, the Yeovil Prize and the Blue Pencil First Novel Award.

"But that is what islands are for; they are places where different destinies can meet and intersect in the full isolation of time."

Lawrence Durrell, *Bitter Lemons of Cyprus*

Prologue

Wednesday 17th July 1974

Dear April,

We have to go now and they won't let me say goodbye. I am leaving you the picture of the tree houses. Remember that we have promised to meet there one day.

Sorry.

Love from, Elena Z
xxx

1

There's a man watching me.

He watched me yesterday as I paused by the wishing tree, its branches decorated with ribbons and scraps of coloured cloth. He was there as I ordered coffee from the kiosk beside the tiny harbour church, a cloudy glass in his own hand. When the sun sank over the distant lighthouse and I closed this balcony door against the evening chill, I could see him on the beach. Indifferent to the floodlit terrace of the Verena Bay Hotel, he was still watching, taut like a mongoose seeking its young. Then all of a sudden he put his head down and bent his body over a sheaf of pages. I could make out the pencil in his left hand, hovering.

He's down by the pool now, doing exactly the same thing.

And the weirdest thing of all? There's an elephant figurine in his shirt pocket, and regularly, on a cue invisible to me, he takes it out and taps it three times. He kisses it then puts it gently back.

I don't know if it's the elephant or his staring that unnerves me most.

I creep backwards, press myself into the doorway, and wait. When I've waited long enough to feel foolish, I take another peek. The man has gone. Inside my room, I check the doors are locked, the hotel phone has a dial tone and, like a bad spy, I sit the stone doorstop on the bed beside me – just in case he tries to get in and I can't get out. This is the third day of him watching, and normal people would have said something by now, but the heady mix of sun, self-interest and sheer incredulity that I'm even here have taken the edge off.

At breakfast, across crumpled tablecloths, sticky with spilled honey and stained with discarded coffee spoons, the picture window frames the man's shaved head and slender silhouette; he's still watching me. Defiant, over a plate of halloumi and olives, I stare right back. He doesn't react. Unsettling? Reassuring? Whatever he sees in me, it somehow isn't *me*. In the circumstances, it's fitting because *I'm* no longer one hundred per cent sure who I am either: me, April Zarney, the last person likely to do things on a whim, is here on a whim in Cyprus.

Here. At last.

And alone.

Oh dear God, what have I done?

I realise I'm drumming my fingers on the table in time to the tapping of my toes. Opposite, my stalker is stroking the toy elephant with his right thumb and shovelling scrambled eggs into his mouth with his other hand. I push back my chair, clear my place and seek out Petros, my host, my friend, who's in the office adjoining the makeshift reception area. He's instructing his newest, shapeliest receptionist in the apparent mysteries of the monthly accounts – or so he says. When he sees me, he sends her off for coffee; she looks affronted and ignores my apologetic smile.

'*Kalimera*, my dear April.' Petros slides reading glasses onto his forehead. He raises a brow that shows off washed-denim eyes; arresting eyes, twinned as they are with his Mediterranean skin.

'Morning – I mean, *kalimera*. Petros,' I hurry on before he can give me an impromptu Greek lesson, 'who's that man over there? The one with the elephant in his shirt pocket?'

He glances across at the restaurant area. 'Ah, yes. I thought you might notice him.'

'Not quite as much as he seems to notice me.'

Petros' lips twitch. 'I wondered when you would mention it. He is Andreas. Andreas Koumettou? I could introduce you but I expect he has fallen in love with you. If I am right, it is better you speak to his wife...'

He lets that hang, but since it was Petros himself who informed me that the best conversation is 'one which charms unreservedly and shocks just enough', I refuse to rise to the bait.

'Well, please tell Andreas' wife...?'

'Nicole.'

I turn to sweep grandly out of the foyer. 'Then please tell Nicole... Oh.' I register the name and my self-righteous face falls. I turn back and Petros is looking shifty. 'Nicole?'

'Yes.'

'The *same* Nicole?'

'The same-as-what Nicole?' His brow creases; all innocence.

It would please him so very, very dearly if I called him out. Instead, I allow myself a tiny glare. 'Nicole, your friend and neighbour. The Nicole you told me I'll love but I've yet to meet. The Nicole who can apparently help me...' There's more but I run out of steam; Petros is grinning.

'Yes,' he says. '*That* Nicole. I'm sure I mentioned her husband was an artist.'

I shake my head. 'I expect you just forgot to tell me he was voyeuristic with it?'

'Andreas is gifted. Perhaps a tad obsessive.' He leans back in his chair, hands behind his head, and grins some more. 'I admit it. I let it slip my mind. Does it matter?'

Yes, it does. What else hasn't Petros told me? 'I suppose not.' I call his bluff. 'Okay then. See you later.'

Petros calls after me. 'April, dear girl, wait. If Nicole does call today, where will she find you?'

I pause again. 'Her husband is sure to know. She can follow him, following me. We'll conga out through the gates and make a merry procession through the sweating party streets of Agia Napa.'

'Hoity-toity!' Petros' shout of laughter is an echo in the wind. 'I believe "party central" is the accolade now given to Ibiza. And remember this is unseasonable April here. And Easter Sunday morning.'

'Alright. I'll be in the garden,' I amend. 'Thinking. Hopefully all on my own.'

'I will have a word with Andreas,' Petros promises. 'And later, I'll bring you elevenses. A peace offering.'

With a blanket over my arm and a book in my bag, I follow the wrap-around terrace to the water's edge, dithering over the perfect spot to sit back and practise doing nothing. If I'm shivering, it's nothing to do with a stalking Andreas – like a dream that vanishes when it's spoken out loud, he's no longer lurking – but the sun is still waking up. With the gulls swooping, the sea lapping and the wind gusting half-heartedly, it's a day to imagine flute music, high and flighty and fun, with maybe a hint of melancholy viola before the orchestra crashes in, triumphant... There's a composition exercise in there somewhere.

'You're the eternal musician, April,' I mutter aloud. Yes. Right. The totally professional, *dependable* musician who has burnt her boats, her bridges, and probably set the Mariana Trench on fire by running away and hiding at the dilapidated edge of a troubled island. I shiver again, hold a half-breath in tense shoulders and count to five. It doesn't help. Instead, I drag a metal table and chair nearer to the shelter of the whitewashed hotel building, sit down and fidget. The book I've brought with me, grandly titled *Running with the Devil: Power, Gender, and Madness in Heavy Metal Music*, is unappealing, mocking me from my old life, and I don't get past page eight.

As Petros reminded me, it's Sunday, and the highest holy

day in the Greek Orthodox Church's calendar. A series of crackles and dull booms then a squawking sound system herald what must be Mass from Agia Triada, being relayed around the bay. Whether this is because the tiny church is already crammed with devout worshippers or a save-the-slumbering-sinners outreach programme, I don't know. As a tone-deaf priest murders the Liturgy, a hooligan cat gang, chasing and yowling like hyperactive boys in a playground, quickly starts matching him shriek for shriek. It cheers me up no end: I can't be expected to relax with that racket going on, nobody could.

I've been meaning to come to Cyprus for thirty years – long, long before I met Petros and he issued an open invitation – but never like this and not on my own. This particular trip was the brainchild of my ex-partner, Jake, and I was along for the ride. Jake is the type with what my mother would have called 'notions'. A cross between a cuckoo and a magpie, snatching up a shiny bright hobby from any passing acquaintance and dropping it hastily when the next one comes along. He is charming and boyish and earnest and at first I found it all so endearing and let myself be swept along.

Jake's attraction to Cyprus was, of all things, wild orchids. Faux jealous of my passing acquaintanceship with Petros – whom I'd only met because his aunt and my parents lived in the same English nursing home – he inveigled himself in. Petros had left his Aunt Ana a book on wildflowers because they both knew the author, Yiannis Loizos, and Jake, bored and restless, affected an interest. He then jumped on an orchid bandwagon, became a self-styled amateur botanist and ended up writing to Yiannis. The upshot was Jake convincing me we needed an orchid-hunting holiday in Cyprus.

When I demurred, he played his trump card. 'You can look for Elena, that little Cypriot friend of yours who you never stop banging on about.'

I was fairly sure I'd only mentioned Elena a couple of times, maybe half a dozen, but back then I said nothing. By Christmas, I'd kind of come round to the idea and the trip was agreed to the extent that we were bickering about it over the mince pies. Me, with island maps spread out on the floor, him with a notebook on his knees, mispronouncing the Latin names of indigenous rare flowers.

'Jake, look.' I flapped the map at him, pointing out where I had traced the zigzag, two thirds up. It showed the Green Line, separating south and north, Greek and Turkish, the slowly unravelling UN buffer zone lying haphazardly in the middle. 'Nicosia is the last divided capital city in Europe. I never knew.'

'Cool. How do you say *Ophys bornmuelleri* properly...?' He was as distracted as ever and I, converted to the trip, held in my breath in case his passion wore off before we bought the tickets. It didn't. In fact, Jake made all the travel arrangements himself, even paying his own share.

Then he spoiled it by taking a wrong turning and ending up on a different island with a different girlfriend.

In a fit of pique more suited to a teenager than a forty-year-old woman, but equally irked that Jake was letting the generous Cypriot botanist down, I took over writing letters to Yiannis Loizos. He – no doubt egged on by Petros – urged me to come over on my own. And in a bigger fit of pique (which really isn't me but then again, a lot has happened in the last year or so) and outright daring, I turned down a contract with the Berlin Philharmonic, and bought a one-way plane ticket here.

I still feel slightly sick when I think about it; I've been forcing myself to sit down and do that every single day and at least now I'm not hyperventilating. The view spread out in front of me certainly helps. Unlikely as it seems, Petros Evagora, half Machiavelli, half ageing Lothario – if you trust his own publicity – and his beautiful, ramshackle Verena Bay Hotel, might actually be my saviours.

I have to stifle a bubble of (slightly hysterical) laughter when, on cue, I hear footsteps, and rounding the corner appears Petros himself, looking like nothing more than a benign butler. He's carrying a large tray with a white cloth and a silver coffee pot, which he places on the wrought-iron table beside me. I feel like the lady of the manor receiving my morning tea.

'Indulge me,' Petros says, as if reading my mind. 'I used to do this for Thia Ana on her rare visits home.' He eyes the coffee pot. 'Although there is somewhat more Nescafé and less whisky involved today.'

'Sugar is more my drug of choice over alcohol.' I help myself to one of the shortbread-esque biscuits as he pours the coffee and hands it to me. 'Here's to your Aunt – ah, sorry.' I swap to my beginner's Greek, 'Your *Thia* Ana,' and raise the cup.

'To Ana, indeed. And to your parents. May they all rest in peace—' My choking sound interrupts the innocuous toast, and he narrows those perceptive eyes. 'What is it, April?'

I could pass it over, blame an errant biscuit crumb, but it feels like a now-or-never moment. 'About my parents... I've a confession.'

'It's good for the soul,' is all he says. Equable.

'My mum and dad are... well... they're here with me. Oh, not literally.' I change tack, I don't want him to think I'm unbalanced, hallucinating. 'I mean their ashes are. They're in... er... a shoebox in my wardrobe. I've been carrying it with me since the funeral.'

'Everywhere?' He stifles a bark of laughter.

'Well, yes. I didn't know what to do with them. I'm still looking for that final resting place.' I feel better now I've said it, emboldened. 'Maybe somewhere here, I thought. Near Ana?'

'Oh, my dear April. Where else?' Petros leans over and squeezes my hand. 'You are all welcome *finally* to Cyprus.'

2

Even without the unlikely and peripatetic presence of Andreas Koumettou, being in Verena Bay is unlike any holiday I've ever had. When I was growing up my parents were devil-uses-idle-hands types, so there was always something to do at home and I don't remember us going away. 'We're staying at home and going out for days,' they'd tell anyone who asked. In recent years I've snatched weekends here and there, even been on short honeymoons (two, in fact – a whole other story), but I'm one of those musicians who never takes real time off. *Was* one of those musicians, I should say. Back-to-back concert performances, masterclasses, practice sessions, teaching – all the elements of a self-employed, good-but-not-great pianist has frequently seen me in seven cities in as many days, escaping the treadmill only to visit my mum and dad. They never complained about my feast-or-famine appearances; they never complained about anything.

Here, now, there are no rules. No timetables. No expectations. I'm drunk on it and scared of it, both. I'm waking late, eating frequently, reading books rather than scores and textbooks (I can't bring myself to ditch *Running with the Devil* totally; Robert Walser is a musicologist I admire, but gleefully I lap up Jilly Cooper and Dan Brown from Petros' leave-one-take-one hotel bookshelf), and thinking as little as I can while I sit in the sun, swim and pass the time of day with Petros and his casual handful of hotel guests. It's a crash course in relaxation. The fixed point of my day is practising for pleasure, not work, on Petros' old but carefully tuned grand piano in the dark and old-fashioned 'good' sitting room. And scales and arpeggios are as automatic as breathing; I've done them every day since I was ten.

But old habits clearly do die hard because today, by the time Petros is ready to clear the tea things, I'm fretting for an adventure. 'Just a little one,' I tell him, by which I mean a safe and contained outing – and he knows it.

'Take the jeep. Drive the coast roads and park up along the sand.'

'What do I do when it breaks down again?' I'm not mechanically minded and I've not been out alone, driving.

'Be spontaneous. Live life without a plan.' He pulls the keys from his pocket and tosses them onto the table. 'Someone will recognise the jeep and bring you home.'

Despite myself, I can't help but rise to the amused hint of challenge. Before I can dwell on the wheezing decrepitude of the battered car, I snatch up the keys. 'Alright, I will.' And as Petros mooches back to the bar, I stride up the hill, under the frothy purple bougainvillea arch of the entrance, to the tiny lay-by he calls a car park.

It's warm now, the sun like an egg yolk in plasticine-perfect blue sky, and I roll up the plastic sides that do for doors on the decommissioned, once-military jeep. I climb in and coax it to start, which it does first time, but grudgingly – a pensioner dragged out of retirement too often. I pat the steering wheel in consolation, and quell my misgivings.

The road is empty with only a grass verge and intermittent crash barrier between me and the shore. There are a few houses – beach huts or whitewashed bungalows, but it's silent, somehow timeless. And getting even warmer. Warm, warm, warm. I fiddle with the radio for something uplifting, thinking better of it when the metal dials all but burn the tips of my fingers. I fumble through my own mental playlist but nothing is right so I make do with a cappella humming: half-remembered arrangements of obscure Easter hymns. Sometimes, Church-like triumphal music fills my head for days and can be enough to move me to great intentions, occasionally actions. I don't think I believe in God, but I want to believe in Easter, or more likely Anastasis, as Petros told me the Greeks here call it: resurgence or renewal; new life. Today, the best thing though is that there's nobody – Jake, for example – to object if I belt out the odd chorus.

Ahead of me, a dilapidated sign tacked to a tree says *Nissi Beach*, then in smaller letters *The Bunch of Grapes Inn*. I've heard that before. From Petros, probably... Ah, no. Jake, again. Of course it was Jake. I yank the complaining steering wheel sharp left and swerve off the road, stopping rather than parking.

There, by the waters of Nissi, I sit down, slip off my sandals, and weep.

I could pretend I'm lamenting thirty years of Cyprus' lost identity, but that's a pretentious Jake-remark, not mine. Yes, I *am* crying for Elena, now I'm here, how could I not? Elena is where my life as I know it all started. So mostly I'm crying for myself. For a career in jeopardy. For touching forty with no family left. For two failed marriages. For... I don't know what else, and I can almost hear my father's gentle rebuke. 'Self-pity isn't becoming, April. You choose your moods and whilst there may be a time, a short time, for anger or fear, self-pity deserves not a second.' He would have sent me for a brisk walk; my mum calling after me to count my blessings as I went.

There's worse advice, I think. Why not walk it off? In fact, why not run? Alright, so it's a very sedate, unathletic 'run' but who's to see, to judge? I splash through the ankle-deep water and then onto the sand, eventually jumping up and down on the spot as if it's a trampoline and I'm conducting an invisible air orchestra in some energetic Mozart. I stop, breathless, bow and look out to sea. From here, I could tread through the shallow waves to the small rock of an island that gives Nissi its Greek name. But beyond that, the vision I've carried of Agia Napa as a simple fishing village is wishful, fuelled only by Elena's childhood memories, shared thirty years ago. It was built into the hill, she'd once said, crammed with stone cottages, all out of shape like too many crooked teeth in a mouth.

But this is 2004, I remind myself, not the early 1970s, so this town is deserted, as silent as the war-ruined ghost town of its invisible neighbour, coastal Famagusta. Agia Napa is waiting for the evening, possibly sleeping heavy with the burden of history and of change, but mostly under the weight of a thousand hungover 18–30 package trippers, turning collectively in someone else's wrinkled sheets and dreaming of the 'All-Day-Breakfast Special' at the Plato Café. 'Snob,' I tell myself, though it's more that I've *never* been 18–30, even when I was. Sensible. Cautious. That's me. Except maybe for that year with Elena.

Nostalgia for a place I never knew is killed by my imaginings of modern Agia Napa so I meander towards the closed Bunch of Grapes Inn where, energy spent and mood levelled, I collapse onto springy turf. Wispy wildflowers – red, purple, yellow – huddle against the stone and moss, and idly I wonder if any of them is an orchid. Yiannis will tell me when I finally meet him; ironically, he flew to England the day I flew out. I close my eyes, let the sun wash over my face and decide, with determination and trepidation in equal measure, to embrace being alone.

Except I'm not. There's a light tap on my shoulder and I blink rapidly at the girl crouching down and placing her purple shoulder bag on the ground in front of me.

'Excuse me?' she says. 'You are April, I think? *Kalimera.* I am Nicole Koumettou, friend of Petros, wife of Andreas. May I sit too? I've brought you cold water.'

I take the bottle she's holding out and absently pat the ground. In settling down beside me, she slides her feet out of purple wedge-heeled sandals and reaches up to let her dark hair free of the purple slide that holds it in place. When she turns properly to me, I see she's not a girl at all, she's probably my age, but with a creamy complexion, pillar-box lipstick and short dark hair that shines in a neat wave about her face. She reminds me of a 1940s film star.

'Of what do you think?' she asks.

I bite back the urge to tell her, saying randomly, 'That Andreas is real and he does have a wife.'

'Wife, mother, sister, friend and muse. Yes, I am all of these things to Andreas. You see, he is a painter.' She pauses, sounding serious but her eyes are dancing. 'A painter of talent and inspiration. He is driven to create, April, and when he sees his next subject, it immediately becomes an object to him. There is little social grace.'

'So when Petros said that your husband had fallen in love with me, what he meant was…'

Nicole fills the moment by lighting a cigarette. She offers it to me, and I'm tempted – though I've never smoked in my life – then she confirms, 'That Andreas wishes to paint you, not sleep with you, yes.'

'What if I say no? Will he carry on stalking me? Kidnap me?'

'God, no.' She shrugs. 'Andreas is familiar with rejection. If you refuse him, he will not pounce or die, just sulk.'

I'm slightly put out that I'm expendable after all.

'But why refuse him?' Nicole goes on. 'We are already going to be friends, you and I, are we not? Is it not decreed by Petros Evagora himself?'

'He seems to think so.'

'Then let Andreas paint you. There's no rush. He does not have to have you right now. He just needs to know that he *will* have you.'

We look at each other and smile, in synch.

'I am truly sorry though, if my husband frightened you,' Nicole says. 'Being his apologist and evangelist is not how I wished to greet you.'

'It's lovely to meet you.' I relax a bit. 'But Nicole, tell me two things?'

She holds out smooth hands, palms raised in enquiry.

'Why does Andreas have a toy elephant in his shirt pocket? And,' I look over my shoulder, 'where is he now?'

Nicole laughs. It's not the beautiful social tinkle I expect, but a throaty, drill-like chuckle that cuts through her neat prettiness and rounds her. 'His elephant is the god Ganesh, his talisman for good luck and opportunity. He carries it when he is searching for a new subject to paint. It is nothing perverted or phallic, this I swear.'

I pull a face, acknowledging she's read my half-formed thoughts. 'And the other?'

'Andreas is in the car park, in the car. I said already that I was his wife, his mother, his sister. Sometimes his babysitter also.' She glances at her watch and then reaches over to gather up her shoes. 'We are on our way to a dreary but necessary Easter lunch, and when I spied Petros' jeep, I expected it had broken down. I diverted to rescue you.'

'You know, I think you've done exactly that.' I mean it.

'Exactly what friends and friends-in-waiting are for.' Nicole smiles again. 'Remember, if you really do not wish Andreas to paint you, I can convince him. It makes no difference to the friendship you and I will have.'

We stand up and she kisses each of my cheeks in turn. When she hugs me, she exudes comfort and warmth and just an undercurrent of excitement, so that I don't want to let her go. But I do, waving her off to the car and to Andreas. ('He is okay,' she dismisses him. 'He will be sleeping.') On impulse, I shout after her, 'Oh, Nicole?' She stops and looks around. 'What do you know about orchids?'

'Orchids? Not one damn thing,' she calls back, cheerfully. 'Ask Yiannis Loizos when he arrives home.'

Well.

I lie down again once she's gone, flat on my back daydreaming. Finally I check the time, scramble up with a yelp, without grace, and take a final, testing look across the bay. My tears have dried, my mood lifted. The idea of seeking Elena has returned to hopeful rather than hope*less* and – I brace myself – the image of Jake, all cosied up in a patchwork Orkney croft with Scottish-Erica-the-storyteller, conjures resignation, not anger or longing.

That's a good start.

The jeep isn't. I cajole it, entreat it, bribe it with Nicole's bottle of mineral water for its overheated radiator. Then I walk away as if it's a naughty toddler. And it works; when I come back and turn the key again, the engine roars. An Easter Sunday miracle, no less. Hmm. I don't believe in miracles like I don't believe in signs and wonders; I switch the engine off, switch it back on. It comes to life again. Then a third time, by which I decide I've had my adventure and I'm not pushing my luck. At the road I turn left, back towards Verena Bay, where Petros will be complacent about the jeep, my 'spontaneity' and, mostly, Nicole and me hitting it off – right down to the fact she has already convinced me to model for Andreas.

3

Of all the places Petros has suggested since my confession, I really thought these caves around Cape Greco would be the place to release my parents' ashes from the shoebox. Half an hour into the boat trip, I can see I'm wrong. Close to the shore, the water looks as if it's lazily bouncing emeralds towards the sun, exactly as Petros described. There's a darkening swell on the horizon though, and beyond that those catch-me-if-you-can waves... No. Not here. If I scatter them here, they'll be, well, *too* scattered and none of us would find peace. Petros swears he decanted his Aunt Ana into a pepper pot and shook her off the bow on a blustery day up the coast; a rollercoaster of ecological confetti to the soundtrack of Stravinsky's *Firebird*. 'I felt her presence right beside me,' he said, 'and I am not a fanciful man. I knew she would be loving it.'

My parents wouldn't. They were very keen on neatness and order. I glance over towards the tiny galley where they're in the safe confines of the snug box. They've waited a year already for their eternal home and, infinitely patient people in life, I'm sure they don't mind being carted around the globe a bit more until I find it.

'No good?' Petros calls over, reading my mind.

I shake my head. 'Sorry.'

'No matter. It's a lovely day to sail.'

We settle under the canopy of the rear deck, sipping

small glasses of Commandaria, a sweet fortified local wine that Petros says will turn our plates of halloumi and grapes into dessert.

'I finally got their – my mum and dad, that is – bits and pieces a couple of weeks ago.' I stab a slice of the cheese with a cocktail stick. 'Their "effects", the solicitor called them.'

Petros nods. 'It is true the wheels of law turn slowly. Thia Ana's valuables remain in a bank deposit box awaiting my collection. It sounds grand, does it not? The reality is costume jewellery and the long-defunct deeds to her old home in the North. Yet…'

'Yet you can't bring yourself to ask the solicitors to dispose of them. I know. My parents' legacy is my mum's engagement and wedding rings, and the pocket watch I never saw my dad wear. I think it was my grandfather's, the inscription is in Polish anyway.' I don't tell him about the accompanying passports, British passports, still in pristine condition in a black leather holder, yet tossed into the kind of exhibit bag detectives use on TV dramas. That was what made me cry. To leave so little, so tidily, without ambiguity, is exactly what Mum and Dad spent their whole lives striving for.

'It's not much to show for a life.' Petros' eyes gaze far away and I'm not sure if he's thinking of his Aunt Ana, my parents or both. Then he snaps back to the present, shrugs and grins. 'It is not sentiment that makes me keep them, not really. It is the wrath of God Thia Ana would invoke if I let those house deeds out of the family. She went to her grave believing that the dispossessed Greek Cypriots would one day have their land returned to them.'

'Was she right?' I might have looked up the historical facts, but my understanding of the island's turbulent past is as hazy as it was when I traced the Green Line through that map of Nicosia last Christmas Day – as it was when I knew Elena, actually.

'Who knows? Not in my lifetime, I think. Her house was

near Kyrenia, in a village called Çatalköy. It was acquired by Turkish settlers, I'm told, and has been passed through their descendants ever since. Who is ethically the owner in such a case? The orange groves around it were bought by a developer in the nineties and now the village is one of holiday homes. The legalities of that are also a minefield, and one I have no wish to pick my way through.'

'Did that happen a lot?' Another image of Elena swims into focus. 'Greek and Turkish refugees commandeering each other's houses, I mean?'

'That's probably a simplistic way of putting it, but yes, I think it did,' Petros says. 'What else could they do? Displaced North or South with no real choice. They all had to live somewhere.' He leans back in his chair and crosses his arms behind his head. 'Why do you ask?'

'I... No real reason. Just making conversation.'

'Hmm. It has nothing to do with your long-lost friend Elena? That would have been her family's world, perhaps?' Petros gets up as he speaks, leans on the guard rail and, before I can gather my words, points across the water. 'Look – do you see him? A cliff diver.'

Distracted, I turn just in time to catch the lone figure hurtling from cliff to water. 'He just jumped? Is that even safe?' My insides plummet at the thought.

'He did not "just" jump,' Petros corrects me. 'Cliff diving is an extreme sport and is regulated. See that small boat over there? Watch long enough and the diver will be picked up.'

I scan the waves but my mind is elsewhere. 'Who told you?' I ask Petros. 'About Elena, I mean. Was it Jake?' Of course it was Jake, a man whose lifeblood is being in the know. A master manipulator with titbits of information; people are lulled into spilling the beans thinking he already knows more than he does.

'It was not Jake.' Petros sits down again, refilling our glasses first, and lighting himself a cigarette. 'I have barely spoken to the man, remember? After that first encounter, he made a beeline for Yiannis, the orchid expert—'

'Then who?' The Yiannis tangent I'll save till later. 'Who told you? And what did they say?'

'Ana.' Petros holds up his hands as if in surrender. 'It was Ana. When your parents learned that she was originally from Cyprus, they recalled you once had a school friend called Elena, who came from here also.'

'And?'

'And nothing. It was a casual remark, passed from your mother or perhaps your father to my aunt, who passed it to me.' Petros takes a long drag of his cigarette and blows the smoke over his shoulder. Then he grins at me. 'Why so defensive? Is there more to the story? Do tell, my dear April.'

I can't help but laugh at him relishing a spot of gossip. 'Sorry. There really isn't much more.' Is there? On the surface, no. 'Elena was my friend, my best friend, when I was ten. She came to my school for a year and I always wondered what happened to her afterwards. That's all.' Or that's all he getting for now, anyway.

'Fair enough.' Petros apparently accepts it at face value. 'Curiosity only. No mystery. No family skeletons. No love affair.'

'No...'

'April?'

A second's hesitation and of course he picks it up. Maybe I want him to. I concentrate on spearing a slippery olive, chewing it and delicately removing the stone from between my teeth.

'You are, as the British say, holding out on me, April.'

'Not about Elena.' I cross my fingers. 'But there is something. Sort of.'

Petros just raises his eyebrows above bright eyes and motions for me to continue. I can see him trying to compute if this is going to be better or worse than the ashes-in-the-wardrobe admission.

'It's about Yiannis. No, don't say anything,' I rush on. 'It's not much, so don't go getting ideas, but when Jake and I broke up, I wrote to Yiannis to apologise for him – Jake, I mean – muscling his way in about the orchids. And, well, we kept on writing. Letters. To each other.' I wriggle in my seat and reach for another olive I don't want, managing to drop this one on the floor, where it rolls across the deck and under the life-jacket box. I watch its progress and only then look at Petros. 'No smart remarks?'

'I'm surprised.'

Actually, he looks winded. What's wrong with Yiannis, I wonder. Or a potential combination of me and Yiannis? I may have a poor track record for picking the right man but Petros doesn't know that.

'You have caught me off guard.'

'Yiannis said nothing to you about our... friendship?'

'No. But I would expect that, his discretion and his reticence are appallingly good.' He shakes his head. 'Really? Our Yiannis Loizos, a romantic scribe?'

'Hardly romantic.' Though he does write a poetic letter; I smile to myself. 'Should I be wary?'

'Wary?' Petros repeats, scratching his chin. 'No. Yiannis is a good man. A good friend.'

'But?'

'There is no but,' he protests, and I want to believe it as I watch him haver. Finally he adds, '*But* it is no secret that Yiannis wants a wife – and I'm not sure, April, that you want a husband.'

'Oh.' I don't want another husband, not now, probably not ever. I flick mentally through the letters: light-hearted, kind. Caring, for sure. Flirtatious, perhaps. Yiannis has been courting me and I've lapped it up – but without considering our end points might be so divergent. 'I didn't know. He never said.' I add lamely, 'Forewarned is forearmed, I suppose.'

My loss of equilibrium has clearly settled Petros'. 'Meet

him. Talk to him. It will all come out in the wash, as Thia Ana might have said.'

'I suppose. Don't say anything to Yiannis, will you?' Something occurs to me. 'You haven't told him anything about me, have you? In general conversation, I mean?'

'Heaven forfend.' Petros makes a zipping motion across his lips. Then he opens them to add, 'Would it matter? In all truth, April, I know little about you. We are bound by the ties of...'

'Tragedy?' I fill in. It's a strong word, but apt. My parents, his aunt – our only remaining family members – died together. That brought *us* together.

'I was going to say "circumstance", though you are not wrong. But I think we are friends too.' He knocks back the last of his wine and stands up. 'The weather is coming in, April, we should get back to the harbour. But in the interests of transparency, I will tell you that I *do* know other things about you, courtesy of my aunt, of course.'

'Such as?' Although I'm not sure I really want to know.

'How you and the little Elena were so fascinated by tree houses that your father built one in your yard.' *Harmless,* I think. *Significant but harmless*. Petros looks at me for a minute, as if gauging my tolerance. 'I know you started to play the piano at the age of ten years old,' he says. 'Your teacher thought it would take your mind off Elena – when she disappeared. Back to Cyprus. Into a warzone.' He lets that hang.

'Well, there's me in a nutshell. The life and times of April Zarney.' I decide to treat it lightly; there's a lot to think about. 'But right now,' I hold my hands palms up, 'isn't that rain spitting?'

'April—'

I shake my head, but I'm smiling. 'Another time. My poor parents aren't waterproof, you know.'

4

Back at the hotel, I tuck their – thankfully dry – remains carefully into the back of the wardrobe, hoping they enjoyed their sedate boat trip. The storm clouds are still gathering overhead, so I pull on a cardigan and run lightly down the stairs. Petros' *Reserved* sign on the drawing-room door makes me smile; I've never seen anyone other than me do more than poke their heads inside. He seems to think I practise the piano under strict exam conditions despite assurances I'm neither a musical genius nor a prima donna and won't lose my temper or my muse if I'm interrupted. But Petros has assigned me a 'gifted' role and I think he secretly longs for that kind of excitement. When I offered to leave the door open and play some popular tunes, he looked horrified and muttered something about 'a select evening soiree' being a possibility. I hope he forgets.

I click on each of the small mock-Tiffany lamps, and lift the lid of the baby grand, carefully situated in the dimness of the closed shutters ('Where neither light nor draughts will affect its tuning,' Petros proudly pointed out). I'm not yet used to the stool, slightly uneven on the tiles, but it's one of those that spins round, so like a child I whirl round a few times – because I can – and start my C major scale like a drunk. I push on, dogged to the nth degree, and gradually close my mind to anything but the black and white keys. It's a mercy, though, nobody's listening to the self-indulgence with which I drift through a medley of my favourite pieces. When the last chord settles and I'm tired playing from memory, I flex my fingers and stretch my legs, soothed.

It's time to find some dinner and have an early night – as the old saying goes, it must be the sea air getting to me.

At some point in the early hours I'm aware I'm dreaming to the soundtrack of Chopin's 'Raindrop', a zoetrope of flickering images, past and present, of half-formed memories and indistinct visions of the future. Petros… Jake… my mum and dad… Nicole… Elena… all jumbled pieces of an unfinished jigsaw.

Then I jolt awake. The digital radio alarm beside my bed reads 7.00 a.m and over on the dressing table my mobile phone is vibrating to the infuriating noise of the Nokia ringtone. I grab it and with an indistinct 'Hello' get back under the covers.

'April? Is that you?' the voice at the other end says. 'April, it's me.'

I sit up straight in bed. There is still just only one *me*.

'Jake?'

Two months ago, maybe even two weeks ago, a good half of me liked the security of his alternately irate and sorrowful messages; he was still the bridge, however eroded, to everything I was blithely discarding. Now, though, I need to pretend I'm in control. I imagine Nicole as she was in my dream; I bet in real life she can discard suitors with finesse.

'April. What are you doing? How's life? Missing me?'

'Sleeping. Intriguing. No.' My determined lack of enthusiasm doesn't penetrate. This is how it goes: stalemate, small talk, the grand pause, then he cracks first.

'I'm going on a crystal tour,' he says.

'A what?'

'Oh, I don't know, something to do with ley lines and runes. It's one of Erica's things. Orkney's not what I thought, to be honest. The rain's horizontal, and it's fucking freezing.'

'It's very warm here.' I notch up the temperature. 'The people are great too. Verena Bay is beautiful.'

'Verena Bay? *Verena Bay?* Like, Agia Napa. In Cyprus. You're in Cyprus.' There's a sharp intake of breath, then, 'April. You went without me. How could you?'

'Of course I'm in Cyprus, you phoned me here…' I realise too late that he called the mobile phone, so he wouldn't have known where I was until I told him, would he? *Fool*, I curse myself. For leaving it switched on *and* for letting him convince me to buy the thing in the first place.

I hold the handset away from my ear and glower at it while Jake rants away at the other end. 'Nicosia records office,' I hear. 'Dionysius and the Tombs of the Kings; bornmuelleri; Elena; Minerva House.' I'm tempted to hang up but common sense tells me to get this over with now.

'Calm down, Jake,' I butt in when he doesn't shut up. 'They were all your plans. Not mine. You lost any say in *this* island trip when you took yourself off on *that* one.'

That hits home because he goes silent. I can feel him sulking through the airwaves and the devil gets into me.

'I've met some people and changed my plans. Andreas, he's Nicole's husband – remember Petros telling us all about Nicole?' He didn't, but this will drive Jake demented. 'I met her yesterday and she is gorgeous, Jake. You'd love her.' I enjoy that dig even more. 'Anyway, Andreas wants to paint me, and Petros thinks it would be a good idea. I've also talked to Petros about finding Elena. It came up when we were sailing towards Famagusta on his boat.' Well, none of it's a total lie. None of it sounds remotely like me either, but I'm banking on Jake being too self-absorbed to notice.

'Jesus, Ape. You haven't wasted any time.'

'No.' I ignore his sarcasm and decide it would be gilding the lily (or the orchid) to mention Yiannis and our letter-writing – about which Jake has no idea. 'And my name is April. Please stop calling me Ape.'

'Sorry, sorry. Habit. Just be careful, April. Just because we've parted ways doesn't mean I'm not concerned about you.'

He might be, but the implied vulnerability makes me fume. 'You don't need to be,' I snap. 'Worry about Erica. Concentrate on your ley lines. Anyway, why are you phoning me so early? Isn't it the middle of the night there? In fact, why are you phoning me at all?'

'It's five o'clock in the morning. Though it might as well be five o'clock teatime or the middle of the effing night. It's pitch-black half the time. I've been trying to get in touch with you for days, which you'd know if you ever checked that phone. The thing is...'

And there we have it, the Jake-shaped beat. He's after something I won't like but he'll talk me into. Or so he thinks, because those days are gone. I get out of bed and, *that phone* balanced against one ear, pull back the curtains to seek dawn breaking over the water. The beam from the lighthouse penetrates a foggy, cloudy morning. There are a handful of stray leaves floating like dead things on the surface of the swimming pool. I shiver and return to bed. Waiting.

'The thing is,' Jake repeats, finally breaking the dead time, 'it was about the holiday with Yiannis and the orchids. But you've kind of stolen my thunder.' Now he's all matey.

'And?'

'Well, it was my idea, wasn't it, not really your thing at all, so I had been thinking... I was ringing to see if you'd mind if I went anyway and took Erica,' he finishes in a rush. 'But I guess that's not going to work so well if you're already there. Er... would it?'

I've got to admire his nerve. And I need to save my outrage for later and nip this in the bud before the two of them are installed in Verena Bay in a double-pronged attack to show me what I'm missing and treat Erica to a sun holiday. If he infiltrates with an oh-so spiritual and earnest Erica, I will inevitably not act my age, humiliate myself and agonise over it forever.

'I don't think so, Jake.' I cut to the chase. 'Look, I just

want to play the piano, not second fiddle.' I thought that up on the plane over here, and I've been dying to say it; he doesn't respond. 'So I'm glad I'm here on my own, and *I'm* the one going to meet Yiannis. We've already arranged it.'

'Well, for fuck's sake, April. I don't know what to say… Hey, what's that?'

'Just a minute.' It's the hotel phone, an old-fashioned high-pitched *ring-ring, ring-ring*. I lean over and lift the receiver. 'Just a minute,' I repeat to the new caller.

'Who the hell is phoning you at this hour?' Jake grumbles.

'You are. And one of my new friends, presumably.'

'Which one? Honestly, Ape, can't you ask them to call back? We're in the middle of something here.'

'Bugger off, Jake,' I say, sweet as Petros' baklavas, and hang up, simultaneously saying, 'Sorry about that. Hello,' into the other phone. Slightly disoriented by my apparent new-found popularity – before I'm even out of bed – I'm not helped by the female voice that responds.

'Bugger. Off. Jake,' it echoes, and I can hear the smile. 'Ah, here is a very interesting story, and someday soon I shall ask you all about it.'

'Nicole? Hello.'

'I want to catch you early to invite you to a party. Andreas would like to meet you properly, his parents too, and of course, I wish to see you again. We thought Georgios' place, the Village Tavern, but Yiannis is keen to trial his house for guests, so we shall arrange a gathering there.' Whilst I am doing my own gathering – of rampant thoughts – she continues, 'Petros agrees but says I should ask you directly. He is a true gentleman in his heart.' Her voice bubbles into her ungainly laugh. 'I must ask – did he try to take you to bed?'

'What? No, he didn't.' I'm startled into answering, laughing with her. 'I'm much too old for him.'

'Bah, you are much too intelligent. Those little receptionist girls of his, they are all looking for rich husbands, and they think Petros is rich. They twist him round their engagement ring fingers then run off to wed builders and travel agents. He thinks very highly of you.'

'Has he taken *you* to bed?' I can't believe I'm channelling teenage me but I blame Nicole, she started it.

'Once. I was twenty-two years old. I planned it. It was comfortable, not exciting. Instructive though.'

Poor Petros, relegated to the role of teacher. Or maybe that's his motivation.

I half hope she'll continue, but, 'It is fate,' she declares.

'Fate?'

'Of course. Fate has brought you and me together... What? April, excuse me.'

Abruptly, she launches into fast and furious Greek. I've no idea who's on the receiving end, nor whether it's good or bad, but it is lengthy. Waiting, I get a long-forgotten urge to poke my index finger through the curly cord of the green telephone, so I do, and it gets stuck. Suddenly, everything, not just Nicole, feels strangely familiar: the voluble shouting in a language I don't understand; the phone with its huge dial; the heavy, tickly bedspread; and the flowery, frayed-at-the-seams curtains that don't quite meet in the middle. There should be a cat, a shaggy black and white moggy, with a bald patch over its left eye, curled up on the armchair and eyeing a plate of Iced Gems beside the lemonade on the bedside table. There should be a scent, patchouli and a trace of frying oil...

So strong is this parallel world, it hardly registers when Nicole switches back to English, saying, 'April? I must go now. A problem with a delivery here. I will see you tomorrow evening, yes? *Yassou.*'

'*Yassou,*' I murmur back. '*Yassou.*'

Her goodbye jolts me from déjà vu to memory. The old-fashioned Verena Bay hotel room morphs into Elena's bedroom: it's above the fish and chip shop, it's 1973 and I'm nine years old. I'm spending another Saturday night with her whole family, about to be called downstairs to eat a greasy bag of fried crispy bits in front of *The Generation Game.*

5

'Krista. Elena. April? Bring Sofia down.'

Elena's mama's voice floated up the stairs as it always did just before six-thirty. It was a weekly roll call that gave me a warm, happy surge because my name was right there in the middle. We tumbled down the stairs, one of us scooping up Fishcakes, the piebald cat, and the other reaching in and flashing the lights off and on, off and on, off and on, in Sofia's room, just in case she was still there, as we thundered past. It was a race to the huge orange beanbag for the best view, a race that Krista won. Sometimes she let Elena and I trade, if we had enough Saturday sweets left, but our proper places were at opposite ends of the corduroy sofa, Sofia jumping in between us.

The television was blaring above the constant squeak-bang of the takeaway door below us, but not nearly enough to mute the snatches of Greek conversation, cheerful and exciting, that came from Elena's mama, and her Aunt Irini, as they drank coffee in the kitchen and took it in turns to help out Stefan in the shop.

'Who is hungry?' Irini poked her head around the door, to a chorus of *'eimai, eimai'*, mine still shy, and she handed round the dregs of the chips and battered sausages, that came, best of all, in paper bags.

'So, what are you eating today, April Rose? My little April

Rosita?' Mama came in too, and perched beside the cat. She always called me that, my whole name. 'Such a beautiful name for a beautiful girl,' she said, starting the game that was meant to teach me Greek words.

I knew the word for sausage. '*Loukaniko*,' I said.

Mama put her arm around my shoulder and hugged me. 'My, so clever. We will make little Cypriot girl of you yet! Yes?'

Krista, licking salt off her fingers, interrupted. '*Loukaniko* is boring. April is really eating...' This was the part of the game I liked best. 'She's eating – *patcha. Patcha.* Yuk!'

Everybody laughed, including Sofia, who clapped her hands too. Sometimes I forgot Sofia couldn't hear what we were saying. Till I met her, I'd thought only old people got deaf.

'April's eating *patcha*, April's eating *patcha*.'

Nobody had ever teased me before, but I knew that was what real sisters did in real families, and I loved it.

'*Patcha* is sheep's head stew, sheep's head stew. Yuk!'

'Enough, enough.' Elena's mama pointed at the television screen. 'It's starting.'

I never understood I was lonely until I met Elena. Life with my mum and dad, by far the oldest parents at the school gate, was kind and neat. In daylight hours my mum mostly wore a cornflake-coloured apron, and I hardly ever saw my father without a shirt and tie. She spent Saturday mornings ironing perfect creases into his pyjamas; he mowed the lawn into perfect straight lines. *Shabby Stepford*, my first lacklustre boyfriend, aged seventeen, once called them, which was too cruel and too near the mark for me to forget. My top-secret compensation was a glamorous, daredevil twin called Rose, who provided a constant vicarious thrill. So what if she was imaginary? All the better to be thrown over without a second thought, for the sake of Elena.

Excitement was rife at my primary school that summer. Almost everyone I knew lived in the same neighbouring streets of semi-detached houses with picture windows and open-plan front gardens. Nothing much changed, which meant newcomers were to the village what the fictional Rose was to me, and that year we were blessed. First was Cynthia, her black skin such a novelty in our then-white world, that she got a special assembly and the fourth-year girls baked her fairy cakes. However, Cynthia brought no kudos to Mrs Gale's class, she was too old for us. Instead, we craved the arrival of Tiffany from London. London outdid African antecedents because it was the big city none of us had seen, and Tiffany was without doubt a big city name. Rumours escalated, and soon we knew absolutely that her dad was a burglar and she was from a broken home. It was as well she never came, she couldn't have reached the pedestal we had her on. Instead, the advent of the wild card, Elena, made Tiffany and Cynthia history.

On the first Friday afternoon of the autumn term, we were roaring out Seekers hits with enthusiasm if not tunefulness, accompanied by the long-haired Mr Clegg and his banjo. There was the *train whistle blowing* – Craig Miller was the whistler, though I've no idea why I remember that – when Mrs Gale came in with what appeared to be crowd of foreigners. She introduced them as Elena, her two sisters and her mother, explaining that Elena would be joining our class the following week. We should be especially kind to her, Mrs Gale urged, because she was from abroad, a faraway island called Cyprus where oranges and lemons grew on the trees. I watched Elena's mother take her hand and squeeze it. Elena didn't pull away, which was amazing in itself: most of us would have been mortified, and teased without restraint, had our families accompanied us into the classroom. Elena, though, looked as if she didn't mind a bit.

So exotic was all of this that when Mrs Gale asked for a volunteer to look after Elena, every girl's hand went up, and even some of the boys squirmed as if they wanted to offer. Mrs Gale caught my eye.

'Where's April Zarney?' she said. 'Ah, yes. Let's put the Zs together, shall we?'

Amidst the ordinariness of Thompson, Miller and Holmes, my surname had been a sore trial, but from that moment my Polish granddad was a hero. Elena and her whole family smiled at me and I felt myself go bright red.

That's when I fell in love.

I've tried to do it again since – fall in love, that is – but it never quite works. I shake my head, literally, as if it will settle me back into 2004, and my fragmented memories into their rightful places. When I first told Jake that story of meeting Elena, he laughed, then he went quiet. At the end, all he said was, 'Can you remember the day you met me, April?'

My beeping mobile phone drops me firmly back in Verena Bay. I let it ring because the message will be from him, of course: *We got cut off. Please phone me back Ape... ril. We can still be friends. Erica understands how important the orchids are to me. Can't you?*

Maddened, I phone him back. Seconds later, I thank the ley lines, the crystals or just the probable lack of mobile telephone masts on Orkney, when the recorded voice tells me to leave a message. Overcoming temptation to be plain rude, at least until I've turned the phone off, I chuck it across the bed.

Then I shower, making a mental note to tell Petros that there's an irregular triple drip from the ceiling into the bath (which solves the Chopin's-'Raindrop'-in-my-dream conundrum), dress quickly and creep downstairs to forage for food.

I know I'm allowed to help myself to breakfast. Petros has encouraged me to call his home mine for as long as I'm here, but still I feel guilty raiding the deserted kitchen. I get butter, honey and yoghurt from the fridge, then ease open the back door, and haul in the plastic sack of bread rolls, dumped on the porch by the baker's boy. Slitting the bag, I steal two for myself before carrying the tray back through the slumbering hotel without seeing a soul; Nicole and I might be the only people awake on the island.

The polite, the refined, thing to do would be to bring in the flimsy wrought-iron chair and table from the little terrace outside my room. I see a fleeting image of my mother and father doing exactly that, me in the middle of them, being gently urged to sit up straight despite the cold and rusted bit jabbing my skin. The comfortable alternative here is to prop myself on my bed and balance my plate on my knee. With the French doors to my room open, I can hear the sea but I can see it only in the faint, monotonous sweep of the lighthouse; it's like the car headlights passing my main-road-facing bedroom at home but on mute. In time, there is an occasional bang of a door, a snatch of conversation, and the ceiling creaks in tune with the footfall of the awakening guests upstairs. I enjoy the auditory footage, enough to feel life around me without the necessity of taking an active part, and let my mind wander over the morning so far.

What a shame, I think suddenly, that Nicole isn't Elena. She's the right age, it's the right location – I look outside again, over Verena Bay, a place that Elena could well have visited. How convenient that would be, how Richard Curtis, if life were like that. Nicole, in a Goldilocks kind of way, could never have been Elena – or one of her sisters: too slight of build to be Elena; not slight enough to be Krista; too old to be little Sofia.

It's a real shame.

6

'Nicole reached you on the phone?' Petros says, when I meet him mid-morning. He's propping up the messy reception desk, apparently working his way through what looks like a sheaf of invoices, yet with a cup of coffee and the *Cyprus Mail* close to hand.

'She did. I'm looking forward to the party.'

'If you have no plans before that, I wonder if I may break into your holiday to ask a favour. It might be to your advantage.'

'You don't have to bribe me,' I say, laughing. We're still arguing over how much bed and board he's charging me and since his suggestion has always been to give me a free ride, anything I can do to help out, I will.

'I am indebted to you.' Petros gives a mock bow. 'I promised to collect Yiannis and a colleague of his from Larnaca Airport this afternoon, but he has phoned to say the colleague was on an earlier flight and took the bus to Agia Napa to meet a family member.' He raises his eyebrows.

'They both need picking up and you can't be in two places at once?' I guess.

'Precisely.'

'Which one of them do you want me to go for?'

'Which one do you want?' If it's possible, his eyebrows go higher.

'The friend.' I hold up a warning hand. 'And before you read anything into that, it's because I know the way to Agia Napa and I'd rather drive your clapped-out old jeep ten minutes along the old coast road than find my way to the airport in a hire car.' That much is true, but I do quail at the thought of such a public meet-and-greet with Yiannis; I'm such a coward.

'As you wish.' Petros winks. 'But you will have to meet Yiannis some time and soon. You cannot survive on letters alone.'

'Who am I meeting, and where?' I ask briskly.

'A man called Red. The monastery at noon.'

'It sounds like a cowboy film... Red – really? I can ask him to push when the jeep breaks down again.'

He ignores the jibe. 'That is the only name I have, though he may have been baptised something less – colourful.' Petros turns the big black-leather reservations book towards himself and adds, 'He can have the room above yours for tonight. That and the old stable block is free now the Eagle Scouts have gone.'

When it's time to leave, Petros abandons his paperwork to walk me up the car park. Feeling like an old hand, I climb into the jeep, check the keys are dangling from the ignition and lean out of the window. 'Oh – how will I recognise this Red?'

Petros looks pityingly at me. 'April, oh April. So innocent. At midday, the centre of Agia Napa is deserted. If you see someone at the monastery, he is bound to be your man.'

I take a few pre-performance breaths as I walk through the town. To be down and out in Agia Napa is probably having insufficient change for the worn-out How Sexy Am I? slot machine on the main strip where it jostles with the Saucy Postcard Maker and Fanny Feather, Fortune Teller. My uneven footsteps trigger their rainbow flashing lights and tinny voices in turn. I can't stop, I'm too busy marvelling at The Flintstones bar, where apparently all comers are guaranteed a *yabba-NAPA-doo-time*; and at the neighbouring Titanic, where the frontage combines a replica of the original ship ploughing into an iceberg. So silent, eerily silent, the many clubs and bars might well be stage props ready for a macabre fairground murder scene.

Sanctuary is at the foot of the old town, the Venetian monastery. A handwritten note tacked to the main door tells me, in English, it's locked until mid-afternoon and an arrow points me to the tiny garden cafe where I might wait. I sit on the grass where, contrary to Petros' certainty of running into Red head-on, I feel like the last remaining real human in an avant-garde collaboration of H. G. Wells' words and Schubert's 'String Quartet in C major'. I'm further from Elena's Cyprus with every move.

Inexplicably, strains of a Christmas carol filter through; if there's a musician's equivalent of schizophrenia, I'm surely incubating it. Then I realise I'm not imagining the hymn, but hearing it and it's getting closer. Rounding a corner, it's embodied by two traditionally collared, crucifix-wearing priests carrying an Irish flag.

They see me. They stop. I stand up. I stop. We spend a few seconds re-enacting an old-fashioned stand-off before the fairer-haired one with the Gucci sunglasses raises his hands in mock surrender.

'We come in peace,' he says. 'We've no weapons bar the voices.'

His friend squints at me from under the visor of his baseball cap. 'Howya,' he says. 'We're looking for a man.'

'So am I.' I'm so far into the twilight zone, dropping another couple of feet won't matter. 'Mine's called Red. What's yours called?'

'Petros,' they say in unison.

'We're Jarlath and Kevin,' the darker-haired one adds, pointing to himself first. 'Red isn't here yet.'

A lot of years ago, newly qualified and broke, I filled the time between auditions teaching teenagers at a residential music camp; they were mostly drunk too. The experience is flooding back. 'My name is April,' I say slowly and clearly. 'Petros asked me to come and meet Red. Where is he?'

'Our father, Red.' Kevin digs Jarlath in the ribs and they both snigger.

'Right... Red's your dad?'

They're looking at me as if I'm the one with cogs too awash with alcohol to grind. 'He's our brother,' Jarlath says eventually. 'The "our father" is a joke.'

'Yeah. He told us to get our arses quick-smart to the monastery to meet Petros, while he brings the bags.'

Jarlath leans forward and tugs at the hem of my skirt. 'We're not really priests,' he says in a stage whisper. 'We're twins. This is fancy dress. We got Red the archbishop togs but he told us no feckin' way and went off to look at the sunset or read a book or something equally mad.'

I open my mouth, then close it because the sensible thing to do is wait. We sit down in a stupefied row, until a man in immaculate jeans and a white shirt, but loaded down with two holdalls, a rucksack and a pair of hiking boots, turns the corner.

'That's Red,' Kevin confirms.

The man – Red, apparently – looks up, sees me, appears to do a double-take and drops the boots. 'Oh,' he says. 'You're... I mean...'

'Not Petros,' I supply. Nonplussed for a second, I realise I'm expecting him to have Little Orphan Annie hair, whereas it's fair and wavy and he hasn't a freckle in sight. He's boy-next-door wholesome, yet grown-up and – this is going to sound so stupid – whereas Nicole felt like a new friend, unknown, he feels like someone I've met before, someone I've always known. And though I'm not usually good at reading strangers, I could swear he feels the same. *Do we know each other?* Taken unawares, I stumble over explaining who I am.

'Hi, April.' With difficulty, he extends a hand from amongst the bags and I shake it awkwardly, while he seems to regain his equilibrium. 'I'm Philip Redmond – Red. And I see you've met my baby brothers. I always start out apologising for them: what they have done, are doing now and will do ever more.' The twins groan as he goes on. 'Please don't hold it against me; I'm adopted and twelve years older and wiser.'

The world tilts back to a semblance of normality and I laugh. 'It's nice to meet you, all of you. The jeep's at the end of the street, and Verena Bay is only a few minutes' drive.' I cross my fingers. 'Petros is expecting you.' I cross them on the other hand.

'It's good of you to collect us.' Red shares out the luggage with the other two, and we all amble towards the car. 'I was supposed to travel with Yiannis – Yiannis Loizos – but I'm sure you know that. Anyway, my mother begged me to come over earlier and check on these two. They only came for a long weekend, about a fortnight ago.' His tone is exasperation mixed with affection.

'Over there.' I point to the jeep, standing back as Red shoves Kevin and Jarlath and all the luggage into the back before climbing in beside me.

'Pray it starts,' I say, turning on the ignition.

The twins titter and Red turns to give them the kind of look only an older sibling can achieve.

The engine coughs and fires up and we set off. It's a more or less silent trip, though not uncomfortable. I have to wrack my brains for small talk at the best of times, without having to coax the jeep along as well, and Red seems content looking out of his window at the view. The boys in the back are lolling against each other, apparently asleep. When we turn into Verena Bay and come to a stop, both Red and I turn to look at them.

'Leave them to sleep it off,' he suggests. 'They'll find their way when they're hungry.'

We make our way sedately along the drive. 'You're in the main house,' I tell him. *Near me*, I'm tempted to add. 'And

Kevin and Jarlath in the... er... extension in the garden? It's a bit rustic. Will that be okay with them?'

'A mattress and a regular supply of sandwiches is all they need to be happy. And they should be gone in a day or two anyway. How long are you here for, April?' he goes on, taking his eyes off the sea and smiling at me as if it really matters.

I hesitate, a naturally glib response dying on my lips. 'I know that should be an easy question, but the truth is, I don't know. Another few weeks? It's... complicated.' I'm willing him not to ask more, not yet, because I've a horrible feeling I might blurt it all out.

'I find life usually is,' is all he says, 'mine suddenly is, anyway.'

And I warm to him even more – while, hypocritically, dying to ask him to elaborate.

'What about you?' I settle on. 'I mean, how long are you staying?'

'Ten days is the plan, but it's not set in stone. Yiannis and I have got some work to do after this conference.'

As we reach the main door of the hotel, I stand back to let him through. 'Here we are. Let me get you a drink and find the key to your room. I know Petros would like to have dinner with you later.' Unobtrusively I hold my breath.

'Great.' Red glances around, looking impressed. 'This is a real relief after the places I saw in Agia Napa. I was afraid I'd have to suffer a *yabba-NAPA-doo-time.*' Then he smiles at me again. 'April, I hope you'll be there for dinner too?'

Slowly, I let the breath out. 'I can be.'

'I'd like that.' He pauses. 'April, we haven't met before, have we?'

I knew it wasn't just me. Slowly, I shake my head. 'I don't think so.'

'It must be in a past life then.'

Or a future one, I think, my mouth firmly closed.

7

Once Red is sorted out, I hurry up to my own room, too wound up to contemplate piano practice. It sounds woo-woo, but something has shifted inside me. I was already buoyed up by Nicole's early phone call, now meeting Red has boosted that threefold. Even if it's temporary, Jake has been shoved into my peripheral vision where he belongs. There are nice people out there, I remind myself, and I'm not too old or too insular to make friends. I feel... brave. Yes, brave, that's the word. It's what motivates me to root around in the back of my wardrobe and once more pull out the shoebox of Mum and Dad's ashes.

I keep calling it a shoebox, which it is, but inside there's a smaller metal box – in lieu of an old-fashioned urn; after all, it's not as if I intend displaying them on the mantelpiece. That's plain odd. *And hauling them around on my travels isn't*, a little voice in my head asks. I know it's not logical. Theirs were lives well lived, according to their terms, and if their deaths were unkind in manner, they weren't untimely. My mum was mid-eighties and my dad nearer ninety. It's life half lived or life cut short that scares me.

And that's why, I acknowledge now, I haven't looked inside the bulky envelope since I tucked it in beside the metal box a week or so after their double cremation.

Sitting on the edge of the bed, I run my finger under the half-sticky seal, and pull out a small white hardback book.

It's slim, not even the size of a mass-market paperback, well thumbed with a creased spine: the 1971 *Travellers' Guide to Cyprus*.

I found it in the tree house my dad built us, oh, weeks after Elena had gone. Back then, we lived in your average semi-detached council house that came with a long, thin back garden. Dad grew tomatoes and potatoes on a patch halfway down and behind that was the tree... My eyes threaten tears at the memory but I blink them away. The guidebook was under a cushion, flattened open to the chapter on Varosha; we must have thrown it down the last time we were there, distracted by dinner or games or whatever ten-year-olds' crisis had intervened. It wasn't the best book, too much text and not enough colour pictures for our liking, but once she was gone, it was the only keepsake I had of Elena's. I put it in my school bag to spirit to my bedroom, telling nobody, in case they said it wasn't mine and took it away.

I open the book now and turn the pages, removing from them my holy trinity: a letter folded in four, a postcard and a photograph. These three things came much later, on the day of my parents' funeral, in fact, and courtesy of my old primary school teacher, Mrs Gale. She'd been mine and Elena's favourite teacher, someone I hadn't seen since I'd gone away to college. In the meantime, she'd risen to deputy head and then to headmistress and when I met her, newly retired ('I knew it was time to go when my new pupils started saying, "You taught my granny, miss",' she said) Gillian Gale was collating an archive of the soon-to-be demolished village school. Nostalgia hit hard, standing in the graveyard surrounded by the last of the mourners, and I asked if she'd saved anything from my time.

'I moved up from the Infants' in...' I squinted and counted back on my fingers. '... 1972 and I left in 1975.'

Gillian Gale pre-empted me, she'd already looked those years up: the netball team, recorder club, library monitors. I hadn't been one to shine, just another grey-uniformed outline in the class photos, and I couldn't reliably name anyone grouped around me. It brought the years back though.

'Elena isn't here at all,' I said. 'Do you remember her? Elena Zacharia, third year juniors?'

'I do. That's why...' She seemed to be choosing her words carefully. 'You were peas in a pod. You became a butterfly beside her.'

'I still think about her sometimes,' I said. 'I waited and waited for her to write. I was so sure Elena would write to me.'

That's when Mrs Gale gave me a long, appraising look – her ability to do that hadn't changed either – then reached in her bag and slowly handed me an envelope, written on in neat cursive writing and with a foreign stamp. She said quietly, 'Oh, April, but she did.'

And that's the letter I'm unfolding now, smoothing out the creases as you would a first-edition heirloom. I'm doing it self-consciously too, as if there's a film camera on me. The paper is thirty years old but the blue ink has barely faded.

Elena was always good at writing, and if I try really hard, I can pretend I still hear her voice across the years.

8

Nicosia Airport, Cyprus
Friday 19th July 1974

Dear April and Mrs Gale's class,

Hello, here is Elena Zacharia writing you the summer holiday letter from Nicosia, the capital city of Cyprus. The sun is hot here and the sky is like the sheets of plasticine we use to make the models for folder work. My big sister, Krista, says she will die of a headache without some sunglasses, and our Aunt Irini won't give her money to buy them so she is being cross. She went to the Lost Property where the lady felt sorry for her and because there were no sunglasses she gave Krista a black umbrella. Sofia, my little sister, wanted to get an umbrella as well but the Lost Property lady gave her a floppy rag doll called Jemima Long-Legs. I got a box of Rainbow Notelets with coloured paper and envelopes in, and I am going to use a different colour each time to write my letters.

We came here on Wednesday, which was already a big surprise, because my mum is very strict about school and it isn't school holidays till next week. When Antony got the car out, we thought it was a special tea at the Little Chef on the roundabout, the one with the playground that is Sofia's favourite. Now it is Friday but we have to stay here in the airport until the soldiers say we can go. This might be an hour or a day or a week. There never used to be soldiers here but there has been something called a coo that is spelled coup. This means the leaders of the country have been fighting and the winners sent the losers away. Aunt Irini says the army is keeping the island safe but I don't think it's working because everyone looks worried. We are very unlucky to arrive here at the same time as the coup. It means my mum isn't here to meet us because ordinary people aren't allowed in the airport any more. April, when you come with us here on holidays, it will be after the coup is gone, Aunt Irini promised.

The soldiers have guns across their stomachs and I think they aren't allowed to smile. The ones with the blue hats are a bit friendly because they speak English and seem pleased to talk to us. They have searched our bags and asked us questions, which Krista says is to be sure we are not spies. She wants to be a spy so she tells the soldiers all kinds of stories. They aren't writing any of it down, except when she says about my mum and Stefan coming here before us to get our tree houses ready and to check Stefan's hotel. (If you have forgotten, Stefan is my stepdad. My own dad died before I was born.) The soldiers liked hearing about that. Afterwards, they took Antony to a separate place to ask him more about it. He hasn't come back yet. They have only asked me my name and age and where I live. 'Do you mean in England or in Cyprus?' I asked and they said, 'Both.'

It is funny to hear Greek and not English everywhere, just like when we got to England but backwards. When they took Antony away, the soldier guarding us said maybe we should talk in English anyway. He said it would be easier for us. I think this is because Antony doesn't speak Greek, only kalimera *and* yassou. *April knows many more words than him. (If you don't know this, Antony is married to Aunt Irini, so he is like my uncle, and Aunt Irini is my mum's sister.)*

Some things are the same as England, like we are eating chips in the airport, and sausages. But the letter box here is yellow not red. I am going to post this letter into it when Antony comes back, and if the nicest soldier says I can go out. Aunt Irini is being allowed outside with Krista and Sofia because Krista shouted she will be sick without fresh air and Sofia is too little to stay here alone. Sofia likes walking to the fence to see the little planes but they say Military *in huge letters and we can't go near them. I can see Krista with her umbrella up. Everybody is looking at her but she likes that best.*

After today, I am going to write my letter every week as if I am in News class with you. Sometimes I will keep a diary too for interesting things that happen. Aunt Irini promised we will be back to England for school next term.

I miss you, and I miss April my best friend most.

Love from, Elena Z
xxx

9

And there you have it.

The one and only letter I ever got from her, and nearly thirty years late.

When we were ten we imagined the trip I would make to Elena's island. We'd go together, we decided, as soon as we were grown-ups; Elena's little sister, Sofia, could come, but definitely not Krista, her bossy big one. For years after she went away and, rumour had it, back to Cyprus – *without me* – I promised myself I'd still go and find her; she was my best friend, she would have had a good reason for leaving me. The dream waxed and waned and in the way life happens, I never made the time. I studied music *forever*. The piano became an extension of me: a safety blanket and one of suffocation until I couldn't tell the difference. I got married and divorced, married and divorced, watched my parents age without ever really knowing them, and fell into the part-time, increasingly indifferent relationship with Jake.

Now I am here in Cyprus but the goalposts have changed. While it really is so much more than getting one over on Jake and being on a promise with Yiannis, chasing Elena feels like a pipe dream. It was no rumour that she and her sisters were brought back here into a warzone; that lost letter is the evidence, and the resultant *why* nags. I'm old enough, and have read enough history, to know that answers will be nigh-on impossible and probably hidden inside a Pandora's box anyway.

As a compromise for now, I put the ashes back in the wardrobe but promote the guidebook and papers to the drawer in the dressing table. Then I let myself out of the balcony door, go down the steps and take a long, solitary walk along the water, accompanied (mentally) by a yearning 'Gabriel's Oboe'.

I did enough homework – when Jake was frowning over the orchids – to learn there's no Elena Zacharia listed as alive, dead or missing in the official records office in Nicosia. I say that, but without proper identifying information, I can't know it for sure. The family spoke of coming from Famagusta, though where Elena's fabled tree houses were, I've not even a vague idea. I look behind me at the shabby whitewashed hotel, wondering. Verena Bay was long established before the Zacharia family went to England but was she ever here? Nearby? Theirs isn't a name or story known to Petros or his Aunt Ana – it would have come back to me via my parents if so. The island was only divided in 1974, of course, so the places she used to talk about could have been anywhere. But Verena Bay is the kind of place Elena would have known, I tell myself: this strip of coast, off the beaten track, no fast road eastwards and still today a century away from modern Agia Napa. But do I magically feel Elena's presence as I walk along the beach? No, I don't.

Petros calls out at the sound of my flip-flops on the stone flags. He appears to be treating the new receptionist to his version of afternoon tea, at the corner table beside the unlit fireplace. She already looks vaguely put out, and then glowers as he beckons me over. I'm sure she expected dinner and seduction, but within the confines of an establishment more upmarket and less empty than the Verena Bay, and not at nursery teatime. However, to complain is, of course, to sneer at her new place of work. For whatever reason, Petros cultivates a persona here, more than one, none of them the man I know. He cared for his aunt, and has looked out for me, opened the doors to Verena Bay for me, without ever dwelling on my errors of judgement or Jake's shortcomings. Petros is astute, a charmer and, yes, he loves women. Judging by his choice of staff, he also has a penchant for haughty girls with hourglass figures but he's neither naïvely avuncular nor a dirty old man. When he *doesn't* send this receptionist off home with a wink and a fleeting hand on the behind, she pouts even more. Petros watches her go, appraising. 'By mid-summer,' he says, 'she will have found a job renting upmarket holiday apartments in Limassol. Good luck to her.' Shades of Nicole's assessment, I think. He turns back to me and indicates the now-vacant seat opposite him. 'What?' He sees my lips twitch.

'Nothing. Honestly, nothing,' I insist, as Petros crosses his arms and narrows his eyes, because I'm never going to admit how Ana warned me off him. It was via my poor mother, whose whisper was disbelieving and scandalised: 'She says to "keep Petros as a friend. Sleep with him, if you must. Marry him for the hotel, but don't fall in love with him. That one is a gypsy spirit, a romancer, but his friendship is solid".' I knew Mum was quoting word for word, even before she added, 'April, I was so embarrassed, but Ana just laughed.' I grin as I imagine the scenario. 'I was just remembering something Ana told my mum,' I admit to Petros.

He puts his hands to his ears and pretends to shiver. 'You win. I do not wish to know.' Then, 'Are you hungry? Dinner tonight is a buffet, a chance for guests to mingle.' He lowers his voice. 'Actually, it's the chef's night off and my cooking was all learned in the Army Catering Corps. So be kind. And choose wisely.'

The food set out in the centre of the dining room is an amalgam of cold cuts, cheeses and salads, plus anything else Petros has had time to chuck into the mix. He's concocted a roasted tomato tart, which is delicious, and a waxy crème caramel – pudding, he calls it – which is not. I taste both before filling my plate. I pour a glass of something that might be rum punch, might be blackcurrant squash, and go and sit back down.

'Was it a successful mission to the airport?' I ask Petros, doing my best to affect indifference.

'Indeed. Yiannis is now at home and looking forward to meeting you tomorrow.' When I all I do is smile into his pregnant pause, he goes on, 'And you found our men in Agia Napa.'

'Um-hmm.'

'Red seems a decent bloke, as you English say. His brothers promise to be... lively.'

'Ah, but did you meet them as priests or not... Oh.'

'Speak of the devil—'

'Speaking of priests—'

We both start, and stop, at the same time.

'I need to talk to you further about Yiannis,' Petros says in a rapid undertone, as he rises to greet the somewhat sheepishly approaching Kevin and Jarlath, leaving me no time to ponder. Fresh-faced and dressed in jeans and t-shirts, they're now advertising their commitment to nothing more celestial than Gap.

'Howya, Petros. April,' Jarlath says. 'April' – he sounds as if he really wants to call me Miss something – 'me and himself owe you an apology. We're sorry for being made fools of by the drink.'

'Our father Red has given us a hard time already,' Kevin adds. 'Sorry.'

'You were just a bit drunk.' I let them off the hook. 'It's a big brother's job to give you a hard time.'

'I could warm to a lady who calls on-our-arses fluthered at midday a "bit drunk". April, will you marry me when I grow up?'

'Oh, oh, conscience alert.' Jarlath's is a stage whisper. 'We'll scarper. Find some dinner. Leave you to the father.'

Sticking their respective thumbs up to an approaching Red, they wander towards the other end of the dining room and are enthusiastically – almost literally – grabbed by the gleeful teenage waitress.

'No lasting damage done then,' I say, as we watch them. 'How did they bounce back with so little trauma?'

'They are twenty-something. Nothing, if only we knew it, is irreparably damaged at that age.' Petros shrugs philosophically, making me feel middle-aged and doubly sensible. 'I was in the army at nineteen, and known to take a drink or two and still be on parade at dawn. Ah – Red.' He looks up and gestures. 'Please, help yourself, then join us.'

As he does so, Petros gives Red a potted history of this corner of Cyprus. Our host would have his guests believe that this stretch of land has belonged to the Evagora family since the Mycenaean-Achaean Greeks became permanent settlers. People believe him because most, myself included, haven't a clue when that was. Even fewer examine the ancient land boundary document on the wall above the bar to discover the map has been photocopied upside down and the names filled in with biro.

'The Verena Bay Hotel and Verena Bay are now one and the same,' Petros boasts, sweeping out his arms to embrace the view.

Red and I follow his gaze. And I think, as I did when I arrived and got a similar spiel, he's a lot to boast about. Life here faces out towards the bay I was recently walking along. From the top of the drive, a visitor who can see beyond the concrete barbecue area (three empty gas cylinders and a half-dozen plastic picnic tables) finds a large stone house, whitewashed and shuttered, that is only steps from the honey-coloured sand. The upper windows have black wrought-iron balconies barely wide enough for a window box each, and the lower ones have doors leading directly to the cracked stone terrace, and so to the water. The old side entrance, once the servants' route to the main hall, is now the hotel reception and dining area. In the orchard, camouflaged by orange trees, a line of concrete huts is the tongue-in-cheek stable block where Kevin and Jarlath, when not flirting at the other side of the dining room, are happily ensconced. Thinking of the twins, my eyes swivel over to them; either one of them speaks rudimentary Greek or the now-radiant waitress has a talent for sign language. *I learned some sign language once,* I think, totally out of the blue. I picked it up from Elena, talking to her sister, Sofia, though I was far too shy for a long time to use more than a modified wave for hello and goodbye...

'It's named for my Aunt Ana,' Petros is saying when I tune back in. 'When she was born, her other grandfather, living in what is now Kyrenia, in the North, bought this specific piece of land for her and said he would name it in her honour. The baby was nameless for months before they settled on Ana Verena.'

'I never knew that,' I say. 'It's a lovely story.'

'Ana Verena,' echoes Red. 'I'll probably look a fool here, but Ana for Grace and Verena for, for... Defender? Protector? Please tell me I'm near the mark or it's five years of higher education and half a doctorate down the drain.'

'Impressive.' Petros claps him on the shoulder and it's on my lips to ask what he's studying when Red beats me, with the inevitable question.

'Is your aunt here now?'

'No. Thia Ana lived in England for years, she never really came back after the island was divided – along with her loyalties,' Petros says slowly. 'She died nearly a year ago. She was very elderly.' He's looking at me now, semaphoring with his eyes, subtly, but I can see Red intercept him.

'My parents died at the same time. An accident,' I jump in. 'It's how Petros and me know each other.'

Red closes his eyes briefly. 'I'm sorry for you loss, Petros.' He turns to me, and I *know* he would have taken my hand if we'd been alone. 'Yours too, April.' He stops there, with none of the embarrassment or curiosity or downright voyeurism I've come to expect. We just look at each other.

Petros picks up a timely glass and, with it, the earlier thread of conversation. 'Here's to Ana Verena. As my aunt herself always said, what other name could have seen this place stand untouched through the many tribulations of Cyprus?' He gets to his feet, calling to the young waitress as he does so. 'Come to the bar for coffee? April, I have filter coffee, just for you.'

'You're not converted to Cypriot coffee yet?' Red asks me, as we re-establish ourselves in the cosy bar area. He indicates two waiting espresso cups, set on a low table and filled to the brim with a grainy treacle. There's a cafetière and jug of milk in judgement beside them.

'I haven't written it off yet,' I say. 'But mostly because the alternative seems to be a sachet of Nescafé and a mug of warm water.'

'When you meet Damaris, Andreas' mother, ask her to make you her *metrios*,' Petros advises. 'It is the perfect introduction.' His eyes twinkle. 'I am sure there is a warm-blooded Cypriot-April lurking under your cool English surface.'

'Remember my parents came from Poland. The whole of me is about as far from Mediterranean as you can get,' I protest. 'In the circumstances, I'd say I'm positively oozing warmth.'

Red, stirring sugar into his drink, says gallantly, 'On first impressions, I think the English-April has a lot going for her.' Before I have to think of a clever and witty answer, he carries on, 'What are your plans now, Petros? For the hotel. *If* that's not a rude question from a stranger.'

'Ah. How do I make Verena Bay more cultured and sophisticated than a faded roadside stopover for transient backpackers—'

'No!' Red and I are in unison but Petros is grinning.

'Do not worry. The joy of the Verena Bay Hotel is that the words "corporate, fine dining, and nightclub" are a foreign language.' Gesturing around the room, he says, 'I was a little boy here; raised by my widowed mother, my grandparents and Ana, perpetually the traditional spinster aunt. They kept the place more as a smallholding and a hostelry for fishermen. From the shadows, we have watched Agia Napa flourish.' He pauses to down his coffee in one. 'And never have we wanted to be part of it. And never will we…' This time the pause is for dramatic effect, he knows he has us eating out of his hand. 'Thia Ana has left her "home" to her only nephew, Petros Evagora, on the understanding…' He makes quote marks in the air and declares, '"He maintains it as an independent boutique hotel, without recourse to mortgage, property redevelopment or tertiary investment". Blah, blah, blah. Basically, dear friends, I cannot sell-out, or buy-in big.'

'But you don't disagree with any of that – do you,' I point out.

'Not at all, dear April. It is only that she has trumped me. She has won not just the match but the tournament. Game, set and match.' He roars with laughter. 'Thia Ana always did have the last word. And now she has had the very last one.'

10

The very next day, Red and I are strolling along the beach towards Agia Triada and Yiannis' house.

'I need to finish some work here. Tax,' Petros announced a few minutes ago, bailing out on us travelling as a threesome. To be fair he did look faintly harassed, refusing all offers of help. 'Why don't the two of you go ahead? It will take only an hour or so, and it is a glorious afternoon for a walk.' He led Red and me, both hovering in the reception area, to the balcony and pointed vaguely. 'Walk as far as the little church and then turn left. April, you have been there – is that not where you first met Andreas?'

'Where I thought he was stalking me,' I corrected him. 'But yes.'

Petros shook his head. 'Dear April, let me say again, it is an honour. Andreas has a remarkable talent for portraiture. It is rumoured he has been commissioned to paint an important political duo. There is much speculation as to whom.'

'A retrospective of Archbishop Makarios and General Grivas, maybe?' I knew I was grumbling stupidly – nerves on all levels.

The sarcasm was wasted on Petros anyway. He merely saluted my knowledge of Cypriot history and shooed us on our way.

If it feels awkward to be meeting Yiannis at all, let

alone in the company of Red and half of the Agia Triada residents, well, it's not something I can put off. I've already acknowledged how my letters to Yiannis started as a juvenile tit-for-tat when Jake ran off with Erica, but I learned to look forward to his words. Yiannis isn't the average wish-you-were-here type, scribbling on the back of a postcard – he's poetic, lyrical and funny. But that's as a writer, and who's to say it translates to the person? The musician-me and the woman-me couldn't be more different. I can't deny, either, that Petros' suggestion Yiannis wants a wife is niggling.

'Could it be a more perfect day?' Red interrupts my tortuous interior monologue, and he's right. 'Beautiful setting, sunshine, good company.'

'It's not what I expected, any of this,' I blurt out, not exactly sure what bit of 'this' I'm referring to. I divert randomly into, 'What are your brothers doing now?'

Red takes it in his stride. 'Studying, surprisingly,' he says. 'I know, you can't imagine it. You'll also have difficulty imagining them as doctors... I do.' He pauses and I do my best to look unsurprised. 'Yep, second year medical students, so a way to go. But if you had a prostate you could look forward to Kevin tinkering with it in a few years' time.'

'What about Jarlath?'

'Hmm. I'm not sure Jarlath is as committed,' Red says, 'but he's clever, and in Ireland if you're clever and get a lot of points in your Leaving Cert, you ride on a sort of law or medicine wave. I have a feeling it was easier for Jarlath to follow Kevin than decide what he really wanted – wants.' Red bends down, selects a flat stone and skims it into the water. It bounces and sinks and we both laugh. 'I expect he'll find his way. Nothing's ever wasted, is it?'

'No... I mean, I hope not.' My own career swims into focus, forcing the honesty out. If things had been different, would I be spending a life hiding behind a piano? Marrying unsuitable men? Wandering like a spare part on a foreign island, chasing the ghosts of the past? Red's looking at me in concern and I force a laugh. 'Don't mind me. Midlife crisis. I was forty last birthday.'

'Ah. I was precocious, I had mine at thirty. But men don't live as long as women, do they, so we're quits, I'd say.'

We walk on for a few seconds, quiet but not uncomfortable.

'Losing your parents, and together, is a crisis at any age,' Red says, after a while. 'Be kind to yourself, April.'

'I am. I'm running away,' I say rashly. 'I was supposed to get on a plane to Berlin but went to the stand-by desk and changed it to Larnaca. I've never done anything so... so unplanned.' I flick a sideways glance at him.

'Why?' he asks.

'Why?'

'Yes. Why?'

'Well, I...' For a second, I'm flummoxed because it's a blanket question nobody has asked me. Yiannis assumes I'm here for the orchids (aka to meet him); Petros would say it's a mix of Elena and Ana's relationship with my parents; Jake, by now, will think I'm putting one over on him; and the Berlin Philharmonic will probably write it off as that midlife crisis. And it is all of those things, it's just that it's also *more*. 'I'm lost,' I tell him. 'Lost among loose ends.'

'Go on.'

Words tumble out of me. So many, I'm not sure they even make sense, but suddenly it doesn't matter. Red may have asked but I'm talking to myself and the words are flying away on snatches of wind, way out to sea. I can almost see them, like crochets and minims breaking free from bars of music on a dancing score. The individual verses are the story of my life; the chorus is Elena. Everything comes back to Elena.

'Do you think I'm crazy?' I follow up the silence when I finish.

'No.' Red doesn't hesitate or ask me to elaborate – the

usual responses. He takes my hand and keeps hold of it as we walk the length of the beach. It's warm and solid and... *understanding*. As if he means it.

'You should be a counsellor,' I say finally. Then I stop dead, awkward. 'Oh. Maybe you are? You're a good listener. Sorry if this is a busman's holiday.' When I attempt to untangle my hand, he tightens his grip and I'm glad of it. He looks as if he's searching for the words.

'I feel... You... You and me... I'm not wrong, am I?' He shakes his head and starts again. 'I'm also not a counsellor,' he says. 'But I am something that's very hard to admit at this point.'

I wait. We walk.

Finally, Red says, 'I'm a priest, April. The whole shebang – a Roman Catholic priest.'

I have a fraction of a second to let it sink in, marshal my feelings, and reject all and sundry clichés. I float down from my cloud a little, as I say, 'Damn,' quietly but smiling.

'Yes.'

I can see he means it. 'A good priest, and a happy one.' I manage to make it a statement.

'I thought I was – no, I *am* happy,' he says, ruefully. 'I hope I'm good – enough. I have *a lot* to learn. I was ordained a curate two years ago, so a new priest, but still a proper-ish one.'

'Our father.' I start to laugh, Kevin and Jarlath in my mind's eye. 'Of course, and the fancy-dress outfits. It's starting to make sense.'

'Glad you think so.' But Red is laughing too. 'They were at a stag do and thought it was a hilarious idea. They also think I'm mad. A lot of people do. It's very all-or-nothing.'

There's an unspoken question in his voice, one I can answer in my own way. 'I'm a good-enough pianist,' I say. 'Unlike you, that's as high as I'll ever reach, and no, I'm not being modest. Sometimes I love it, sometimes I loathe it, but it's what I am and nothing will change that even if

I... I... *do* stay hidden in Verena Bay forever, tinkling the keys on Petros' ancient baby grand. So,' I squeeze his hand, 'I understand exactly.'

'You do, don't you?' Red stops and looks at me, then lets his gaze wander over the beach. 'My life was simple and clear, right until I rounded the corner yesterday at the monastery and there, between my idiot little brothers, saw you. I floundered, April.'

'I know,' is all I can handle, heart hammering. 'I felt it too. Even though I don't believe in *feelings*.' When he grins, I make a snap decision to make light of it. 'And it's just as well you're a priest. I always pick the wrong man, always for all the wrong reasons, and it always goes very, very wrong.'

At that, Red laughs out loud and pulls me sideways towards him in a hug that is not as brief as it should be. 'So we bury this... this connection, or whatever it is we have?' he asks into my hair.

'Or we explore it, find an acceptable way to "connect".' I pull a face. 'Now I sound like a counsellor.'

'You sound sensible.'

'And that's the story of my life,' I tell him.

'Is this the shortest love affair in history?' he says. 'If so, it makes *Brief Encounter* seems like a saga.' We walk on, and after a little while he adds, 'It's not though, is it?'

'A thwarted love affair?' I shake my head and try to find the words. 'No. I don't know what it is, but it's not romantic. Is it?'

'No... I don't think so.' He looks as uncertain as I do. 'I don't know.'

A few more steps, then, 'We're old souls,' I settle on. 'That's what Thia Ana would have said. Not soulmates exactly. It's about intuition or instinct.' I'm making it up as I go along, half believing it.

'Down to some kind of physical time blip in the universe?'

We look at each other and laugh.

'It's not a love affair,' I repeat. 'This wouldn't be so easy if it were.' And I think we both believe it. Or maybe we're both simply sensible.

Nicole is waiting for us at Agia Triada church, to take us to Yiannis' house; Petros arrived there a little while ago. There's no implied rebuke or even query that Red and I have taken so long to walk the beach, but still we avoid each other's eyes. I greet Nicole, no doubt led by her effusiveness, in a most unlike-April way – English-April, anyway, maybe the Cypriot-April is worth cultivating – as a long-lost sister. She's swapped her purple outfit for an emerald-green shirt and pale jeans and I'm relieved that I fit in, even if I don't wear clothes as well as her or Red.

We cross the old dirt and concrete road and head up a rocky avenue away from the sea. Halfway up, we see Andreas coming towards us. He greets Red first, with a perfectly normal handshake-and-kind-words welcome. Then he turns to me, looks me up and down and nods, looking relieved. It isn't rude or disrespectful, more as if I'm a treasured possession, briefly taken from him and now rightfully and properly returned. It's weird but not unpleasantly weird. There is, as far as I can tell politely, no sign of Ganesh the elephant god anywhere about his person.

'Yiannis has a leak,' Andreas then announces, mostly to Nicole. 'I have invited people to gather instead at our house. Maybe twenty guests, Yiannis thinks.'

Nicole's brow creases, though nowhere near as much as mine would if landed with a score of guests at a couple of hours' notice. 'Has he called a plumber?' she asks. 'Andreas? Did you ask Yiannis if he has telephoned a plumber to deal with the fault?'

'He says it is under control. He is repairing it now.'

'No,' says Nicole. 'No, no and no. Give me your cell phone. Quickly, Andreas.'

Meekly, he hands it over.

Nicole, dialling rapidly, turns to Red and me. 'Excuse me while I avert a crisis. Yiannis is one of the kindest men you will meet,' she explains as the phone rings. 'He is also one of the most inept. He cheerfully tackles all irritations that come his way and he elicits chaos. Last year his lights fused and he managed to plunge not just Agia Triada, but the coast as far as Agia Napa, into pitch-blackness for several hours. This time, we cannot allow a flood— Ah.' She switches to Greek and, a few minutes later, says *yassou*, makes a second briefer call, then clicks the phone shut and hands it back to Andreas. 'The plumber is on his way here,' Nicole says. 'Yiannis has promised to find the stopcock and switch off the water and to do nothing else.'

'Where would we be without my beautiful and efficient wife?' Andreas touches her hair admiringly.

'You would be left catering an impromptu party for dozens of guests with no idea how to achieve it.' It's the first cheerful indication that she even heard the other part of Andreas' bombshell.

'I will get out the glasses,' Andreas offers. 'And I will go back to Yiannis and see what food and drink he has planned.'

'Just bring the alcohol,' says Nicole. 'Lots of it. We have plenty of meze in the deep freeze.'

He ambles off and we three watch him.

'Well,' says Red. 'This is a side of Yiannis I've never seen.'

'Certainly not how he comes across in his letters,' I murmur.

Nicole covers her mouth in mock horror. 'Oh, my goodness, I am so indiscreet. Please forget what I said. I seem to have taken upon myself the mantle of village-auntie bossiness. I am very fond of Yiannis. He is an expert botanist, and he was always a thoughtful priest but he has so much to learn as a host... April, what is wrong?' She swings off at a tangent. 'And Red? Why are you laughing at her?'

'Not at April, at the situation.' Red's broad grin lies somewhere between amusement and sympathy as he watches my face. 'April? You didn't know, did you? It never occurred to me to say that's how Yiannis and I met. We're writing a theology book together.'

'Yiannis is a priest as well?' Why the hell didn't Petros tell me? Before I blurt that out, Nicole corrects me.

'He *was* a priest,' she says. 'But still – April? Red? What is the problem?'

I just groan. Coming here in the steps of Elena, I thought, was eccentric, but before I start I'm deep in the twilight zone.

'A double whammy of priests,' says Red.

11

Two hours later, the double doors between Nicole's sitting room and dining room have been pulled back to create a single large space. I wander over from the guest room, one of two joined by a bathroom and tiny lounge, purpose-built in light wood, at the far end of the site.

'Consider this your room for as long as you wish,' Nicole said, as she showed me to it. 'If Petros has an overflow of guests or if you need a hideaway.' She urged me to rest, as if I'd trekked the Sahara on a camel rather than strolled along the beach, and I wonder if I looked as winded as I felt. Now I've got my brave face on, ready as I'll ever be to socialise.

The glass doors to the garden are open too, and the strategic outdoor lights-cum-heaters give the impression of infinity. The furniture is pushed back and small tables, tall ashtrays and a selection of rugs are scattered about the tiled floor. The baby grand piano, a middle-of-the-range Steinway, remains, thankfully, in situ. It's an ornament, rather than a musical instrument; it gives this space an air of the *salon*. I wonder if Andreas or Nicole designed the house. From the front and rear, it resembles two neighbouring cottages, small and traditional, yet the centre is modern and minimalist in the extreme. It would take an expert eye to explain *how* it works, but it does.

There's a smattering of people, all strangers. I can't see

Nicole, and Andreas is in close conversation with someone whose back's towards me; all I see are yellow shoes. I haven't yet set eyes on Yiannis – leak fixed, apparently – or if I have, he hasn't made himself known. Feeling out of place, I resist the compulsion to sit at the piano and instead examine the artwork on the walls. It's a legitimate reason to turn my back on the room; not a wallflower but looking at flowers on the wall – inwardly I groan at my own pun – until I feel a tap on my shoulder and whirl around to find Red proffering a flute of champagne.

'You deserve a magnum of it.' He lowers his voice. 'You really can have too much of the Church, even at Easter. Though if you quote me on that I shall have to convert you.'

'Don't be daft.' I brush it off. 'Why should it make any difference if Yiannis was once a priest too? I barely even know him.'

'It always matters,' Red's voice is neutral, 'when the priest in question is quite smitten by you.'

I can't tell if his ambiguity is deliberate so I take him at face value, to stop it getting complicated. 'Did he – Yiannis, I mean – did he tell you that?'

'Not in so many words. Yiannis is the soul of discretion.' Petros had said as much. 'He mentioned that there was a woman he was in contact with, that he was going to meet her soon and had... hopes.' Red shrugs and half smiles. 'I didn't realise until today, but it has to be you, April.'

I sigh from the soles of my feet.

Red looks, I don't know, amused? Sympathetic? Sympathetically amused about covers it. 'There's only one thing for it,' he says.

'What?'

'A refill of the fizzy stuff. Wait here. Don't run away – again – because if you do, I *will* come and find you.'

I turn back to the paintings, bracing myself.

Red returns quickly, with two more drinks, and a shadow in tow. Even without the barely discernible wink – maybe it is a genuine twitch – I know this is going to have to be Yiannis and I call on all my PR skills.

Sure enough, Red turns slightly and pulls the shrinking figure forward. 'Yiannis, this is April. April, Yiannis.'

'Yiannis.' I put out my hand, hoping I sound warm enough. 'It's lovely to finally meet you.'

'And for me to meet you.' He shakes my hand jerkily up and down. 'Welcome to Agia Triada. I hope Petros has been looking after you well. The Verena Bay Hotel is a very special place.'

'Yes, it is. Thank you. He is.'

'Good. That is very good.'

We look at each other. My performance skills are shot and Yiannis' have rigor mortis. Red, clearly adept at defusing awkward moments, grabs the safe and mutual subject of Jarlath and Kevin and their exploits in Agia Napa. I nod and smile and attempt to regroup my thoughts. When there was little but a grey English day and the increasing drudge of work to fill my thoughts, Yiannis' letters were a ray of potential. Seeing him in the flesh, I try to locate a similar warmth and faint excitement in this small, thin man in an ill-fitting suit. He looks shy. He looks eager. He looks – and I despise myself for this – like an ex-priest on a blind date. Why, oh why – I try to stem the forbidden, adolescent thought, but it's off like a runaway train – couldn't Yiannis have been a straightforward Red package?

'I'm looking forward to seeing a lot more of Cyprus.' I blurt out something, anything. 'You know this is my first visit here?' Of course he does. 'And you know I'm ignorant about orchids. That was Jake's thing… But I suppose you're never too old to learn…' I run out of steam again.

'Perhaps I might convert you,' says Yiannis, oh-so polite. He can't know his innocent choice of word has me all but wincing. 'Cyprus is a wild garden, and the contrast between orchids of the mountain ranges and coastal plains is breathtaking. I hope I may be able to show you, if you have the time and inclination.' His whole speech is seeking approval, which I hasten to give. It's impossible, even if I wanted to, to picture this man preaching in front of a congregation, certainly not hellfire and damnation. But Yiannis is warming to his theme. 'I have a microbus with eight seats,' he's saying. 'We – all of us, I mean, with Petros, Andreas and Nicole – could take a short trip, orchid hunting, perhaps. To Trooditissa or even the Karpass Peninsula.' He looks between Red and me.

'I'm in.' Red saves the day and I think Yiannis is probably as relieved as me that he and I won't be a default twosome.

'It sounds good.' Only a beat too late I agree. 'As to where, just tell us what *you* think is best. You're the expert.'

'Oh, no, no. Not an expert.' Yiannis looks more shell-shocked than bolstered in the face of my positivity and conversation dries up again.

Afraid he'll discreetly leave us, I let Red steer us towards Andreas and the sideboard where the drinks are set out. As well as the champagne, which I need to slow down on because I really don't drink, there is a cloudy aniseed ouzo, carafes of wine and a large punchbowl that must be the brandy sour concoction so famous locally.

Unwisely, I let Red fill my glass again and we each spear a couple of olives. Andreas turns, sees us, and brings over his companion with the yellow shoes. 'April, Red, this is Georgios of the Village Tavern,' he introduces us. 'He does not speak much English.'

'Better than my Greek. *Kalimera… Kalispera.*'

I raise my glass to Georgios, floundering, but he replies with an apparently delighted, 'Good days,' and we do lots of manic nodding and smiling.

Yiannis coughs beside me. 'I would be pleased to teach you some Greek,' he says. 'It would be my pleasure.'

'Well, thank you,' I say – lamely doesn't cover it. 'But I'm sure it would be a chore. I don't have an ear for languages at all. Even though I know that's a terrible excuse. I started an evening course in college, about twenty years ago now,' I don't add that it was fuelled by fond memories of the odd words picked up from Elena and her family, 'and lasted a term.'

'Maybe a classroom is unhelpful for you?' Yiannis suggests. 'It was certainly unhelpful for me, but then I was the teacher. And I do not have an ear for that, at all.' He goes on, smiling, self-deprecating, and suddenly – though maybe it's the alcohol – I see a glimmer of the man hidden in his letters.

It's an old joke but I laugh. He's encouraged.

'We could speak informally, perhaps during dinner. Perhaps at Georgios' tavern. Would that be acceptable to you?'

Since refusing will demonstrate I've written him off after five minutes and I can't do that, I nod and grin, hearing a burst of Ignaz Pleyel and a few violins in the ether.

Poor Yiannis looks hugely relieved, then elated. He blushes and wrings his hands together. Half agreeing to dinner seems shockingly close to agreeing to marry him. I need to be careful.

Red turns from Andreas and Georgios, back to us. He's holding out a bottle, and I, usually so temperate, thrust my glass forward. Yiannis shrinks back and covers his with his palm. When I realise that Andreas has reverted to type and is sketching me on his napkin, I try to focus on him. Things ease further when Nicole makes an appearance.

'What is happening?' She's bearing fragrant plates of a meaty stew, which she places carefully on the table. 'Eat,' she urges, inclining her head. 'The *Psito*, please eat it. We have cooked much too much.'

She comes to stand close behind me, her hand gently on my elbow. I ignore the food, relax into the moral support, and explain I'm having dinner with Yiannis and looking forward to Andreas painting me.

'That is good. Very good, in fact.' She stands for a moment, watching her nearest guests attack the food. Then she surveys the room in general, and swoops on the empty canapé bowls. 'April?' she says. 'Would you help me?'

I could kiss her. Instead, I follow her what seems like a long way round to the huge country kitchen. She dumps the dishes in one of the sinks, and I ask what I can do.

'Nothing.' She leans against the counter. 'I was rescuing you. I spied Damaris, my mother-in-law, just arriving. Do not misunderstand me, Damaris and Orestes are a delightful couple, but Yiannis, Andreas – I think you have met enough new people for one day. Yes?'

'Yes, oh, yes.' I sink down onto the nearest chair, a battered sofa in the corner and supremely comfortable, and ease my shoes off.

'It is only a temporary reprieve,' she warns. 'Damaris is the original village auntie – the heart of the community, the gossip, the caretaker, the matchmaker. Before you even know it, she will have your life story. Now, what may I serve you?'

'Could I have a glass of water?' I rest my chin on my right palm.

Nicole fills two sparkling glasses from the fridge, plops in ice and adds slivers of lemon. She ladles *Psito* into two deep bowls, hands one to me, and suddenly I'm ravenous. We eat quickly and she serves more, pushing a breadbasket towards me too.

'What else?' she says, looking around. 'Anything you need, just tell me. April?' she adds as I don't respond, my attention snatched suddenly by the pattern on the matching bowls. They're images of matryoshka dolls, those ones that nest inside each other, crudely printed and gaudy. 'Awful, are they not?' Nicole follows my gaze. 'A gift from Damaris. She bought a box at the market to use as water bowls for her precious pets. These were the spares.'

'I've seen them before,' I tell her. 'Somewhere…' And then it comes to me: Elena's mama had them too, three of them, kept on the high shelf above the kitchen sink. They were for the keys to the shop, to the storeroom and to the freezers. There was a broken chest freezer they used for chip wrappers and Stefan, Elena's stepfather, was afraid – irrationally so, when I look back; he was always warning us – that we'd climb in, get stuck and suffocate. Without thinking how oddly I'm behaving, I pick them up, move over to the dresser and arrange them one, two, three, on the top shelf. That's it; they were just like that.

'April?' Nicole sounds more uncertain this time.

Briskly, I take them back down and pile them up. I owe her an explanation. 'I had a Cypriot friend once. Elena. Her family had these bowls. I'd forgotten.'

'A long time ago?' she asks.

'She left England in 1974. To return here.'

'Oh.' Nicole gets the significance straightaway. Slowly she comes and sits beside me, tucking her feet underneath her, and looking as if she was just waiting for me to say something like this. 'Will you tell me about her?' she asks.

I pick up a spoon, lay it down and wonder what's got into me. Is it more than the drink talking? Probably not – I'm a cheap date, according to Jake; I think he was being affectionate. But a dam burst open with Red today and here, sitting with Nicole, in her quiet kitchen, the muted buzz of a party beyond, it feels... not familiar this time, but somehow safe. A moment in a million.

'I can tell you my story,' I say. 'Elena's though...' I picture the letter tucked into her old guidebook, her ten-year-old confusion at arriving in a warzone, then – nothing more. 'Elena's story, I just don't know.'

12

Agia Napa, Cyprus
Saturday 20th July 1974

Dear April and Mrs Gale's class,

Already I am writing my number two letter and it is just the next day. There is no news but there is nothing to do either, so really this is a diary. The soldiers have let us leave the airport but they were not pleased. They wanted us to get back on the next aeroplane to England but Aunt Irini argued and cried so long that it went without us and there isn't another one. Everyone is evacuated, which means sent away from danger. We are going home and homes are safe, so don't worry we will be okay. Antony paid some money to a soldier who brought a car and now we are driving.

Actually, Krista says, we are not driving, and if I'm keeping a diary then I should be correct. The car is stuck because the main road to where the tree houses are is shut. It is blocked off by a red and angry STOP sign being held up by a policeman, who is even redder and angrier. Krista says he looks like he should be married to the lollipop lady outside our school because she has the same face on when the big boys play Chicken in the street. I am not talking to Krista. She pretended our mum is in prison after the coup and that's why the soldiers *didn't want us to go, in case we helped her escape. Why would Krista say that? She's mean. She said she heard the airport soldiers tell Antony, but it is not true because we are on our way to meet my mum and Stefan <u>right now</u>.*

Antony also has a red face and Aunt Irini a white one. Maybe they are carsick or sun-sick. Antony has not got the right papers for the policeman to change his STOP sign to GO, so the policeman wants money instead but I don't think we have enough. We have to take the car to the side of the road and wait and wait and wait. There are some donkeys and an outhouse but nothing else. It is funny to think that last Saturday was chips and The Generation Game. I hope you are not too lonely watching it without us, April. When we get to the tree houses and I see my friend Mamun, I will tell him all about you.

Love from, Elena Z
xxx

PS After I wrote this I have seen a lizard. Lizards are like the stick insects in the classroom tank, but are more curved and green with scales and they twitch themselves.

Elena watched the lizard and the lizard watched Elena. It watched her as if its sliding sideways eyes knew the game they were playing. Elena held her breath but the lizard breathed quickly, its long body going in-out-in-out at the sides, the way her *papous* made his accordion play.

If the lizard moves first, I win, I win. If the lizard moves first I win... In the dank privy, Elena sang a silent song. It was a game of If: if she won, the sign would change from *STOP* to *GO*. They would roar down the road and turn the last corner and there would be the sea, with Uncle Costas' little blue and white boat bobbing in the harbour. If the boat were there, he would be resting on its deck, his head under his handkerchief hat. If Uncle Costas were there then Aunt Zara would be on the road, wobbling to Mass, her rosary beads clicking in time with her best false teeth. If Aunt Zara were there, then so would be the tree houses standing proud on the beach, reflections all dizzy in the water. And if all that happened, please, please, *please*, St Mary the Theotokos, Mama would be waiting too.

'Elena, Elena, daydream girl. Come out, come out, whatever you do. We're very desperate.'

Elena's breath gave way and she tipped from her squatting position. The lizard vanished. Who was the winner? The lizard or the girl? Or was it a tie? If it was a tie, did that mean they both won or neither?

'Elena, Elena. Come out, now, now, now… Too late, we're coming in.'

The voice got louder. Quickly, Elena pulled up her knickers, smoothed her dress and yanked open the door of the dark, damp lavatory. Her two sisters, the oldest hauling the smallest behind her, crashed inside.

'Sofia, pee.' Krista pushed the little girl in the direction of the hole in the ground, making hurrying motions. Then, hands on her hips, she turned and stared at Elena, half trapped behind the door. 'I've got news,' Krista announced. 'I've got big news, daydream girl.'

Elena's heart jumped of its own accord. 'The *STOP* sign is *GO*? We can go?'

'No, silly. They're still talking. Yap, yap, yap.' With her narrowed eyes, her tongue poking out, just a bit, and her chest rising and falling in excitement, she looked exactly like the lizard, Elena thought – only a whole lot more cunning. 'Ask me what it is then,' she demanded.

'What?' Elena was unwilling. She didn't want to play the game today, she couldn't. But saying so would just make Krista worse. 'Alright. Tell me. Please.'

Sure enough, Krista stood grandly. 'I *might* tell you. I haven't decided.' She poked her toe out and jabbed Elena on the leg. 'First, you can hold the mirror for me. My face feels shiny. I'm afraid I look like you.'

Elena pulled the half-hearted cross face that Krista expected, but didn't bother arguing that she wanted to wash her hands. It saved time to follow Krista's orders first and then do what you really wanted. The square of glass, cracked and sharp at the edges, spotted with brown marks, hung on the back of the door attached to a pin by a piece of string. For enough light to see themselves, the girls took it outside where the sun was brightest.

'Hold it higher, higher,' Krista commanded. 'I need to comb my hair.'

Elena swallowed a sigh, and with it a wish that April was there with them; Krista showed off more, but bossed less when April was there. Obediently, she angled the makeshift mirror away from the dancing, blinding sunbeams so that Krista could admire herself and see how like Twiggy she looked. Elena wished she had that glossy, straight hair inherited from Aunt Irini. Hair as long and sleek as Black Beauty's tail, hair that never tangled and never lost its almond-oil scent, even in England. It was straight hair, which looked so nice with Krista's heart-shaped face. Even the brand-new pixie cut suited her, though Elena still got a shock when she saw it and Aunt Irini had nearly dropped dead. What was Mama going to say?

Krista was thin too, skinny so that the fat village aunties had always sighed and pinched her cheeks and given her food. They had done it to Elena as well, but with a chuckle not a sigh and Elena knew it was because she was one of them; Krista was the oldest sister but Elena was the biggest. Elena looked like Mama, with big bones, and curling hair that never settled; a fine big girl, she had heard the fat village aunties approve, a fine wife and mother-in-waiting was what they said. She wondered if they would still say it now, now that they were back after one whole year away. Would everyone remember them? Elena thought she had forgotten Cyprus but as soon as they left the airport and Nicosia behind, it was England that started to get blurry. She tried to paint a picture of April in her head, but the village aunties were already getting in the way. And what if April forgot her? Elena hadn't even been able to say goodbye. She didn't cry much but in the dark on the aeroplane she had cried for that.

Sofia, peeing done, clamoured to look in the mirror too. Down, down, she signed, jumping like one of the skittish donkeys hee-hawing by the side of the road, one second stock-still, the next braying their business over fields of corn, trampling the yellow flowers. With Sofia, the village aunties pinched both her cheeks, gave her sweets and said *poor little Sofia,* crying or laughing depending on the taste of the day. Elena didn't understand them, there was nothing poor about Sofia. She was always happy and always got what she wanted.

'We look like Russian dolls,' Elena said, the three of them in matching cotton frocks and sandals; *three little maids in a row*, Mama would sing. They had a set of the dolls on the dressing table at home; one of the grown-up cousins had sent them from the USSR, not from Moscow, from a town that Elena didn't know.

'Catch me wearing a peasant pinafore and a shawl, day-dream girl.' Krista twisted and turned. 'I want my jeans from the suitcase. This dress is too tight, I can't breathe.' She pulled at the armholes and panted like a dog. 'Anyway, it's you and Sofia who look like proper Russian dolls. I look like the one who was shrunk in the wash.'

'Krista is the runt of the litter,' Elena said, daringly, in case Krista stopped being normal and remembered she was acting grown-up now.

'That makes you both two fat piggies. Two fat piggies ready for market and I'll have to eat you all up to get fat too.' Krista leant down and grabbed Sofia round the middle, whirling her in a circle. 'What do you say to that, Miss Sofia? Shall I gobble you up? All up?' She nuzzled Sofia's ear and snuffled like a piglet. Sofia giggled and signalled to be twirled again and again until: 'Elena, you fling her around,' Krista gasped. 'This runt is too small. My littlest sister is so heavy and it's so hot. Why is it so hot here?' She dumped Sofia on the ground, where she lay, laughing up at the sky, and turned on Elena. 'Go on. Guess.'

'What?'

Krista glowered. 'Durr. Have you forgotten already? The *big news*, daydream girl.'

'Is it about the tree houses?' Elena gave in.

'No. Guess again.'

'Is it about April?'

'April?' Krista repeated, sounding scornful. '*April*? Why would I have big news about your silly friends? Last guess, stupid.'

Elena didn't want to say it, in case it wasn't true, but she knew Krista wouldn't give up until she did. 'Is it about Mama?' she whispered.

13

'We were nine years old, and then ten, and Elena Zacharia was my fairy-tale friend.' I gaze beyond Nicole, off again into the distance and into the past; my past this time, not the meagre pickings of Elena's. I almost want to start, *once upon a time*. 'She was short and plump and had the hair of a princess: long black wriggly waves of it, so unlike my mousy-gingery head that it had to be magic. She arrived overnight and we played together for a year. Then, on another night she was gone.'

Gone *whoosh* like the vanishing worlds at the top of *The Faraway Tree*, the Enid Blyton stories we read, reread and acted out – allegedly for her little sister, Sofia; we were far too grown-up.

Elena stayed real to me for a long, long while; it was only much later she became dreamlike, ethereal. I used to lie in bed, curtains open, wondering where she was, what she was doing. Could she see the same stars that twinkled above me? Maybe I had magicked her up; I used to stare hard into the darkness willing her back. Over the years, I pictured Elena fleetingly and without context, happy, jumbled childhood memories. As I got older, she didn't cross my mind for weeks or months, and then a random news snippet (*Kofi Annan's Cypriot Plan Deconstructed*) or book title (Lawrence Durrell's *Bitter Lemons of Cyprus*) caught my eye and I'd wonder all over again.

'That's the gist of it,' I tell Nicole, feeling awkward. I

don't know if she's judging me for being here on the whim of a childhood dream; I judge myself. *Is there so little else in my life?* My mind flits back to Red saying that nothing is ever wasted. When I chance a glance at Nicole she's just looking thoughtful.

'Little Elena, a Greek Cypriot, escaped from the wars,' she says, uncurling her legs and stretching. 'The military coup that unseated Makarios and was followed by the Turkish intervention. There were thousands of people displaced from their homes. Hundreds of refugees, some to Greece, Turkey, and to England.'

'That's what's so strange,' I butt in. 'Her family was, I'm fairly sure, from Famagusta, and her stepfather had this brand-new hotel in Varosha – which was a new town, a strip along the nearby coast?'

Nicole nods.

'They left there to come to England in 1973. September 1973. It was the start of the school year.'

'Why strange?' Nicole asks. 'That is sensible, no? It was a time of great unrest. Many people saw that trouble was likely and if it happened, the island was doubly vulnerable to invasion. Elena's family saw ahead and left before they could be forced to flee.'

'*That* makes perfect sense,' I agree. 'What doesn't is what happened next.' I sit up straight, because this is important. 'Why did they suddenly return to Cyprus in July 1974, just after the coup and only days before the Turkish invasion?' I wonder, as I always do, if there is an obvious answer, some explanation lost in the chaotic historical and political record of that time. But I see from Nicole's face, she has no answers, and I slump down again.

'Maybe they had concerns for their family left behind, or for their land and property,' she suggests finally.

'I expect that's true.' I shrug. 'Although I still can't understand the whole family going back. Who would take three children into a warzone when they didn't have to?'

'Ah, but do you know *for sure* they didn't have to?'

'No. No, I don't...' My mind ticks over Elena's letter, dated the nineteenth of July, right in the thick of it. There had to be *something*.

'But?' Nicole asks gently.

And I frown at a memory that's always just outside my grasp. 'Elena's mother had already gone away – somewhere. Now I know it was back here. She and Stefan, Elena's stepfather, left about a month before, but it was all so vague. Her Aunt Irini was left in charge; she was always with them on and off in England. Her partner too.' I shake my head, as if, kaleidoscope-like, the pieces will make a perfect picture. 'I was ten. It was the seventies. Nobody told me anything. Then Elena had gone and it was too late.'

'Hmm.' Nicole gets up slowly and crosses to the fridge-freezer. It's on the tip of my tongue to refuse more of the champagne I expect to see, when she turns round brandishing a plastic container of something bright blush pink. '*Triandafillo* ice cream.' She wrinkles her nose. 'A rose cordial ice – sorbet, you call it? Very refreshing.' She chips away at it, sharing it between two miniature glass dishes. 'It's Damaris' recipe. Try it.'

I do as I'm told, relishing the cold sweetness enough to lick the teaspoon clean.

'Good, yes? It clears the head.' Nicole smiles. 'Too much sugar and it becomes icy, too much water and it's slush, too much cordial and it turns to syrup. Or so Damaris says. My cooking skills amount only to reheating and presentation.' She licks her own spoon. 'Your story of Elena made me remember the ice cream man, Georgios' grandfather, who rode through Agia Triada on his bicycle selling ice cream and *mahalepi*. So long ago.'

I can see her forming the obvious question, but hesitating over how to phrase it. 'You want to know why now,' I say. 'Why I've come to Cyprus looking for Elena now?'

'I can guess.' She says it so softly, as if she doesn't want to break the reminiscence spell. She won't; the story's spilling out quicker than I ever thought possible.

'A midlife crisis,' I confess. 'Time out; taking stock; finding myself. Give me a cliché and I'll raise anyone a stereotype.'

She laughs at that.

'Except...'

Nicole settles back down beside me. 'Except?'

'Except that I'm not really sure I *am* looking for her. I'm not sure that I do want to find her.' It's the first time I've admitted it aloud and of course the world doesn't crack. Still, I take a deep breath. It matters how I tell it. I don't want Nicole to think I'm either needy or heartless. But she gets it, she's already nodding.

'You are curious. But you want to find what you *want* to find, a happy ending.'

Exactly. I drink the last of my water. 'I'm not naïve, Nicole. I know my lovely rose-coloured idyll is bound to be muddied with the starkness of dirt, displacement and death.'

'That is war, April. Nobody is untouched by the horror of it. Yet sometimes, you know, there *are* happy endings. We are all seeking them.' There is some nuance in Nicole's tone, something that smacks of experience rather than theory, but she doesn't expand. Instead, she says, 'You will find an Elena, or her cousin, her sister, her friend, in every town and village on Cyprus.' She pauses. 'Some people will talk to you about that time, some will say things you wish not to hear. Others will stay silent.'

Which is how we stay for the next few minutes, my thoughts punctuated only by the rumble of the party: a snatch of laughter, a flurry of footsteps and someone running quick fingers over the piano keys. I'm locked in two time zones, jolted back by talking about Elena and forward talking to Nicole; the two are muddled, like the aftermath of a dream, leaving me disconnected. I sway slightly as I stand up and start pacing, trying to relocate myself in the present day. 'Sorry,'

I say to Nicole, 'sorry,' realising I've probably shared thirty years' worth of musings in thirty minutes, and under the effects of unaccustomed-to alcohol. *That's* starting to wear off and I'm suddenly resolute that the rest of the story will keep. I should face Yiannis again, and Red. I place our bowls and glasses in the sink and then balance on one leg to put each shoe back on. 'Nicole, I'm keeping us from the party. Come on.' I gesture towards the other room. 'You can hear multitudes more any old time. If you want to.'

Nicole touches my cheek, pulling me to her in a warm hug. 'I want to,' she says. 'I am honoured you have shared it with me and there is no need ever to be sorry. But right now, you have good timing. If we do not reappear, Damaris will come looking and she is best met unfuelled by champagne. Although…' Nicole pulls back and searches my face for a long second.

'What?'

'Damaris. As you spoke, an idea unfolded. Help is at hand. But not now.' She gives me her radiant smile, warm through and through. 'Right now you are feeling nostalgic for a voluble, excitable, gossiping Greek community, yes? Who needs your Elena when you have the Koumettou clan in Agia Triada?'

14

The after-effects of the party are still ricocheting when the time comes for me to start posing for Andreas. I've a temporary reprieve while he washes his paintbrushes and fills his palette or whatever artists do to prepare, so the rest of us regroup, this time at Yiannis' no-longer-leaking Minerva House. We're going to arrange the trip Yiannis suggested. It wasn't a throwaway remark, I've learned from Petros (after he apologised for not mentioning his botanist friend was a retired priest; he'd meant to, the evening Red had arrived, but got distracted. I mostly believe him) but something of a business plan. Yiannis, like me, is reconsidering his whole future.

We're in the conservatory, a rustic glass and wood extension that runs the length of the house's rear, and which in a grander establishment might be labelled the orangery. There are orange trees and lemon trees, neatly potted, and a wealth of other greenery I can't identify, its only colour arises from single birds of paradise here and there. Sunlight hasn't yet penetrated the room and the rhythmic drips from a recent watering give a pleasant, if too quiet, sense of dawn in the rainforest. The furniture is the kind that has been there from the year dot and will last forever, huge sofas and endless cushions to sink into. Yiannis' mother, the great matriarch (I assume), has left him the vestiges of enviable shabby chic.

It's a big house for one man, and this clearly bothers

Yiannis. It's his catalyst for action, he explains to an audience of me, Nicole, Petros and Red. He's planning to turn it into a B & B for flora-enthusiasts. He thinks he'll run *actual* orchid-hunting tours, he says, looking in my direction but not quite catching my eye.

'Your, uh, that is April's um ex... April's friend, Jake, gave me the idea.'

I don't comment beyond a lukewarm smile because Yiannis is a nervous wreck, as if expecting hecklers, and I wonder how he ever held the attention of a church congregation. He finishes collecting up miscellaneous crockery and piling it on a small table inside the door, then starts to shuffle a folder of papers.

'My friends... the microbus...'

'Spit out your wishes,' Petros calls; they're a good double act. Yiannis' intensity and advanced work ethic balances Petros' studied laissez-faire. 'We are all aware of your intentions but you must sell them to us, inspire us—'

'He is teasing you,' Nicole says. 'We would all like to take a trip with you, wouldn't we?' She nudges me. 'April?'

'Yes, of course.' I nod vigorously. 'That was our... my... original plan, before... well, before.' I'm not mad at Jake any more, I'd rather orchids than ley lines any day.

Red offers a murmur of approval too, and Yiannis begins to look less like a child struggling with the sight-reading in his grade one piano exam. He looks to Petros, the supportive parent, who nods encouragingly and suggests they retire to Yiannis' office to make some arrangements. As Yiannis passes me, he crouches down, his knuckles clenched white on the arm of my chair. 'Ah, April. Our, ah, first *Greek lesson*. Would tonight be convenient? Eight p.m. in Georgios' tavern?'

In anyone else, it would be superlative innuendo, with Yiannis my heart sinks at the ominous 'first' and I actually wonder if he expects me to buy a dictionary and copybook.

'Okay.' It seems a bit short to leave it at that, but then I have a spark of inspiration. 'Yiannis? I'm an ignoramus. Have you got a copy of *Bluff Your Way in Orchids* or some kind of *Idiot's Guide*?'

He looks blank.

'What she is asking you, Yiannis, is if you have any simple books about orchids. Preferably books with many large pictures,' Nicole interprets.

His face lights up. 'I have the perfect book. In my office. I will leave it with Petros for you.' And off he bustles.

'Yiannis just needs a little more confidence.' Nicole approves my request. 'He really is an expert, you know. He has written books on botany. I am ashamed to say I have never asked him about them.'

Am I digging a bigger hole for myself here? 'Jake bought a pile of them. He says he got them specially from the head gardener at Kew Gardens. I expect he just bought a ticket, looked round and picked them up in the gift shop, like anyone else.' Nicole nods for me to go ahead through the door into the hall. 'When he's being normal there's a decent enough man in him, but when he decides he's *an expert* at something, or gets one of what he calls his "obsessions", he's infuriatingly pompous.'

'No love is lost then?' Nicole smiles.

'Definitely no love lost.' I consider that, and realise it's more or less true now. 'Oh, I was upset and hurt when he broke it off. Humiliated that I hadn't done it first,' I admit as we wander down the hall and into the garden. It's hot now at midday, though there's a breeze that means we'll need to choose a careful spot. 'But Jake wasn't the love of my life. He was a nice habit for too long, but I'm glad, if apprehensive, that I'm here and on my own.'

'You need not be on your own any longer.' Nicole takes my elbow. 'I promised I would deliver you to Andreas today,' she adds. 'And I will. But first, a detour. I want to show you something.'

She motions me forward and leads me around the side of

the hotel, down a ribbon of pebbled pathway and into what feels like a miniature forest, a cluster of trees still in their adolescence, spindly trunks dense with leaves. It seems as if we have reached a dead end, a wall of greenery, when Nicole ducks left under a twisted but non-accidental arch and into a small garden. A secret garden, a sign tells me; a natural folly, with a squat stone Buddha guarding the entrance from inside. Within the clearing, it's like a miniature spa with a big swing seat and a double-sized hammock, the grass springs underfoot and there is a mosaic-topped table and chairs and wind chimes eerily still. The sudden shade is startling but not gloomy and it doesn't seem too fanciful to say I feel peace settle around me like a silky cloak. There is room for us to sit, legs in front of us and facing each other at either side of the huge swing, and let it move gently under our combined weight.

'This is the creation of Yiannis,' Nicole says after a while. 'Whenever he is driving me crazy with indecisiveness, and Andreas is being the obsessive artist and Damaris is wanting grandchildren and Petros is being Petros, I come here and remind myself of my need for patience. And to tell myself that I am not always right about everything all of the time.'

'It's beautiful,' I agree. 'I could come here for many similar reasons... except I'd be reminding myself that I'm not always wrong about everything all of the time.'

'Yin and yang.'

This space has been formed by the letter-writing Yiannis, almost chatty, more forthcoming, the thick cream paper and black-ink script almost coming alive. It will be interesting, I think in passing, to discover what he and Red are writing about and how that works out. This garden is perfect; I look around again. Beautiful, enclosed, safe but with a sense of light and freedom... *This* is it. It's exactly right. If the sea was too infinite, Yiannis' secret garden is perfect. And suddenly an ex-priest is a bonus; surely he'll see the promise of eternity rather than a small box of cremated remains? Nicole is the test case. I sit up and look at her expectantly.

'Do you think Yiannis would let me bury my mum's and dad's ashes here?' I'm almost blasé mentioning them for the third time and, to her credit, Nicole is the third person who takes it in her stride, nothing but a few rapid blinks. I wonder if Petros or Red has tipped her off. 'Discreetly, in a corner or under a bush. All I know is, they can't stay at the bottom of the wardrobe in Verena Bay Hotel forever,' I gabble on. I've spoken more here, shed more secrets than I have in the last three decades, since Elena. 'My parents were never here but they lived beside Ana Evagora for five years, and Ana was one of the few people who understood them. I didn't, not really,' I admit. 'I often think Ana brought them the same kind of colour as Elena brought me.'

Nicole gently rocks the swing. 'I think he would be honoured.' I wait for her to say more, to ask me for *this* story, on top of Elena's, but she doesn't. She just holds out her hand. 'You can ask him later. At this moment, Andreas is expecting you. Come.'

'Never a dull moment for Cypriot-April,' I murmur as we retrace our steps.

From the outside, his home-made studio resembles a wonky shoebox with windows, glued awkwardly to the roof of the main house where it juts out across the courtyard. He's waiting for me there, smoking a morose cigarette, which he stubs out immediately after he sees me.

'April. Come and view my initial creation, my homage, my shrine. To you.'

Trailing behind him, up the whitewashed steps that hug the side of the house, I shiver; his invitation – his order, rather – is oddly sinister.

Inside, the studio is like a police incident room in the aftermath of a major incident. I know Andreas has been watching me, intermittently, since day one. I know – now – he's been sketching me. I also know he's been taking photographs as

I've moved to and from Verena Bay and Agia Triada, but somehow I failed to notice how his tiny, state-of-the-art digital camera must have been flashing away with all the speed yet none of the flamboyance of the paparazzi. I say that as if the press follows me around. They don't, generally, but it's a side effect of important concerts and, harder to bear, the interest into the official enquiry of my parents' death.

Anyway, one wall is covered in snap-happy photographs and crude line drawings: front and back views, side-on angles, upside-down shots and enlarged bits of body that can't be identified without holding them at a squinting arm's length. Some of the photos and drawings are torn in half, in quarters, in postage-stamp squares and taped back together like a mosaic, others are filtered until the pixelation renders them abstract. Since they're all, without exception, of me, I'm not sure whether I feel like victim or suspect.

Andreas takes a few minutes to tack up his latest glossy printouts from the evening of the party – he must have a tiny darkroom hidden away – and then stands back and closes his eyes. He's radiating satisfaction.

'All in your honour,' he tells me.

'It's like a fairground hall of mirrors.' I'm unwillingly fascinated, but more than that, *relieved*. Relieved I've seen the non-stalking, non-obsessive side of Andreas: friend, husband and host. Andreas is Jekyll and Hyde. If I'd known this exhibition was his intention, as he watched me from the swimming pool at the Verena Bay, then as I spoke to Nicole at Nissi Beach, I may well have refused. As it is I'm curious. 'What happens now? Will you start painting me?' When will I have a chance to start looking for Elena, I wonder.

'Soon, soon. First, we will discuss the motivations I wish to capture. Next I will arrange you. My art,' he states, 'is dependent upon my capturing the graceful musicality of my subject's movement: no staging, no expectation, totally unencumbered.'

I turn round to stare at him, wondering if he's joking, but

his face is unselfconscious and earnest. Sadly, there's nothing particularly graceful about my movement, and my musicality is stored in my brain and ends at my fingertips. In all of his pictures I look stiff, startled and on the brink of running further into the hills to disappear into one of the deserted EOKA bunkers. Andreas seems content though.

'The look on your face is immaterial,' he says. 'I am not interested in your face. I shall make art of your personality.'

At a loss how to answer, I cross the small space and look out of the window. Two floors below me, the stone-flagged courtyard is cluttered with terracotta pots, out of which deep burgundy fuchsias explode to dress the length of the wall and frame the arched entrance. At the head of the long refectory table, a cast-iron bread oven is recycled into a barbecue, and at the foot, oblivious to me, is Nicole. For a happy minute I pretend she's the adult Elena, untarnished, living a simple life in this quiet idyll. She alternates feeding leftover souvlaki to a grinning red setter, and grains of millet to a pair of rainbow parakeets. When she finishes with them, she sets their green cage casually on the wall and disappears inside. The birds flutter and sing in unison, careless of their free cousins in the trees. Neither are they fazed by the lolloping dog who thrusts his nose between the bars, nudging them that bit closer to the void.

I tense up on their behalf and, behind me, Andreas applauds. 'Excellent,' he calls. 'Do not move. I need that expression…'

I tune him out, my head filled with 'Waldszenen'. It's the fourth piece, the 'Haunted Place'. It's rare that I itch to play Schumann but it's the secret garden, of course, and there's no question that, later, my fingers will benefit from the workout of triple-dotted crotchets and double-dotted quavers. In the interim, I do a handful of mental scales and arpeggios, fingers tapping on the windowsill, promising I'll make up with extra practice tomorrow. I think myself through the whole 'Opus 82', enjoying the flow of all eight vignettes, then sigh and settle to flexing the fourth finger of my left hand, a long-standing weakness.

I'm distracted by a figure weaving its way across the road through the garden and up the steps into the courtyard. A woman wearing a denim jacket over a pink gingham overall, whose wiry hair is tied back with – a broken dog's lead? She settles underneath my window, starts humming, then crooning something that sounds like a hymn, and in the space of a few bars she's singing aloud in a cracked but powerfully trained alto. Surprised, I easily recognise Rutter's arrangement of the 'Magnificat'; sung in Greek and transposed from the soprano lead, it shouldn't work, but it does. I lean out for a closer look, listen till the woman holds the final note and fades.

Andreas' sigh lodges in my ear. I turn to him, see him frowning.

He shakes his head. 'She will sing until we stop, so we stop right away.'

'Who...?'

'She is come to tell you about old Famagusta where her family once lived. She will take you home to her *kind* menagerie, where she will sing some more and tell you her war stories.'

'You mean, this is Damaris?' I piece it together. 'Your mother?'

'Yes. Yes. Go and meet Damaris. My mother.' He sighs again. 'Nicole will serve figs and *metrios* now, so all is not totally lost.'

15

By the time we get downstairs, Andreas dragging his heels, Damaris is semi-buried in the embrace of the red setter she's trying to haul onto her knee. When the dog sees Andreas and me, his massive tongue flops over, his panting body close behind. I'm smothered.

Damaris' eyes, black pinpricks in the ruches and crinkles of her leathery skin, grow brighter. She turns to me, and takes my hands. 'You are April, of course. Concert pianist and friend of the Evagora clan. We would have met at Yiannis' displaced party if my daughter-in-law was not keeping you to herself. This time you will come and take your coffee with us at Loxandra, yes? If my son has finished his work for the day, you shall come now.'

Andreas gives a wave of dismissal. 'I will explain to any concerned party how Damaris spirited you away. Go.'

With a semi-apologetic smile, I let myself be drawn off. Arm in arm, Damaris leads us through the gate and up the hill.

'Loxandra Inn is our family home,' she explains. 'Although it is rarely used as an inn now. What a loss.'

'That's a shame.'

'A shame?' Damaris snorts. 'A folly. The health inspector,' she confides, as if the connection is obvious. She launches into a complicated story from which I gather that the former Loxandra Inn is only defunct as a B & B because the health inspector, and myriad false guests he sends her incognito, are against house pets.

'What is this problem?' asks Damaris. 'Always before my guests arrive, I ask if they like animals. If they say no, they do not come. In future, I will send them to Minerva House, where they will wallow in books and flowers. Quite simple. I keep only dogs and cats. I am not mad,' she assures me.

'I like dogs and cats.' I'm unsure where else to go with the conversation. We seem to have bypassed the usual pleasantries – like mother like son? – as we make our way along an unpaved lane that splits into a V-sign, and where I hear the chorus of barking dogs and yowling cats before I see them.

'My babies.' Damaris beams.

The farmhouse is not pretty or rustic, it's a grey single-storey rectangle to which an ill-fitting extension has been attached. Originally a Turkish family home, she mentions tight-lipped, abandoned during the war and requisitioned for Greek Cypriot refugees. The fence is a modern-day moat, barely restraining the swarming cats and dogs within.

'We will keep them outside.' Damaris ushers me through the gate, opens and slides shut the glass doors to the kitchen, doors smeared and sticky with years of twitching feline noses and damp dog breath. 'Let us make coffee,' she adds. 'True Cypriot coffee, to sit and savour. I will convert you where Petros Evagora cannot. Instant Nescafé is a poor substitute to be drunk in a hurry over the kitchen sink.'

Is there anything about me she doesn't already know, I wonder, as she stoops and lifts a sleepy-looking grey cat from the warming oven of the immense cooking range, pouring it a bowl of cream.

'She just had kittens,' Damaris explains. 'In human age she is an elderly mother, she needs special care. Are you a mother?' She turns to me.

'No, I'm not. No children. No animals either. I travel too much.'

'There is still time. I have three daughters quick, quick,

quick. Then – delay and boom! Fourteen years later Andreas is born. I am blessed.'

'I have two ex-husbands,' I admit. I don't mention Jake. 'It probably would have happened before now.'

'Maybe. Maybe not. Life goes along, tick-tock, tick-tock, then suddenly it speeds away and you are on a different path into the unknown.'

She might be talking about her own situation or mine, but she doesn't elaborate; the ritual of the coffee is underway. Damaris boils up the fine, sour-smelling grinds in a tin jug, long-handled, and well blackened from the gas. When it turns to muddy bubbles and starts to froth like a live volcano, she spills it sideways into espresso cups and pushes the sugar bowl towards me.

'The cats like sugar too.' She runs a finger round the rim, checking for hairs. Then,

'Welcome,' she repeats. 'Welcome to Loxandra. What do you think of my home?'

Beyond the functional clutter of this kitchen are an open-plan dining room and a sitting room. I'm caught up in a revolution of colour and texture, louder by far than any impact the animals could make. The walls are invisible behind fiery Aztec tapestries, muted gold and ochre woodcarvings of the Stations of the Cross, enormous oil canvases, thick with seas and skies. Smaller watercolours, sketch pads and history of art books are in piles on the floor; Gombrich's *Story of Art*, a book I remember from school, is a handy doorstop. If the National Art Gallery of Cyprus had an attic, this would be it. What it is not, even to my untrained eye, is the work of Andreas.

'No, not Andreas.' Damaris reads my mind. 'His father, my husband, Orestes. He is a very good artist and a very great doctor.' She sighs, then continues, 'Ah, he is an old man now. Long retired. And he seldom paints – the cataracts, you see. He is also too soft here.' She taps her chest. 'Here, in the heart. Not tough, not like me. Wait, he will come…'

Damaris calls out a long greeting in Greek and, at the same time, starts to rummage through the various packets and tins atop the teak dresser. 'Honey cake,' she says. 'The family recipe. Ah!' She brandishes the remnants of a bun, breaks it apart with her fingers and tips it onto a plate.

Only then is there an answering echo from a room out of sight. Slowly, an elderly man shuffles into the room, and for a second I see only a lifetime of hard experience weighting his stooped shoulders and in the liver marks that seep like spilled ink over his hands. Then I look again at his carefully knotted tie and the shine on his smart shoes, the way he pulls himself up straighter, coming forward to me, holding out his hand.

'I am Orestes Koumettou. My home and my family are humble, but they are always here for you.'

His dignity... well, all I can say is I have a lump in my throat.

'He is an old man, eighty-two years. But a handsome man, yes?' Damaris pulls out a chair for him, pours more coffee and shares the cake between us, rich and nutty, only a hint of sweetness and one or two rogue cat hairs.

When Orestes asks me about my trip to Cyprus – why here, why now? Is it correct I'm looking for someone from the past? – I falter. There is something, something in the air, maybe in their unspoken history, that makes me oddly ashamed. My half-hearted journey towards Elena is towards a person I don't know and will never really know, even if I do find her. Sincere as I am, it's still something of a game, a puzzle; the story of Damaris and Orestes though, whatever it may be, is *real*.

Damaris must recognise my discomfort because she leans over and pats my hand. 'Never worry that you will offend us,' she says. 'The only offence is that people are too quick to forget their history.'

'Thirty years, my love.' Orestes looks at her. 'There is a time to remember, yes, and also a time to move forwards.'

'The time to move forwards is when we have learned from

the past. Can you say we have done that? Our country? Our people? Ourselves?'

If the words themselves are not enough, the way their eyes lock in the ensuing silence tells me how well rehearsed is this dialogue. Damaris yields first, she looks down and brushes some crumbs onto her saucer. 'I try,' she says. 'My God above knows, *you* know, how I try.'

'My darling, of course He knows and I know, but April does not.'

And on some tacit cue, here, uncontrived and either side of the filthy kitchen table, they open their mouths and begin to sing, in Greek, in perfect harmony. I'm surprised how this spontaneous action is not sentimental or embarrassing to my uptight English soul. I imagine the torment, for all of us, if my mother and father had even threatened to hum along to my piano practice. This, though, is perfectly natural, something that Damaris and Orestes probably share whilst they are doing the dishes, feeding the dogs and cats, gardening.

'That song we sang every Easter back in Famagusta,' says Damaris, when they close. 'It was the happy time when our families came home and we sat together remembering our lost ones and planning our futures. Our dreams waited for us to catch them. Now, Easter has come once more and it is still hard to celebrate.' She is matter-of-fact now, collecting up cups.

'My children are the brothers and sisters of this child you call Elena.' Orestes says this to me but is looking at his wife. 'It is for this reason, I wish and Nicole wishes, that Damaris returns to Famagusta.' Damaris freezes. 'She should look again at the place they started to call Varosha. It is important that she goes, not to forget but to make peace. Thirty years,' he repeats.

Damaris. Help is at hand. I shuffle Nicole's words, from the night of the party, in my mind: me helping Damaris, not her me. Or maybe it's mutual, but I know immediately what Orestes is asking and it's so much easier that Elena is peripheral. 'Damaris, I want to go to Famagusta. I want to look at Varosha. Will you come with me and Nicole?' I ask her. 'I know it's a big thing and I know I can't possibly put my feelings about Elena in the same league as yours about your whole family, but we might be good for each other.' I hesitate. 'This is the first time I've really admitted aloud that I want to look for Elena, to… to…'

'To tread where she trod, to see what her eyes saw.' Orestes closes his eyes and nods.

'Yes,' I say, startled that he's expressed it exactly. 'And I think I need you, Damaris.'

She purses her lips and glares between us. 'You think I give in so easily to your manipulation, that I say yes, fine, let's go. I need time to think.'

'My darling, there is a season,' Orestes tells her. 'Every year for fifteen, twenty past, I ask you. Time is not to think but to do.'

'Andreas will not like it,' Damaris says.

'I, *we*, believe it is our duty to tell you the story of our Famagusta,' Orestes explains to me. 'But you will understand not everyone close to us agrees.'

'Andreas was born so much later in England,' Damaris says. 'Our family story is not his story, just history. He is not talkative about it; he lives only now. That is a gift, he believes, for then there is no pain. I think no pain makes less joy. And I know, as a mother knows, that Andreas is not true to himself.' She wipes her eyes, quickly, on her sleeve. 'Sometimes we sing,' she says. 'Sometimes we cry. For your little Elena and her family, it will be the same.'

'And sometimes,' Orestes takes her hand and reaches across for mine, 'we all even laugh.'

16

Agia Napa, Cyprus
Sunday 21st July 1974

Dear April and Mrs Gale's class,

Letter 3. The next day.
 It is early in the morning after we have slept all night in the car. Antony drove into the trees so we would not disturb anyone and also have shelter if it rained. Aunt Irini called it Brownie camp and promised if we didn't fuss, we would get our Hiker Badges. April knows, but if you all don't, Aunt Irini was going to be the new Tawny Owl when Mrs Talbot left to have her baby. (Maybe, April, your mum could do it? I don't think she is too old.) I didn't fuss, but Krista said it should be called Holy Hell not Holy Dell, and got into trouble. To understand this you have to know Greek, as this place is near a village called Agia Napa and that means Holy Dell (a dell is a valley of trees, Aunt Irini explained it to us) so Krista was being rude.
 We are here in the pretend campsite because we are not doing Plan A, which was to go straight to the tree houses for our holiday. Krista was bursting to tell me this news. More roads are being closed or only army trucks are allowed. Instead we are doing Plan B and going to Stefan's hotel. These

aren't written-down plans, just ones in Antony's head, but he says they are in my mum's head too, so we will be sure to meet her soon and not to worry...

Clutching her paper and pencil, Elena scrambled down from the low branch she'd perched on; Aunt Irini was calling them from outside a tiny whitewashed room on the side of the road, a resting place for travellers. It was a place for shepherds and goatherds to swallow thick syrupy coffee and flat rounds of bread, and Elena recognised it as somewhere Mama would never stop. Longing for lemonade though, she had said nothing, and Krista didn't care.

'Krista. Elena. Sofia. Are you ready?' Aunt Irini called, and it sounded so like Mama on Saturday nights in England, Elena felt a big pang in her tummy. All that was missing was April. 'Girls?' her aunt's voice went on. 'Antony is waiting.'

'Antony.' Krista made *kiss, kiss* sounds. 'Irini loves Antony.' She nudged Elena. 'Kiss, kiss.'

Elena laughed then, knowing that April would have laughed too. She was guilty because she loved her aunt nearly more than anyone else in the whole world, but truthfully, Irini was soppy with Antony. Even Krista who declared she was grown-up and pleased to leave England behind and couldn't wait to make friends and sneak into the new hotels on Varosha beach, whispering about boys and breasts, made sick noises when she saw Irini and Antony together.

'Kiss, kiss,' she signed to Sofia, who giggled and blew them right back. She squealed as both Elena and Krista grabbed her and smothered her and tickled her.

'Kiss, kiss,' Sofia signed back as they chased each other to the car.

'Irini, can we get a drink first?' Krista shouted. She nudged Elena, nearly toppling her over, to get her to agree.

'Please may we?' Elena added, 'It is so hot, Aunt Irini.'

'*Please, Auntie, please.*' Elena could hear Krista mimicking under her breath. 'Good little girl, good little swot. *Drinkies, please.*'

Elena, ignoring her, leaned against the door of the old car, avoiding the burning metal bits and thinking about being squished into the back seat again. Either side of her, her sisters, their legs touching hers, would be sticky and sweaty, even with the windows all rolled down as far as they would go. The wind that blew in was hot, like when Mama opened the big bread oven in the bakehouse, but without the sweet, soft taste... Elena squeezed her eyes shut to stop the thought. Her mouth was dry.

They had only been back in Cyprus for – she counted on her fingers – five days and already she was remembering things that happened before England better than their life there. England was like a long dream, a happy dream, which was disappearing as she woke up. Nothing here was right.

'Elena, Elena.' Irini was snapping her fingers and trying to laugh. 'Come back to earth, darling. I was just saying that Antony is buying lemonade for us all. We'll drink it out here.' She waved at the garden, a tired patch of dried grass where there was a little shade from the weary and drooping orange trees.

'I hate lemonade,' Krista grumbled. 'Lemonade is for kids. Why do I have to sit out here? Why can't I sit in the cafe with you?'

'Of course you can.' Irini gave her a brilliant smile. 'I thought you liked to be outside in the fresh air instead of that smoky, smelly bar, but maybe you're too grown-up now. Next time, you can sit with Antony and me and we'll take coffee.'

Elena felt Krista deflating like a balloon beside her. Krista loved to fight, to argue, but Irini was much too clever for her. And when Antony came out of the tiny *kafenio*, carrying a tin tray loaded with lemonade bottles, Krista was first to snatch hers. There was a whole bottle each, which Elena knew pleased her sister – Krista always complained about the oldest having to share – and she even said thank you. Antony nodded and smiled but he was silent. Elena noticed that Antony did most things silently until he was alone with Irini, then she heard their voices non-stop: on the aeroplane; at the airport when she was too stuffy and too uncomfortable to sleep on the floor; in their new old car. He wasn't unfriendly, he just seemed nervous. So it was strange when Irini drained her lemonade and said, 'Girls, Antony has something to say to you.'

It was like an announcement at school. Elena had a clear flash of Mrs Gale standing in front of the class and clapping her hands before telling them something about PE or not hanging around in the toilets at home time, or the announcement that Mr Reynolds, who taught the fourth years, had died.

'Is Mama alright?' Elena's sudden train of thought took on a life of its own.

'Your mama is fine,' Antony said quickly. 'There's nothing to worry about at all. Nothing. But it is about her. You see, she and Stefan have been delayed a little while.'

Elena felt the little bounces of excitement she'd been feeling all day puncture into a heap around her. She wanted to cry.

'Where are they? Why are they delayed?' Krista demanded. 'It's not fair. They promised. Do we now have Plan C? What happens if we get to Plan Z and run out of Plans?'

'Krista, we know how much you're looking forward to seeing them. We don't want you, any of you, to be upset...'

'But they promised. Mama promised she would be waiting for us. She did say that, didn't she, Elena?'

Elena swallowed and nodded but her voice felt too small to push any words out. Antony looked down at his hands, and laced his fingers together. He sighed. When he looked up again, he said, 'It's not their fault, girls, they miss you too. But they had to go to—'

'Limassol,' Aunt Irini butted in.

'Yes. Limassol. For some... some business...'

Elena watched a glance pass between him and Irini. It was as if she was warning him to say, or not say, something important. 'What business?' she whispered.

Her tiny voice was drowned by Krista's loud one. 'So what? Why can't we go to Limassol and meet them there? It's only a few miles down that road. Or that one.' She flapped her hand vaguely around her head like a cowboy with a lasso.

Irini took over in her teacher's voice. 'It's more than a few miles, Krista, even if we could turn round and go back. You know that very well. And particularly now...'

For a second, in that hesitation, Elena felt what it was to be Krista: annoyed by everyone and frustrated by not being told things. She wanted to stamp her foot and tell Irini and Antony to start talking in proper sentences, ones that finished. Instead, she asked, 'Why is the other road longer now? Is it because of all the soldiers?'

Even after the *STOP/GO* barrier, they had been halted twice on the other road by men in uniforms checking who they were and where they were going. Elena was sure that never used to happen, not on the fast main road. She remembered it one time in the villages, just before England, when they had gone to visit their friend Aysel for his birthday and a soldier there had said Greek Cypriots weren't allowed. Even when Mama had argued and shown her special papers, he said no. They had taken Aysel's cake, specially baked by Mama, home and eaten it themselves. Elena still hoped somebody had time to make him another.

'That's right, Elena.' Antony looked at her as if he was grateful. 'When the government was attacked last week, it meant that all the important people in the country, not just Archbishop Makarios, were put in danger. So there is extra security everywhere to make sure everyone is safe. It's nothing to worry about but it does take longer to travel, and that's why so many routes are closed. We're going to have to be very patient.'

Irini backed him up. 'Yes, we heard on the radio that it's best if people only go out for real emergencies. You know, to the hospital if they are very sick. Times like that. We all want to be good citizens, don't we? Mama too.'

Elena was unsatisfied but nodded reluctantly. Krista didn't.

'That's stupid,' she said. 'They're stupid idiots. I think it's an emergency for us to find our mother after a whole month. Or is the army too mean to care about that?'

'The soldiers we see here, and on the other streets, are just following their orders.' Irini was brisk. 'You will see your mama very soon, but it won't be in Limassol and it won't be today.'

'It should have been at the tree houses yesterday,' Elena heard Krista mutter, but they all ignored her.

'We will get to Varosha and we'll wait for them there. It will be just a few more days.'

More? Elena had been counting down the days for four weeks now, and they suddenly were not getting any fewer. A curious thought entered her head.

Krista got there first. 'If I were a stranger listening, I would think you knew all of this in the airport, maybe even London airport not Nicosia, and you must have because there is no telephone here to talk to Mama. So why wouldn't you tell us, your nieces, all the Plans then? And if I were another stranger I would ask why first our mother and now us had to run away from England in the middle of the night anyway? And...' Krista looked triumphantly around the little group sitting on the grass. 'Why didn't we take the newest road straight to the tree houses? Mama said there was one. She showed us on the map. The *STOP* sign is on the old road.'

Picking through that complicated speech, Elena realised her sister was right, right on every point. Krista did this: just when you thought she was being extra silly, she said or did something clever and you had to twist your thoughts around to accept it.

Not waiting for an answer though, Krista jumped up and prodded Sofia, who was nodding to sleep against an orange tree; Sofia could sleep through fires and flood and wars, according to Mama. Krista tugged hard on the long black pigtail that had fallen forward over Sofia's shoulder as her head lolled against the trunk, then took the end of it and tickled her little sister on her cheek. Sofia, awake immediately, grinned and sat up straight, always happy. She put her thumbs up to Krista, who stuck out her tongue, and said, 'Let's get to Stefan's fancy hotel. I want to swim. If that's still allowed by stupid soldiers and even stupider – other people.' Krista didn't say 'aunts' but Elena knew that was what she meant.

Irini, too, ignored the challenge. Instead, she brightened and rooted in her big pockets. 'Look, girls. I found this tucked down the side of the suitcase. To remind you of the tree houses until we can get there, and to keep our spirits up.'

Krista pretended not to be interested, but Elena leaned forward and took the photograph. She remembered, if she screwed her mind back far enough, it being taken, and they looked so happy. So free of cares. 'Can I keep it?' she asked Aunt Irini.

'Of course you can, darling. We'll take another one when we arrive there. We'll take one every year. I promise.' But Irini was already distracted. 'First though, we must move on and make new memories in a new place.'

It was much later when Elena remembered nobody had answered Krista's questions.

17

The evening finds me sitting on my tiny terrace at Verena Bay, facing the sea and some home truths. Meeting Orestes and Damaris has made the idea of a grown-up Elena much more real than ever before.

I look down at the old snapshot on my knee. Families. History. Life… Zarney, Zacharia, Evagora, Koumettou: does it matter? Was Elena's happy family all a sham? Was it really all sweetness and light on the outside and a murky, maggoty core within? Or not even that, just a fairy tale I concocted all by my lonely, sad little self. Except it wasn't a fairy tale really, because I did live it for a few months; I was part of something that made me happier than I ever had been before. Or since. But I was barely ten years old back then, of course I saw only the sweetness and light.

We didn't dwell on unpleasantness in our house. If life were a colour it would have been an easy shallow beige, and it means – I've said it many times since their deaths – I never knew my parents, not as people independent to me. Petros' Aunt Ana did, probably the only one who pushed hard enough at their self-made barriers. From the day she moved into the same residential home, Ana became their spokesperson, their champion, their (in so much as anyone was) confidante. She transformed the last few years of their lives but my place was too established on the fringes. I could always ask them about their unspoken pasts tomorrow and tomorrow and tomorrow, I'd reassured myself. Until I couldn't. And with Ana gone too, the one person who may have had something to share, so was my backup.

Yes, I'm suddenly scared to lose out with Elena in the same way.

Except that with Elena, it's always been a very real possibility that I'm *more* scared of finding her.

Oh, the grass is always greener on the other side, the sky bluer, the sun warmer and the drinks colder – everything you could want. Then you get it, but you don't realise it because actually the grass is spiky and full of bugs, the glare from the sky screws your eyes up until they ache and blur, the heat from the sun is sticky and breathless and the ice has melted and weakened your lukewarm lemonade. Maybe Elena's family were not the all-singing, all-dancing von Trapps, escaping over the mountains – the Troodos Mountains, in this case – to their new life in a new country. Instead of being led out of a warzone they were taken into one, and taken by the very people supposed to protect them. Would that even be allowed nowadays? If I checked the library, or an internet search engine, I bet there's some act of law that could seize their passports and stick Krista, Elena and Sofia Zacharia on a Child Protection Register. Maybe my parents were right (Andreas too, according to Damaris) that forgetting or not knowing the past is better. It can't be helped that, if so, then I've only half inherited the gene. Of course, a tiny voice in my mind reminds me, nobody is forcing me to look for Elena while I'm here. I *could* call it a holiday and be done. But that feels worse than never coming to Cyprus at all.

I should stir myself and do my hair or my nails, conjure up the right outfit for my dinner non-date with Yiannis. I need to get into a mindset for company and conversation. I'm sure he's doing the equivalent. I shake myself; I need to give Yiannis a chance because it's not his fault he and I didn't immediately click in that sudden way of me and Red. God knows (their God) I'm no great prize and anyway, behind his meek and mild exterior, Yiannis, no doubt talk of the village for *his* life choices, must have a core, battered or not, of steel.

Instead, I glance again at the photograph of Elena, Krista and Sofia in front of what they called their tree houses, the shacks on stilts that look like defunct UN lookout posts. Behind them is the sea, but it's impossible to make out much more. The grainy black-and-white square has faded; Krista's long, sleek hair, nearly to her waist, has a yellowish hue and there is a paper tear across Sofia's chest, but the girls have their arms around each other and they look happy and carefree. There are no date or location clues on the back, just *The Zacharia girls at the tree houses* scribbled in pencil. In contrast is the bland tower block, *Hotel in Varosha New Town* postcard that Gillian Gale also handed over. Three smiley-face dots are drawn on a window towards the top of the seventies-style high-rise building and the message, in Elena's neat, rounded writing says, *To April and our class, I have sent this card for if you are bored with the letters. The smiley dots are me and my sisters in our bedroom. Love Elena Z xxx*.

If nothing else, I decide, I'd like to find the tree houses and the Varosha hotel. I cross-reference both with the 1971 *Travellers' Guide*, but there's no eureka moment. I slip the pictures of both into my book, marking a page I've not read, and put them in my bag. I'm sleeping in Nicole's spare room tonight, in case it's a late one, and she might like to see them.

'Right,' I say aloud. 'Onwards and upwards.'

We meet at the entrance to the Village Tavern – he's punctual, I'm punctual – where a beaming Georgios gives us our pick of the empty, midweek and out-of-season, tables. He takes an order and retreats for the rest of the evening. Yiannis is vegetarian, so out of solidarity I duplicate his order of fasolada, which he says is some kind of bean stew, and syrupy walnuts. It's as lacklustre as the décor, and the company – both of us – is little better. It's nothing to do with the unexpected symphony of meeting Nicole and then the encore of Red; with or without them, Yiannis leads me straight back to that safe beige boredom of childhood. We just don't click in person. I'm sure he feels it too but his earnestness is infectious and we've no common ground to confront it, shake hands and move on. The stilted dialogue and lapses into silence make us look like a middle-aged couple that has already said all there is to say and are trying not to contemplate the next thirty years together. Earlier, Nicole commented how she had been on an innocent lunch date with Yiannis once, when he was still a priest, and 'oh-so guilty about it'. As far as I can see, he still is.

That said, he's not without passion; he's warming to a long – very long – description of the *Tulipa cypria*, growing near the village of Polemi, down near the Pafos coast.

'The wildflowers are known as *Tulipa agenensis*.' His eyes light up and he drums his fingertips on the edge of the table. 'The original name, though, is prettier and more appropriate: *Tulipa oculus-solis*, eye-of-the-sun tulip. It is that the outer petals are red, with yellow and black inside, thus resembling the sun. Whether they are considered vulnerable or endangered is a most interesting debate.'

He goes on to explain, at more length, the classification system of *The Red Data Book of the Flora of Cyprus* as approved by the International Union for Conservation of Nature.

Then, 'I am boring you,' Yiannis says, finally, matter-of-fact.

'No!' I shake my head too hard. 'No. I'm sorry, Yiannis. It's interesting – great information for your B & B botanist guests – but I was just thinking...'

'Yes?' He nods encouragingly.

'We've been talking for hours,' I say. Well, it's forty minutes but seems longer. 'And we still don't really know each other. We said so much more in half a dozen letters.'

'You are disappointed.'

Aren't you? I want to snap but instead choose the words carefully. 'I'm disappointed we don't have the easy relationship we created in print.' I reach for my untouched (like his) wine glass, think better of it, and fiddle with the plastic vase of dried flowers.

Surprise and then dismay flicker across his face; gone in an instant. He raises his thumb to his mouth and rubs his lower lip; his nails, his scrupulously clean nails, are rough and bitten down.

When he doesn't reply, I bulldoze my way on. 'The tulips are interesting. So are the orchids and the history of Minerva House. But they don't tell me anything about you. I know that you are polite and kind and thoughtful... but that's the, the *packaging*, not the inside *you*.'

He inclines his head slightly, as if digesting the point. He says, suddenly, 'You are wrong, April.'

'About what?'

'This *is* me. This.' He parodies a *head, shoulders, knees and toes* action. 'In my letters I said everything. Tonight, I've said everything. There is nothing more to know. I am a very simple man. And,' he goes on, clearly seeing me open my mouth to argue, 'I am happy with that.'

'But you left the Church. You left your vocation and started again. Isn't that complicated?' I'm puzzled, genuinely, looking at the endless, tortuous self-reflection wheel I've put myself on over my own life choices.

'That was *very* simple. Not easy but simple. I did my best for a long time but my unhappiness grew and I thought, "Would God want an unhappy priest or a happy botanist?" If life is God's gift then the answer is obvious. If it isn't and there's no deity, then it does not matter.' Yiannis smiles and for the second time I see a flash of his literary persona. 'You find that hard to understand.'

'Only because everything in my life is complicated,' I say. 'I've got enough baggage to sink Cyprus.' I hurry on because my next, spontaneous, thought – *Have I though? Or is it all of my own making?* – is less palatable than Georgios' food. 'Are you happy now? Do you have what you want?'

He thinks for a minute. *'Fertilior seges est alieno simper in arvo.'*

I know it's Latin not Greek but that's as far as I go.

'The desirability of another's circumstances... greener grass, I think is the English?' *Déjà vu.* He stirs his coffee, meditatively. 'Yes, I am happy. When I see a true man of God, someone like our friend, Red, I know I made the best decision I could. I have a home, a business and a career.'

I wish he hadn't mentioned Red. The fasolada churns in my stomach, but it was an innocent compliment, not a dig. I concentrate on his glaring omission, but I don't help Yiannis out.

'I would like to marry.' He addresses it. 'To enjoy the consolation of living and sharing with another human being but...'

I take a breath in and hold it.

'But, I have not yet found her. The village aunties must keep matchmaking.' He smiles again and it takes years off him. He raises his wine glass, still full. 'A toast, April.'

Wondering, I pick up my glass and swirl the red liquid.

'To the orchids,' he says.

'The orchids.'

With all the cards on the table, the evening jogs on nicely, and I do learn half a dozen Greek words. When I go on to admire the vision and tranquillity of his secret garden, Yiannis uneasily brushes off the compliments, but when I broach the subject of putting my parents' remains there, he's totally at home with it, not only agreeing but making suggestions. I imagine him in his former life, counselling the bereaved and thoughtfully planning a funeral, especially when he offers to say a few words, or ask Red to do so, making it a semi-formal occasion, but I shrink rapidly from that – I might be trying to tap into Cypriot-April but I'm still my parents' daughter, and 'words' teeter on the edge of 'fuss'.

I try to match his reverence but have to smile at the absurdity when we get into the nitty-gritty of digging a shallow grave versus scattering the ashes, and the merits of sunlight or under a shady tree. Earwigging diners would think we were planning a murder, so it's lucky we're alone and the virtually absent Georgios has negligible English.

It's later than I would have thought possible when we prepare to leave the tavern and walk back towards Minerva House and Nicole and Andreas' guest room. It's a cool night on this part of the coast, the sky is mottled with cloud, a crescent moon playing a lacklustre game of peek-a-boo. Trying to contain a shiver, not wanting Yiannis to offer me his jacket, I stumble on the uneven road so that he takes my arm anyway.

'I'll say goodnight here.' Yiannis inclines his head towards the side of the Koumettou courtyard where a porch light is glowing above the little guest cabin.

When I thank him for the evening, it comes out like something you'd say at the end of a job interview and I don't want to leave it like that. 'Yiannis, I am truly sorry that... Well, you know.'

'I know.' He puts out his hand towards me and we shake hands awkwardly before I move away to cross the road, go through the garden gate and over the stones. At the bottom of the steps to the room, I bend down and slip off my sandals and wiggle my toes. Hooking three fingers over the straps, I use the other hand to press down the unlocked door handle. I look back as I turn to go inside and see that Yiannis is still there, seeing me safely home. He raises a hand and turns back towards Minerva House.

'Would it be too late to wake Nicole?' I'm muttering to myself, before catching my breath, startled by the silhouette in the middle of my bed. I creep forward and, as if I've magicked her up, I see it's her. I place the sandals on the floor, beside a pair of flip-flops that don't belong to me, and put my bag on the chair. Let her sleep or wake her? She's clearly been here a while; the cushions on the chair are indented and my copy of the Robert Walser book is open, face down on the arm. I wonder what she made of that. Elena's photo, the letter and the postcard are neatly side by side on the small table and a glass of water or ouzo – something clear, anyway – is beside them; a bunch of keys has fallen to the ground. I pick up the key ring and put it on the dressing table, then slip the Elena notes back into my book and shove that in my handbag. I tiptoe around the side of the bed, bend down and hesitate. Nicole is lying on her side, her knees drawn up so that her maxi dress covers her feet, just one silver toenail poking out.

'Nicole?' I murmur. Neither her slow, even breathing nor her position alter. I put out my hand to shake her shoulder, but she looks so settled. She'll still be here in the morning, plenty soon enough to tell her about the events or non-events over dinner. I pull up the throw from the bottom of the bed and lay it loosely over her. In the bathroom, I brush my teeth and put on my pyjamas, then slip, carefully, under the duvet beside her. She still doesn't stir; I've never met anyone who sleeps as quietly and neatly. Waking Nicole's alter ego, I think as I drift off to sleep myself, the calm, unconscious side that gives the energy to her days.

18

'I really do sleep the sleep of the dead, do I not?' is the next thing I hear, and I struggle to open my eyes. It feels like a few seconds later, but a slant of light across the shutters and through the gaps in the door suggests hours have passed.

'The sleep of the just, you mean.'

'That I can only wish.'

I turn my head and Nicole's sitting up, smiling at me. Her arms are raised, plaiting her hair.

'Good morning, April,' she says. 'I am so sorry to have invaded you as I did. I was restless last night. I calculated the time I thought your meal would finish and I came over to wait for you. Was it a liberty?' She narrows her eyes and I shake my head, it not having occurred to me. 'Andreas said entering your room without invitation was not appropriate, but I was certain you would think it fine.' Her brow creases. 'I should add, it is probably not fine to put myself on your bed and fail to wake when you arrive home. I picked up your book too, but when the papers fell out, I thought it might look like prying, so have left them folded for you, unread.'

Still chattering, she pushes back the blanket and stands up, draining her glass, tidying up the book and her car keys as she goes. She opens the little fridge and removes a bottle of water.

'I calculated, also, that you would not bring Yiannis back with you for a night of passion. But if you did, I am ashamed to say it would be worth the potential embarrassment to watch his face, and wonder if the term ménage à trois occurred to him...' She slips her feet into her flip-flops and comes over and perches on my side of the bed, placing the water on the night table. 'My plans are awry. April, you are not a morning person. I knew that the first morning I spoke to you by telephone.'

'Just give me a minute to wake up properly.'

'Certainly not.' She puts a finger to her lips, then leans over and tucks a stray hair behind my ear. 'Sleep. Come to the kitchen later. I will make you breakfast.'

Dozing, I unpick last night and start to tick off Yiannis on my mental 'to do in Cyprus' list. He is patently the writer, rather than the man, of my dreams and he's equally aware I'm not the woman for him. I spend a few minutes readjusting my headspace to put Yiannis in the 'friend' section, grateful that, on the flip side, he's sorted my mum and dad's resting place. Both things feel right. I bring Red into the frame, and feel something like a warm pang, akin to nostalgia, maybe. *In a different life...*

By nine o'clock, a litre of cold water inside my body and a shower of hot water over it, I'm happy with the nocturnal events and playing the 'Allegro appassionato, Opus 70', in my head; Saint-Saëns this early is a definite indicator that I'm ready for whatever the day might throw at me.

The first thing it throws at me is Petros.

He's sitting in Nicole's kitchen, drinking coffee and smoking. Andreas is at the other end of the scrubbed refectory table, astride a chair turned backwards, and he's leaning a sketch pad on the high back of it. It reminds me of the evening I looked down on him from my bedroom at Verena Bay; the stalker that wasn't. It occurs to me again how I'm reframing and refocusing my Cypriot expectations and assumptions at an alarming rate.

Andreas merely waves at me, that proprietorial air. It's Petros who speaks. 'April, my dear, come in. Nicole was about to seek you out. Excuse an old man's manners, but I am a subject under orders only to sit and to smoke.' He shrugs. 'It is not a challenge.'

'Morning, Petros, Andreas.' I move around the table to kiss Petros' proffered cheek.

'Tell me what he is drawing,' he begs. 'If it is a caricature or an abstract in which my head is an apple and my cigarette an erection, I must be prepared.'

So must I. Though it's less artistic interpretation than the wrath of Andreas if I lean over his shoulder that makes me hesitate.

'Come, come. See.' Andreas looks up at me, challenging. 'Do you fear I am a child who screens his picture so that others might not copy?'

'You might be.' I decide to be brave. 'You refused to acknowledge me when you were following me.'

'Not following, merely observing,' Andreas insists. 'I worked to capture your spirit, the essence of you. This old man has no essence left.'

Petros guffaws. 'I assure you, my friend, I have plenty of *essence*.' He mocks the word. 'If you cannot depict it, then your skills as an artist are waning.'

'Perhaps I have drawn you too many times,' Andreas counters. 'Come. See,' he repeats to me.

I've still no idea what Andreas will make of me on canvas. His sketches look skilful, but what do I know about painting? To be honest, I'd never heard of him before I demanded his name from Petros and I definitely didn't recognise it then. If there was a library to hand I'd look him up. In the meantime, there are plenty of examples of his work around this house, all portraits of people I don't know, but enough to tell me he's not an impressionist or abstract painter. However, watching what Andreas has done with Petros in a few pencil strokes at the kitchen table, even an art virgin can see outstanding talent in action. Andreas has drawn two men sitting either side of a table, each holding a cigarette, and with a small cup and ashtray in front of him. Both are undoubtedly, physically, Petros, but at the same time they're different men, or more accurately, opposing personalities of the same man. The one on the left is a benign gentleman, a kindly uncle or father, a straightforward man; the one facing him is far more complex, contained and more knowing. Light and dark shine through the tilt of the cigarettes, the slightly altered body posture. It's as if the artist has seen into another's soul, and most importantly, is able to show that to an audience. It demonstrates exactly why Andreas is a great artist and why I am a good-enough musician.

That must show on my face because Petros, the living, breathing version in front of me, fakes a Mona Lisa smile. 'He is good, is he not? He sees the parts of a person that most of us hope we keep hidden.'

'It's remarkable.' I'm stunned into honesty. 'Almost unnerving.'

I keep staring — what *is* he going to make of me? — until Nicole breaks the spell, whirling into the kitchen and dumping a cracked ceramic pitcher on the table. She grabs me round the middle and gives me a quick kiss on the cheek.

'I was about to come for you, April,' she says. 'You returned to sleep okay?'

'I did. I—'

'Ah, yes, my poor April, you awoke alone after your long-awaited date?' Petros, the devil version, twinkles.

I glare at him but expect the effect is spoiled by an unexpected blush. 'I awoke exactly as I would have chosen to,' and smile to acknowledge the tiny wink Nicole gives me.

It's not lost on Petros. He looks between her and me and then gives another pretend-secret smile. 'I know better than to involve myself in the complexity of female nuance.' He grinds out his cigarette.

'For once, sensible.' Nicole snorts. She turns to me. 'Don't indulge the voyeur in him, April. Or the gossip.' Hands on her hips, she surveys the scene. 'Look at them, they have turned my kitchen into the *kafenio* – coffee house,' she adds for my benefit. 'All the villages once had these places where old men whiled away their day, playing cards and chatter-chattering.'

'Me? Never. I came here only for your fresh goat's milk.' Petros indicates the jug.

'And you forget this is my house too,' Andreas protests. 'I am waiting only for April, so I may continue the portrait. I care nothing for nights of passion with Yiannis Loizos.'

'There was no night of passion—'

'He is teasing.' Nicole shakes her head. 'He is well aware that unlike these two,' she glares at them but without meaning it, 'Yiannis is a gentleman. You,' she turns to Petros, 'take your milk and go to check your hotel is still intact. And you,' this to Andreas, 'you can have April today – if she agrees – if you promise to care for your mother's dog tomorrow. It has adopted us, the one that looks like a giant fox, and it is not accompanying us to Famagusta.'

'Famagusta?' Petros and I chorus, while Andreas looks mutinous.

'Yes. April, Damaris has telephoned me and tomorrow we, that is you and I,' she indicates us both, 'will accompany her to Famagusta.'

There's a question in her tone, but it's directed at Andreas, not me. He affects indifference, but his pencil stabs the paper a little bit harder. I see the miniature Ganesh figure is back in his pocket and wonder if that has any significance, but now clearly isn't the time to ask because his voice, when he does speak, makes me jump. He stands up and scrapes his chair legs in a circle until it fits under the table. 'History,' spits his one-word farewell. He bangs the door behind him.

We all glance after him, but I'm the only one who seems remotely perturbed by his temper.

'The red setter. Tomorrow,' Nicole calls, shrugs slightly,

then picks up the jug of goat's milk and pushes it towards Petros.

'Ah,' he says, ignoring her obvious instruction. 'You have put Yiannis to bed – metaphorically, of course, dear April – and are now searching for Elena? Tick, tick.'

'I've also found a place to bury Mum and Dad's ashes.' I smile, taking his remark at face value. 'Tick, tick, *tick*.'

'Oh?' Petros raises his eyebrows. Nicole looks interested too, and I give them a quick rundown of the secret garden plan. But Petros isn't distracted. 'Even better. More time for chasing your Elena.'

I'm not sure why he's pushing it, or why it bothers me that he is, but Nicole saves me. 'Damaris is going to visit Famagusta for the first time since 1970-something,' she says, looking evenly at Petros. 'Orestes has wanted this for years, but she has agreed only since hearing April's story of Elena. If we can piece together anything of Elena's story, then all to the good. If not, maybe Damaris can lay a ghost to rest and we enjoy our day trip across the border.'

'Very good,' Petros says, meekly for him.

'Elena's not a mystery,' I relent, knowing that in fact I've made her one and shown myself full of contradictions. 'And I'm not chasing her, I'm... I'd just like to see what her world was like, or what's left of it. She talked about Cyprus being home, all the time, all sunny colours and warm feelings.' I shake my head. 'We made such mad plans to come here together. I...' I make a quick decision and root in my bag. 'This is Elena and her sisters.' I leave the letter and the postcard behind but take out the photo and lay it on the table. Nicole comes and leans over my shoulder and Petros cranes his neck, reaching out to pick it up. 'Elena, Krista and Sofia.' I point them out in turn. 'I don't know where this place is. I've told you they came from Famagusta, I know that much, but the more I see modern maps of Cyprus and hear the place names, I think they must have moved around a lot.'

'You have no idea where this is?' When I shake my head, Petros turns over the photo and sees the legend, *The Zacharia girls at the tree houses*, then turns it back and squints again. 'It's on the sea,' he says, 'but then we are an island. And when this was taken, Cyprus was not divided so…'

'It could be anywhere,' I finish for him. 'I've always thought it's the old north part though. As well as Famagusta, Elena used to talk about her Uncle Costas and his boat in Agia Napa. But she made it sound as if that was also near Apostolos Andreas,' I pronounce it carefully, 'which I know is a monastery at the farthest northern point. Elena called it the pointy finger.'

'Between Agia Napa and Apostolos Andreas,' Nicole repeats. 'Tree-house-like constructions that are on the beach. It is a start.'

'Probably flattened for a concrete conference hotel. With a nightclub and eighteen-to-thirty holidays.' I know I sound despondent, so I cheer it up with, 'I thought I might recreate *Journey into Cyprus*, you know, like Colin Thubron, the author? Just keep walking.'

'Or,' Petros' eyes twinkle, 'you – we – can ride in style in Yiannis' microbus and save our feet.'

'We can.' Nicole puts her hands on my shoulders and squeezes them. 'But only after me, April and Damaris have first seen Famagusta.'

19

Varosha, Cyprus
Saturday 10th August 1974

Dear April and Mrs Gale's class,

After a long time, here is my next class letter. Number four, I think. A lot has happened but mostly it's all the same things so this is a <u>summary</u>, like we learned in English, so you won't be bored.

We travelled all that last day, and for two more after we knew the tree-houses road was staying closed. At first an army jeep was behind us, then it drove away, then one came in front, so that it was like playing What's the time, Mr Wolf? Rushing steps forward, then stopping, then little creeping steps. The soldiers watched to make sure we followed the airport signs, but nobody said anything, not even Krista, when Antony waited for the dark and turned round again. We started to camp behind a broken barn in one village, where there was a rooster crowing and crowing, and the smell of jasmine flowers, my mum's favourite perfume, was everywhere. I was picking some to crush in my hanky, when something exciting happened!

A rat-tat-tat sounded. Rat-tat-tat. Rat-tat-tat-tat. Like that. Aunt Irini rushed back from looking for milk and bread screaming that a man with a machine gun was on the roof of the school. And he was firing the gun at the police station. It was like Bonanza *on the telly, April! I was only scared for a minute, because when the man saw us he stopped shooting and waved his flag at us as we drove away.*

After that we did a lot more zigzag driving until Aunt Irini said in her bright and shiny teacher voice that we needed exercise and fresh air, so were going to walk a little way. I think that actually the car broke down or maybe we ran out of petrol because she and Antony were whisper-arguing all the time and we had to walk a very long way and our bags were so heavy. Aunt Irini said maybe I shouldn't write more letters till we got to Stefan's hotel, just in case they got lost.

We walked for so many hours along the road, then across some fields, until our feet hurt and Krista and me got matching blisters on our pinky-toes. It was easier for Sofia because she got carried a lot. Sometimes a car or a cart stopped for us but it was as if Aunt Irini and Antony were looking for something that I couldn't see and they wouldn't tell us, they kept waving the drivers on. Then the mysterious right sort of car came and it gave us a lift to a truck and then a tractor and then, like as if it was a hundred years later, we saw the sea and the sand of the beach.

This means we are now in Stefan's hotel in Varosha, which you might think is the end of the story with 'They all lived happy ever after', but we are not happy and we are waiting. At least I can write my letters to you again.

Love from, Elena Z
xxx

They were bored. Bored and hot, so hot. For once they all agreed: it was too boring and too hot. It made the room so still, there being no bickering or squeals or stamping of feet. Like they were faint copies of themselves, or statues. Krista hadn't slammed the door all day. She lay on her back, spread out like a starfish, taking up the whole bed that they had dragged underneath the open window, hoping a breath of air, even warm air, would stir around them. Krista's hair was sticking up like a hedgehog's prickles. She had ordered Elena to braid it into tiny, tiny plaits, tying each one of the ends with Antony's cigarette papers. It was so short it was impossible, but Elena didn't mind trying. It felt nice. It reminded her of afternoons long ago when Mama and her friends sat in the cool of the back room and knitted stockings for winter. Elena's fingers couldn't knit, and she didn't want them to learn if it meant wearing scratchy and thick black stockings that needed mending every wash day, but they could braid without needing to be told how.

She liked sitting on the floor here and still being able to look over the sea and dream and plan. Sofia was sprawled beside her, a little pile of felt-tip pens discarded. She'd been colouring in the cigarette papers, decorating them with heart shapes and flowers, but was now clutching her doll, kicking up Jemima's too long and stripy legs against the glass. The three sisters were all as limp as that horrible rag doll, Elena thought, and it gave her a hot shiver, a goose over her grave, Mama would say; that made her shiver again.

Elena had never before been in a room where the window took up one entire wall. She had never been able to see so far. They were ten floors up in one of the newest hotels on John F. Kennedy Street. There were two rooms, one for them and one for Irini and Antony, with a bathroom between them; there was a card reminding you to lock both doors when you used it. Irini was in there now, having a bath. She had said she would do that whilst Antony made some phone calls down in the lobby, as long as the girls promised they would be alright on their own. 'We're not on our own really,' Krista had pointed out. 'You can hear us through the bathroom door. Well, you could if the water pipes weren't so noisy.'

The hotel was so new that the gardens hadn't been finished yet. The swimming pool stood empty of water but full of plastic tables and chairs. Looking down, the sun umbrellas were as tiny as the ones Charlie, the barman, put into their bright coloured drinks. In the evenings Irini took them down to the bar and he sometimes added sticky cherries from a tin or made them lemonade floats with a scoop of ice cream. Elena looked at her watch, but it was another two hours to go till then. It was as if Krista had read her mind; she loved Charlie. Aunt Irini called it a crush, but Krista said she really, really fancied him. Charlie was from England and his accent reminded Elena of April. She missed April so much. But writing her letters was harder than Elena had thought because mostly – except for The Machine Gun Man, as they'd started to call him – there was nothing interesting to say. Maybe she could buy one of the postcards in the lobby. Elena brightened up, there was one with a picture of the hotel on it, an *Artist's Impression*, it said it was, which meant it looked like a photograph but was really a drawing. She could circle a window on the tenth floor and draw three smiley dots to show their faces looking out.

'Why do we have to stay in here?' Krista was still grumbling. Then she wriggled. 'Ouch – you're hurting me. Why do you do it so tight, daydream girl?'

'Sorry,' Elena murmured, not bothering to respond to the first question, it was something Krista had said and Aunt Irini had answered a hundred times.

'It's stupid to say it isn't safe to go out,' Krista insisted. She struggled upright, shaking her hair free of Elena's hands, saying 'ouch' again. She flung her arms out wide. 'Look, look out there. What do you see? What do you see, Elena? Huh?

Sofia.' She poked her little sister with a toe and signed, 'What do you see?'

Sofia scrambled up and the three of them leant forward and pressed their faces against the window. Elena knew what she was supposed to say but instead she considered the view.

The hotel was right on the seafront. Beyond its gardens, the beach was a few strides across the road and down a flight of concrete steps. The sand was yellow and flat, laid like a huge carpet, and there was a roundabout and set of swings right in the middle. The tide was so far out, it looked like the sand was holding the sea and the sky back. The distant water sparkled underneath the sun but it barely moved, so hot and still was the day. It looked like a painting.

'I see sea,' signed Sofia. 'I see sand and sun. I see swings and a see-saw.'

'There's a dog,' offered Elena.

'Yes, yes, yes.' Krista wriggled impatiently. 'But that's like the, the setting. Like in the theatre before the actors come on. Nothing is happening.'

'No people,' Elena and Sofia agreed.

'That's what I mean.' Krista was triumphant. 'Where are the people? Where are the girls sunbathing and the boys playing with their stupid Frisbees? Where are the old people in their deckchairs? Where are the mothers unloading picnics and the fathers buying ice creams? Huh? Where? Where are they? I don't know.'

Elena didn't know either. There was only a handful of guests in the hotel too, and those that were there seemed all wrong. Elena had seen tourists on holidays; she had seen them here – well, in Famagusta, which was here really, before they went to the year in England. Tourists were usually relaxed and slow. They wandered along the promenade, fanning themselves with hats and sweating under heavy coloured bags full of things for the beach. The people staying in this hotel weren't in big, noisy family groups, they were in ones and twos and they scurried from room to restaurant looking as if they were being chased by a growling but invisible wild animal. There was nobody to play with, nobody to talk to. Aunt Irini had said that the hotel was so brand new, there hadn't been time for people to arrive yet; she said that in a way they were special guests, testing it all out. 'This is Stefan's hotel, you see,' she explained the day they arrived.

They had stood, grubby and dusty, at the kerb right here on the road below them, and they had craned their necks and shielded their eyes to see the top of the white building.

'Stefan owns all of this?' Krista loved to know what things cost, especially expensive things.

'He runs it,' Irini had corrected her. 'He's the manager. And we are very lucky to be able to stay here.'

'But he's not here running it now, is he?' Krista had said. 'He's running away with our mother instead. Is he scared of here because there's going to be fighting? Should we be scared too? Is that why we have run away from the tree houses' direction, seen The Machine Gun Man, and are pretending we have been on an accidentally long walk? Because of the fighting?'

'There's no fighting here,' Irini had snapped. 'We're on holiday. And the only thing you should be scared of, young lady, is my wrath if you don't behave yourself and stop answering back.'

Krista had almost fallen over. She couldn't have looked more shocked if her aunt had slapped her. Elena herself felt as if she *had* been slapped. Aunt Irini often got cross with Krista and Krista knew she would, she expected it, it was like a game, but this time Irini was furious. Even Antony seemed taken aback. There had been a second of silence, then Krista muttered, 'I'll take Sofia now,' which was her way of saying sorry. Irini had just nodded, handed over her youngest niece, and then run up the wide steps of the hotel entrance. Antony rubbed his fingers over his nose and cleared his throat three times. 'Don't mind her, she's just a bit edgy today. You know, tired and anxious,' he said, not looking at them. 'All the travelling and then trying to sleep in all the different places and waiting to see your mum...' He cleared his throat again and smiled apologetically at nobody in particular.

Since then, Elena had thought about what Antony said, and she understood. It was how she felt too. And now, sitting in the bright hotel room on the tenth floor with nothing to do but think about it again, she realised it was probably how all the other people that were there were also feeling. It was like time had slowed right down and they were waiting for something, but that the something might not all be good. Suddenly, with a spark of understanding she didn't want, Elena realised that Irini had shouted at Krista with the same hunted look that Jerry the mouse always had on his face before Tom the cat caught him. It was the same look as the few other guests had. Irini hadn't just been a bit tired and nervous, whatever Antony said. Aunt Irini was scared.

'I think the nothing is why it's not safe,' Elena said slowly.

'What? That doesn't make sense. What do you mean?'

Elena concentrated to get the words exactly right. 'You said just now we weren't allowed out because it's not safe.'

'So? It's true.'

Elena shook her head. 'Nobody has said that, Krista. Aunt Irini didn't and Antony didn't. They never said it's not safe. It's just we know that's what they mean because of the way they are acting.'

'You're muddling me, daydream girl, and I don't like it.'

But Elena carried on as if Krista had never spoken, she was thinking out loud. 'And we know it can't be safe because there is nobody outside. Everyone has either gone home or is hiding indoors.'

'Like us.'

Elena nodded.

'So I was right. There is going to be fighting here.' Krista sounded pleased with herself. 'That's why Aunt Irini got so mad with me.'

'I think so.' Elena felt a familiar curl of fear inside. 'What should we do, Krista?'

Krista looked mutinous. 'What we should do,' she announced, 'is be at the Palm Beach having fun. If it's not safe on the beach then it's not safe in a skyscraping hotel made out of glass, is it? Stupid, stupid, stupid.' But she said it quietly, because the water pipes had settled down and Elena knew she didn't want Irini to hear her.

20

'April, relax your shoulders a little more,' Andreas bellows, all temper abated.

Red, crossing the street below, his arms full of folders as he makes his way to Minerva House, looks up, and is treated to a scarlet-faced me managing a half-hearted wave. He laughs out loud – with me, not at me – and I watch his back until he disappears. I can't get away from that sudden thud of familiarity his fleeting presence brings. What—

'April! Where is your attention?'

I sigh and try to concentrate on Andreas' exacting directions. A morning in his studio has confirmed there is nothing artistic about being an artist's model, and by now my expectations of lazing around – magically toned limbs tastefully draped over the time-honoured chaise longue – are long thwarted.

Andreas threatened to arrange me, and arrange me he has. For someone whose sole experience is the arrangement of music, this is illuminating and not totally dissimilar. He sits on a droopy wicker armchair in the centre of the room and directs. It's the human equivalent of sheepdog trials: 'Lean forward, step backwards, up on your toes – less, less. Now look out of the window, no, to the right. That's it – stay there.' He bounds over, manhandles my knees, bends an elbow, props me up against the sill and pats me on the head. 'Good,' he approves. Finally. And as if he's muddled me up with the red setter he's due to dog-sit.

At this stage, I'm leaning out of the window looking down towards the courtyard – hence the perfect view of Red beyond its cobbles – the toes of one foot grazing the back of the other ankle, and with my back to his canvas. When I twist my head, Andreas is behind me holding up two crossed pencils and muttering; he says he's defining perspective. I amuse myself by deciding he's warding off anti-art demons as befits a man on hugging terms with the god, Caerus – his second idol, he tells me, after Ganesh. The figurines now sit side by side on a high shelf, watching over him.

Andreas wants me casual, in a white summer dress he borrowed, in anticipation, from Nicole. It would be long and flowing on her, on me it's knee-length and more fitted. Overnight he apparently decided I should look as if I'd just got out of bed, eyes cloudy with sleep and hair meticulously tangled. Nicole's other reason, I learn, for camping out in my room; Andreas wouldn't be above coming and waking me personally so that the image would be genuine. He's had to make do with a natural, tousled look that's as contrived – if not as polished – as any airbrushed movie star's: Nicole's make-up.

Now he's setting what he calls the painting scene.

'Imagine,' he says, 'it is early morning, just light. Your lover is leaving you as the sun rises. You do not know when you will see him again. You run to the window and are watching him go. You feel…?'

Out of my depth. 'Regret?' I do my best to join in. 'Relief? Anger? Love?'

'All those,' he agrees. 'Think of your heart's desire. Think of the ones for whom you hold much longing,' he urges. 'The ones left behind.'

There's something in that simple phrase that makes me catch my breath, brings me to unexpected tears. I blink them away and in the resultant blur let myself imagine Elena as I knew her, appearing round the corner as if time had stopped.

Andreas gives a grunt of satisfaction. 'Let us paint,' he says. I settle into the position, daydreaming. Time crawls.

'You are in character, yes?' Andreas periodically checks. 'You see your loved one greet another through the trees and your envy is inflamed.'

When the mirage of Elena fades, I while away the morning, running through scales in my head, the majors and minors in sequence: andante... legato, pianissimo... forte. Andreas is not inclined to chatter whilst he paints, instead he grumbles and hums to himself, the constant vibration of machinery in an underground mine. And he does it off-key, a semitone flat, which jangles my nerves. Eventually, I ask him if he is praying.

'I am a communist, not an Orthodox,' he rebukes me. 'When I work, recitation blocks my mind so my eyes only see. Interpretation will come later, with the colours.'

'So, what are you reciting? The AKEL manifesto?' I hazard, fascinated he's doing the same as I am, less tunefully.

'Today, I am retelling myself the Greek myths. But my Latin grammar and multiplication tables wait in the reserve.'

Eventually, Nicole's voice floats up the stone stairs. 'Andreas. April,' she calls. 'Are you still alive? It is late. Red is coming here. Andreas, let us have her for a while. I give you one hour more, okay?'

Andreas grunts, then shouts something in Greek. He keeps working, I think, I can't really see what he's doing. It's broken my concentration and I desperately want to scratch my neck. I marvel again that I'm doing this. It might appear frivolous, but it's really a challenge; to still my body, to still my mind.

'April? Your shoulders are rising, your breathing is too forced. You are aware of the Buddhist vipassana? The training of sati? You must be in the moment, in *this* moment, April.'

Veneration of Greek gods, communism, and now he's releasing his inner Buddhist. Andreas is a philosophical lucky dip, I think, pleased with my turn of phrase. My roaming thoughts flitter from there to Christianity, courtesy of meeting

Red and Yiannis, I suppose. I might not have a faith but I do respect it in others and Yiannis' defection from his Church, for his reasons, I understand. But Red? I've never known a priest, or a man who would want to become one. My hypothetical priest is either a saintly man of God, distant and inscrutable, or, shamefully, that media favourite, the one too familiar with altar boys or quietly seducing his housekeeper. Red is ordinary – well, other than being friendly, uncommonly perceptive, kind and – I think wryly – the 'soulmate' that can't be.

I run through the number of times, ever, I've been to church for anything liturgical: weddings, including one of my own, fewer funerals and a baptism, a handful of occasions at school when the choir sang at Christmas. Yes, I've played concerts in places of worship, beautiful places, but the music, secular mainly, is always the thing. I've never considered it being in a house of religion, the setting is a backdrop, and the clergy and their entourage bit players. Now I've met a priest, and an ex-priest – oh, and not to mention two fake ones. Faintly surreal, it suddenly strikes me as hilarious, and I smother a hiccup of laughter that makes me cough.

'What are you doing, April?' Andreas calls.

'What are you doing to April, Andreas?' I hear Nicole's voice. 'Please take a break now?'

'There is no need. I am finished,' Andreas shouts back. 'Nicole? Please fetch a bottle of Maratheftiko.' Then to me, 'April, you may unbend. Are you hysterical?'

'No.' Stiff, I stretch this way and that, and then quickly pull on a cotton jumper over the sheer white dress. I hesitate, one eye on the canvas, which is angled away from me. Andreas is busy sloshing brushes through a murky brew and says he'll follow me down and I don't dare to peek at the work in progress.

Downstairs, I find Red alone, and drinking coffee.

'April.' He looks up, smiling broadly. 'Er, apologies for laughing earlier. It was in solidarity, I promise. You looked...'

'I looked like a medieval woman who forgot to shout gardy loo before launching water out of the window.' I sink down onto the chair opposite him.

'You looked like a perfect study. How *is* the immortalisation process going?'

'Apparently, the painting's going well. We're finished for today.'

'No.' I hear Andreas' voice behind me.

'Oh?' I twist round, fanning myself with my hand. It's hot out here.

'Not finished for today. Finished, in full.' He opens his arms wide, palms upwards. 'I have much work to do, but your presence, April, is no longer physically necessary to the process.'

'That's it?' It's really all done in the equivalent of a long weekend? Red gives me a discreet thumbs up. Andreas doesn't notice, having made his statement, he's staring distractedly out over the road, but Nicole, appearing from the kitchen with a bottle of red wine and four glasses, overhears and laughs.

'I knew Andreas had finished, he always celebrates with this.' She holds up the bottle. 'It comes from the Pitsilia region, east of Mount Olympus, and is cultivated in only one per cent of our vineyards here,' she recites as if reading the label. 'We own a small part of them.' Then: 'Poor April, you feel short-changed, no?'

'Am I the shortest-reigning muse in history?'

'No.' Andreas slides his eyes between all of us. 'I am very good, is all. She, April, is embedded in the depths of my soul. The creation of the art is just beginning.'

'How long will it take?'

'Not long. Days. Weeks.'

I want to know what I'm going to look like, wishing now I'd had a good look before we came downstairs, but I doubt Andreas will be very forthcoming; he might not even know. I'm beginning to see that his work – from the sketch of Petros to the portraits on the walls – is largely traditional but set in landscapes that go off-kilter: a boat half on land; a flight of steps to nowhere. It's his signature style, I suppose, so I'm unlikely to end up as an orange blob or a set of wavy grey lines, but the window could well be an aeroplane porthole or something.

'What will you do with me?' I ask. 'The painting of me, I mean?'

Andreas shrugs; he has a catalogue of shrugs. 'It is dependent on the end result. Exhibit. Sell. Burn.'

'Burn?' Red and I ask in unison.

'If it is second-rate work. Yes. What else? You prefer your image poorly reproduced on a thousand thank-you cards?' He snorts, before gulping his glass of wine. '*Yiamas.* Cheers.'

'He talks nonsense.' Nicole is sipping more daintily. 'Tell her, Andreas. When is the last time you painted a portrait you hated?'

'January 1990. It did justice neither to me nor my subject.'

'It was a picture of me, in my wedding gown,' Nicole continues. She watches me struggle for an appropriate response, then laughs, easily. 'I am teasing you, April. Oh, yes, it was a picture of me so dressed but Andreas is right. It was not good. I would have burned it if he had not.'

'There were so many contradictions.' Andreas murmurs as if he is back there, seeing the image with fresh, still-frustrated eyes. 'I could not get the spirit, the soul…' He snaps back and unexpectedly smiles at me. A normal smile, one that makes him look like the ordinary boy next door. 'My wife is right though. Your picture will be good, maybe great. I know it here.' He taps his head. 'And here.' His heart. 'I have an exhibition planned next year in Athens. It may be the missing piece.'

'Perhaps you will see yourself in a London gallery.' Nicole pours the wine. 'You'll be even more famous.'

'Rather a London gallery than imagining myself above the mantelpiece of a total stranger's bedroom.' I suppress a shudder and wonder if I could afford to buy me.

'I'd buy you.' Red reads my mind. 'If you weren't well beyond my price range.'

'I could not allow that,' says Andreas. He looks so serious, I ponder what kind of superstition he has; even Nicole looks mystified. 'A life-size triptych of a foreshortened and naked arse is quite unsuitable for a Roman Catholic presbytery,' he adds.

It must be a full three seconds before he roars with laughter, his face as wolfish as Red Riding Hood's granny. Nicole and Red both look relieved and start to laugh; I'm last to join in and mine is tinged with hysteria. I never thought I'd feel nostalgic for my taciturn almost-stalker.

When the wine bottle is empty and Andreas has been dissuaded from opening a second, Red drives me back to Verena Bay. Both of us hesitate, looking first along the coastal walk, and half at each other, coming to the immediate and tacit understanding it's too dangerous. *Lead us not into temptation*, I remember – sourly, I admit – from school assembly days, and bang the door of the old jeep harder than I need to.

'You know my parents' ashes? I'm going to bury them in Yiannis' secret garden,' is the cheery way I initiate conversation. Surely you can't get safer than talking death to a priest. 'Early in the morning, I think. Their favourite time. My dad always did his gardening first thing, and Mum wouldn't dream of staying in bed after him.'

'Good for you,' says Red as we judder onto the road. 'At the risk of sounding the father-confessor, I think you'll find an immense sense of relief.'

'I already have.' I consider that, and it's true. 'Just finding the right place has made all the difference. Silly, isn't it, they died almost a year ago, they didn't believe in an afterlife, so why would they care where their mortal remains end up?' The sea flashes by on our left, wild and infinite, not like a safe little burrow under a native shady tree.

'Funerals, memorials, whatever, are for the rest of us left behind, April.' Red crunches one of the gears and winces. 'Sorry. I don't think this thing likes me much.'

'It doesn't like anyone much, it's a crotchety bundle of nerves.'

'But it's got us here.' He swings into the car park, slows down and lets the engine stutter and cut out. Before we get out, he says, 'April, you don't have to do any of this alone. You do know that, don't you?'

It's a novelty for someone who's *always* done things alone, but I nod. 'I know that, and if there's anyone I'll turn to it'll be you...' I do *and* don't want to single him out. 'And Nicole. Petros too. Honestly.'

Red nods too. 'That's okay then. And you also know I'm saying it as Red the friend. Don't let the P-word put you off.'

'The what? Oh, of course,' I realise. 'I wasn't even thinking the P-word.'

'Good.' We make our way to the house. 'Usually, people can't forget it and either don't know what to say, or they launch into the evils of the Church and ask what I'm going to do about them.'

'What do you say?'

'That I'm on a fast-track programme to join the Vatican and when I become Pope Philip I, I'll rewrite every article of faith ever known.' Red grins. 'Well, I have been known to say that but mostly I put on my priest face and act patient. The Church does have a lot to answer for.'

We stop at the door to the hotel; the reception area is lit but deserted. Noises suggest dinner preparations in full swing in the kitchen.

'Hear that?' Red gives a mock sigh. 'Jarlath's in there, "lending a hand", I'm told. He's been there all day. And with Petros' blessing.'

'But not yours?' So that's how Petros managed to be in Nicole's kitchen at breakfast time.

'Hey, as you now know, I'm not his dad. It might be a

sudden interest in hotel management or maybe a certain hotel waitress, but he's happy and allegedly useful. Want a drink?' he adds.

'I'd love one... but later? I think I'll play for an hour,' I decide. 'I've had a piece of music on my mind since I was hanging out of Andreas' window: Gerald Finzi, "Eclogue". English, pastoral, but it will *so* fit here.'

I've no idea if he recognises the composer or the piece but he nods and as we wander over towards the drawing room, he says, 'When Nicole said that you might be *more* famous, does she realise that you are—'

'I'm not famous now, Red,' I can't help interrupting, 'if that's what you're saying. At least, my name is reasonably well known in a very specific bit of the world of music but ordinary people don't stop me in the street, and I'm not invited on to TV game shows. Thank goodness.' Red grins at my mock-ish shiver. 'Stop. It's a horrific notion.'

'You'd be great, I'm sure, but I can understand why you wouldn't want to. No,' he goes on, 'I was just going to ask...'

'About me coming here?' I open the door and click on the nearest light. 'If it's a publicity stunt? Or a midlife crisis? It could be just a slightly odd holiday, you know.' It's my turn to grin. Looking over my shoulder, I watch him scratch his head.

'Actually, I was going to ask if I could listen to you play sometime,' he admits. 'Or is that the last thing you want? Busman's holiday? Too personal, one-to-one?'

'I can't think of anyone I'd rather play for.' I mean it. 'You can sit in now, if you like? As long as you don't expect a performance and I get to veto any requests.'

'Deal. I won't clap, fall asleep or ask you if I can have a go.' He looks at me evenly. 'And I'll sit at the back of the room. A good professional distance.'

'Probably best.' I smile.

It's one of the nicest evenings I could wish for: no pressure, no agenda. Just the shared music.

21

The next morning, Damaris struggles into the back seat of the car, a huge tapestry bag in one hand and a wicker basket in the other. She slings the first in, the other she places gently on the floor and settles herself beside it. She's swathed in an orange shawl against the cool whiteness of the dawn. 'It is too cold today,' she says.

'It is too early. Even for me,' Nicole corrects from the driver's seat, turning around and squinting over her shoulder. 'I need more sleep. This morning I drank a litre of green tea and still I look like a troll. Maybe God is telling me I am too old for entertaining and keeping goats.'

'You are looking as beautiful as every day, my darling,' Damaris says. 'Always so elegant. If only you would stop your smoking.' She fiddles with the luggage at her feet.

'I did. I do. For a little bit of Lent every year. I don't like it,' Nicole says. 'Wait, why are you distracting me?' She squirms around some more and fixes on the wicker basket. 'Mother-in-law, tell me it is not possible you have one of your horrible cats in that basket again? You know the rules.'

Damaris' face flickers from guilty to wounded to smug as she leans over and opens her bag and then the basket. No cat.

'This is the thanks I get for agreeing to this little trip and for making us a lovely picnic so that it is bearable,' she complains. 'My home-made spanakopita, all warm and flaky;

sweet, ripe oranges picked from my own orchard; a flask of good coffee ground by my own arthritic hands. April, does that not sound like the task of love?'

'It sounds perfect. My stomach is rumbling already.' I'm only half joking.

'The green tea is my penance for too much coffee and red wine. We drank the second bottle of Maratheftiko after you were gone. It was not a good decision,' Nicole chips in, also eyeing the picnic basket. Then she squares her shoulders. 'We can eat as we drive,' she announces.

'She is afraid I will run away if we do not get started,' Damaris says to the air.

Not answering, but not hanging around to test her either, Nicole guns the car to the main road.

Sipping hot, sweet coffee from a thermos and catching pastry flakes where they fall, we also eat up the miles. It reminds me of school trips when I was little: starting on our lunch boxes before the coach driver had sped up to fourth gear. There was one time, the only time when Elena and I went to London together, we sneaked fish and chips from the takeaway and wrapped them up for the next day, swapping them with the corned-beef-filled rolls waiting in the fridge. Neither of us wanted to admit that yesterday's cold and limp fish supper was truly disgusting at ten o'clock on a rainy Tuesday morning. We didn't say a word when Mrs Gale, nostrils delicately twitching, confiscated it all and handed us the sausage rolls and crisps she carried for emergencies.

'The spanakopita is delicious.' I choose another triangle from the warm nest of them, and hand one to Nicole.

Damaris beams. 'It is the nutmeg sprinkled through the spinach leaves and the salt in the cheese,' she says. 'Take one more. No? Then I will peel the fruit. Green tea, indeed.'

'I would not have made a breakfast so good,' Nicole owns up.

'You can cook fine, my Nicole, but today you are chauffeur. Drive, if drive you must,' Damaris says.

'You see, April? You see that one of the many reasons I married Andreas is for my mother-in-law.'

I begin to smile but there is something in the pause after Nicole's remark that takes it beyond the realms of a fond joke. An unspoken note of challenge perhaps, but if so, it's one that Damaris doesn't take up. She's frowning at the oranges, and doesn't meet Nicole's momentary gaze in the rear-view mirror. Nicole slides her glance towards me but a lifetime of curiosity and misunderstanding trailing my own family and love life makes me circumspect.

For a minute or two, we all concentrate on the road. 'How far is it?' I ask.

Nicole shrugs. 'It depends on the border formalities, how long it takes to swap over the car and then the state of the roads on the other side. We can see the old town of Famagusta first, and look at Varosha from the ramparts. I suppose you would call Varosha a suburb if it were still alive now. Then, it was going to be a new town. A brave new world, even. That is right, Damaris?'

But Damaris is looking vaguely out of the window and humming to herself.

'Damaris?'

'What was that?' Damaris says. 'I do not think I was listening. We can make our plans later on. I was thinking it is time overdue that Georgios cleans and paints the tavern. Agia Triada is looking shabby.'

Nicole allows herself to be diverted. 'If I was not there to stop it, Georgios would have Andreas decorating the whole building and painting murals of the Dionysius mosaics in the bathrooms.'

'It's a living,' says Damaris mildly.

'Oh, mother-in-law, I do not expect Andreas to turn down good and simple work, but I object when he is agreeing to payment in tired kleftikos and pickled walnuts.'

'There was a time when barter was more important than money. Maybe it is not so strange an offer.'

'Not so strange if you exchange first-class food for first-class art, but I swear to you Georgios has the same menu as his great-grandfather did.'

'The vegetarian option was... okay,' I offer.

Damaris claps her hands. 'You ate there with Yiannis,' she says. 'It is good for his confidence,' she tells me. 'But,' firmly now, 'you are not the wife for him.'

'Why not?' challenges Nicole. 'It is a universally unacknowledged fact in Agia Triada that an ex-priest of a certain age must be in search of a wife.'

I am not quite sure what to make of that. Damaris laughs and, after a second, Nicole does too. She leans over and pats my knee.

'April, I am sorry. This was an ill-considered remark and unpleasant. A terrible misquote, of which my father, he's professor of English and Greek, would be ashamed. Although it is true all of the older ladies this side of Agia Napa would like Yiannis Loizos married as much as he would like to be married. It is the only way to make sense of his desertion of the Church.'

'Even then it will be many years before he is forgiven,' Damaris says. 'We are an old-fashioned kind.'

'But he could have got married and stayed a priest, couldn't he? I'm hazy on the rules. 'Not like the Catholic Church.'

'Not like Red,' Nicole murmurs, eyes flicking from me to the road.

Ouch. I say nothing, pretend not to hear.

'In the Greek Orthodox Church, one can be married first and become a priest, but not vice versa. And Yiannis was very young when he entered,' Damaris explains. 'I think for him, however, it must always be one option or the other.'

'Oh. Well, I'm afraid I won't be his Redeemer.'

'It was very lucky for us, if not himself, that Yiannis found you.' Damaris leans forward to pat my shoulder.

'You make it sound like a dating agency. We sent letters

about the orchids, and that was courtesy of Jake, my ex.' I sigh. 'Alright, I did quite like the sound of Yiannis. But.'

'But. That was before you met him and realised that if you date an ex-priest you want him to be of the Red variety, not the Yiannis variety,' Nicole says.

Ouch again; far too near the mark. What is it with her today? 'You don't think I'm interested in Red?' I say, heart hammering.

'Oh no. No more than he is interested in you,' she says. Sly. 'Although, April, you surely agree it is a shame he is so unavailable.'

'I'm glad he is,' I say, feeling reckless. 'I'm a sucker for unsuitable, so unavailable is the best way.'

'Were both your husbands unsuitable?' Damaris asks.

'From the start.' My marriages aren't something I usually dwell on but there's an air of expectation in the car and, after a minute, I go on, though I'm not sure why. 'The first I met in college when I was nineteen. I married him because my parents loved him and because he needed a visa to stay in the UK.' Neither of them says anything. 'The second, well, he had the most amazing singing voice I'd ever heard. It was seductive, strong, clear, full of emotion and promise.' He's quite famous now and it still gives me chills when I hear it.

'What happened next?' Damaris sounds as if I'm recounting film scenes.

'It took a year to find out *he* wasn't any of those things. We divorced before I was thirty.'

'Third time lucky in Cyprus. Hmm?' Nicole says.

With that, I know I'm not imagining an edge to her. On the surface she's as cheerful as ever but every now and then one of these 'witty' remarks feels knife-sharp. I rack my brains and eventually dismiss it as something as simple as her need for nicotine; I don't think I've seen her go more than half an hour without a cigarette but she's scrupulous about not smoking in the car. Or perhaps she and Andreas argued over the second bottle of wine and she's smarting about relationships.

Damaris is a good buffer until she starts growing quieter with each mile we cross, which in the circumstances makes sense. I feel myself overcompensating and being too bright, chattering to Damaris, trying to draw Nicole out. It's something I don't think I've done for half my life, not since my mother and father shared one of their worried silences prevalent during my – innocuous – teenage years. I only now recall that I used to do it at all and how unsettling, *exhausting*, it was.

Nothing today is as I expect it to be. The formality of the border crossing from Greek South Cyprus to Turkish North Cyprus is a surprise. Despite my original pontificating to Jake, I clearly hadn't grasped how divided is the city of Nicosia, island and people. We wait in an outdoor no man's land, plastered with political posters and images of atrocities carried out by 'the other side' and the passage isn't quick or friendly. When our visas are stamped we're ushered across a barrier to undergo more of the same in the northern half of the island. Eventually we're in a hire car following road signs in Turkish instead of Greek.

Damaris breaks miles of silence to grunt, 'Huh,' and shake her head. 'Ridiculous,' she says. 'Ridiculous the trouble it takes to visit my family's home place.'

'Whilst the North is under Turkish control and the Turkish Republic of Northern Cyprus is recognised only by Turkey, this is the way it will be, mother-in-law,' Nicole says. 'Cyprus is about to join the European Union and to vote on the next phase of the Annan Plan. Maybe that will forge a common bond.' She sounds as if she's reciting from a political memo, which I realise she is; and so cautioning Damaris. Damaris knows it too.

'Do not worry, Nicole,' she says. 'My lips are buttoned. In bitterness maybe, but buttoned nonetheless.' She bangs one fist on the window. 'It is nothing like my home, anyway.'

I find myself thinking that this place – Famagusta – if it's so strange to Damaris, it would be alien to Elena. The Elena of thirty years ago, that is; maybe the contemporary Elena takes it in her stride, maybe she, herself, dons a military uniform and helps maintain the status quo. Who knows? It isn't the Famagusta of my imagination either. I was expecting an oasis of calm stuck somewhere in the 1950s, but the approach to it is just another tatty road.

'Be patient,' says Nicole. 'This is modern Famagusta, the old town is more what you imagine.'

Sure enough, old Famagusta is a walled city, a mix of historic buildings and ruins, and an everyday residential place where life is being lived and work is being worked. At the large and ornate roundabout, the old walled city and its ramparts lead off to our left where we can ride around with impunity.

'Cyprus has a very laid-back attitude to health and safety, and to preservation,' I comment, used to countries with *Do Not* signs and a more definitive demarcation of the historic and the modern day.

'We are not as obedient as Europeans nor yet as interested to sue as the Americans,' Nicole says. 'It makes life more interesting.' Then: 'Two legs good, four wheels better,' she goes on as she slides around a narrow corner. 'And four wheels with AC is better still; it is never usually this hot and dusty in early April.'

'The cats are the kings of the road.' Damaris, more animated, looks through the windscreen between the front seats, as Nicole slows to an impatient crawl behind a stalking feline family.

'What is this? Loxandra pets on vacation?' I hear her mutter, gripping the steering wheel tight. She leans out of the window with a pointless, 'Shoo, shoo,' at the high-tailed specimens sauntering down the middle of the road. They turn round, lazily, but don't move. 'If they had fingers they would make a piss-off sign at us,' she complains.

Without casualties, we stop in an amateur parking lot beside the church of St George of the Greeks, where the light and shade make curious shadows over the Petra-coloured stone. There is nobody else around, save an old man mending a tyre on the car parked next to us.

'April, you must use the cream,' Damaris says. 'Nicole, give her the cream. You are still so pale in colour and the freckles can catch cancer so easily.'

'She doesn't have sun freckles. I bet she has freckles even in the winter in damp England. They are matched with red hair.' Still, Nicole rummages obediently in her bag.

'It's okay, I have my own stuff here somewhere,' I say. 'You're right about the freckles. Not that I have red hair, not really. It's more reddish-browny.' I pull down the sun visor and frown into the tiny mirror.

'No, it is definitely red,' Damaris insists. 'Red like the English rose.'

'My parents named me April Rose.'

'April Rose, such a clever name for you.'

'But red like gold, not like carrots.' Nicole is still looking at my head and reaches over to smooth a stray hair out of my eyes. 'It is beautiful hair.'

I feel a tremor; a fleeting memory or some unspecified, untenable longing. I don't know if it's Damaris echoing Elena's mama or Nicole's touch, but instinctively I back off from it. 'Thanks.' I snap the sun visor closed. 'Now where's my bag?'

We walk through narrow and cobbled streets where paint is flaking off once-white buildings and dilapidated cars; a veneer of fatigue not masked but heightened by the unseasonal weather. Damaris steps inside and blesses herself as we pass a huge medieval building. 'St Nicholas Cathedral,' she says with a defiant look at Nicole.

'Yes. And also Lala Mustafa Pasha Mosque.'

'Whatever you say.' Damaris shrugs and points to an ancient fig tree towering over us. 'I will sit here a while.' She turns her back on us. 'You girls must go and see the view.'

It's a dismissal and we watch her walk away. She's the

one who, from behind, resembles a girl. Her thin back is bony under the striped cotton dress, twisted with the weight of the carpetbag, and the strap of her left sandal is flapping around her heel.

'Into her seventieth year and one hell of a life.' Nicole makes it sound like another quote. She turns to me, almost accusatory in her gaze. 'Do you know how long it is since she was here? Did she tell you?'

I shake my head.

'No. Me neither. Orestes has told me this. One time she has been here since they were evacuated in the invasion. One time in 1997 when she receives permission from Turkish authorities to attend the funeral of her mother's sister. She did not have news till then that this woman had survived.'

'Nicole—'

'Today Damaris comes here with a reason that is not her reason. It is for you she comes, maybe for Orestes; this she can bear. But we must not forget, it is her day. Not for you or for me or for your Elena. For Damaris.'

She turns and strides off in the direction of the old city ramparts. I hesitate, guilt and responsibility, also confusion, hanging as heavy as the afternoon sun. It's the first time I've heard Nicole's impeccable English desert her. My inclination is to slink away, give her time to gather her thoughts, but my feet know better; Nicole needs an audience even if she's fighting with it. I catch up with her down by the quay and at the edge of the water where the headland curves round into a fading crescent. She's in front of a Greek sign, which she translates as if our previous conversation had never happened.

'Listen to this. "Much of the ramparts cannot be walked as they are military controlled",' she reads, '"or are inaccessible through the neglect of the Turkish authorities. The Greek government promises to restore the city walls as a tribute to its people".' She jabs at the final line. 'Dated 1985. How very Cypriot.'

We haul ourselves up the steep stone steps that lead to

a tower staggered with lookout points. The bay beneath us is sandy, deserted. With the thick blue sky as its ceiling it is postcard-perfect. Then, in the distance like a mirage, the seaside buildings begin, in low-rise ones and twos at first, eventually turning into a shimmering cityscape.

'That,' Nicole points out, 'is new Famagusta. The 1970s jewel named Varosha. From here it looks like any Mediterranean holiday resort, no? It is only up close you see it is empty and forgotten.'

'Not forgotten, surely.' Something in it appeals to my imagination and I can't drag my eyes away from the curving, abandoned coastline.

Nicole shrugs, scrabbling for her cigarettes. 'Not by the thousands who were driven out – or evacuated, let us be objective because I have no fight with either Greek or Turk – no. But it is my doubt the rest of Europe knows of it. It is a mirage,' she says. 'You will see.'

'Nicole, I don't want to upset Damaris—'

'April, it is okay. I am sorry for shouting. I am angry at myself for forgetting how real all of this is to her. For you and for me, it is,' she hesitates, 'not a game, not that—'

'A puzzle.'

'Yes, a puzzle. Our lives will not change because of this visit, will they? Damaris' life might. Or at least, how she views her life. Yet, she does need to be here. I feel that strongly. She does too, I think. Your journey is the excuse – the catalyst, is it?'

I can see that Nicole is struggling to express herself, again, but she doesn't need to keep trying. 'I know. I do understand.'

She raises a sceptical eyebrow and I laugh, but not with much humour.

'That's the problem, Nicole, my journey is an excuse because I want my life to change.'

'How?' she demands, taking a final drag of her cigarette, her long hair blowing backwards in the wind, framed by the ramparts. I want to take her photograph.

'If I knew that,' I take my camera from my bag and point it at her, 'I probably wouldn't be here, and that would be a great shame.'

'Yes, it would,' she says, posing. 'Done?'

'Done.' I tuck my camera away, and squint up at her. 'Are we friends again?' I realise too late that I must sound uncommonly like the ten-year-old me falling out with Elena, and Nicole hears it too. She grins.

'Friends forever. Pinky-promise. Forgive my disagreeableness, I was very out of sorts,' she says, grinding out her cigarette. She looks at the mess in distaste. 'My mother-in-law is right. I must give up these things.' She motions me to lead the way down the steps. 'Dear Damaris. Let us go to her now.'

22

Varosha, Cyprus
Tuesday 13th August 1974

Late in the afternoon, Aunt Irini took them down to the hotel bar for a Coke float. But even that didn't please Krista because it was Charlie's day off and she said the ice cream had gone off. It tasted fine to Elena.

'Krista, please quieten down.' Irini shifted slightly to accommodate Sofia and her rapidly spilling drink. 'Think of the other guests.'

'There aren't any.' Krista said it without looking around. 'Not even that fat man in the yellow anorak. The flasher,' she added. Then she put her head down and slurped noisily through her straw.

'Krista, you can't say things like that when they're not true.' Irini spoke hastily, looking over her shoulder, but there really was nobody else in the bar. Then she frowned. 'I mean it's not true, is it? He didn't… he didn't…'

'Show his yellow-anorak willy to me?' Krista's voice was raised. 'You are very shy for a schoolteacher, Aunt Irini.' For a few seconds she looked innocently at Irini's half-alarmed, half-exasperated face. Elena held her breath, waiting. Then Krista gave a huge smile. 'No, Aunt Irini, he didn't do anything bad except wear horrible clothes. But if he had—'

'What?' Irini sounded reluctant, but as if she didn't dare not ask.

'If he had, at least it would be interesting,' Krista burst out. 'It would be something new to look at and talk about. Actually, I am disappointed the fat man in the yellow anorak didn't flash his willy at me.'

'Krista!'

'But, Aunt Irini, it's so boring here. I'm so bored. Why else would I want to see an ugly old willy? Elena is bored too. She probably would like to see the willy as well. Sofia is too small to see the willy though, I bet she doesn't know what a willy is, so she will have to stay bored.'

Elena knew that Krista was just showing off and seeing how many times she could say that word aloud. Through the big mirror behind the bar, she could also see the barman who wasn't Charlie trying not to laugh as he wiped glasses that didn't need wiping and held them up to the light to check for fingerprints. Krista was grinning around the room. Elena wanted to laugh too. It was silly but it was funny and nothing funny had happened for days. Silly wasn't always silly, sometimes it was good. Suddenly, Krista jumped off the bar stool she was perched on and leaned over and hugged Irini.

'I am teasing you, Aunt Irini. Don't be cross with me. Pleeease…'

Aunt Irini returned the hug, shaking her head but smiling, just enough. 'You are incorrigible, madam. What am I going to do with you?'

'You could let us go over to the Palm Beach Hotel for half an hour. Then we wouldn't be bored and the willy talk would stop,' Krista said, quick as a zip.

'Krista, we've had this conversation dozens of times. You know the answer.'

'Yes, but this is a free country, you can change your mind at any time.'

Irini's lips twitched. 'Is that so? Anyway, precisely what entertainment is there at the Palm Beach that you can't get here?'

'The. Swimming. Pool.' Krista spoke like a lawyer resting her case; Elena had seen it on *Crown Court*. She and April didn't like *Crown Court* that much but it was April's mama and papa's favourite programme so sometimes if they were home on school lunch time they all watched it together. Then Krista spoiled it, by visibly kicking Elena for backup.

'We don't mean we want to go on our own,' Elena obliged, earning herself another kick – she knew that was exactly what Krista meant – and ignoring it because Elena was on her sister's side, just being cleverer. 'We could all go. If you and Antony come, you can't worry that we're not safe.'

'Yes, that's what we meant.' Krista was shameless. 'Think about the lovely cool water, Aunt Irini. You could swim off all your tired anxiousness. Then have a Bacardi and Coke. Or we could all have tea there.'

'All of that in half an hour, hmm?'

'Maybe an hour then, or even two—'

'Don't push your luck, Krista,' Irini warned. 'I might be convinced...' She frowned. 'Wait a second. Who said I was tired and anxious?'

'I did.' Antony arrived right on cue, like in a film. He entered the bar, dropped a kiss on Irini's head and scooped up Sofia, pretending to pull a face when she gave him a smeary ice-cream hug. 'And you are. Too much travelling and too much sun. You're not used to it any more. She isn't, is she, girls?'

'We've been in this hotel for a million years,' Krista objected, 'with nothing to do except play Happy Families and now we can't even do that because Mrs Bun the Baker's Wife is lost...'

Lost because you tore her up and flushed her away, Elena thought.

'... and you haven't even let us put our noses out into the sun. We might as well have stayed in England.'

'I suppose a walk over to the Palm Beach would be okay. What do you think, Antony?' Irini sidestepped Krista.

'Really?' He raised his eyebrows at her. 'Well, why not, if you say so. Last one there's a sissy.' He hoisted Sofia over his shoulder and headed back out of the door.

'Come on then. Get your swimming costumes before I change my mind.' Irini didn't sound enthusiastic so neither Elena nor Krista stopped to finish their drinks. They giggled their way up in the lift without even pressing buttons for all the floors they pinged past. They snatched their swimming things and Sofia's from the messy bag that was spilling clothes onto the floor.

'We've got everything, Aunt Irini.' Elena, with Krista just behind her, gave a quick tap on the second bedroom door and peered round it.

Irini was standing with her big patchwork handbag in one hand and what looked like their passports in the other. Hearing Elena, she dropped the little books into the bag and looked up. 'Right. Good. Then let's go,' she said. 'Why don't you go and call the lift back?'

Antony and Sofia were waiting for them at the empty reception and they went out of the front of the hotel. A right turn, and the Palm Beach Hotel was only a few minutes' walk. At six-thirty in the evening, the hottest of the hot was gone out of the day. It was warm and breezy and felt like fluttering butterfly wings on Elena's skin. The street wasn't quite as empty as the beach although they were the only ones on foot. There were three cars parked and another was driving slowly along the road as if the men inside were looking for a particular address. It slowed even more as it passed Elena and her family, and she expected the driver to stop and ask for directions, but he didn't.

'Kerb-crawlers,' stated Krista, but not too loudly. Elena knew she was careful enough not to be frogmarched straight back to Stefan's hotel. Still, Irini heard her, grabbed Krista's hand and yanked her along.

'Ow,' shrieked Krista. 'First daydream girl, my own sister, pulls out my hair by the roots instead of braiding it, and now you, my own aunt, dislocates my shoulder. If you are not all kinder I will be taken into care.'

'There is no children's home which would keep you,' Aunt Irini assured her. 'Really, Krista; flashers and kerb-crawlers. It's not nice talk. Where do you learn these things? What will Mama say when she hears this language?'

'She'll only hear it if you tell her,' Krista said. 'And it's what you must expect when you get to be a parent anyway. Chill out, Aunt Irini. You really do need your Bacardi and Coke.'

23

The Patek Patisserie is on the edge of another pedestrian square, not more than a few minutes' stroll. It's clearly long established, somewhere labelled an 'institution' in tourist guides and extended over the years. I should have brought my *Travelers' Guide*, I think, maybe it's in there. One half of the building houses a sweet counter but, tempted, I remind myself that chocolate-covered coffee beans and jellied orange peel coated in icing sugar will be a gloopy mess after a few hours in my pocket.

Under an arch, in the marble interior of the cafe-bar, Damaris is seated at the edge of a central fountain, a half-drunk glass of orange juice on the table in front of her. She's watching a turtle peer out of its watery home, a replica of a mountain chalet, and eyeing the slices of ham and lettuce left on a small tray by the model front door. Above the fountain, above Damaris' head, hang a clutch of cages in which small and bright birds – I don't know anything about bird species – twitter incessantly. Damaris is the only patron so close to the menagerie, the only one who looks totally at home there.

'There is still a turtle in the fountain,' is how she greets us. 'Maybe even the same one. I asked but the waiter is too young to know.'

We sit beside her and order more fresh orange, and pitta breads stuffed with lamb and olives. Damaris asks us if we enjoyed the city, but otherwise is apparently distracted by the turtle. Anyway, the overhead cacophony precludes conversation and, once the food is gone, I'm mentally begging Damaris to suggest moving on. It takes until the turtle has worked its way through the salad and scorned the meat.

'Shall we now go to the Palm Beach?' She picks up the napkin from her lap and places it on her empty plate.

'If you are ready, mother-in-law?' Nicole looks as relieved as I feel.

'It's the reason we have travelled so far.' Damaris pushes back her chair and stands up. 'So let us go.'

Slowly, we retrace our steps back to the car. The walk probably takes longer than the drive, snaking the perimeter of the old town and round the coast until we can go no further. We abandon the car once again, this time amongst a convoy of tour buses, the drivers all trying to reclaim their rightful passengers from a milling crowd.

'Do you really need to bring that huge bag?' Nicole asks Damaris, as she watches the older woman hoist it over her shoulder, wincing slightly.

'Yes,' says Damaris.

'Then may I carry it for you?'

'Not now, Nicole. I will ask you if I need help.' Damaris is firm.

With what feels like an entire coach party accompanying us, we walk alongside a scruffy, partially sealed-off building site – strange, I think, for prime land in a holiday resort – heading towards the beach.

'That was once Varosha. It is now the Turkish controlled zone,' Damaris says conversationally, indicating the building site. 'The Palm Beach Hotel is the last one outside the military area.'

Sure enough, I can now see the barbed wire through the tarpaulins and the electric fence above it; the red-ringed *Keep Out* signs, featuring fierce dogs and even fiercer armed soldiers, and the written warnings nailed up in three languages. But the wire is damaged, the tarpaulin torn and the notices are faded and askew. It's far more dismal and neglected than threatening, and it's also a tourist attraction, judging by the number of singlet- and shorts-clad spectators taking blatant photos of one another in front of the *No Photography* cartoons.

'It looks like the photoshoot of some trendy urban designer and his young and beautiful models.' Nicole pinpoints it exactly as we push past. 'Imagine a centre-page spread in a Sunday broadsheet, commenting on urban decay and the Zeitgeist of Generation X. Andreas has contacts who specialise in mocking up such scenes.'

'I don't know whether to smile or wince,' I admit. 'I want to sneer at the gawpers but I'm no better. I want to stand and gawp too.'

My voice is as low as Nicole's, but Damaris hears us and gives a thin smile. 'Do not bother to loiter here,' she says. 'There will be much better gawping opportunities from the beach.'

Ahead of us, to the left and set slightly back, is the vast, whitewashed and shiny-looking Palm Beach Hotel. It looks like any four-star beach resort anywhere, flanked by an outdoor restaurant and an open bar, its golden sand and glorious blue bay, knee-deep in holidaymakers on their sunbeds. The difference is in the view from the terrace, the balconies and the beach: the roped-off, burned-out, derelict wrecks of the high-rise buildings of the so-called dead zone.

Most of the people eating their casual kebabs, downing beer or taking in the rays seem immune to the looming backdrop, but others are making the pilgrimage to that part of the beach framed by the barbed wire. Here, there are yet more red and black posters, now depicting soldiers with big guns; apparently in lieu of any real military personnel.

We hesitate at the top of the half-a-dozen steps on to the sand. We look at each other. What to do? I feel, and I think Nicole does too, the voyeurism of being here may be disrespectful to Damaris and her peers. But it's Damaris herself who speaks.

'Go and look,' she says. 'Go. Why be coy? Nobody else here has your reticence. And why should they? Varosha is as much a part of the history of this island as the purpose-built museums and the pretty landscapes. Not looking does not make the nasty things go away, it just makes us ignorant.' Her voice cracks but her face is deadpan; I can't tell if she is furious or distressed.

'Damaris—'

'Mother-in-law—'

But Damaris flaps her hand as if irritated by a duo of persistent flies. 'I am perfectly fine. I will not swoon or fall to tears. I will not start to hack at the security fences. I would like just to sit, be quiet and think for a minute. And,' she pre-empts any further objections, 'thank you for caring, my darlings, but I would like to do it alone.'

'Is she really alright?' I ask Nicole, as we leave her seated ramrod-straight with her past and present stretched out fore and aft. We make our way down to the boardwalk, and then step gingerly into the grainy sand.

'Yes,' replies Nicole. 'If Damaris says she is fine, she is fine. If she is not, she will tell us.' She looks back. I do too, and Damaris sees us and waves. 'She might have spent many years of her life in England, but she did not catch your famous British reticence.'

'Maybe if I stay here long enough I'll lose some of it.' *Cypriot-April*, I think.

'Do you want to?'

I shrug. 'Some things are better said, some not.'

Nicole shakes her head. 'April, you are... what is the word I want... wait – unfathomable? Yes, that is it. Unfathomable. I have never met a person I understand less, but am curious to understand more.' She pushes up her sunglasses and squints at me. 'What do you say to that, Ms Reticence?'

'Sometimes,' I'm honest, 'I don't say anything because

I just don't know what to say. It's all stuck in my head. I'm one of those people who thinks of the right words hours later in the bath.'

She lowers her sunglasses and smiles. 'Then I will ask you later.'

It's on my lips to ask, what exactly? We're back at cross purposes, or else I'm still missing something. Then again, this is no ordinary walk along the beach and it's no ordinary place. Frankly, it's weird. And maybe that's making *us* weird. It's *Koyaanisqatsi, Life Out of Balance*, for real. We walk slowly around the perimeter, my feet almost burning in the hot sand, which seems right, a penance, but why I think that I can't explain. We might be literally in the sun but we're in the shadows too. Varosha looms. It's almost possible to view the tumbleweed drifting through the deserted miles of an ex-seaside town. There is nobody moving beyond the perimeter fence. Nobody watching the photographers this side of the wall. Small knots of people stand around us, looking, so that it feels like a vigil – a group of mourners who didn't know the deceased well, but pick up on the mood and regret the passing of something; something ordinary that has become special in the wrong way.

That was where Elena lived, I tell myself. One of those hotels was the 'Hotel in Varosha New Town' from her postcard. The beach was where she and Sofia played, Krista would have watched loftily until temptation became too great and she joined in, screaming loudest. Maybe it was that street right there, where she came from and to where she returned. And then moved again, evacuated, disappeared. I consider the apocryphal stories of dirty breakfast dishes left in the sink, the bare light bulbs left burning, tattered curtains at jagged broken windows, cars still in the salesrooms. When all of that stopped, Elena's life, for me, at least, stopped too. *That was where Elena lived*, I repeat inwardly, *and that was where Damaris lived*. I'm trying to evoke some kind of reaction in myself, but I just feel a sense of unreality.

'There is still a sense of despair, is there not?' Nicole says, slowly, and I'm glad it's not just me. 'Somehow it is still alive here. There has not been long enough for it to die and simply be a curiosity. I do not doubt that is a good thing, uncomfortable as it is.' Her gaze sweeps over the people around us. 'I wonder what they all see?'

'Hopefully none of them booked two weeks at the Palm Beach in complete ignorance.'

'Shall we go?' Nicole asks. 'I think I've seen enough. I think Damaris has been alone long enough.'

'Come on.' I have no more business here. And it's not *Koyaanisqatsi* at all, it's Khachaturian's *Gayane*; Scene 6 'Conscience'.

'Do you feel a sense of Elena?' Nicole asks as we walk back.

'I want to... but I'm trying too hard, I think. I feel much more for Damaris.' I try to explain. 'Cyprus was a mythical place for me before I came here. Now it's real, and Damaris is real and you're real and—'

'And?' She laughs that filthy laugh of hers and the day immediately lightens.

'And, I don't know.' I laugh too. 'Just that Elena is, maybe, less real.'

'Why?' Nicole demands, but she's still smiling.

Because I've found you pops into my head, but that sounds all wrong, too much. 'Maybe because I've met you and Damaris and Petros and Red. Yiannis too.' I temper it and cast around. 'Maybe you're sort of filling the Elena hole.'

'Thank you, April,' says Nicole. 'I'll take that as a compliment. But it must be a very large hole then, would you not say?'

She links my arm into hers and we're smiling when Damaris comes into view, still on her bench, but she's no longer gazing at the view. She's bending over and stroking a large golden retriever, its head docile in her lap, feeding it something from a packet in her bag.

'I wish I had let her bring that horrible old cat in its basket,' Nicole says, watching.

'You'll wish it even more when Damaris tells you that dog is a stray and she's taking it home with her.'

Nicole looks horrified. 'Dear God, no. She'll give it to me and Andreas and we already half have that giant red dog and Damaris' parrots.' Then she brightens. 'It is far too well groomed to be a stray, and look, Damaris is speaking to someone who must be its owner.'

Sure enough, by the time we reach the steps, a plump, dark woman, my age but lined and tired-looking, is clipping a lead on to the collar of the animal and saying her farewells to Damaris. Damaris gives the dog one final stroke and turns to us.

'I would like to visit Salamis,' she says. 'That woman with the dog, Elena Balis, says it has not changed at all, not like here. I have seen enough here. My duty is done.' Her lips set in a firm line and I realise she is not going to talk about Varosha, nor allow Nicole or me to do so. She does turn to me though. '*Elena* Balis,' she repeats, with emphasis.

'Oh…'

'But not your Elena. I made sure to ask her.' Damaris shakes her head. 'Her only daughter is called Maria. It is as well. God above help her if your Elena was here then, or is here now.'

That postcard, three little smiley dots, dated August 1974, weighs heavier in my pocket than ever before.

24

Varosha, Cyprus
Tuesday 13th August 1974

They were all smiling as they approached the stone steps down to the beach beside the Palm Beach Hotel. It was one of nicest places to go, Elena agreed with Krista about that. The Palm Beach had always been there, even before the rest of the big hotels like Stefan's started to be built. It had a swimming pool shaped like a kidney and a terrace where they served strawberry ice-cream sundaes and each one had a real strawberry on the top. At teatime and on Saturdays there were family games on the beach and the winners got their ice creams, and a big plate of chips, for free. Elena remembered it from before. She looked around. There was nothing like that there now. The beach and the pool and the terrace were empty. Krista seemed equally confused.

'Where is everyone? Why are there no games?' she demanded, glaring at Irini and Antony, as if, Elena thought, they had cleared the hotel just to annoy her.

Neither of them was listening. They were watching the progress of two men in uniform who were plodding slowly towards the family. They were the National Guard, Elena knew, she had seen the big recruitment posters on the side of the road. But these were not the young and sexy – according to Krista – men in the advertisements, these looked nearly as old as her *papous* and he (her mother's father, her other grandpapa was dead) was already sixty years old. One carried a gun – a rifle, Elena corrected herself – but it sat awkwardly across the bulk of his stomach.

Aunt Irini put her hand out to stop the girls walking. 'Wait here,' she said, sharp as a pin. 'Elena, keep hold of Sofia and none of you move even a step.'

'Not fair,' muttered Krista, but she did as she was told. She even took hold of Sofia's other hand and the three stood in a row, waiting. Irini and Antony were talking to the guards.

They are not going to let us go to the beach, realised Elena, watching the rapid gestures and craning to hear the muted conversation. *I expect they are saying it isn't safe and we should go home,* she thought, and a cold dread filled her because where was home now?

Krista must have understood too, because she nudged Sofia and, turning her back so that Aunt Irini could not see, she signed to her: 'Sofia, act mental. The soldiers are stopping us playing, but if you act mental they will be sorry and let us play.'

It did often work. It had got them the best spots by the swimming pool and to the front of the lines for ice cream and lemonade, even front seats in the pavilion hall for the variety show. It had got them sweets and even money, small coins, from strangers. It was only recently that Elena had begun to think maybe it wasn't a nice thing to do, but Sofia didn't seem to mind and Krista just put on her superior voice and said 'the meanness justifies the ends' which she'd heard on telly.

Obligingly, Sofia started to jump up and down and shake herself. She made noises in her throat and squeaked, which was the only talking she could do, and she waved her hands in the air as if she was signing badly. Then, as Krista had taught her, she let her tongue flap out of her mouth and rolled her eyes. Sofia looked crazy, for sure, Elena thought, and Krista *was* mad to think it would work today.

'No,' said Elena, suddenly. 'No.' She signed 'Stop' to Sofia, who didn't even notice, and she glared at Krista, who glared back. But it was already too late.

Aunt Irini was beside them in seconds. Her teeth were set and her face was turning red she was so angry. The way she clenched her fists, Elena could tell she was trying her best not to slap all three of them, the way she had promised (at the variety show from which they were very nearly marched home without seeing it) she would if she ever, ever caught them at this again. They all wilted in front of her; Elena wondered which of them, Aunt Irini included, would cry first. Elena braced herself for the telling off: Krista for starting it, Sofia for doing it – she did know it was naughty even though she was little – and Elena for allowing it.

It never came. Aunt Irini took a deep breath, rubbed her eyes, and said in a quiet and dangerous voice, 'We are going back. Back to the hotel. Now. You will have some bread and cheese in your room and you will go to bed.' Krista's mouth opened, but Irini's hand was already up to stop her speaking. 'You will say nothing. Nothing.' She turned and walked away, quickly, the way they had come. In single file they followed her, Antony last. In less than ten minutes, they were back in their bedroom at the hotel.

It was several more minutes before any of them dared say anything, for fear Aunt Irini was listening behind the bathroom door. Krista's eyes were glinting and Elena's heart sank at the thought of having to listen to her for ages; when Krista was mad she was like a dog with a chewy toy and would not, not, not let it go.

'Charlie promised me his radio,' was what Krista said though. 'I'm going to get it. I am. Just because *she's* in a bad temper,' she jerked her head in the direction of the other room, 'and won't let us make a joke or go to the beach doesn't mean we should miss out on nice things.'

'Krista, you can't,' began Elena, not even bothering to

listen to Krista's version of the events. 'You don't even know where Charlie is today. If Aunt Irini finds out…'

'If she finds out – what? She will slap me? Who cares. And she won't, she was pleased to shout at us to shut up so that she didn't have to explain why we weren't allowed on the beach. I'm not stupid. And I'm going. So there.'

Elena watched her sister toss her hair and march out of the room, careful not to bang the door. *I know you're not stupid,* she thought; sometimes Krista was so right it was scary, though mostly she was wrong. Like now. Elena couldn't even begin to think what Aunt Irini would do to all of them if she caught Krista on the stairs. She tried to distract herself by turning to Sofia, who wanted to know where Krista had gone, and why, and could they go too? Or, if not, would Elena play the monkey song with her and Jemima? *Pleeeeeease?*

Elena sighed. Both Krista and Sofia were miles ahead of her in being able to get their own way. Okay, she nodded, and resigned herself to watching Sofia bounce the horrible spidery-leggy Jemima up and down a zillion times.

'*Five little monkeys jumping on the bed,*' she began to sing, wondering again how Sofia could possibly know – and she always did – if Elena mouthed the words instead. '*One fell off and bumped his head…*'

Twenty-five little monkeys later, it was Elena who jumped.

'I have a secret.' Krista's head came suddenly around the door and she bounced in, grinning. 'Look.' From behind her back, she took out a small transistor radio. 'Charlie gave it to me. Forever. A present for me because he's leaving.' Krista faked a sob but her eyes were gleaming.

'Charlie is leaving? Why?' The fear twisted in Elena's tummy again.

Krista was concentrating on the radio. 'The curfew. He says the reason we couldn't go to the beach is a curfew. Nobody is allowed out in the dark. He doesn't like that. I asked him if it meant the fighting was here, but he said to ask Aunt Irini and Antony. But now with this,' she held up the transistor like a trophy, 'we can know ourselves what is happening. We'll listen in the morning.'

Elena could only nod.

'Oh, and I got you this, daydream girl.' Krista pulled a postcard from her jeans pocket and held it out. It was the one of the hotel that Elena had decided to send to April.

'Thank you,' Elena said, surprised at Krista's attempt to be friendly.

'Oh, I just took it off the rack of the counter.' Krista shrugged, but looked even more triumphant. 'It's their stupid fault if there's nobody in the reception to take the money. You can pay for it tomorrow if you like. I'm not.'

25

We're on the way back to Agia Triada, the return border crossing thankfully behind us, the hire car swapped back for Nicole's, when Damaris begins to talk.

Spread out on the back seat of the car, she lifts her old carpetbag onto her knee, and carefully removes from it a brown paper package, loosely tied with string – Julie Andrews singing on a stormy night pops into my mind. Inside is a photo frame. I'm in the front of the car, looking over my shoulder, and she twists it round to face me.

'This,' she says quietly. 'This is your Elena's Cyprus. This is my Cyprus.'

This is a garish artist's impression of the suburb of Famagusta in the early seventies; the picture could be the frontispiece to my 1971 travel guide – I'm kicking myself even more now that I didn't even think to bring it. I'll show it to Nicole, and to Damaris if she wants to see it, later. The sand is yellow, the sky blue and the high-rise buildings are brilliant white. The families on the beach and walking the promenade are happy and prosperous, their hopes and dreams of a bright future implicit. Damaris says nothing, I say nothing, but I squint to check and the signature in the corner is that of Orestes Koumettou.

Methodically, she unpicks the painting. Hidden between the canvas and its frame, she pulls out another picture. It's a blurred snapshot of a large house on a grassy street, the shutters hanging off and the downstairs obscured by overgrown hedges. She holds it by its corners and murmurs, 'All that has been left of number three, twenty-eighth October Street for thirty years. The only way I have seen it in thirty years.' She lays the pictures side by side on the seat next to her.

The silence is thick, the car engine white noise. After a full five minutes, Damaris unleashes the past three decades.

'I took the children,' she says. 'A colleague of Orestes drove us. We heard that the soldiers stopped him and killed him on the way back. We had a picnic, one change of our clothes, one toy for each. I thought we would be back in a very few days; I left twenty-four jars of strawberry jam setting in our larder. When I felt stomach cramps, I remembered I had no sanitary towel, and I worried that blood would show on my dress. We drove past men with blindfolds, down on their knees. The guns pointed at them and I hid the children under blankets so they would not see. God above forgive me, I made it into fun for them.'

I sit as still as I can, not looking at her. Nicole just keeps driving.

'Orestes stayed behind, working,' Damaris goes on. 'He had a tiny boy in intensive care, his heart enlarged and newly operated upon. Derin. I remember it as well as I remember my own children's names. It saved Orestes' life, of course, but his choice worries me still, it was once a rift between us.' She pauses, then matter-of-factly she adds, 'We lost everything we had, every *thing*.'

She touches the bright utopia-on-sea, tracing the almost architectural figures.

'This was not the new Famagusta any more than what is over there now,' she says. 'This was a simple dream, a simple hope of a simple man for sunny people on sunny days. This,' she points to the other one, 'this was, is, the reality.' She's quiet for a minute and then she shrugs and gives the ghost of a smile. 'But can I not pretend? A fiction is fine as long as I know it is a fiction, yes?'

She looks at Nicole's back as she says this. She's talking about much more than just her situation, I think, but it's something bigger than me. Bigger than this trip.

Nicole looks at Damaris levelly, holds her gaze. Suddenly I am in fade-out. Nicole is the first to speak. 'Next time, mother-in-law,' she says, 'you can bring your horrible mangy cat.'

'Next time?' Damaris sniffs, back to her usual tone. She starts to rewrap her precious cargo. 'Take it.' She thrusts the painting, Orestes' painting, at me. I draw back. 'Yes. Take it, April. Prop it up on your dressing table in Verena Bay and think of Elena in happy times. Imagine her a happy life. Take it.'

In the early hours, they leave me back at the entrance to Verena Bay. I turn to wave, when Nicole jumps out of the car. 'April, wait,' she says, catching my wrist. 'In the morning, you are going to—'

'Scatter the ashes? Yes, I am. And honestly, Nicole, before you ask, I will be okay and I do want to do it alone. Though you don't know how much I appreciate you asking.'

I expect her to try harder to get me to reconsider, but she just nods. 'I knew you would say that,' she agrees. 'Okay, but you will allow me to arrange breakfast afterwards? A tiny celebration to mark the occasion. That is, to mark their deaths, I mean, their lives – oh, shit!'

I can't help but laugh; she looks anguished – Nicole, of all people. 'It's fine. I know what you mean, and that would be perfect. Thank you.'

'Perfect,' she repeats, gives me a brief hug and dashes back to the car. They are gone in a – literal – cloud of dust.

I walk very slowly down the drive, eyes turned towards the stars, the descendants of those I quizzed thirty years ago. So that was Famagusta. That was Varosha. Inside, in the quiet of my room, I prop up Orestes' painting against the mirror of the dressing table and stare at it, drinking in the bold colours and thinking out loud.

You weren't there, Elena. Nothing of you was there. I should be grateful because Varosha is a shell, not even that; I wouldn't like to think of you trapped forever there. But I have had a glimpse you today, Elena, courtesy of a stubborn old woman who might finally be laying her own demons to rest. When Orestes Koumettou painted this image of Varosha, he captured something of your life. Elena, I know he did.

Please tell me you emerged similarly unscathed. Please tell me something.

26

Varosha, Cyprus
Wednesday 14th August 1974

For a moment Elena wasn't sure what had woken her. She didn't want to wake up. She'd been dreaming about Mama, just an ordinary dream where they were all having an ordinary breakfast together on an ordinary morning. Except where they were didn't seem to be ordinary, it was a cross between Nicosia Airport and their flat above the English chip shop. Her father was there too, she remembered, and that wasn't ordinary either. Elena tried to recall what he had looked like in the dream, because how could she have known it was him? That's what dreams did though. Elena didn't remember her father in real life; Krista pretended she did but all she ever said was that his hair was brown and he laughed a lot. One thing Elena was sure of, though, was that when she was little, Papa had carried her on his shoulders so high she could touch the clouds.

Elena lay still, her eyes shut and her fists clenched, willing herself back into sleep. It didn't work. An orangey wave of daylight was already playing on her eyelids and pulling her into the new day. There was a noise too, a muffled boom and a vibrating grumble alongside it. Ah, Elena thought, thunder, a thunderstorm. That's what had disturbed her. She didn't mind thunder but she was scared of lightning; one day last year when Mrs Gale had been away ill and the supply teacher never arrived, the whole class went to the assembly hall for a film. The projector broke down three times so they only saw about how lightning worked: a cracking bright slash in the sky and zigzag that threw itself downwards and sliced a tree in half, dead. It was a big oak tree, but the trunk just split and the insides were black with burn marks. Now Elena waited, taut, for the flash, but there was nothing, just more of the distant thump-thump... thump-thump-thump. The air had been so very thick and heavy – oppressive, Antony called it – that she supposed a burst of fatly wet raindrops would make everyone feel better.

The window was open, the curtains only half pulled, so she sat up to close both. The bed was still under the window – Elena remembered then that Irini had told them to move it back before they went to sleep; they'd better do it before breakfast – and the sheets were thin and white. She didn't want the mattress to get wet. She wished she was more like Krista, who never worried about things like rain coming in the window.

The thunder rumbled again. It was not any nearer. Elena leaned out of the open window and looked for rain clouds but there was just the haze of another hot day. The sky was blue across the sea, and only far away to the right was it shadowy. But that was smoke, she realised, a grey mushroom billowing upwards, wisps of angel hair disappearing into the sky. Something was on fire at the other end of the curve in the bay. Elena blessed herself, Father, Son and Holy Ghost, and hoped it wasn't a hotel. Imagine being stuck ten floors high with flames licking the soles of your feet and fumes choking your breath away. She shuddered. She left the curtains showing only a chink of light, climbed down from the bed where Krista and Sofia still snoozed away, and went to rummage in her suitcase for her pink diary folder. There was still a letter to post, and two days of her diary to catch up on as well as her postcard to write. She looked at the overflowing bags and sighed. Yesterday, before the Palm Beach, Elena had pretended it didn't matter, but it did – to her, Krista scorned tidiness – so she spent a few minutes folding the clothes and putting them neatly away. Elena shook out a damp towel and a face cloth that looked clean and went to hang them up in the bathroom.

Picking up Sofia's swimming costume that had fallen from the rail into the bath, she wondered if she should wash and dress now; she thought she would and began by squirting toothpaste onto her brush. Elena listened, but there was no sound from Aunt Irini and Antony's room. However, she could hear her sisters stirring. Krista coughed twice and groaned, and then Elena could hear the whirr and squeak and interference from Charlie's transistor radio as Krista tried to tune it. Krista's muttering would be because she was stuck on 692 rather than a pirate station that had music. Elena liked the pop music too; the Cyprus Broadcasting Corporation was very talk-talky and serious, so she braced herself for Krista to get mad and come and interrupt Elena to twist and turn the dials.

But she didn't. Elena had buttoned up her blouse, and was brushing her hair when she realised how quiet it was. Too quiet. What was Krista…? Elena's neck prickled and slowly she put down her brush and went to the bedroom door. Something was very, very wrong.

Krista was sitting on the edge of the bed, right on the edge as though she might fall off any second. She had the little radio tight to her ear.

'Krista?' Elena said. 'Krista?'

But her sister sat still, Elena had never seen her so still, even when she was asleep. Elena almost ran over to her, and shook her shoulder, ready for a telling-off for accidentally kicking Krista's leg and leaving a mark on her pyjamas. Krista simply looked up as if she hadn't noticed. She looked confused, not cross or sulky.

'Elena,' she said, sounding as if she hadn't recognised her. 'It's you. Elena, you need to wake up Sofia. We need to get Irini and Antony.'

Elena felt her stomach clench. 'What? What? Is it Mama?'

Krista looked at her, then carefully she switched off the radio, leaned over and stood it on the ground. She pushed it a little with her foot, as if it were a bug that might bite her.

'Krista, tell me.' For the first time in ages, Krista seemed like the bigger, more sensible sister that Elena thought she should be. 'Tell me.'

Krista spoke as slowly and clearly as if she was a newsreader. 'The Turkish army invaded the island of Cyprus at eight o'clock this morning.' Then her voice altered, and she became the familiar, dramatic Krista once more. 'It means the war is here. It's here now, this minute,' she wailed. 'Elena, we're all going to die.'

27

I expect to dream of Elena but I don't. Like a metronome I'm swinging side to side: Yiannis to Red; Elena to my mum and dad; past to present; yesterday to today. Today demands – deserves – all my attention. I read somewhere once that every ending is also a beginning and that's what I want this memorial to be.

They died together, my parents, with Petros' Aunt Ana just down the hall. The nursing home was devastated but, small mercy, the fire never reached them; suffocation killed them long before anyone could intervene. They lived quietly and they died quietly; Mum and Dad, that is. Ana was loud, opinionated and clearly adored through and through.

It was a shock, of course it was, a terrible shock, and for a while I wanted to rail at the world over the unfairness of it, but I didn't because I knew they would have liked to go together that way. An electrical fault, smoke inhalation: no trouble to anyone, not their responsibility, no violence or dramatic scenes. When my father was previously diagnosed with angina, it was his worst fear that he'd have a heart attack and die on the street, spoiling the day for passers-by and medics alike.

I was born when my mother was forty-four years old, my father almost fifty. It's only occurred to me recently what a shock to their peaceful and ordered lives I must have been.

Our council house, first rented, then saved for and bought, they lived in all their married lives until my mother was eighty and both growing more and more fragile. They sold up and moved to a residential home, impressed by the professional and neat arrangement of being beholden to nobody, certainly not April Zarney, their acclaimed concert-pianist daughter.

'Were you happy?' Petros asked me, a day or so after the funeral. 'Were they happy? I mean, when you were a child.'

I didn't know the true answer then and I don't know it now. We were each in our own quiet world and I've no idea whether their worlds connected or whether they were eternal strangers living side by side. I could never have asked. According to them, we had no other family. Their own parents were Polish, and that they were both born in Poland was understood. Their birth certificates, they hinted, were lost during the war but they had a British marriage certificate and, somehow, those British passports. They always had passports despite the fact, as far as I know, they never went abroad. They sounded English enough to me. We, as a family, were English. Just English. I didn't think to question them, and more recently when I thought I should, I couldn't. It would have been cruel.

I wasn't *un*happy. Dullness brought routine brought stability. School brought enough excitement. I had space to think and to imagine. I never knew it any other way, until Elena and her big, noisy, stereotypically Greek family caught my attention. It was like a light going on, or watching colour TV after a childhood of black, white and that insipid beige – 3D as opposed to 2D, we'd say now. And then Elena disappeared and it faded again. Oh, there were still pockets of colour; there still are, in the memories. And of course, her legacy is my music.

Unlike Ana's complicated novella-length creation – fondly berated by Petros – my mum and dad had short, identical wills that specified a simple cremation for both of them. What I hadn't expected was the hope that: *Our daughter, April, will play a piece of music*. I could imagine the hours they had puzzled over the etiquette of that, probably seeking Ana's opinion too. 'Showing off' was anathema to them, and it touched me – it still does – this posthumous display of pride.

My parents were not musical. I picked the 'Moonlight Sonata' to play at their joint funeral, because they would have recognised it: not complicated or clever or strange. It was also the first classical piece I learned (and all but murdered in the process). It meant I could – and I *have* – played it blindfolded, backwards and backwards blindfolded. Playing it at the funeral calmed me too; I didn't have to picture them hovering in some limbo world, agonising in case I fumbled a note. Nor did I have to watch the coffins slide eerily behind a black velvet curtain.

It's all running through my head again now, 'Moonlight Sonata' included, as I leave the still-sleeping Verena Bay, retracing the walk Red and I took along the beach a couple of distant weeks ago. Dawn is only a ghostly strip of light close to the horizon, eclipsed in the monotonous sweep of the lighthouse. It's a cleansing hour: cold, colourless, even the wind is still; satisfyingly ritualistic. I feel I should be carrying the box of ashes out in front of me, like an offering, but that would cross into the realms of spooky witchery. Petros still swears he shook out Ana from a pepper pot. 'Out at sea, a sudden squall that did not allow for dignity,' he insisted again last night, when I mentioned today's plan. I'm not convinced, but I always imagine Ana herself enjoying the rollercoaster.

I wonder again at the serendipity of Gillian Gale being at my parents' funeral, and being there out of friendship rather than duty. Her allotment was next door to my dad's, she'd told me, laughing at my surprise. 'Your dad was getting too frail to do much, but he and your mum liked to sit and watch the birds. I'm a complete novice in the garden but it's one of my retirement challenges – yes, really. I used to bring a flask of tea and we'd all sit and talk about you. They were very proud of you, April.'

'Did they ever talk about their pasts?' I asked her, after

she'd handed me Elena's long-lost letters. I suppose I was hoping for more surprises, but really I knew her answer before she shook her head. My meagre family was now totally depleted and it bothered me, too late, that I knew so little. It had always been as if they'd apparated from Poland into middle England in 1950; no past at all. It was making me feel increasingly like a building on a fault line: looking fine but at risk of crumbling any second.

I still feel that way but, here in Cyprus, not all the time.

I pass by Agia Triada church, squat and sleeping, but barely registering it, Mrs Gale's next words ringing in my ears.

'It's me who should talk more about the past,' she'd said, looking – guilty? Worried? 'I did something, April.'

'The music?' I guessed. 'I know I've you to thank for the piano lessons.' My parents, who had inherited a serviceable old piano from the previous council tenant, and hated to see it unused, were also very keen. All I remember is the teacher sniffing that I was a 'late starter', and I decided to prove her wrong.

'In a way,' she said. 'Actually, it's what I *didn't* do.' I watched her hunt for the right words. 'I was very practical, back then. Talking cures were still a way off, and you were so sad after Elena Zacharia left, I wanted to make it better. I'd watched you blossom with her, and then you withered. I had no idea that the piano would be the making of you.'

Or the unmaking, I think now, as I head up the inland path, beyond Nicole's house – all deserted – and slowly round to the rear of Minerva House. The piano has been a distraction, an obsession, a heaven and a hell, ever since I took it up. It's been my career and contributed to my ill-fated love life, not least the relationship with Jake, who always has had a weakness for creativity in his women. Music hasn't been my life but it's nearly taken over my life. Until now.

'I made it fill the Elena-shaped hole,' I'd replied to Gillian. 'It bothered me that she never wrote. Of course, it was silly when I look back. She was ten, I was ten, it was the 1970s, no mobile phones, no computers. Without a grown-up to help, it wouldn't have happened. But at the time, I thought that if she was really my best friend she would have sent me a letter somehow.' That had been almost worse than her leaving. Elena's was the kind of family which did unexpected things, so I could believe she was whisked away, but illogical as it was, I was sure that between them, she and her sister, Krista – shades of the Famous Five – would have been resourceful enough to smuggle out a letter. 'And now I know that she did.' I smiled at Gillian Gale through tears and the warm pang of nostalgia rippled through me again. 'It's silly how it's still important to me after thirty years. But…' It had taken me a few minutes to put two and two together. 'But… the obvious question is why only one? What happened that she didn't write every week like she promised? Was it so good she just moved on or bad enough that she couldn't?'

'That's just it.' Gillian looked torn. 'April, I'm so sorry.'

'Why?' My heart sank. 'You know what happened to her?'

'No. Not that.' She shook her head. 'I don't know, but I should, and so should you. Look, April, Elena *did* send you another letter. She sent you more than one. The first – the one I've just given you, with the postcard, was here waiting when school restarted in September. Both were addressed to you and Mrs Gale's class. I didn't know what to do for the best; you'd settled down; the news from Cyprus was awful; I knew what your parents would say.' She looked straight at me then. 'I'm sorry, April. Time went on, I did nothing, you went from strength to strength with the piano and your schoolwork… I only found those again when I was putting together the archive before I left. And it's worse than that, I'm afraid. There were three more letters, maybe more, that all arrived together in the autumn. They were fire-damaged, from one of the sorting offices along the way.' She sighed. 'I took one look and threw the lot away. It might well have been a local accident but I… well, if they had been the remnants of what was happening in Cyprus at the time, I couldn't contemplate that. I regret it now, April, but it was a split-second decision.'

I bit my lip. Far too much time had passed to be mad. Back in the seventies, education wasn't particularly child-centred and, as Gillian implied, 'least said soonest mended' was the proverb we all lived by. I had a sudden memory of the fourth-year teacher, Mr Reynolds, dropping dead on the school playground. We were all shepherded inside (furious for missing the ambulance) and the next day the only allusion was to him leaving and to welcome his replacement.

'Who's to say it wasn't the right thing?' I shrugged. After all, Elena had written, she really had. That was something to take away and treasure. 'What could the *right* thing possibly be? I just hope that it was only the mail that got burned.'

'Exactly.'

It must have been the Christmas of 1974 before I accepted Elena wasn't coming back, before I stopped waiting for the post every morning, gave up grabbing the ringing telephone. I was too young to care about newspapers or television bulletins, and wrapped up in my personal loss, I knew there was a 'war' but I had no idea of the trouble Cyprus was really in. It seemed, too, that everyone else at school had forgotten Elena, especially when the Dillons, new boys and almost-identical triplets, replaced her. In hindsight, Gillian Gale probably did do the right thing. And if it wasn't, well, that's life.

And this, I look down at the box, is life going on.

I duck into the secret garden, only realising I hadn't confirmed with Yiannis the practicalities of digging a hole when I see someone has been there before me: hole, trowel, pile of earth all in a row. There's a small black plaque too, un-engraved as yet, as marker. Yiannis has thought of everything.

I don't want to make a ceremony of this so I fill my mind with simple scales while I fill the hole with the urn and the earth. I make sure it's neat – neither of them would ever rest easy in an untidy room – and that's that. I sit back on my heels, waiting for the wave of sadness, but it's not overwhelming; again, that both of them are together makes it bearable. To horrified outsiders the way they died was a cymbal-filled finale ending moderate, andante lives, something the newspapers called a double tragedy. From the inside, a single tragedy would have been so much worse: just one of them gone, leaving the other one leaning on me, bewildered and out of step.

I'm not sure what to do now. Nicole had said breakfast, but she didn't mean at a dark seven o'clock, and I don't much feel like the lonely, wallowing walk back. There's a dim light in Yiannis' conservatory, and his un-invested kindness is probably just what I need (selfish, I know). I try the garden door, find it open, and there, in the half-light, undrunk cups of her green tea in their hands, are Nicole, Red and Yiannis.

For the first time, tears threaten. This is why I didn't—

'Play for them, April.' Red gets up and comes to me, taking my hand. He indicates the clunky upright piano in the corner. 'Play for them and then play for yourself.'

Without hesitation I go back to the Beethoven. I doubt anyone has ever, will ever again, play the 'Moonlight Sonata' like a drowning woman saving herself, but I do. Then I swap moods and play *with* some Rachmaninoff, crashing the chords like never before.

It's exactly the right thing.

When I look up, tears banished, Nicole is opening a bottle of champagne, and Yiannis is hastily trying to temper it with a jug of orange juice.

'Take a deep breath, Yiannis,' Nicole is saying, handing glasses around. 'It is not actually illegal to be decadent at breakfast time.'

'Soak it up with some bread.' Red holds up a huge oval platter, possibly one of the late Mrs Loizos' antiques, piled with buttered toast and honey. 'My speciality. I've put the coffee on too.'

'It's like Christmas.' *No, it's like the Christmases I always wanted but never had, except for the single year with Elena's family.* I juggle the food and drink and clear my throat. 'Thank you, all of you... Um, cheers?'

'It is our privilege, April,' says Yiannis.

I'm terribly afraid he's about to make a speech, but we're saved by a perfectly timed commotion outside: ferocious banging on the front door. A couple of minutes later, Jarlath and Kevin crash in, a tall brown bag, the kind that American grocery shops hand out, clutched between them.

'We heard there was a wake in lieu,' Jarlath says. 'We've come with condolences or congratulations, or whatever's the thing, to April's folks.' He holds up the bag. 'We've brought breakfast.'

'Petros let us in the kitchen,' Kevin adds, 'because Jarl is like his right-hand man now. He's coming too but a guest was just arriving. He'll be here now in a minute.'

'Want one, April? Nicole?' Jarlath offers us both the bag. 'Rasher sangers.'

'Bacon rolls,' interprets Red. 'I wouldn't look. It'll be like a six-car pile-up in there. Ketchup,' he explains.

They plonk themselves down, refusing alcohol like pioneers, and it *is* a bit like a party, especially when Kevin spies the piano and says, 'Give us some tunes, April. OF, here, told us you can play it a bit.'

Red groans. 'Kevin, I don't know—'

'It's fine.' I smile confirmation around the room. It's going to be a long while until the piano stops being my safety net. 'Of course, I'll play. Happy music. What would you like?'

An hour later all reserve has vanished and I'm belting out show tunes, with Jarlath and Kevin helpfully warning me when there's a fiddly bit coming up. Nicole and Red are humming along, even Yiannis has mellowed with his splash of alcohol, or maybe he's just given up; it's by no means raucous but I doubt Minerva House has ever been this exuberant.

And this is how Petros finds us. He taps briefly on the

garden door, stepping inside swiftly. It's me he's seeking out, apparently trying to semaphore a message with his eyes.

'I'm fine…' I begin, then see I've misread him. Petros isn't looking for reassurance, he isn't alone.

There's a loaded pause.

The second man stands there, triumphant but shifty, like the scruffy boy in the playground who's just stolen somebody else's marbles; he knows he'll be found out, but it's worth it for this moment of glory.

'Surprise!' Jake says.

28

When excruciating (to me) introductions and small talk are over, Yiannis goes off to prepare a bedroom for his unexpected guest. Petros says, very apologetically and with the merest flick of his eyes towards me, that he hasn't room at Verena Bay but he knows Yiannis has plenty so…? These arrangements conveniently require the help of everyone else, and Jake and I are left alone.

'Hello again, April,' he says.

'Hello, Jake,' I reply. 'Did you lose your way to Lerwick harbour in all that darkness?'

'April, April, that's not very nice when I've come all this way to see you.' He tries for a brave but wounded smile. 'A bit more of a welcome would be kind. I thought Petros was going to chuck me out before I got my foot in the door and now, this. And actually, April, Lerwick's on Shetland. Kirkwall is the main town on Orkney; I'm sure I told you… Oh. I see. You're being clever.'

'Yes, Jake. Which is more than you are, turning up here. What are you thinking of?' I keep my tone light, conversational, and I see it disconcerts him. Jake likes fireworks. He'll have spent his journey relishing – ridiculous – scenarios, like me running into his outstretched arms delirious with joy and begging him to take me back, or screeching like a fishwife and clawing at him for the scent of Erica. All because his feelings are hurt.

'You told me to bugger off on the phone,' he blurts out. 'You put the phone down on me. That was really hurtful, Ape.'

'Don't—'

'Call you that. Sorry, April. But, still.'

That's what really rankles with him. He doesn't want me but he doesn't want to be rejected by me either.

'I think it's your pride that's hurt, not your feelings,' I say. 'And now your bank balance. You've come here for no good reason, for nothing.'

'Not for nothing.' Jake plays his trump card. 'Yiannis is here and he's still planning to set up orchid holidays for enthusiasts. And da-da – here I am. I can't have missed much.'

'Nothing in the line of orchids.' I'd almost forgotten them over the last couple of days, though when Jake learns the rest of what I've been up to, it won't only be his fingers that are green.

'And all these people, April. There's a whole cast. It's like trying to work out characters in a film halfway through.'

'Is it? What a shame Erica couldn't come too.' Even as I say it, I'm overcome with weariness at such pathetic one-upmanship. It's always been a feature of the relationship Jake and I have, except once it was affectionate and we called it banter.

'You looked happy when I arrived, April. Light-hearted,' Jake says, unexpectedly. 'This place is good for you.'

'I like it here.'

'Well, you deserve to be happy,' he says finally, when I don't expand. 'You've had a tough year.'

'We all deserve to be happy, Jake.'

'Even me?' He grins his best little-boy grin.

'Everyone.' I ponder the real point of him being here and how soon he will come to it; Jake is not the A-direct-to-Z type.

'How does it work around here, anyway?' he asks. 'I mean, could we – just you and me – have dinner tonight?'

'I'm sure we could, but why would we?'

Jake sighs. 'I've treated you badly, April. I wish I'd

spoken to you properly before I left. So this is selfish – I know, I know, sarcastic response taken as read – but there are things I need... no, things I *would like* to say to you...' That smile again.

'Fine.'

'That easy? I don't have to beg?'

'Not if eight o'clock suits. Yiannis will point you in the direction of the local tavern.' I push down a sense of déjà vu and wait for him to argue for somewhere more upmarket and discreet. He doesn't.

'Just us?'

'Just us.' Whatever 'just us' means, with Georgios cooking up a storm in the kitchen, Petros being paternal, Yiannis and Red across here and in my head, Nicole protective in my room. And Elena closer but forever unseen.

'Thanks, Ape... ril. I appreciate it.'

There's a lull, then Nicole pokes her head around the door.

'Come in, come in.' I beckon madly. 'Are you ready to go? Remember? Didn't we say... er, mid-morning?' I will Nicole to catch on.

'Oh, I am sure we did,' she replies. 'We must go immediately, or we will be late.'

We could win awards for ham acting, but Nicole bluffs it out.

'Would Jake like to come, do you think, April?'

'Where—'

'Jake always has a little nap when he arrives somewhere. Don't you, Jake? He's sensitive to reconditioned air on planes.' I'm too old to actually roll my eyes.

'Well, yes, I do, usually.' Jake is clearly torn between his hobby horse of recycled air and germs, and his desire to gatecrash whatever.

'Exactly. I'll see you tonight then.'

Even Jake must be able to hear the full stop in that, and I hide behind wanting to spend some time with Nicole, to thank her for this morning. Of course I do want to do that, but underneath I'm not that nice. Really, I just want to annoy Jake. Who, I note, has shown no interest why we were all congregated in this tiny corner of the island at cockcrow. For once his self-interest serves me because I don't want to explain.

'Should I speak of him or not?' Nicole asks, as we scamper across the road and disappear into her guest room – looking back to check that Jake isn't watching. I have a flash of memory, Elena and me dashing down the garden and into my tree house to escape Krista's bossing.

'I just wish I knew why he's really here.'

'Is he really interested in orchids?'

'Jake is a graphic designer turned PR man. He wanted to "manage" me – my career – for a while.' I shake my head. 'As if I'm Celine Dion or someone who needs a posse. Anyway, he gets so enthused with his projects, he ends up vying with his clients' specialist knowledge.' I flop down onto the bed and Nicole takes up residence in the big armchair. 'He did some work on a BBC gardening programme, met an expert and charming botanist, and suddenly orchids were Jake's latest passion. When he met Petros, who was carrying Yiannis' book... Well, it was a sign, wasn't it?' I pull a face. 'Except now he's moved on.'

'So why *is* he here?'

'I expect he thinks he's missing something.' A bit awkwardly, I change the subject. 'Nicole? I want to say thank you, you know – for this morning.'

'You are welcome,' Nicole says. 'It was a small thing to do, but we all thought it would be – fitting.' Then she, too, changes the subject. 'April, I have a confession.'

'I would have thought I'm the least qualified person here to hear it, but go on.'

'You are very funny. The last day, when Andreas had finished his painting of you, I made a silly comment, about you being famous—'

'Ye-es.'

'I know you are famous already,' she says. 'Petros told me.

I think, maybe, I was aware of your name before that. I know very little about music though.'

I repeat what I said to Red. 'I'm not famous, Nicole. I am, I *was*, a concert pianist. Quite a good one. Certainly not great. Some people know me for that, but I wouldn't expect it and, really, I like it better when people don't know. Truly. No false modesty.'

'Petros said that too.' She nods, then her face creases. 'Wait, you said "was"?'

'Yes.' I wait for a pang that doesn't come. Good. 'As of last month when I ducked out of a European concert tour to come here instead. I'm trying out retirement from the professional scene.' I recite the party line. 'I shall play for pleasure and by special request—'

'As you did for Red?'

I'm not sure if she's joking. 'For Red, this morning for the twins, even for one of Petros' threatened soirees,' I say evenly. 'I'll play for you anytime, Nicole, if you want me to. But,' it occurs to me, 'I generally play the piano when I have no words. You and I have so much to talk about instead.'

'Yes. We do.' She looks pleased. She adds, 'What else will you do?'

'I may teach. I like teaching. And I don't doubt I'll still practise for hours every day, and worry always that I've done the wrong thing in giving up. But basically I am free.'

'Are you?' Nicole is very astute; of course, she's married to an infinitely more talented artist than I am. She knows how it is.

'About fifty per cent and working on it.' It's important I tell her the truth. 'I'm not a natural performer. I'm technically proficient, I interpret well. I've done alright in my career, but the, the spark of that indefinable extra is too intermittent. I've struggled for years with that. Now I've stopped. And it's getting okay.'

'I will not be polite and argue.' She smiles and holds her hands up. 'What do I know of music? There is not an ounce of creativity in me; I told you my father was an English professor and from him I quote other people's words very badly. But I understand what you say. Andreas does have the spark, does he not? I see it. I am not sure which is more uncomfortable, to have it or not... But does Jake know this? Is he here to convince you otherwise? So he can "manage" you?'

'Jake is a loose cannon. Who knows?'

We grin at each other.

'Nicole? Nobody, ever, ever, has known all my secrets before,' I tell her, half joking but realising the truth of it.

'Not since Elena.'

'Okay,' I concede.

'One day I might even tell you mine,' says Nicole, jumping up. 'But now you have laid your parents to rest and formalised your ties to Agia Triada.' She sees my face and smiles sympathetically. 'You had not thought of that, had you? There will always be part of you here now, April. Thank goodness you turned down Yiannis before you found his secret garden.'

'Don't.' I shudder. 'I feel terrible. I wasn't even thinking ahead. Have I just insulted Yiannis beyond belief?'

'Did this morning suggest that? No. Yiannis and you are mismatched like broken china. He knows that as you do. He is *thrilled* to have helped you in the way he has, but being restrained Yiannis, he cannot show it. Anyway, that is not the point I set out to make.'

'No, you were going to tell me your secrets.' I make a huge effort to calm down, knowing how right she is.

'Oh, no, no.' Nicole shakes her head. 'I was going to say that now your parents are settled, surely it is time for Elena? Do not be like Damaris and live in a limbo land. April, find her, or find her not, you need to make your peace with Elena.'

'You're right. I know you are.' But, I can't help thinking, it would be much easier to do that without Jake here.

29

Somewhere in Cyprus
Monday 19th August 1974

Dear April and Mrs Gale's class,

If you have seen the Cyprus news on television please do not be worried. We have seen the smoke of the Turkish invasion and heard some bombs but we are not injured. The soldiers came and said that Varosha and our glass hotel was not safe so we have been driving again. Backwards, from where we came.

Our trip is like the Snakes and Ladders game we take from the cupboard at wet playtimes. Every time I think we are getting a little way nearer to my mum, she is in another spot. Like a mystery. Before we came here I wanted to be like the Famous Five so that me and April could have adventures. Now I know I don't like mysteries or adventures.

My Aunt Irini says we must be cheery though, and Antony tells us to keep our chins up. Krista is cross about that because she is worried she has a pointy chin, but really I think she just likes to be cross. Also, she is now scared of dying....

Dying. Elena shivered and breathed deeper, her breath wet and stifled under the tickly blanket provided by the small lonely rest house. She didn't think they were going to die. She couldn't even imagine not being here. But she was still scared. But of what? Elena put her pencil down and thought. She was scared of nothing being the same any more, that her life wasn't there and if her life wasn't there where was she? Who was she? The thoughts frightened her but, like blocked ears after swimming, however much she shook her head they wouldn't go away. She was waiting for the pop, but of understanding. And for that she had to think. There was nothing that could not be solved, Mama always said, by thinking it through from beginning to end.

'Like a recipe,' she had said, long ago, before they went to England, in one of the village houses. Mama knew that Elena, almost clever enough to bake her own cake and ice it, would understand. 'You think through all the ingredients, you mix them together and from all of the muddle, out comes something new and tasty. See?'

Mama had been at the other end of the scrubbed wooden table when she said that. Her face was shiny with heat from the oven and slick curls of hair tumbled from the white net that covered it. She had bent over to take out her tray of scones and howled to find them risen the size of the Troodos Mountains but with the fruit all sunk to the bottom.

'Holy Mother and all the saints, when will I learn how this furnace works?'

Aunt Irini and Elena had laughed and laughed. Mama too. She had cut the doughy scones in half and they had eaten the cooked bits with orange jam.

'See, Elena, it looks like a muddle, it doesn't work how you think, but still it tastes good, yes? Like life.'

Elena, her mouth full, and one eye on her own cake, which was cooling on a high shelf, had nodded. It was Irini who had pointed to the dissected buns, discarded in the corner. 'What happens to them?'

Mama had stood up and retied her apron. 'We learn from them, and we do better next time, Irini. The crumbs we give to the chickens. Come, Elena, let's make scones as beautiful as your cake.'

Elena did see what Mama meant; she had never forgotten it. Even if her worry didn't unravel easily, and she picked at it night after night, eventually it made sense and she found the answer. But this time it was different, as if the ingredients for this recipe were all written in a foreign language with a blunt pencil. As if she couldn't make sense of any of it and the dictionary was too high on a shelf with nobody to lift it down. It must be because she was in a war now and nobody could fix that.

The tree houses, she thought fiercely. *Think of the tree houses and pray to God that everything will be right there.* A whole world going on as normal. Quietly, and rooting in the dark, so as not to wake her sisters, Elena felt for the photograph of the three of them, taken just before England. She couldn't see it, but she didn't need to. Holding it was comfort enough.

Elena didn't know, nobody seemed to, why they were called tree houses. There were no trees. Antony called them stilt houses. Elena had tried to describe them to April and her papa and he had made them a special one in April's garden; Elena had promised she would bring April to see the real ones one day. 'They have brown wooden legs with a square box on top and are reaching into the sky,' she remembered saying. She had even drawn a plan. You climbed up a ladder and inside the door was a bed with a net for mosquitoes, and a window with no glass that looked out to the sea. Underneath the ladder was a bathroom but it was really just a hole and a tap, no bath. The ground was all sand from the beach, and Yorghis who owned the tree houses and the food shop said sometimes the water came in so far that they were in the sea. Krista said then they would be boathouses. Elena had never seen that; she wished she could.

Beside Elena, Sofia snuffled in her sleep and made little rasping noises in the back of her throat. On the other side, Krista lay flat on her back, her arms by her sides. A white band kept her hair off her face. Krista said that sleeping on your stomach like Elena did gave you wrinkles and puffed-up eyes. Elena didn't mind that, but she minded that Krista looked like a dead body all laid out and waiting for God's angels to swoop down and take her soul away forever. That wasn't a thought for the night-time. Or for wartime. Elena pulled the covers over her nose and concentrated on breathing. Her sisters never worried about the dark or about the secrets. Krista always wanted to have secrets and Sofia made them up all the time. Elena didn't want there to be secrets at all.

It was funny that people could be opposites, especially sisters, she thought. Even though she and Krista had the same mother, the same dead father, and the same life, it wasn't the same life because they were different girls. Elena wondered if Sofia was going to be like one of them or just like her own self. She was too little to tell yet and maybe Sofia being their sister but not truly being their sister changed things anyway. There was nothing bad about being adopted. Elena knew that for sure, Mama had said it often, but sometimes outside people didn't like it, so they never talked about it. It helped that Sofia looked exactly like Aunt Irini who looked like Mama and she looked like Elena and a bit like Krista. It all worked out...

But it didn't, Elena thought all of a sudden. She wanted to stamp, like Krista would have. It didn't all work out, it didn't make sense. Like being in England then not being in England with no reason for going there or leaving there, when everyone else in her and April's class had lived there since their very first day at school. Like her mama disappearing away to work while English mothers sat in the cashier desk at the supermarket or were nurses or dinner ladies. Like how they were *all* called Zacharia. Sofia, she was okay, but why Stefan, who wasn't from Cyprus at all?

Elena couldn't sleep and now the torch was flickering. She

could hear the sea whooshing and rolling, and sometimes a donkey was crying. Yorghis said it would have a baby soon. She staved off the dark by staring at the stars, tiny silver sprinkles that stayed the same whatever happened. She wondered if April was looking up and wishing on the same stars, wishing that Elena hadn't gone away. She wondered whether April had forgiven her for leaving without saying goodbye.

The stars stayed the same, and the sun came up and the sun set the same in all of the places she had lived, but the dark was different, different everywhere. In England, it had been grey and grainy mostly and the street lights meant she could always see out. In Famagusta, the place Elena used to call home, until Mama looked bruised and hushed her, Elena knew the darkness; it fit her like a cape. It was like a finished jigsaw puzzle, the shape of one house joined to the next and the next. There was the shadow of the laundry, the hulking bread oven in the yard, big enough to hide in – if you dared – the old tractor, bought the same day as Elena was born, and the cats that streaked from one to the other chasing their tails and playing tag in the night.

What frightened Elena was not dying but living if all of that was gone.

30

Splashing water on my face and brushing my teeth, I recall what I wore to dinner with Yiannis; to put on the same things to go to the same place at the same time to meet a different character would be far too like acting the lead in an experimental play. My lips twitch at the thought of the gourmet Jake scanning the tavern's laminated, pictorial menu. Before I met him he'd got through to audition for *MasterChef* and still has his signed photo of Loyd Grossman, and to be truthful he can be a decent, if overly complicated, cook. Perhaps Erica has converted him to the simpler things in life.

I'm already late, fallout from a couple of hours wrestling with Balakirev and his 'Islamey'. Still, I pause in the village to watch the distant sun set: an orange globe which, framed with pale streaks of light from the sky, looks uncannily like the retina of an eye as it slides into its hiding place. When I was a little girl, I used to think the sun was like a huge coin being dropped into a money box and that it was this daily, endless collection of coins that were collected for the pot of gold at the end of the rainbow. Funny, I haven't thought of that for years, but the image hasn't changed; I can still conjure up the impression of that wonder.

I look out for Jake but presume he's already fidgeting in the restaurant, sniffing the carafe of house wine and grilling the confused Georgios about shoulder of lamb versus its crown. This thought has the dual effect of making me speed up and shape up; I will be nice. I know Jake – that will be the way to bore him back to Orkney.

And then, when I arrive at the Village Tavern and go in through the side door to the dining room, I find nobody there to be nice to. The clock behind the bar reads eight-twenty; it *is* possible Jake got waylaid, and more probable that Georgios is somewhere in the back assuming potential customers will stick their heads into the kitchen for service.

Not quite liking to do that, I hang around for a few minutes, looking at the random knick-knacks on the shelves: a chipped ceramic Aphrodite, a snow globe of the Acropolis and a thimble collection of the Dionysus mosaics. I imagine the young Georgios and his siblings counting out their limited pocket money on school trips and proudly bearing home souvenirs. The prints on the walls may be of the same generation but years of summer sunshine have faded and yellowed both them and the flock wallpaper they blend into.

It's a shame. They're all images of Cyprus and look as if they've been cut from newspapers and magazines and cheaply framed; a pictorial scrapbook that once told a story. There are no borders, no captions, but some destinations I can guess: Bellapais Abbey, the fort at Pafos Harbour, Kantara Castle, and the expectant Varosha coastline, albeit a shadow of that vibrant living impression painted by Orestes. The remainder are anonymous: a mountain range, a deserted beach, a village square… Then something catches my eye: the last picture in the line and almost impossible to view without moving a dusty old spider plant and the furniture.

Wanting a better look – what else is there to do? – I squeeze behind a table for four, close to the fireplace. I think, at first glance, it's a row of UN lookout posts, the type still standing today along the Greek–Turkish border. It's definitely military: a jeep and a mound of kit in the background, a raised flag of indistinct origin and a couple of uniformed personnel grinning from what are *not* UN lookout posts.

What they are, are the tree houses.
Elena's tree houses.

I bet Georgios won't mind if I take down the picture and have a closer look. If he were here he'd no doubt get it for me. If he were here... temporarily diverted, I remember I'm waiting for Jake and he's not here either. And it's now, I squint at the clock, nearly half past. That gives me illogical justification for pulling out the table, climbing up onto the chair – fairly shakily, it has to be said – nearest the wall and unhooking the flimsy frame. Holding it in one hand and grabbing the back of the chair to steady myself – I'm neither naturally graceful nor agile – I step down and then sit at the table, angling the picture under the adjacent wall light.

It's certainly the tree houses, but it doesn't give away any more secrets. Two uneven rows of them, well, not rows necessarily but a cluster of six, and perhaps more out of shot, exactly the same as the one in Elena's photograph. The evidence of bedding hanging out of the glass-less windows and boots at the foot of the ladders confirms military digs. I can't name the picture, I can't date it; I undo the catches on the back of the frame but underneath the cardboard liner there is nothing other than the carefully trimmed sheet of newspaper. Still, it *is* the tree houses. Cyprus was probably once littered with army billets like these, I tell myself, but surely press archives or military records could fill in the blank—

A sudden sound makes me jump. I look up guiltily, resisting the temptation to slip the photograph under the table. Georgios, beaming his signature beam, crashes through the door behind the bar.

'*Kalispera, kalispera,*' he cries, as if welcoming home the prodigal. 'April, welcome. Drinks for the house and menus immediate. Jake is arrived,' he announces. 'He, and Red-man, and I, Georgios, take a comradely drink while I am cook. Then Jake has a call.' He mimes a phone. 'Girlfriend. He is being one minute.'

'No problem.' I'm barely listening. 'Georgios, this picture...' I indicate the tree houses, now on the table. 'Do you know anything about it?'

He peers over my shoulder, not seeming to care it should be on the wall. 'Ah, yes, yes,' he says, nodding intently. 'This picture.'

I experience a flash of hope, instantly extinguished.

'No,' he goes on. 'No. I know nothing. Is always here. All pictures always here. I can ask my mama and papa but they are dead. You like it? You like to take it, yes? Yes?'

'May I borrow it?' I start, when Jake barges in, an unconscious parody, from the door behind the bar, and I don't want him to know; he'll take over, claim it as his find. I put my fingers to my lips, and say, 'Sshh. Secret?' into Georgios' astonished face.

'Yes, yes. Secret,' Georgios repeats, and neatly whips away the photo and frame as if they were uneaten soup and he trained to silver service.

'April,' Jake says, 'there you are.' He seems anxious as he makes his way over.

Georgios, on the other hand, looks like he's just remembered he's a restaurateur, and taps his pockets as if to bring forth a notepad and pencil. Neither is there, causing him to slap his head and turn on his heel to the bar.

'*Fawlty Towers*, the Cypriot edit,' Jake murmurs.

He's not wrong but I don't respond, it would be disloyal to Georgios, owner of the tree house picture.

'Sorry I'm late, I didn't realise the time.' Jake sits down opposite me. 'Actually, Red and I – he walked over with me for a drink, sound bloke – came early and Georgios said come into the kitchen, and he got in a knot with his filo pastry and then, well, then Erica phoned and, you see, Erica doesn't like to be kept waiting or being asked to phone back.' Jake is gabbling; Jake never gabbles.

He looks hunted. Or haunted. 'What *is* the matter?' I hold my breath.

'Erica's pregnant.' He puts his head in his hands.

I let my breath out. 'Oh. Well. Congratulations.' I sound too neutral, and try harder. 'Lovely news.' At lightning speed I search my soul, experience a faint wash of regret, an even fainter one of envy – of Erica, not Jake – and conclude that I mean it.

Jake looks at me through parted fingers.

'Isn't it?' I add. He's far from the image of a joyous father-to-be. And he's over here.

He slides his hands down his face and, elbows on the table, supports his chin. 'Well, yes. I suppose it is.'

I raise my eyebrows and he visibly collects himself. 'I mean, of course it is. It's great. It's great for me but,' he looks at me earnestly, 'but is it great for you, April? Is it really? You don't have to pretend with me, you know,' he goes on. 'You have every right to feel hurt or sad. Even jealous.'

'Strong words there, Jake,' I say. 'Hurt? Sad? Jealous? About what exactly? Your new relationship? Motherhood?'

He shifts uncomfortably, his counselling veneer inadequately polished. I get the impression he was expecting me to dissolve into tears and now doesn't know what to do.

'Well, both of those,' he decides. 'Let's face it, Ape... ril, this time last year this was us. You and me—'

'No, Jake.' I sound sharp and I mean to. 'This was never us. I was never pregnant.' I cross my fingers. 'There was never a realistic chance of us, you and me, settling down. We got along for so long because I was touring so much.' I steer the conversation in a way I'm happy with. 'Is that what you're going to do? Get married? Make a proper family?'

'When you put it like that, then I guess so.' Jake sounds a little sulky. 'It's what Erica has decided. She... I... well, we wanted to make sure there's no unfinished business.'

'Between us? Not on my part.'

'No regrets? I'm very fond of you, April, and this doesn't have to be the end of us. Of course, things can't be the same, there will always be Erica and the baby—'

'Don't, Jake.' I shake my head. I would guess Erica has given him a very reasonable ultimatum and this visit is about him hedging his bets. He doesn't know what he wants – except it all. 'I'm not exactly sure where *you* think you're going with this, but *I've* reached the end of the road.' I sit back in my chair, summon all my willpower and a friendly smile. 'Let's start again, with me saying congratulations, lovely news and meaning it, and you accepting it graciously.'

Slowly, Jake nods his head. 'If that's what you really want...' I don't fill his expectant pause. '... then fine with me, April. It's your call.'

I can hear the 'and your loss' in his tone. 'It was good of you to come over and tell me in person,' I relent. 'That couldn't have been easy.'

'What? Oh, yes. No problem.' He looks over my shoulder. Again, shifty is the word that comes to mind and I know there's something he's not saying but I tell myself to let it go.

'Have you told the others about Erica and the baby? Just so I know.'

'Don't be silly, April.' His angst is gone now he's on firmer ground. 'Naturally I'd tell you first. Okay, I did tell Red. But he doesn't count, does he? Confessional sort of thing. He's a priest, you know. He and Yiannis are writing a book. Sound chap, Red. Very sound.'

'So you already said. And I agree.' I set a little wager with myself: by the end of the week Jake will almost certainly fancy himself a priest and be emulating Red like a committed understudy. Of course, the odds might lengthen when he meets Andreas the artist, but either way his botanist ambitions have a limited shelf life. I want to say something about fatherhood, being a dad, not being a short-term project, but don't. It really isn't my business and we'll end up arguing.

'So,' says Jake, finally. 'Shall we order?' He twists around in his chair.

Georgios pops up from behind the bar like a jack-in-the-box, it's so on cue I wonder if he's actually been crouching there, waiting. I'm still not hungry, and it seems daft to drag the evening out, but if I leave now, Jake will forever believe I'm running away to cry myself to sleep, and Georgios will take it personally. Instead, I watch Jake pick up the menu, study it, hesitate, and clearly bite back a litany of questions and demands. Maybe he is growing up, slowly.

'Er, what do you recommend, Georgios?' Jake asks.

If Georgios says chips and beans, I'll insist we both have it.

'Kleftikos. Speciality of the house,' is what he does say. 'Very good choice. Beautiful dinner. Best for two persons.'

'Fine,' I say quickly, before Jake can spoil Georgios' enthusiasm.

He lopes off to the kitchen and leaves us in silence.

I rack my brains for something to say. 'So. Erica must be thrilled about the baby.'

Jake mulls it over like a cryptic crossword. 'I wouldn't say thrilled, exactly. Erica doesn't do thrilled. She's very practical and efficient. Except for her thing about ley lines. She's pleased,' he settles on. 'She's bought lots of baby books. She likes a woman called Gina Ford. And real nappies. And breastfeeding. She's going to express milk so I can do the night-time feeds.'

'Well. She seems very organised,' is the best I can offer. 'And she knows what she wants. Very useful with a baby.' I can't help myself asking, 'Didn't she mind you coming over here?'

He doesn't reply. He's looking at a point over my shoulder again. He might just be overwhelmed with it all. He might not. Then I understand.

'Jake, she does know? Jake!' He looks increasingly as if he knows he's in freefall and his parachute is jammed.

'She knows I'm away on business. It's true.' He can't help but hear my intake of incredulous breath. 'And I needed a break. I told you already I would have brought Erica with me over here, if you hadn't come first. It was my holiday. I'm the one interested in orchids, April.'

And what about my interest in Elena? It being a trip for both of us? I open my mouth, frustration bubbling, when Georgios saves me. He appears at my side, holding aloft two oval dinner plates, and, oblivious to the atmosphere, he places them in front of us with a flourish.

'Kleftikos. Speciality of the house.' He beams. 'Enjoy, please.'

'We will,' I lie, gazing down at the uniform chunks of lamb standing like building blocks in a sea of thin gravy. I spear one. 'These are the perfect size for you to choke on, Jake,' I say quietly. 'But you know what? We're both here. We're both happy. Let's both enjoy the holiday.'

31

Being so reasonable is a strain, but it's the only way forward. The sparsely remaining scales about my ex have well and truly fallen from my eyes. We leave the restaurant, waved off by Georgios, whose parting shot is to show us his karaoke machine. 'Sonny and Cher?' He points between us, encouragingly, which about sums up the evening.

Like Yiannis before him, Jake leaves me at the entrance to Minerva House – I'd expected him to take more persuading to go but he says he promised to catch Red for some spiritual interchange over a nightcap; I hope God is looking over his own. Jake watches as I cross the road.

Him, a dad. I can't yet visualise it, and I don't think he can either. Bemused is the term I'd use to describe him, but that'll soon change. Erica has the upper hand at present but once Jake wrestles those baby books from her and works himself into the role, he'll be in his element. Deep down, he needs to be needed. As for me? I do the brief soul-search again, and am still ninety per cent sure that any residual feeling is my pride not my feelings under attack.

It really is a beautiful night. I haven't been drinking, I'm calm, so I could drive back to Verena Bay tonight. I pause at Nicole's; on the other hand, I have an open invitation and nobody waiting up. There's only one person I want to talk to about this. I cross the courtyard, push open the door and pray my instinct is correct.

She's not asleep on my bed this time. She's curled up in the armchair, having another go at *Running with the Devil*. She looks at me gravely. 'This man,' she holds up the book and speaks like a child who has learned a recitation, 'compares electric guitar riffs with the cadenzas of Vivaldi. What do you think of that, April Rose?'

'Some heavy metal songs do use the sonata-allegro format,' I start, unthinking. Then, 'Hold on, what's that got to do with anything?

'Just an interesting fact.' She snaps the book shut, sets it on the table, uncurls her legs and smiles up at me. 'Hello, April. Did you have a good evening? And are you not going to come in?'

I don't know why I'm still standing on the threshold. I enter, close the door, drop my bag and fling myself on the bed. 'Take me from this world of madness.'

'Ah. It was that good?'

I can hear the smile in her voice. I groan for effect and then push myself up to lean on my elbows. 'Jake's new girlfriend is pregnant. Reading between the lines, he's still in two minds, but knows if he doesn't shape up, she's quite capable of going it alone. She doesn't know he's here, seeing me.' I pause for breath. 'I *think* he came over to check that there's no chance of he and I getting back together, although his argument is that it's not fair I've got the "orchid holiday" and he – with or without Erica – hasn't. Shall I go on?'

Nicole's face is a picture. She's sitting upright now, and her eyes and mouth are forming a triangle of Os. 'Of course, go on.'

I flop down again and look up at the ceiling, reflecting. 'Actually, that just about covers it. Mostly his nose is out of joint.'

'His nose...? Oh, I see.' She comes across and sits beside me on the bed. After a lengthy pause, 'April? May I say something?' she asks. 'Jake is an idiot. And if I might be so blunt, April, why did you not tell him to get to fuck?'

Why didn't I?

'April, the best thing of all is that none of this is your concern. Jake's commitment to fatherhood is not something about which you must worry. Let this other woman have the job. You have me, and Petros and the others. A whole life of your own to plan. You have Elena to seek out.' She smiles at me. 'You can hide here at Verena Bay forever, if you like. We all are doing so.'

It's exactly what I need to hear. Another little spring of relief uncoils somewhere deep inside, another item ticked off the list of English-April's convoluted life. 'I've had enough of it all for one evening.' I spare a thought for Red who might well be in the midst of Jake's philosophies for hours to come. 'Let's change the subject.'

'I can do better than that.' Nicole roots in her bag and takes out a DVD and a big box of Cyprus Delight. 'A dose of sugar, and a movie where it all ends happily ever after. We can be teenagers again. Complaining about boys and all about Girl Power.'

'*Four Weddings and a Funeral* and sugar. How did you know? I feel better already.' I crawl up the bed and prop all the pillows into a comfortable mess while Nicole starts the DVD player and then tears open the sweets. We settle back and wait for the opening sequences.

There's something I've forgotten to tell her, but it won't come, I'm too wound up. I think of something else instead.

'I didn't know you were a lawyer, Nicole?'

'I trained as a lawyer,' she clarifies. 'I did it because it pleased my father, but I didn't enjoy it. It was conveyancing most of the time and so boring. By accident, I became an events manager, then I began to run the international business that is Andreas Koumettou, Artist.'

'Did your father mind?'

Nicole straightens up. 'No, he didn't. I could have stayed

as Andreas' assistant but instead I married him, and my papa is an old-fashioned man. He liked having a professional daughter, he loves having a son-in-law more. He is a romantic at heart. And my mother,' Nicole grimaces, 'she is a narcissist. Her dream is that Andreas and I will return to Athens, where we both studied, and she can boast about him to her friends. Her nightmare is becoming a grandparent; I think she is relaxing a little now. I am their only child and...' Nicole shrugs and lets the statement hang. She adds, nonchalantly, 'You and Jake. Or, or... your husbands, you did not think of children?'

'Damaris asked me that. No.' I take the edge off it by reciprocating. 'What about you and Andreas?'

'No.' She is equally brisk.

We look at each other: a flash of understanding that the conversation could take a specific turn – or we could watch the film. The credits start to roll and we both relax.

'You know,' I tell her, 'I really haven't had a friend like this – sweets and films and a sleepover – for years, since I was a child. Like you said about sharing secrets, since Elena.'

'When you used to sit in your tree house and talk about when you'd visit *her* tree houses?' Nicole hits the nail perfectly on the head.

'It was our happy place.'

'And this is your new happy place. Mine too. Sshh.' She nods at the screen. 'It's starting.'

32

The Tree Houses, Cyprus
August 1974

Dear April and Mrs Gale's class,

We are at the tree houses.

I do not like to write this next thing but I have learned that wars are not just soldiers and guns they are about telling lies so it is important for me to tell you the truth or this would not be a good News class. It is that I waited so long for the tree houses and they are different now to what I said. I am especially sorry to April for this. The good things about the tree houses are (1) the beach (2) the turtles (3) my Uncle Costas (4) the war is not here yet. The bad thing is just one: they have stopped being happy. And so have I. Mama is not here and my friend Mamun is gone from me like I have gone from you.

I won't say the worst thing as I do not want you to be sad like me.

Love from, Elena Z
xxx

PS It is something bad and maybe very bad about my friend, Mamun.

PPS If you don't understand about the tree houses, ask April. She knows everything.

The worst thing was the secrets. No, the worst thing was the dark. The secrets kept coming like InterCity trains and there was always a new darkness to lay awake in and worry. This night Elena was curled up tightly on her corner of the mattress. The sisters were – finally – in bed in the tree houses. Their special, safe place. Except it didn't feel special or safe any more. Elena and her sisters had been disappointed by the Palm Beach Hotel, but arriving at the tree houses and seeing how they looked the same but felt different was like a pain in the heart. It was a grown-up pain, Elena thought suddenly. Too big for her. She could never meet April here now.

Now the tree houses didn't seem as magic or as safe as they used to be, but the war wouldn't come this far, Aunt Irini had promised them that, but Elena had seen her eyes flicker and her hands make fists when she said it.

Elena was worried. Just before Mama left, Elena had listened when she shouldn't, and heard her tell Aunt Irini that the house in Famagusta was gone, they couldn't go back, and that Varosha was a stopgap, but that the tree houses were still a safe place. She'd been wrong – *Mama* had been wrong. Now what if Irini was wrong too? There were secrets and darkness everywhere, as if they all expected a thunderstorm and the only shelter they had was the trees, heavy with fruit, their trunks wide open to the lightning that could strike them in two.

Like today, when they were all out catching the fish that Uncle Costas sold for breakfast. He wouldn't take them on his boat, that wasn't safe either, so they were fishing on the pier. Two army trucks came trundling past, and the Greek soldiers were so jammed together inside that they were like a whole bag of Sherbet Pips gone sticky and you couldn't get them apart. They stopped and the driver asked to borrow the car. Antony didn't want to let them but Uncle Costas whispered it was better to say yes or they would command it anyway and not give it back – Elena thought command was the English word. They had to take out all the suitcases and stack them in an empty tree house. Aunt Irini was scared to leave them outside in case they were stolen, although there was nobody else staying there. She made the girls go inside too. They could hear the soldiers across the road in the hotel then. There was lots of banging and shouting and then flames and the smell of fire; Krista peeked out and said the soldiers were taking out furniture and making a bonfire. She wanted to go and join the fun, she said the soldiers were laughing, and that they had called Irini and Antony over to show them something in the car before it roared away. But Irini and Antony were misery-guts and didn't seem to be enjoying themselves.

Irini was tight-lipped when she got back to check on them and when Elena asked about her friend Mamun, whose papa owned the hotel, she had snapped. It was fine, Aunt Irini had said, fine. Mamun and his papa had gone away to Turkey and the hotel was empty so the soldiers were moving in.

It was wrong, something was all wrong. Elena sat up, unable to resist temptation any longer. She checked carefully that Sofia and Krista were fast asleep, and then she struggled out from beneath the mosquito net and felt her way to the door. Her heart thumping, *bump,* one beat for guilt, *bump,* one beat for fear, she tiptoed down the ladder, and beside the simple bathroom, she knelt down. As her pyjamas got dusty, and the still, hot night pressed darkly around her, she listened.

They were just on the edge of the sand, propped up by one of the legs of their tree house next door, and talking long into the night. Both were smoking cigarettes, the little glows like two lonely fireflies grown lazy in the stretch of the summer.

'We should have left here straightaway,' Irini was saying, her voice muffled, and Elena could picture her aunt's face buried in Antony's shoulder, her legs tucked over his. 'It was disgusting, Antony. What they did, what they said. And we have girls. Girls, Antony. I can't bear—'

'Ssh. Ssh. Don't even think it. It's better we go in the morning. Just as if we're taking a picnic for the day, we'll walk along the beach, we can get far enough and pick up a lift on the main road and head into the mountains. Okay? We'll tell the girls it's another adventure...'

With that, Elena lost her temper, something unheard of; Krista was the temper-sister, Sofia had baby-tantrums but Elena was goody-good, just like Krista always said. She got up and ran onto the sand and stood in front of Irini and Antony, breathing hard, her hands on her hips.

'Elena – what's wrong, darling?' Irini jumped up. 'Are you sick? What is it? A horrid nightmare?' There were tears on her cheeks and she was wiping her nose with the back of her hand and trying to be smiley.

Elena deflated and started to cry too. She just wasn't good at crossness. 'Scared,' she muttered as Aunt Irini wrapped her in a huge hug. They stayed that way for a long time but nobody asked her why she was scared. Elena unravelled herself and said, 'Sorry. I'll go to bed now.'

'You don't have to say sorry, Elena,' Antony said. 'It's okay to be scared. And come to me and your aunt any time. Any time, okay?'

Elena nodded and hesitated, about to ask, when Aunt Irini spoiled it. In a bright voice, she said, 'Get a good sleep now, darling. We're just planning a picnic tomorrow, we'll leave early. Along the beach and up into the mountains. Won't that be lovely?'

Elena didn't even nod that time. Just turned sadly and crept back up the ladder to her mattress, almost there, when Krista sat up suddenly and shone her torch into Elena's face. Elena just managed not to shriek out loud. Krista grabbed her arm and pulled her down, the springs on the bed wheezing.

'What did they say? Were they talking about me?' she asked.

'Why would they talk about you?' Elena said. 'I didn't hear much. They are arranging a surprise picnic for tomorrow, that's all.'

'Cool.' Krista snuggled back down. 'The war must be going away. Why isn't that good news, daydream girl?'

Elena stayed quiet. She was thinking about Mrs Gale's

class when they did good secrets and bad secrets. They didn't learn what to do when you weren't sure if it was good or bad. She couldn't even write to April and ask her because they had no proper pencils or paper left, and Aunt Irini had forgotten to buy some in the grocery. April would probably have a new best friend by now anyway, she thought sadly.

A single tear, like a fat raindrop, ran down Elena's cheek. Instead of letting others follow it, she reached for the last pencil stub and added a *PS* in thick black writing to her letter.

33

Tonight, I do dream of Elena, an Elena who is no more a child nor yet adult. She's in Georgios' tavern, which is silent, no music playing, looking sad rather than her usual cheery self because I forgot to tell Nicole about the picture of the tree houses. All the while she's in front of me, speaking, her voice doesn't take away the silence, and Elena herself, she's familiar and different at the same time – still ten years old though and I'm not. 'You see,' she mourns, 'you do not remember me. You are not interested to be my friend any more.' Then her hair is wild about her face, and she isn't Elena any more but a stranger. 'Do you not want me?' Do you not want me as I want you? Why did you not tell me?' So says this stranger, and when I look again it's a smiling Nicole.

I wake with a jolt, Georgios' photo of the tree houses in the forefront of my mind. How could I have forgotten that? I let Jake distract me to that extent. All I can do is go back to the tavern and collect it in the morning. It feels an age to wait; I'm itching to compare it with my own photo. Sleepless, I try and cross thirty years to happen upon a dormant clue. I asked Elena for stories about Cyprus as if they were fairy tales, drinking in exotic and distant worlds where colours were bright and magic happened. Elena was good at telling stories; fact or fiction, we both believed them implicitly. One day, Elena told me, when we were grown-up and could do what we liked, she would show me her island, we would stay in the tree houses, play with her friend Mamun – who Krista crowed was Elena's boyfriend but that was plain silly – and bring our Easter baskets to the monastery, riding on donkeys, wearing the flowery bonnets that her Mama and Aunt Irini always made. All I could visualise was a distorted Nativity scene but it sounded wonderful.

'Don't you miss it?' I asked, wistful on her behalf, homesick for her.

'Yes,' she said, 'but I would miss you more if I were there without you.' She still looked a bit sad though.

It gave me a great idea: I would give Elena a present of a tree house right here, in England. There were no trees in our close – that didn't matter, Elena's tree houses didn't have trees either – and I had a garden, a long, thin one with my dad's shed at the bottom. Dad listened carefully to Elena's description of her tree houses – she finally conceded we didn't need a bathroom – and even drew a little plan. He built us an extension behind his shed: five steps up to a platform where a little house sat, and the little house had a window where we could squeeze out and get onto the roof of the shed. It was a tiny space, room enough for us to sit side by side under a shelf holding two SodaStream bottles and a packet of crisps each.

I unveiled it for her at Easter; I remember exactly the Cadbury Creme Eggs we took up there, the first we'd ever had, and later, back in the house, playing Elena's gift to me of 'The Wombling Song'. I was speechless. The Wombles were big that year and I'd never owned a record before.

It was bliss. For three months, it was bliss. Then it ended.

'Well, it would, Ape, wouldn't it? Had to. Think about it.' I hear echoes of Jake, the kind of pseudo-philosophical debate he professes to love. 'I mean, if bliss were constant we wouldn't know it was blissful so it would be just ordinary...'

No. No, no. Bad enough he's across the street, he's not invading my dreams any longer with the tortuous arguments that might be theoretical concepts or pretentious prattle. I'd rather have 'The Wombling Song' in all its glory. Or there was another record… whatever was it? The one Krista loved so much she slept with the sleeve under her pillow.

I give in. I climb out of bed and gather up my picture of Elena and, with a lot of effort, I wake up Nicole. She doesn't seem to mind, though it takes her a while to comprehend why I've shaken her awake at four o'clock in the morning when there's no evidence of fire, flood or pestilence.

'Is it Jake?' she asks, groggily. 'You do not have second thoughts?'

'No, no.' I'm impatient. 'I dreamed about Elena. You and Elena. She was cross because I forgot to tell you about the best thing of the evening.'

'There was a best thing?' That rouses her.

I explain, she comes to life, and we both pore over the scraps of history. Nicole is bemused she never noticed Georgios' print before.

'Why would you?' I ask her. 'You didn't know about Elena till a few days ago. You and I only met…' I count back. '… three Sundays ago.' I look at her in disbelief, it really is disbelief, and I see it mirrored in her eyes. 'And we might be calling these things tree houses, but they're not really, not in any true sense of the word.' I picture Georgios' tavern. 'And I had to climb to see that particular frame, anyway.'

'I do not know if there were many places like this.' She taps the photo and answers the question I formed earlier. 'I think not, but I really know so little. So very little,' she repeats and shakes her head. 'I am intrigued by you… by your story, April. By Elena. And, belatedly, by the story of Damaris. Remember, in 1974 I was a little girl then too, although I lived in Polis, far on the west coast, and then went to Athens to school and to university. Of all Greek Cypriots, people like me were affected least.' She wriggles under the blankets and looks down at her hands. 'Perhaps it is hard for you to accept, and it is shameful for me to admit, but I have rarely thought of the life of my contemporaries.'

'You forget you're talking to the only known surviving member of the Zarney family,' I say. 'The one who knows nothing, truly nothing, Nicole, about her past.'

She stabs the black-and-white picture with a long pink nail. 'We will make it a mission to find out about these tree houses, yes? We will beg, borrow or steal the newspaper cutting from Georgios, who will take great pleasure in being involved. But in the daytime, April. Remember, tomorrow is another early start. This time to the mountains.' Then she sits bolt upright. 'Did I really say that? Did I let such a middle-aged remark escape my lips? I am spending too much time with Yiannis. Save me, April Rose, save me.'

'Seasons in the Sun'.

It was Terry Jacks back then, the original. Krista's favourite song – those sentimental first lines – comes to me when we're in Yiannis' minibus part way through a 'Maybe two hours, maybe more' journey towards the Troodos Mountains. I've reluctantly filed away the tree houses for the day, as they're on the sea and we're heading inland, climbing higher with every twist and turn. And Elena never, ever mentioned Troodos or the mountain range anyway. This trip is Yiannis' baby.

In the minibus with me are Nicole and Red, who's been conspicuously absent, working hard to a deadline. There's also Kevin and, to my surprise, Petros – he's freed up by leaving Jarlath, in whom he has 'every faith', in charge at Verena Bay. And Jake, who has replaced Andreas. (He seemed only too relieved to give up the last seat.) We are stand-ins for the intrepid orchid hunters Yiannis imagines taking on future tours. In years to come I *can* see him hosting small and dedicated groups of experts, keen to share photographs, watch slide shows, make copious notes and traverse the island searching the unique flora endemic to Cyprus. Kotschy's bee orchid, for example, or maybe Casey's larkspur, probably the rarest plant on the island.

Pleased with my study of Yiannis' botany guide, I settle further down into my seat, and rehearse those names some more, saving them up for a casual conversation drop later on. I haven't a clue about Kotschy or Casey, or the flowers named after them, but overnight have belatedly skimmed Yiannis' textbook. In my world, orchids will always be the exotic hothouse variety in a pot, sitting on the windowsill. Jake bought me one; it came with a list of instructions (plus his own) which made me think a pedigree puppy needed less care. I'm cheered to think how the flower actually sits happily at my kitchen window, sucking up the tepid water I splash on it whenever I'm passing, and blooming copiously when inclined. I hope my sub-letting tenants don't upset it.

Poor Yiannis though, dumped with a set of ignorant flora-philistines who are hijacking his cause at every turn. I'm by far the worst culprit: once his romantic hope, I've been distracted with amateur modelling, burying human remains in his garden, dates in the local tavern and memories of Elena. Yiannis accepts it all with grave politeness. Jake, of all people, has given him a new lease of life, bounding in, spouting Latin and enthusing over Yiannis' own learned publications. Right now, Jake's up front, approving Yiannis' use of 'The alphabetical rather than taxonomic order of the binomial names.'

'My sentiments exactly,' Petros calls. 'That is precisely how I arrange my pantry for ease of stocktaking.' Beside him, Kevin – who is 'along for the craic' (he had to explain that very carefully to a worried Yiannis) – sniggers like a schoolboy.

Beside Yiannis, who's trying to concentrate on driving, Jake's now nodding like a scholarly professor. 'Obviously, Yiannis, we'll be seeing the *Ophrys kotschyi*, and personally, I'm hoping for the *Orchis punctulata*.'

'We can hope,' Yiannis agrees. 'The bee orchid is relatively common, more so at Karpass but the punctate orchid is a rarer species altogether, so I cannot guarantee it.'

'Of course you cannot.' This is Nicole from next to me. She leans forward and gives a beaming smile, switching it between Yiannis and Jake. 'Personally – forgive me for this, Yiannis – I would like to see the *Chelonia mydas* and the *Caretta caretta*. Do you agree, Jake?'

Jake nods some more, but impatiently, as if viewing those species is obvious. He doesn't fool me; he's got no more idea what Nicole has said than the rest of us in the back and he's itching to note down the Latin and go and look it up. Yiannis looks uncomfortably at Nicole. He opens his mouth, but she beats him to it.

'We arrive shortly in Platres, do we not, Yiannis?' It's blatant misdirection. 'So we should concentrate on today's sightseeing, yes?'

'What did you say? The Latin, to Jake just then,' I ask Nicole in an undertone a few minutes later as we get down from the minibus in the deserted square of Troodos village. We've climbed steadily higher on ribbons of roads and into green forest, the whole landscape altered from beach life below. Here, we need fleeces and sweaters to compensate for the cooler temperatures – Petros remembers skiing in March or April, but there's no late snow this year.

Nicole looks at me, and at Red behind me, from under her lashes. 'Do you think Jake understood me?'

'He didn't.' I couldn't be more certain. 'Yiannis did, but not Jake.'

'I was being clever. Actually, I was being unkind,' she admits. 'I said I wanted to see the *Chelonia mydas* and the *Caretta caretta*,' she repeats carefully. 'These are not orchids or any other kind of plants. They are sea turtles. And they do not lay eggs or hatch until later in the year anyway.'

I laugh. I know it's not kind, but Jake sounded so pompous, it serves him right.

Red grins too. 'You are a wicked woman, Ms Koumettou,' he says, adding, 'All I will say is that Jake is a man who could dole out confidence to Yiannis and still have reserves galore.'

'Ah. You've managed some long-into-the-night chats with Jake, have you, Red?' I pat his arm in consolation.

He nods. 'Indeed, I have.'

'Interested in theology, is he?'

'I think you could say that.'

'You'll just have to offer it up as a test of faith.'

'Another one?'

We both grin and Nicole narrows her eyes. 'Now the joke is on me,' she complains. 'Come on, the day awaits. It might be interesting.'

What Yiannis has done, very smartly, is scale down any lingering intellectual aspirations. Instead of a diehard hike into the forest interior, seeking rare species easily missed and even more easily trampled, we're going to spend the morning strolling gently around the Persephone Trail and the afternoon at the Trooditissa Monastery. 'Few endemic orchids in April, even fewer rare ones, but a solid introduction to the topography of Cyprus,' Yiannis explains.

I almost feel like a carefree holidaymaker, wandering and watching – and noticing every now and again I'm still humming 'Seasons in the Sun'.

Apparently, we're walking through black pine trees and junipers, and Yiannis identifies sage and St John's wort, dog rose and catmint. It's a beautiful morning in a beautiful location, and we're regrouping at the Makria Kondarka viewpoint, the most spectacular spot of all that Yiannis says marks the halfway point of the trail. It's the kind of scene that pans out of a black-and-white movie, plaintive violins swelling out into a grand orchestral finale as Cary Grant sweeps Audrey Hepburn into a romantic clinch and *The End* fills the screen. I stand and stare and wish... well, I'm not sure what I'm wishing. Right now, this, being here, is enough.

The others peel away and when I reach the top, Petros is already unpacking a picnic, and Nicole and Red are nearby, sitting against a tree, Nicole's legs stretched out in front of her. Their heads are close together and she's gesticulating as if describing a large and distant object beyond the vast tracts of Southern Cyprus visible below. I feel a sudden, ridiculous pang of envy, slow down again and bend, apparently comparing some floral gem with the illustration in Yiannis' guidebook. There's nothing to stop me joining them, my two suddenly, newly favourite people, nothing but an invisible and inexplicable barrier of oversensitivity. So why do I have my nose to the grass, minutes away from being caught out?

'April. April? Come on up here.'

I snap the book shut and jump up. Nicole is standing now, shading her eyes against the sun. She's waving at me.

I'm a fool. All that nonsense I was spouting to Red and Petros about finding a more laid-back Cypriot-April; she keeps going AWOL.

'Kevin. Yiannis. You too.' Nicole's looking past me now and I glance over my shoulder and walk on slowly enough for them to catch me, steering away from the orchid-less piece of ground in which I was scrabbling. We all three troop up the slope together.

'Was there nothing of interest, April?' asks Yiannis. 'You looked so concentrated. I said to Kevin you must have found something.'

'He did,' Kevin confirms. 'I thought meself I had one of the orchid lads back up the way but it was a variegated daisy or a tulip or something.'

'We need to study more, fellow dunce,' I tell him.

'Oh no,' says Yiannis. 'You need only to enjoy your holidays. For me, this is pleasant. Most relaxing. You may laugh, but seeking out the rare and beautiful becomes very competitive between those who would be experts. It is often rewarding, but less fun than this.'

I can see Kevin musing on definitions of 'fun' as we reach the others.

Yiannis indicates the food and then the vista around us, pointing out the old Amiantos asbestos mine, and up to the summit of Mount Olympus. 'Chionistra, as the Cypriots know it,' he says, then, 'Coffee, honey cake and a view; perfect for one's body and spirit.'

Jake is the laggard this morning, it's unlike him, and I'm just about to comment when there's a cartoon yodel and he rounds the corner, camera ahoy.

'I got it.' He runs up, breathless. 'I'm sure I got it.' He beams at us. 'The *Platanthera holmboei*. Holmboe's butterfly orchid.' Jake is triumphant, and waves his camera again. 'I'll get the film developed back at Troodos village. You'll see.'

'You want to get one of those digital ones,' Kevin says.

'What does it look like, Jake? The butterfly orchid?' Nicole asks him. 'I don't think I've ever seen one.'

'Personally, I'd rename it the elephant orchid. It's not flowering yet, of course, but it's one of the larger stems and it has a horizontal spur...' The description trips off Jake's tongue. He must realise we're none the wiser; he looks around and spies Yiannis' book on the ground in front of me. 'April, pass me that.' He flicks through it. 'See? Here.' He stabs the page and we look in turn, with various murmurs of interest.

'It looks like the kind of embryonic beanstalk Jack would hesitate to climb,' Red says.

'What do you think, Yiannis?' Jake turns to the – noticeably silent – botanist who has been collecting up cups. He sits back on his heels and takes the book.

'Your description sounds correct,' Yiannis agrees. 'And if it is a sighting, it is worth documenting as very unusual. The Holmboe is rarely seen here, so high up and so early in the year. I have seen it only on the Artemis Trail in August.'

'Oh.' Jake is a study in outraged versus crestfallen. 'You think I'm wrong.'

Yiannis shakes his head. 'Like people, nature constantly surprises us, Jake. Of course it is possible. We must get the photograph developed with haste. The key is in these markings, here, under the stem. You see?'

Mollified, Jake munches cake, swigs coffee and launches into a rundown of the tricky way he had to lean in, over, under and down to capture his shot. I wonder if I'm the only one who notices how Yiannis doesn't jump up and start immediately retracing our steps to find the so-called orchid. When I catch Nicole's eye and she gives a faint wink, I know I'm not. Still, Jake's enthusiasm is infectious; we all clearly hope he has struck gold and are more than prepared to recognise it as such in his photo.

When Yiannis proposes we move on, we stand up obediently and start gathering our belongings. Red nudges an apparently sleeping Kevin with his foot; Kevin opens half an eye.

'These things called Morning Time and Fresh Air do take it out of you until you're used to them.' Red hauls him up.

'Yo-ho, bro. Isn't "Stop it with thy sarcasm" one of the Ten Commandments?' But he too jumps up, takes the heaviest rucksack from Petros, and we're soon on our way back to Troodos village, paired off in a neat crocodile.

'Those two make a perfect couple, don't they?' Petros says, beside me. He's watching Nicole and Red, together again, ahead of us. Then he looks at me, the game-playing Petros. 'Oh, I mean in looks,' he says, after a pause. 'Both so handsome but such a contrast of fair and dark.'

'Shame they're both engaged elsewhere.'

'Indeed. Life would be dull if we all matched so conveniently.'

'Are you making some kind of obtuse point, Petros?' I ask him.

He raises his hands, palms up. 'Me? Never. A simple observation. We've had so little time to talk recently, you and me. And, now we have a little time, there is something I'd like to say.'

'Okaaay?' I don't mean to sound so tentative but these few short weeks have been an outpouring of the unexpected. Of course, Petros picks up on my tone, and roars with laughter – which is immediately reassuring.

'No marriage proposal, or suggestion that you invest in

my business, or whatever other unholy invitation is going through your mind,' he says. 'What a low opinion you have of me, my dear April.'

I smile at that. 'Then what?'

He looks serious suddenly. 'I just want to say that for as long as Verena Bay is in my hands, and I hope that is for many more years, you need never be alone or lonely. You are always welcome, for long periods and short. It is only fitting that if your parents have their final home in Cyprus, you do too. No,' he adds, as I go to open my mouth, 'say nothing, just know it. We are family, in an odd sort of way.' He wrinkles his nose, breaking the tension.

'Very odd.' I give a sort of dry sob, then giggle, leaning in to hug him. 'But oddly perfect.'

34

Midday, and Yiannis leads us like a latter-day evangelist, from the village of Platres through the forest. It's a tranquil and somehow timeless place, like a remote annex of Minerva House's secret garden. On a day charged with low cloud, looking up through the pine trees to Trooditissa Monastery is like glimpsing Narnia, in my mind accompanied by the dissonant flute arpeggios of 'Peter and the Wolf'.

Yiannis opens his arms to it expansively, as if in supplication. 'So, friends, the monastery was founded in the thirteenth century where resided a hermit monk during the years of the iconoclasm. The present church dates back to the year 1731. It is Orthodox in belief, dedicated to the Virgin Mary...'

I practise the art of looking politely attentive whilst actively tuning out. I'm interested but I never find it easy to retain tour-guide-type facts and Yiannis has it off pat.

My brain is only dragged back by his teaser to 'Take care before trying on the silver-coated belt at the Trooditissa altar. Children, possibly a whole brood, are sure to follow.'

'Thia Ana wrote that off as a religious *Cinderella*,' Petros notes, taking a pack of cigarettes from his pocket and offering one to Nicole.

'*What?*' I mouth to her, as she shakes her head at Petros, and he moves off to the side of the trail to smoke alone. The others have already wandered off. I can see Red at the other side of the monastery's courtyard and making for the main door, either eager to pray or to shake off Jake, I think. Or to avoid me. I'm sure he's keeping a circumspect distance, which is probably sensible.

'I knew you were dreaming,' Nicole says to me. 'By tradition, women who want to conceive come here and ask the Virgin Mary to intercede.' She raises her voice. 'Come, Yiannis, it is simply an example of positive thinking. I have deliberately tried it on five times and there is no effect.'

'Each time with a genuine desire for children?' Yiannis says with such ease, he already knows the answer.

'Never,' says Nicole. 'Merely to challenge the nonsense.'

'Which is why it does not work.' Yiannis smiles at her. 'Without faith, your actions are meaningless.'

'This is my argument exactly.' Nicole is triumphant. 'Positive thinking.'

In the grounds of the monastery, Nicole and I stroll around the outside of the buildings, all framed by the towering forest. Rain spits in the air and we duck into the chapel. It's like another world. Not just beautiful and intricately decorated, but... I search for the word... *golden*. It's golden. The simple, spiritual space that once was home to a hermit is a sophisticated religious museum, albeit a working one. I expected a simple hymn-tune and I've got a symphony.

Red is sitting in a pew about halfway up the aisle, his right foot moving infinitesimally to some internal beat. With his eyes fixed on the altar he might, indeed, be praying or dreaming. When Nicole and I slide in beside him he jumps slightly and grins.

'Sorry,' he whispers. 'I was half asleep. Don't tell.'

'Does it not instil a sense of reverence?' I ask him, half serious.

He matches my tone. 'Ah, April, one of those eternal questions: can a place instil reverence or does it come from within?'

'You've definitely been spending too much time with a certain mutual... friend,' I say.

Red grins again, but he doesn't deny it. I turn to Nicole, who's looking slightly perplexed.

'We're mocking Jake,' I admit. 'That's the kind of light, philosophical banter he likes to indulge in during the wee small hours.' Not for much longer, I bet. I can't imagine the baby or Erica wanting it alongside 3 a.m. feeds.

'Actually, you weren't far off the mark, April,' Red says. 'I was wondering what it's like to be part of monastery life here. Living, praying and working for the greater good in surroundings like these. Would it be uplifting or distracting?'

'Less distracting than the outside world, no?'

I flush and twist around to hide it, apparently making a study of the icons spanning the walls and glad that Nicole's words are cut off when the outer door clatters open. The three of us turn as one to watch Jake's entrance. He grimaces and creeps up the aisle on tiptoe, where we obediently shuffle up the pew. His hair and face are wet with rain; he must have left his outer coat in the porch and I can't help but notice how clerical he looks, dressed head to toe in black with the line of a white t-shirt at his neck. Unlike Red, in his stonewashed jeans and greenish wax jacket.

'It's coming down a storm out there.' Jake gives a mock shiver. 'You all found sanctuary ahead of it.' He looks around approvingly. 'Isn't it something, all of this. It must be so much easier to keep your faith in such a stunning place.'

We all titter, and Jake looks mildly affronted – as well he might.

'What? What's funny?'

Red gives him the gist and Jake nods, as if it were exactly as he suspected.

'Well, it does it for me,' he declares. Then he looks at me. 'Go on then, April. What's the soundtrack?'

'Tchaikovsky. "Hymn of the Cherubim".' I don't hesitate.

It might be Russian rather than Greek, but it's been on the fringes of my mind since we came in.

'Choral music?' Nicole hazards.

'The only Tchaikovsky I know is *Swan Lake*.' Red sounds apologetic. 'That was him, wasn't it? Can you hum—'

With the faultless timing of a French farce, the porch door clunks open again and this time four of us turn to see Petros and Yiannis, Kevin on their heels. Like guests seeking out the appropriate side at a wedding, they troop down the aisle and squeeze into the pew behind us. I brace myself for the same conversation, take three, but Yiannis is here by design.

'At this hour there is a short service in the chapel,' he explains in a low voice. 'The monks sing the noon office, the Angelus. All visitors are welcome, but if you prefer not to stay…'

'Yous can hop it,' Kevin finishes cheerily, but his voice is moderated too. 'Literally. The rain's hopping frogs out there; cats and dogs, you name it.'

'A spring shower.' Petros shrugs. 'The fanciful might say it's a sign to rest here and reflect.'

I don't know if any of us would have left, but it's too late. A *ssh* from Jake quells the nonsense and we sit, the only congregation, as an octet of brown-robed monks enters the choir stalls from a side entrance and with perfect precision and absolute pitch engage in a Byzantine chant I've never heard before. It'll be from the Orthodox Liturgy. Yiannis probably knows, but it's so beautiful I'm glad I didn't attempt to hum a few echoey bars of the Tchaikovsky for Red.

Actually, beautiful doesn't cover it. This music is haunting, mesmerising. It grows overwhelming as the sound rises and falls and tugs me with it somewhere else, somewhere beyond, somewhere—

I gasp and stiffen, so much so that Nicole looks anxiously at me before moving gently to put her hand over mine. But the moment – no, not even that, a second or two – has passed and I turn my palm up and squeeze her hand in reassurance.

As the music fades, so does the feeling, leaving only a shadow of… of… regret? Euphoria? Relief? I've both too many words and not enough because, musician or not, I've never had such a visceral response to any music ever before. It's less déjà vu than a past-present collision that I can't explain.

Whatever it is though, I'm convinced that for the first time Elena is, fleetingly, tantalisingly, here.

35

A church in Cyprus
A night in August 1974

They came by night and now they were leaving by night. That was how it worked and it didn't even seem so strange any more. But where they were, Elena still didn't know. It was the second time they had moved after the tree houses, and the fourth time since those men had come to the hotel in Varosha with their guns and their loudhailers, ordering everyone to get out – or else. They moved from village to village pretending it was a normal thing to do, even though it was the oddest trip ever. In the days they kept inside, in the kitchens or playing in the cellar if the house was bigger. Sometimes the animals wandered in and out of the houses, more at home than they were. The night Elena slept on a straw cot on the floor, she was sure that pigs or cows had been put outside so she could take their bed.

They weren't hiding, Aunt Irini said, not really, just being careful.

'But where are we?' Elena had asked the first time, and the second, the third...

'In the village,' someone, Irini or one of the aunties, would answer quickly before they asked Elena or Krista to wash the vegetables or put out the tea things. Elena's 'What village?' was never heard in the general hubbub of preparing the endless food. It was Antony who took her aside and whispered, 'Best not to know, Elena. I'll explain why one day, I promise, but for now just be a good girl and pretend everything's okay.'

So, the next time, she said nothing. She waited and she pretended.

Tonight, this place was different. They had trundled off in a covered farm wagon, which in sunny days would have been a haven for counting and sorting the lemons or oranges picked from the trees and thrown into baskets and into the trailer, but in the dark it rumbled and shuddered like a distant earthquake, bruising their bodies and bones. When they jumped down, one at a time, onto gorse-like grass under a canopy of pine trees, Elena was as unsteady as if she'd been on a ship, the vibrations still coursing through her. She gritted her teeth, ready to walk uphill for silent miles, *pretending* she was alright and that the distant sound of rushing water – maybe a waterfall, she thought, beside a bridge and a picnic site laid out with halloumi and olives, cups of goat's milk to drink... Then she blinked and shook her head. The image was so strong Elena wondered if she had been here in her before-life, and it was a few seconds before she realised that Antony, leading them, had stopped.

Their feet crunched across the hard ground towards a white building with a red roof, which loomed over them as if it were pushing the trees back. Aunt Irini hurried them towards a big arch, one that Elena guessed was the entrance to a church, and she thought suddenly how she and April had watched *The Sound of Music*, sung along and willed the von Trapps to freedom as they sought sanctuary in a church. Was this what the Zacharia family were doing? Elena sighed. It would be an interesting thing to write in her next letter but it was nothing like the films.

She tugged at Aunt Irini's hand, hopefully. 'Are there nuns here?'

'Not nuns. Monks,' Irini whispered. 'Panagia.' She put her fingers to her lips. 'Come.'

It was dim inside but once their eyes adjusted, Sofia shrank back and had to be picked up by Antony. She buried her head in his shoulder. Elena could see why: from the walls, a line of stern and bearded old men glowered down at them, 'Putting the fear of God into you,' Mama would have said. They were icons, she knew, holy pictures of saints.

'Why do they have to be so mean-looking?' Krista nudged her. 'Probably they're mad they're not as important as Christ and the Holy Virgin.' Clearly pleased with herself, Krista stared up at them, humming under her breath as if she wasn't bothered by hiding in a church in the mountains in the middle of the night.

Elena looked around for the altar, wondering if they were expected to pray, but Aunt Irini pulled them into a pew at the back.

'We're only waiting here for a little while,' she said. 'Until the sun comes up and we get another lift. We're perfectly safe, so you should try and sleep.'

'Er... where?' Krista looked round scornfully.

'Here. Lean on me.' Irini had her brisk teacher's voice on, even in an undertone. 'Or you can read a Bible. Or you can pray.'

Krista huffed but she didn't argue. Instead she shuffled along the pew to the far end away from their aunt and Antony who was next to her, Sofia on his knee, and motioned for Elena to follow her.

'Can I write?' Elena asked first. 'I can write my prayers,' she added, knowing that Aunt Irini couldn't really argue with that and then wondering if little half-lies were turning her into Krista.

Feeling guilty, Elena took out her pencil and paper from her pocket. Maybe she wouldn't write a letter to April. She had a flash of inspiration. What if she wrote to God or to

Our Lady of Troodos? Nobody had said they were in the mountains but they were high up, with valleys beneath them, so it was her best guess, even if her lips were sealed. Elena chewed the end of her pencil and decided to be cautious.

Dear God and all the Saints,

This is Elena Zacharia. We are in one of your houses, and I think I know which one but I won't write it because then if someone asks me I can't tell the truth or a lie because I don't know. Not knowing is safer. We are hiding here to be safe. Please keep us all and my mama and Stefan safe. Please also look after my friend April in England. And...

And what? Elena read back over what she'd written, disappointed that it wasn't very good and that she couldn't think what else to say. Maybe it was enough.

She must have nodded to sleep because the next thing she knew, the paper had fallen from her knee and fluttered to the ground. Just in time, Elena caught her pencil from clattering down too and waking the others. There was a scratching sound... a mouse? She tensed and drew her feet up, before looking to one side and realising it was Krista. Her sister was kneeling on the ground, her head resting on the back of the pew in front of her. Was *she* praying? Elena shifted along her seat as quietly as she could, causing Krista to raise her head.

'What are you doing?' Elena signed – knowing sign language was very useful sometimes, even when the other person wasn't deaf.

Krista sat back and smiled what she thought was her mysterious smile. She shrugged. 'Look,' she signed back.

Elena leaned over, noticing there was a single loose screw abandoned on the little shelf that ran along the back of the seats. She had a bad feeling about this. When Elena saw what the smug-looking Krista had done, she gave a sigh. Saying nothing, she went back to her piece of paper and added a postscript, hoping if God was there watching, he wouldn't send a thunderbolt down. Or a war.

And... Please God forgive Krista for scratching <u>my</u> name in the wood of the pew in the back row.

Elena Zacharia in August 1974

36

On the way back from the mountains, I try to relive whatever it was I experienced in Trooditissa but it's gone. 'A goose walked over my grave', isn't that how the saying goes? Something to do with goosebumps, I guess, which is true; it wasn't creepy, not spiritual either, just startling, and Elena flashed into my mind. I can recall the music note for note but not the feeling, just a faint echo of connection or recognition that's cooling with the miles we travel. I don't discuss it with the others because it's obvious I can't find the words. Two hours later, pulling into the grounds of Verena Bay, I've filed it away as an atypical déjà vu, the power of suggestion.

It's not late at all, it only seems that way because we left before dawn to make the most of the day. Petros took over the drive home and, flooring the engine on the main road from Limassol, he cut a good half an hour off Yiannis' hands-at-ten-to-two sedateness. Everyone's comments are turning food-related, when Petros calls for hush.

'Dinner will be ready and waiting,' he calls over the hubbub of doors opening and slamming. I might be the only one who hears him follow that with a muttered, 'At least, I hope it is so.'

I catch his eye and Petros gives a discreet fingers-crossed sign. Of course. I'd forgotten it was Jarlath's time to shine. Red and Kevin seem to remember this at the same time as they disappear together into the main door, looking as if they're off to offer moral support – or damage limitation.

Nicole, who has moved to the passenger seat of the minibus, winds down the window. 'I am going to bring Andreas and Damaris and Orestes over. Yiannis alone will take no for an answer but I think they will enjoy themselves. *Yassou*.'

'A good day?' Petros says as he and I make our leisurely way inside, me seriously admiring Petros for not barrelling off to the kitchen to see what's going on.

'A lovely day,' I agree. 'I think Yiannis will do really well with the orchid holidays.'

Petros opens his mouth to reply, when who but Jarlath emerges from the bar area, looking neat and cool. 'The man of the hour,' Petros says. 'Is... er...'

'Is there anything you can do? Is everything under control? Is the kitchen, bar, hotel in general all in one piece?' Jarlath grins. 'It's all mighty. And the brothers have already been in to check. How're yous both?'

Good, fine, we're agreeing, when Jarlath's face changes.

'Sure, there is one thing,' he announces. 'It's you, April.'

'Me?'

'Yeah. I'll be needing your room from tomorrow, if that's okay?' He holds a hand up. 'Nothing personal. I'm kicking out our father too.' He beams at me.

'What...?' Petros scratches his head.

'I've let both rooms and the rest of the stable block. At double your rates, Petros. How's that then? I'll make sure your stuff's moved for you, fair dos. You to Nicole's guest room and Red to Yiannis' place. Alright?' Without waiting for an answer, he gives a general wave and sets off towards the dining room. Then he stops and looks back over his shoulder. 'You know, I might just have found what I want to do when I grow up,' he says before disappearing round the corner.

'Well,' I say.

'Well,' Petros agrees. Then he gives a bark of laughter. 'I

think Thia Ana will be dancing with joy in her grave tonight. Who would have thought her mantle would fall on an Irish boy who came in fancy dress?'

In the room that won't be mine for much longer, I decide that whereas English-April would change hurriedly and be back in the bar in ten minutes, hovering anxiously, Cypriot-April would take a refreshing shower, choose her nicest dress for the evening and arrive for dinner in perfect time. It takes most of my willpower to hold back, but I manage it. I stand in the doorway to the semi-private room (aka 'the overflow') between the bar and the dining room, watching all these people: friends – Petros aside, oh, and Jake, of course – that a month ago were strangers. Even Georgios is here, his back to me, while he fiddles with the knobs on something that looks like a giant ghetto blaster.

Damaris sees me first. 'April, there you are.' She sounds pleased and everyone else looks up at her words; they all smile too, except Andreas. I have a sudden rush of belonging.

'I should have painted her framed in that doorway,' is what Andreas says. 'She has The Look.' He points a butter knife at me accusingly. 'The Look I had to force from her at the upstairs window.'

'Sketch it now.' Nicole pats his shoulder briefly as she squeezes past to place a tray of drinks on the table. She's wearing a long yellow dress that makes her look like sunshine.

'It has gone,' he grumbles. 'It disappeared when she knew we had seen her. Never mind. I have it in the eye of my mind. I will go to trace it now.' He gets up with such haste that his chair scrapes like an agonised violin against the floor tiles and a couple of knives clatter to the floor as percussion.

Everyone else is unmoved. I hug Damaris, Orestes too, who struggles up from his seat at the table, kisses me on both cheeks and then holds me at arm's length, as if sizing up a favourite niece.

'April, let me look at you,' he says, winking faintly. 'The person responsible for the return of my wife to Famagusta. She is a changed woman.'

'Such sentimental nonsense.' Damaris denies it. 'People do not change, they just become more of themselves. It was a plan of double convenience, April, was it not?'

'Serendipitous?'

She snorts again. 'You are as bad as he.' She turns to Nicole. 'What have you to say, daughter-in-law?'

Nicole holds up her hands, palms out. 'Do not involve me. I was simply the chauffeur.'

'Simply nothing, madam. You were the, the – conductor?' Damaris points at me. 'Do I mean conductor?'

'Orchestrator?'

'Yes, that is it.' Damaris sits down, self-righteously, hands clasped in front of her as if she has won something.

'We will not argue the semantics,' Orestes says. 'But,' he leans over and puts one of his hands on top of Damaris', 'I shall concede. Perhaps not a changed woman, but one who has unbent a little and walks easier for it?'

'If you think such miracles occur in one day after thirty years of displacement, then it is a relief to medicine you are not a psychiatrist,' she shoots back, but she does not remove her hands, she turns them over so she is holding his and I see him squeeze her fingers.

'Decades of stubborn thread is not unpicked in an afternoon,' he agrees quietly.

Damaris speaks again, quietly, and it's at Orestes she's looking. 'My grudge remains justified; what happened to us, to our home, was a travesty. What I *have* lost, what is best lost, is my longing for the life we had. Because I saw that life does not exist. I saw it in the St Nicholas Church. I saw it at the Palm Beach Hotel. I saw it in Salamis. I saw it in one split second. I am a foolish old woman.'

'No—'

'A foolish old woman. But today, I am beginning to be a

little less foolish.' Her lips twitch into a semi-smile. 'A little more accepting.'

'It has been a long time coming,' Orestes says, and they continue to look at each other, in their own private world, until Orestes puts his hand out to me, and Damaris hers to Nicole, and their world becomes big enough for all of us. Consciously, I check my feelings and it's not embarrassing, not sentimental, just real. I even find myself a little disappointed that they don't start to sing like last time.

Damaris breaks the mood. 'Enough of such bonding or disclosing or whatever is the American psychobabble. Now it is my turn to... orchestrate. You two,' she nods at Nicole and me, 'tomorrow at noon. It is a mystery tour.'

Before either of us can comment – not, I'm sure, that it would do any good – a cheer goes up from Georgios and he claps his hands. 'Music!' he shouts.

Nicole looks at my face and laughs her ungainly laugh even louder than Petros did earlier. 'Karaoke,' she says. 'A speciality of Georgios. And it is your fault, April.'

'Mine?'

She nods. 'He says how you and Jake were very interested when you had dinner at the tavern, so he has come tonight to... er... "pleasure" your ears.'

Kevin overhears that and also laughs. 'Me an' Jarl had better get a few jars down us, so.' He looks speculatively towards his brother, who's overseeing the buffet. 'If he's not on the wagon.'

'Do not worry,' Nicole says. 'Georgios is more than happy with a one-man concert. He is a frustrated performer. You will see after dinner.'

Dinner is pure Verena Bay. Jarlath hasn't masterminded a new menu and whipped up haute cuisine, he's done what Petros has been doing for years, with a cheerful, 'If it ain't broke, don't fix it,' and has managed to hit the right spot, and Petros' stiff shoulders (which he insists are from the unaccustomed minibus driving) drop as the evening progresses.

'You are not indispensable after all, old man.' Andreas raises a glass and calls down the table.

'I am, however, an excellent judge of character,' he replies, and calls a toast to Jarlath, who brushes it off even as he looks pleased – and as relieved as Petros.

'Do you think Petros has just found himself an assistant manager?' Red murmurs to me.

'It does look like the medical profession is fighting the hospitality industry and losing,' I reply. Red's on my right and, okay, I admit I was really pleased when he sat down there. I think he's been avoiding me, and while I've been practising 'out of sight, out of mind' (it's not like I haven't plenty of distractions), his proximity tests my good intentions. The whatever-it-is between us is solidly there but it's not uncomfortable. I can't explain it more than that. 'Did you know he's kicked us out of our rooms?' I add. 'I'm moving in with Nicole and you're going to Yiannis.'

'Thanks for the warning.' He pauses. 'We'll be neighbours.'

'Yes.' There's the frisson, the flicker, the electricity thing again, and this time I can't think of anything to say that wouldn't be construed as flirting. 'Any time you need a cup of sugar, you know where I am,' I blurt out, then wish I could hide behind my napkin.

'You'd be my first choice,' he says.

And for a few seconds the background noise dulls and we just look at each other.

Then Red clears his throat. 'It's not for long. Our work, the book, it's done. I'll be heading home in a few days...'

'Stay,' I say. 'With me. Please. You know you want to.' Actually, I don't say that at all, or at least not out loud. What comes out is a feeble, 'Oh.'

'Look, April, I was thinking...'

But I'll never know what he was thinking because Georgios chooses this moment to clatter a spoon on a glass and call for silence. Red gives me an agonised glance, quickly replaced with a wry smile and a sort of story-of-our-lives shrug, and obediently we turn towards Georgios. And it appears that Georgios wants me up there first; he's peppering his Greek speech with 'April' and gesticulating in my direction.

'It's not what you think,' Nicole hisses across the table, and sure enough here's Georgios, with the toothiest grin ever, handing over a wrapped gift, painting-sized, and it's not going to be Andreas' portrait so—

I rip off the covering and there, in a new wooden frame, is the neatly trimmed newspaper photograph of Elena's tree houses.

'Secret!' shouts Georgios, and I'm guessing he's muddled up that with 'surprise'. No matter.

It's the same tree houses, I'm even more sure this time around, but I hesitate – wishful thinking and all that. I turn it round to show Nicole and she nods vigorously.

'It is identical to your original.' She creases her brow. 'I think so, anyway. Where is your photograph? Let us check.'

'It's upstairs.' I hand the frame to Red, watching Jake squeeze in to look over his shoulder and start to nod like an art historian viewing a lost Monet, and hurry to my room. I grab the photo, pick up the postcard of the Varosha hotel too, and then, muttering, 'What the hell,' add the *1971 Travelers' Guide* to the pile.

When I approach the dining room again, Jarlath is asking, 'Will one of yous ever spill the beans?' and my shabby little heart is delighted that Nicole (backed up by Petros, in Greek, mostly for Georgios), is filling him in before Jake can utter a word.

I pass round the book and the pictures, with a bit more explanation, and with that, the thirty-year-old half-secret of Elena is suddenly right there in the open. Nobody seems to think I'm an oddball, and everyone has an opinion. It's just like being back in the back room of the Zacharias' chip shop on a Saturday night and, it occurs to me in a flash, that's all to do with family, not with being Greek, or even with Elena herself, but with *belonging*. Something the ten-year-old (or the twenty- or thirty-year-old, it seems) me would never have understood.

The hubbub is interrupted by another spoon clattering on another glass. This time, it's Red, he who has probably had the least to say, getting to his feet.

'There's something I want to say,' he announces. He glances around before going on, and though he hasn't raised his voice, the silence is stunning. *Now that*, the performer bit of me notes, *is how to work your audience – or, in his case, congregation*. 'We all come to a crossroads in life,' he says, 'that often appears nothing much to an outsider, but to ourselves it really is a point of change, of decision-making. Think about it for a second. I know I have.' I hear what he's saying but I'm not thinking about it because my eyes are glued on him, wondering what's coming next. 'Well, fate, life, God, whatever you want to call it, has brought us all here at the crossroads of April's past and present. And so,' he's looking straight at me and smiling as he comes to his punchline, 'and so, I propose a prize for the person who finds the location of Elena's tree houses.'

37

*Somewhere in Cyprus
A night in August 1974*

Dear April and Mrs Gale's class,

This is my last night-time letter to you. Tonight we are doing the last of what the village aunties call our 'moonlight flits', which sound like something fun and dancing and happy, but aren't. I can't write with actual words while I'm waiting to go so I'm writing in my head and will remember this and copy it out later...

Aunt Irini took Krista, whose eyes were popping with excitement and the effort of keeping quiet, up the stairs out of the cellar. Then, minutes or maybe an hour later, she came back for Sofia, who barely stirred, burrowing into their aunt's shoulder as she was lifted up. Elena cuddled her knees and wished April was beside her. Outside, it was a hot, breathless night but the worn flagstones on which she sat were cold and smooth. Elena remembered being little, how the tin pitchers of milk, then as tall as her and fatter, were lined up like marching soldiers. Four times four times four, they stretched into the place Mama called the pantry at home but the dairy to the neighbours who bought milk from them. Elena, leaning against the churns, had pretended to sip her hated beaker of strong goat's milk, pouring teasing little puddles just beyond the old cat's whiskers so he had to stretch and twist his neck to lap them up. She still remembered the day the cat died. Not because she was sad, he had been old and nippy, but because it was the day they learned that baby Sofia's ears didn't work properly.

This place could be their old home in Famagusta. It looked like it, but Elena had only been four or five then; yesterday's place had looked familiar – and different – as well. She ran her hands over the smooth coolness of the stones, pressing her palms down into the shallow grooves. Her feet grew chilly, the cold creeping from toes to heels to her ankles, but in her heavy grey sweater the top half of her was sweating and itchy.

The scullery was full of blackness, black that seemed solid, touchable if only her arms were longer. April was good at not being scared. Mama said this was because she was an only-one child and had independence; she had no sisters to take care of her. Elena tried to imagine no sisters. Imagine Saturday night in England with her and April all alone, in the yellow beanbag like toads in the hole, no Krista to pinch them and kick, no bouncing Sofia. They could share their chips and tell secrets and not be interrupted by Mama and Aunt Irini to run the carpet sweeper over the lounge or go into the shop to help Stefan. They could eat other dinner too, mince or stew, which Elena didn't like very much but they were plentiful, and different to always chips. Krista said fried chips made good skin bad...

'Elena? Elena, are you ready?' Irini's soft voice made Elena jump. 'Shh,' she whispered and put her forefinger to her own lips then to Elena's. Her finger was dry and cold, soft. She shook her head slightly. 'Don't speak, just follow me. Okay?'

Irini pulled Elena to her feet, hugged her briefly and motioned her through the kitchen, strangely silent and tidy – no draining dishes piled high, no iron-ready laundry stacked precariously on the old rocking chair – and out through the back door. Irini closed it gently, turning the key in the lock with difficulty so infrequently was it used. She let her hand rest there momentarily, as if she was reluctant to go.

Hand in hand they walked slowly across the yard. Elena half expected they would crouch in the shadows, darting from bush to bush when clouds crossed the moon, fearful that the bushes would rise up as militiamen and shoot them dead. But Irini's gait was leisurely – they might have been returning home from Sunday Mass, ready to pass the time of day with villagers old and young. Only the tightness of her grip indicated that Aunt Irini was 'being careful'.

'This is it, Elena.' She bowed her head so that she was speaking like a whisper into Elena's hair. 'One more ride and tomorrow we will wake up in a new place, a place we can stay. The worst is over, darling. It's over.'

Elena wanted with all her heart to believe Irini but she couldn't. She'd finally put a name to the feeling that sat on her shoulder and weighed her down even in the ordinary parts of life. It wasn't all fear or worry or sadness. She'd looked it up in a dictionary left on the dresser shelf. It was suspicion.

38

This time, Damaris sits in the front of the car beside Nicole and I sprawl across the back seat as we bump and swerve over the narrow roads on Damaris' 'mystery tour'. She has instructed Nicole to aim for Nicosia.

'The journey to Famagusta was for me,' is what she says. '*Your* quest was the push I needed, April, and I am grateful for that. This trip today is of benefit to me but I hope also to you. And that is all I will say until we get closer. Except,' she adds, 'I have not found any tree house. Now, let us divert the subject and you can tell me how you enjoyed last evening.'

I catch Nicole's glance in the central mirror. 'I'm still wondering which part was the most surprising,' I admit. 'Jarlath's expertise, Red's challenge,' which I am definitely overthinking in private, 'or Georgios' voice. Actually, I'm lying,' I add. 'It was Georgios' voice. I'd never have thought it. I'm ashamed.'

'Nobody does,' Damaris agrees. 'A buffoon with the voice of an angel.'

'Mother-in-law! Not kind.' But Nicole is laughing.

'I only say what others are thinking,' Damaris says loftily. 'You are a musician, April, of course you agree.'

I don't know what I was expecting from Georgios when he started to sing. He'd been so kind with the picture, I was willing him not to make a fool of himself when he started up – and, okay, a bit surprised that his friends weren't protecting him but presumed because they were his friends he was safe – but the joke was well and truly on me. Georgios is the most unique tenor I've ever heard. The overtones, the resonance, of a baritone colour it. 'Think of it like caramel and honey highlights in light brown hair,' is the way I explain what I mean to Damaris and Nicole. 'When he launched into Charles Aznavour's "She" and in perfect English, it was, well, perfect.'

'Yet here he is, in Agia Triada, running his dead parents' and grandparents' mediocre tavern,' Nicole says, far more harshly than I expect.

'*Yet* we do not all have the courage to make change,' Damaris says mildly.

'Yes. I know that.'

It sounds like a rehashed argument and I wonder what the subtext is. Not wanting it to hijack Damaris' outing, I plough on, 'Tell me: does it ever actually turn into a karaoke session, Georgios' singing?'

'No,' they say in unison.

Fifty miles later, when Nicole needs more directions, Damaris navigates competently and tells us that we're going to visit her friend, Soussana.

'You will hear what she has to say about that time of war, when your friend Elena was a child,' she says. 'My friend is more balanced than I am. And my visit to her is overdue.' The remainder of the journey is a potted history. 'Soussana lives in a village on the Greek side of the divide. It was my mother's home place too, where we lived when I was a child.' Damaris changes tack to point: turn off the main road; take this side road; go along the donkey track.

The more turns we make, the more it feels like a world left behind. Here, in the old stone houses clustered around a dusty square, comprising a coffee house and bar and a small shop and dairy, is the Cyprus of my imagination.

Here, I can see in front of me, one of the unnamed 'villages' Elena and her family used to talk about.

'Stop here,' Damaris says. 'Our home was here, bought by Soussana's husband to make their home bigger. It looks well, still. Come.'

Soussana is of Damaris' age and height, twice her width, and walks on uneasy oedemic legs. She's been a widow for forty-odd years, still living in the house in which she grew up, saddened it was never filled with children. She says all of this as she squashes first Damaris, then Nicole, then me, into an all-enveloping, citrus-scented hug.

'Bah, do not feel sorry for her.' Damaris beams at her friend and they clasp hands, looking like young girls; if Soussana were not so heavy they might be dancing around in a joyful circle. 'Did she not make it her life's work to become the supreme village auntie? The oracle of all things domestic, the heiress of secrets, the gatekeeper of gossip.'

Soussana is nodding. 'Thia Damaris speaks the truth,' she agrees. 'I would have it no other way. My life is rich and does not need a fast body or a quicker mind.'

Damaris sniffs, but it doesn't hide her smile. 'And the rest of your cosy witches' coven?' she asks. 'Where, dear Soussana, are they? I have come so far to see you all.'

'It has taken you too, too long,' Soussana retorts. 'Why do you not come sooner? Why must these beautiful young women be forced to chaperone? There was a time when you came every month. What happened? Me, I am a village auntie, I do not go beyond the boundary of my land, but you, Damaris, you are a travelled woman…'

Soussana and her friends, four other equally happy and outspoken women, greet Damaris like a long-lost sister and literally gather her back into their fold. Their menfolk have been banished to the cafe, the usual evening ritual, leaving Soussana's kitchen-sitting room to the women, cackling, chattering and industrious. The traditional sewing and embroidery is piled up at one end of the table, but the other is taken up with a laptop and printer. Their mobile phones never stop ringing.

'It really is a coven,' Nicole says. 'I think they do all kinds of magic. If government was devolved here, resolution would come in days.'

I don't doubt it even as I follow only snippets of the conversation. Their speech is in loud and rapid Greek, two or three of them at a time, gesturing dramatically.

'They are fussing,' Nicole says, as we sip coffee and nibble baklavas. 'About the poor cell-phone service here, it seems their calls are constantly interrupted and the erratic dial-up connection to the internet interferes with Soussana's work.' She wrinkles her brow. 'I think she writes or maybe edits a church magazine for rural women.'

The women work like a well-oiled engine, one getting up here, one there, so that as the evening draws on, the range is checked and rechecked for the slow-cooking souvlaki, sauces stirred, salads assembled, and a meal is set out as if by magic. The men drift in, responding to some silent gong, eat, and disappear again, apparently to smoke and play backgammon. Then the women really get down to business.

Why is Nicole not yet pregnant? Does she need prayers, a special brew for her man, or an appointment at the new fertility clinic in Nicosia? Damaris looks slightly anxiously at Nicole as the interrogation is thick and fast, but Nicole laughs and takes it in good grace. At one point she blushes furiously and the assorted women roar with laughter ('They were matching penis size with the best sexual position,' she tells me later. 'I refuse to repeat the details even to you, twice-married April with admirers galore. Where do they learn such things, these old ladies?')

Nicole gives me a wicked smile and I know she's about to deflect attention to me; suddenly it's not such a hardship to be ignorant of the common language. I brace myself for the third degree but, between them, Damaris and Nicole appear to give a comprehensive résumé of my life to date. Given that they know so little of it – I've barely spoken about my relationships before Jake, I never do; I've no idea what even possessed me to tell Damaris I've been married twice – and given it takes so long, I dread to imagine the embellishments and conjecture. But the warmth and humour that radiates from Soussana and her friends is worth it all because these, as Soussana herself said, are the 'village aunties'. Elena said it too, but I hadn't understood then. Other people had aunties and uncles like they had sisters and brothers and dogs and cats, I assumed that these aunties were all of a oneness. Now I see.

'Show them your picture of the little Elena,' Damaris encourages me. 'These women, they know everything.'

I unfold the increasingly tattered letter for them, and Nicole translates it. With care, they pass around the photograph and the postcard. Each one of them inspects both closely, putting on their spectacles or holding the pictures at arm's-length, Damaris too. Gradually, the decibels rise again and soon all of the women are speaking together. Elena's postcard is set down on the table but the photograph is pored over. It's a replay of last night. Until they look expectantly at Soussana, I assume to translate.

'What is it?' I ask lightly. 'Do they recognise anything?'

'April, this is not what you think—' Nicole starts, a warning in every syllable, but Soussana interrupts her.

'Yes, yes,' she says, clearly delighted, clearly sincere. 'We recognise. Of course we recognise.'

1974 was only yesterday. Soussana's 'coven' was there in Nicosia at the time of the military coup, they saw Archbishop Makarios exiled, General Grivas disappear. They were there when the Turkish invaded, in Famagusta, in Varosha, in Pafos. They saw the naval fleet on the horizon, heard the radio news, watched people, Greek and Turkish, friends and neighbours, leaving, running scared. One of them was Elena Zacharia and her Greek–English family, of course it was. Yes. Yes. How could they forget the Greek family with the little deaf girl? But no, wait, she was blind, that little girl, surely? They remembered the child's white half-closed eyes shaded from the light. She was always so beautifully dressed, always clutching her long-legged raggy doll. Those dolls from England – they all wanted one, so difficult to buy, so expensive. Ah, forget the doll... It's a red herring, they were mistaken. It was the English family, the widowed mother had married a Turk and their child was deaf – a boy, wasn't it? He was much younger than their other children and not a son, no. A sort of cousin, illegitimate and unwanted by the disgraced aunt, passed over to her older sister. She left the island. Who? The aunt, no, the new mother, both of them. Who knows? Then there was the mother of the three little girls who had been a spy, they would never forget her. No, surely the spy was the dead father and his widow did a little proselytising for EOKA B... Though it was definitely the wife who was finally brought in. Expecting, was the rumour, and the new husband – was he really the husband? – only half her age. They remembered her with two daughters, one went missing during the trouble, from the Troodos mountain camps, wasn't it? No, no, that was the spy's eldest son, he was older. He joined the army and was killed before he had served a month. It was hushed up but friendly fire was rumoured. Stop digressing, remember the girls, three of them, wasn't it? Their auntie was a schoolteacher, she took them to school in England...

Oh, it was a closed world. Tight lips, know thine enemies, be suspicious of thy friends. It wasn't certain that a fellow Greek was your brother, he may have led the coup, he many have sent the great Makarios, God rest him, into exile. Trust those only who walked with you.

It was a lifetime ago. It was yesterday. It was thirty years.

'We are still here and so many others are not,' Soussana whispers, swatting at her tears. 'We survived. We *survive*. But to what end?'

On the way home, Damaris talks constantly about her animals and the damp in the conservatory, a leak from a bathroom repair hopefully, she muses, not the same plumber as Yiannis employed, as that's a botched job. She chatters on about a forthcoming exhibition for Andreas and wonders whether Orestes could be encouraged to a modest show of his own. I see it's her way of debriefing, bringing herself into her present, an acting technique after an all-consuming role. Nicole feeds her expertly, and I offer to drive, feeling out of it, superfluous. Besides, I need something physical to do; my fingers are itching for the piano.

We leave Damaris at the Agia Triada crossroads, her step light, her back straight, pleased to be almost back to Orestes and the cats and dogs. Parking in the courtyard by Andreas' studio, I feel a pang, I wish I had someone waiting for me that I wanted to be waiting for me.

'What is going through your mind, April?' Nicole asks. 'Those old ladies, did they upset you? It is just their way. I knew they could not know Elena...'

'It's alright, I knew too.' I know my tone is flat; almost resigned. 'But actually, they did know her, didn't they? She was in every one of those stories. And in Damaris' stories too. So, I have found Elena, haven't I? That's it. Surely I've found her – as much of her as I ever will.' I hesitate. 'And maybe that's okay. Maybe that's what I want.' *Is it?*

Something is different within me. It's been shifting with the travel over the island and meeting the people I've met. Even in my thoughts I can't quite articulate it yet but it's been crystallising over the miles. I started out half wanting to find my friend Elena and somehow carry that – *her*, I don't know – into my future and half hoping there were no traces left to follow. Selfishness versus cowardice. Now it's more like the desire to find a piece of a jigsaw puzzle and being satisfied seeing the main picture. It's curiosity. And hope.

39

Somewhere in Cyprus
Another night in August 1974

This time the ride was in Uncle Dmitri's spare truck, spattered with stinking cow dung and chicken poo, that was parked on the road but with its back wheels angled on to the field. Antony had propped himself against the grey-green cab, an unlit cigarette balanced on his lower lip. He gave Elena a thumbs up and a lopsided grin. He jerked his head towards the back of the truck, which appeared to be packed with crates of stunned hens blearily peeking out from underneath a loosely tied canvas. It took him only a minute to hoist Elena over his shoulder, sagging just enough to remind her how much heavier she was than Krista, and almost tip her into a gap between the cab and the chicken boxes. It was lined with another tarpaulin, but it did little to break her fall and Elena winced as her knees and elbows clunked against the corrugated metal. Yesterday's instructions ringing in her ears, she made no complaint – she wondered had Krista had been so reasonable? – but rolled under the plastic sheets and shuffled into the hidey-hole formed from a careful arrangement of straw-filled crates and horse blankets. Elena felt the vibration of doors slamming. She shuddered involuntarily alongside the splutter of the engine and the jerking movements of Antony's inexpert driving as the truck hit gravel and picked up speed.

'Mind my hand, daydream girl,' hissed Krista, even as she helped pull Elena into the space. 'That's your place there. Don't invade me. You're to stay awake and keep me company,' she ordered. Kicking her leg in the direction of Sofia, she added, 'She's no good.' Sofia opened her eyes sleepily and half smiled at Elena before her lids drooped again.

'We should try to sleep also.' Elena was mindful of Aunt Irini's clipped advice and unconsciously parroted her. 'It might take hours to get to the mountains. Lots of the roads are closed and it's better that we avoid the checkpoints.'

'No,' said Krista. 'I won't sleep. I'm too scared.' She paused. 'I'm scared shitless,' she whispered proudly.

Elena ignored her; Krista was just practising until she was brave enough to say that to Irini. Anyway, she didn't look scared. Krista's eyes were still bright and she buzzed with energy. Elena wriggled herself more comfortable and crossed her arms over her chest, muffling her thumping heart. Till now, Elena had forgotten how the village aunties had always talked – in low, special voices – of palpitations and thin blood. Nobody in England seemed to have such illnesses. But the next time the aunties crowded identically around the coffee pan, one hand on their bosoms, the other in the small of their backs, she would be part of the secret. Tentatively, Elena reached out and touched her sister's hand and when it wasn't snatched away, she curled her fingers around Krista's thumb. With her foot touching Sofia's, Elena took comfort in the closeness of her sisters and tried to breathe. 'Holy Mary, Mother of God,' she prayed for them all and willed herself to doze through the miles. She didn't dare hope any more that the miles over the roads to the mountains would bring them closer to Mama.

Later – she had no idea how long, but the pickup now bucked and spun over a road that had clearly stopped being a road so she knew they were heading for the dirt tracks that spiralled like spider's webs out of the foothills of the mountains – Elena jerked out of a half-dream. She gagged and spat out the hair, it might have been hers or Krista's, which was tangled with them under the blanket. She thought she was drowning in evil air. With her eyes closed, she counted to 500, tapping the numbers on the back of her hand like Aunt Irini had suggested, but Elena's heart pounded on and her stomach heaved, she fought a wave of vomit back down her throat. Krista would call this the hell-smell; the hell-smell of Uncle Dmitri's outhouse, not his neat pig tunnels but the unspoken sheds at the back where he hid disease-riddled porkers awaiting the knacker-man. The counting didn't help. It didn't help at all.

Suddenly, the truck slowed down, she felt the pressure of the brakes as Antony applied them too fast and too late; Elena pictured the telling-off look on Aunt Irini's face. She felt a surge of hope that they were arriving, claiming the sanctuary of the magic forest where Red Riding Hood had outwitted the wolf and they all lived happily ever after. Tense with anticipation, Elena waited for strong hands to delve beneath the layers of tarpaulin, to heft the hen cages aside and to free the sisters from their tiny prison. Nothing happened. Car doors slammed but the engine remained ticking over and she heard nothing beyond Sofia's snoring and the squawking of a dozen waking chickens.

Breaking all the rules, Elena crawled to the edge of the makeshift tent and wrenched at the string that fastened the tarpaulin to the side of the truck. It loosened slightly and she forced her head out. Her mouth made a round O, gulping like Krista's English goldfish when food was sprinkled over its bowl. The new day was racing their journey and winning, clean light suspended in streaks from the sky where it met with a smoky haze. A strong scent of woodsmoke caught at the back of her throat and she had to stifle a cough. She sniffed again and it reminded her, suddenly, of charred souvlaki on an open grill. Better than the hell-smell; her stomach heaved and rumbled at the same time. At least it meant they must be on the outskirts of a village, even one where they ate souvlaki for breakfast. Yes, straight ahead of her was the sign for Tochni – she thought it said Tochni – but it had been damaged by red graffiti that ran like blood over the letters and into a pool on the uneven ground.

They were not in the Troodos Mountains at all, not even in the forest, but in an open clearing with a proper concrete road alongside.

Elena heard a sound from the other side of the truck and, with a struggle, twisted herself round. It looked as if Irini and Antony had stopped to pee or stretch their legs. Both of them were stumbling back to the pickup from the direction of the hedgerow, both looked very pale and Aunt Irini had a handkerchief to her mouth; Elena felt sorry for them but was comforted that the bumping and revving of the car hadn't made her alone feel sick.

Her aunt was saying something, saying it over again: 'But they're Turkish, Antony. Turkish. Not Greek...'

Antony's face was strained, almost angry. 'Get in the truck, Irini. Now.' Elena heard him make the order like he never had before. He had hold of Irini's elbow and he almost shoved her towards the cab.

'But, Antony, don't you see what that means? You don't understand...'

'I do. Bloody hell, I do. And we need to get the fuck out of here now, right now, Irini. And especially before the girls wake up.'

'Oh, my God.' Irini's head, half in, half out of the car, whipped round. Her eyes locked with Elena's, slid back to the hedgerow, and met with Elena's again. 'Get down,' she cried out. 'Get down, Elena, and stay down.'

40

After that initial, communal burst of interest in the location of the tree houses, there's a lull while everyone goes about their legitimate daily business. Life here might look all laid-back, even touching on the eccentric to the stranger, but work, routines, commitments are established. I might be wrong but I'm convinced someone (I mean, we all have motive, but it wasn't me) has paid off Kevin to get Jake out from under our feet because the two of them are doing a PADI diving course along the coast.

I'm the sore thumb, the one still to find her place. Settled in Nicole's guest room, I've quickly established a pleasingly lacklustre pattern of practising, swimming and reading, either in Yiannis' secret garden or on the terrace of Verena Bay. Each time I offer to do anything to help anyone, the response is, 'Just relax and enjoy your holiday, April. Research Elena.' I've become familiar with the 'libraries' that fill Minerva House and Loxandra Inn: shelves of dusty books collected over years, and a great resource on the history of Cyprus. Studying some of the lighter tomes fuels my fantasy that I'm doing something useful and at the very least there's a novelty in being – surely – the only classical pianist in recent times who can discuss enosis ('union with Mother-Greece', as one book puts it) and the genesis of Lefkara lacemaking as fluently as reading a score. The records office in Nicosia apparently has a stash of newspaper archives, partly on microfiche, and Nicole is going to arrange a day when we can go and look; I need a Greek speaker/reader for that.

My latest find is *A Lady's Impressions of Cyprus in 1893* by Mrs Lewis. Thirty pages in, she hasn't got here yet, so I'm skipping through seeking a sign of disembarkation when footsteps, followed by Yiannis, appear through the avenue of trees, and he does a sort of knock-knock gesture on the nearest of them.

'I am taking a leap of faith,' he says. 'The biggest one since I left the Church. I am hoping you will come with me.'

I can't help but imagine us holding hands and running into the abyss; a tandem cliff dive off Cape Greco. But when Yiannis says 'you', he's talking plural. Buoyed by the success of the trip to the Troodos Mountains, and conscious of Red's impending departure – with Kevin (Jarlath is an unknown quantity as yet) and, fingers crossed, Jake – Yiannis is striking out.

'To the northern part of the island.' Yiannis lifts his left hand and makes a fist, extending his index finger like a child pointing a pretend gun. 'Right down to the very end of the fingertip that makes the peninsula. One night, maybe two, if you have sufficient free time.'

I smile at that. 'I can bring Mrs Lewis with me,' I say, holding up the book.

'Good. Good. Then it is the same party as to the Troodos. Flora, fauna and… er… tree houses.' He rubs his hands at his little joke and then looks serious again. 'Ah, your parents.' Yiannis indicates the memorial spot. 'This is the peaceful resting place you hoped for?'

'It really is.' I nod. 'You know, when I sit here, it's like being in their garden, with my mum in the kitchen and my dad in his shed. Just out of sight, but present.'

Yiannis swallows and looks as if he's searching for something profound or meaningful to say, before settling on, 'I'm glad,' and that about covers it.

* * *

Entering into Turkish Cyprus for the second time (for me) has a very different feel to my visit with Nicole and Damaris. Different company, with a different intention, stamps its own imprint on the journey, affecting even the landmarks I remember with a different slant: less portentous history and more physical geography. Orchids, still on the agenda, are joined by landscapes, views, castles and ruins; Yiannis branching out of his comfort zone.

It's starting well. *Peacefulness* must be my word of the week because if it's possible for stone ruins to instil a sense of life and warmth, Kantara Castle, our first stop, does so. The north-east tower, according to Yiannis, has the most spectacular views over both sides of North Cyprus: olive groves and carob trees to the north and arid plains and Famagusta to the south. I separate myself from the others, wanting to hear the distinct elements of silence: the wind whistling, grass rustling, the occasional footfall and snatch of voices.

The stone steps are shallow and grassy, and orchids may well nestle amongst the myriad wildflowers protruding through the crevices. I'm on a path to nowhere; it ends in an almost perfect arch – I think Yiannis said *kantara* is arch in Arabic – where I sit down, close my eyes and open my ears. I'm not sure if I'm lost in the thrum of the atmosphere for seconds or a few minutes when a shadow subverts it and I blink to see Red backing off.

'Sorry,' he says. 'We obviously had the same idea.'

'Great minds and all that?' I draw my legs up, indicating the other side of the arch. 'There's plenty of room. I wasn't particularly intent on being alone.' It's a half-truth but Red knows exactly what, or whom, I mean. He sits down opposite me, stretches out and closes his eyes.

Today, his is a restful presence; whatever connection we have is not gone, but muted here. I let a flute solo – Brahms

– wash over me, taking with it a wave of petty annoyances: Jake volubly eschewing coffee and brewing something pale, pink and insipid, just waiting for me to ask why. He's also wearing black chinos, a black turtleneck and black street (that is, not running-around-grassy-ruins-suitable) shoes. Very priestlike. I sneak a look over at Red, whose boots, jeans and old suede jacket aren't. I admire him a bit longer; what would he say? The sin is in yielding not the temptation itself. I suppress a sigh.

There's Nicole too, blowing hot and cold. Since the visit to Soussana and her cronies, she's been – distant? Preoccupied? I can't quite place it. When our paths cross she's as friendly as ever, but I get the impression, like Red, she's limiting the crossings. Maybe I'm being hypersensitive again. She has work to do, a real life to lead, whatever running their home and Andreas' business entails. I've not liked to ask her again about the records office and the tree houses, it's starting to feel a childish occupation in comparison with everyone else's real lives.

Thank goodness for Petros and his reliable peccadilloes; I always know where I am with him, even if I don't like it. His sledgehammer references to 'home' have been few and far between since I opened Ana's letter, but their imprint is distinct. With my to-do list shrinking and a growing sense of resignation over Elena nibbling away, I need to stop and acknowledge the crossroads.

What am I going to do next week, next month, next year?

Play hotels with Petros with my quarter of the Verena Bay? Or go back to what I know, simply tweaking it a bit?

Oh, for a moment of clarity. Or a coin to toss.

I look over at Red again. Part of his attraction, his charisma – if it wasn't such a smarmy celebrity word – is his certainty. It's nothing he says or does exactly, it's just what he is. In a parallel world, he and I would have got together the day we met. It's no accident we've had so little time together, Red has made that decision, I see that now, and I've been complicit.

The difference is, he's been testing our attraction, I've been avoiding it.

How's that for honesty, a moment of clarity?

Not fair, the four-year-old inside me stamps; I want the parallel world where we might be soulmates. Then again, the adult me mediates, Red wouldn't be who, what, he is, and neither would I, so there'd be no spark. Aargh. I close my eyes again and turn up the volume on the Brahms. Try, April, try. Flip over to Bizet, maybe...

'Can you hear that?' Red asks after a few minutes.

'The silence? I'm trying,' I say. Irritated, floundering, I blurt out the kind of question I promised I wouldn't. 'How do you *know*?' I say, half wishing the words would be carried away on the echoes of those who have asked before. 'How can you be sure?'

'I just am,' Red says eventually. Of course he knows what I mean. 'I can't rationalise faith, April. I've studied divinity, philosophy, history and logic so it's not blind faith, but it's plain old-fashioned faith all the same. And,' he sits up a bit and looks at me, 'it's just *right*, April. I don't mean it's always correct or easy and it's not perfect, but it's right. Like any good marriage, maybe?'

'I wouldn't know,' I say. 'I've made my music into such a smokescreen that, behind it, I've never really been certain about anything. Definitely not when I got married – either time. The first time was literally the boy next door and it didn't last beyond my PhD, and the second time, I really did think I was in love.' I pull a face. 'But it was his voice I loved most. I quite liked the sex too.' I look at Red sideways and grin.

He grins too. 'Believe me, April, I do know what I'm missing. I promise I did *a lot* of research in my early twenties. I don't think desire or temptation ever goes away... Who am I kidding? When I look at you, April, I know it doesn't. As for being in love, I understand what I'm giving up and it's not too big a sacrifice. The love I have found is more than a fair trade.' He stands up and comes over. 'Budge up,' he says.

I move over. He squeezes in beside me and I wish simultaneously my thighs took up less space and that my thoughts were on a higher level than that.

'I do sometimes wonder whether I'll come to miss having someone to share it all with,' he admits. 'And don't look so coy, Dr Zarney, you know very well I've wondered it since the day I met you. All I can say is, I don't shy away from challenging myself and right now...' He hesitates and I think he wants to take my hand, so I hold it out, palm upwards. He takes it. 'Right now, even at this very minute, I still feel that the only way to be truly committed to God is to be alone with Him.' He runs his thumb over the back of my hand. 'But will there come a time when I'm old, sick, upset, lonely, overcome with lust, that I'll bemoan the Church's stance on celibacy? There might. There probably will.'

'And that's when the faith kicks in?'

'Yup. And friends. Good friends.' He looks at me. 'It might be harder if someone, yes, someone like you, for example, wanted more from me, but deep down that's not the case, is it?' I don't need to say anything; he knows my answer as clearly as if he's read my thoughts. We sit in silence.

'This must be where the violins come in,' I say, after a while.

'Or the credits roll. What soundtrack do you recommend here, April?'

There's a question. But we're interrupted by a shout in the distance. Neither of us can make out the words, but it's a fair guess that one of our party is looking for us.

'Come on.' I release Red's hand and haul myself up. 'No time to pledge our troth, or whatever it is, in blood.'

Red follows me, but at the mouth of the arch, he puts his hand on my shoulder. 'April?'

I swing around. 'Yes?'

'I promise I won't do this very often but can I take the liberty of saying something a bit priestly?'

'Of course you can.'

His hand tightens. 'Forgive yourself for not being perfect

and let people near you get close. It might help you find what you're looking for. I think you just haven't found your certainty, maybe even your real self – yet.'

I relax and smile up at him. 'Not much of a sermon,' I mock. 'And nothing I don't already know.'

'Hey, I didn't promise to be original!'

'It's about being back at the crossroads, isn't it? What you said at dinner, about the tree houses. That, I might add, nobody has found yet.' I lean in and hug him, flippancy hiding how near to tears I am. He holds me tight, and for a second I give in to that possibility of another time and another place.

'This is something I miss,' Red says into my hair.

I tilt my head up to nod. 'I expect snogging your parishioners is frowned upon.'

'Hugging a beautiful woman,' he corrects me. 'But it's probably as easily misconstrued.'

From below us, there's another cheerful shout that seems to choke in the middle. We separate and look down. It's Nicole. For a second her face is frozen.

'Come on,' she shouts. 'We are leaving.'

We step down towards her, but she's already turned back, stumbling on a couple of uneven steps. Red and I look at each other.

'So easily misconstrued,' he repeats.

'Oh, not by Nicole,' I say, uncertainly. 'I'll explain. Don't worry, Red. She won't think I'm seducing you from your vows, I promise.'

'It's not that.' He looks closely at me. 'April, you really don't see it, do you?'

'See what?'

'That Nicole might be jealous—'

'Never,' I interrupt. 'Red, there's no way Nicole is jealous of me. You can't mean that.'

He looks at me a bit longer, then draws me in for another hug. 'No,' he says. 'No, I don't mean that at all.'

41

Somewhere in Cyprus
Another day in August 1974

Over and over in her dreams, nightmares, Elena saw the lines of wire hung from one telegraph pole to the next and a line of scarecrows hanging from them. They were flapping and twisting their horrible faces, it sounded as if they were groaning in the wind. *I'm a dingle dangle scarecrow with a dingle dangle head, I can wave my arms like this, I can wave my legs like that...* the song went on and on. It didn't stop even when she was awake, not since she'd seen the scarecrows.

She knew it was a trick of her imagination, of course they hadn't been scarecrows. Not so many, not so close to the road, but why, she thought, would someone hang their washed clothes there, in public, and so far from the laundry?

'Why are you still humming that stupid song?' asked Krista, her mouth full of pie, her breath cheesy. 'It's for kids. Sing ABBA. *Waterloo*,' she crooned, '*I was reheated, and you were poor. Waterloo, probably pouring it on the floor...* Can I eat yours?'

Elena nodded. She had no energy to fight with Krista over the right words and her tummy was full with a big lump of being scared, even though Aunt Irini had said it was okay now, nearly okay. They were still being careful but it was daytime and they weren't hiding in this jeep. Sofia was sitting on Aunt Irini's knee and Elena and Krista were on the back seat. Finally, they were getting higher and higher up into the mountains. High up in the mountains would be safe, Irini said, past the monastery and through the forest, the forest where more scarecrows hung with their dingle dangle broken-necked heads...

'The cat's name,' Elena said in desperation. She needed to get back to a place where it was safe. The mountains weren't working. 'Krista, what was the cat's name?'

Krista stopped chewing for a second. 'What cat?'

'The one when we were little. He slept by the milk churns and had blind eyes. We had a funeral. The day Mama cried and Aunt Irini was there and she cried too.'

'Oh, him.' Krista looked at Elena. 'Who cares? Let's sing, daydream girl. Mine first and then I'll do your stupid "Womble Song". Come on.' She took a deep breath and poked Elena in the ribs *'We joined in all the fun, we had secrets in the sun...'*

Elena's voice was little but she joined in – with the proper words. It helped a bit. It reminded her of April. She thought of April's tree house. Her garden. School. It helped a bit more.

They had just finished helping Sofia to pee accurately into a plastic container put there for the purpose and Elena was hoping she wouldn't have to use it herself, when the jeep slowed down even more than its struggling snail's pace. It bumped over what felt like giant marbles, and came to a halt. A crowd of people ran forward to meet them. This time Elena froze and stayed where she was, Krista and Sofia either side of her. This time firm hands lifted them down and the next minute the sisters were being hugged and squeezed breathless by people they had never seen before. This time a stranger pulled off Elena's sweater and swept back the hair from her face, tying it deftly under a headscarf in a style she had never used before. Someone else was doing the same to Krista who was scowling and squirming, and to Irini who was sobbing. Antony was cuddling Sofia, his face buried in her hair; Elena watched his shoulders heave. The woman chucked Elena's chin and offered her cold water. She drank cup after cup until she felt as if her insides were loose and swimming.

They had arrived in a village, but this one was different. Elena knew she had never been here before, even before they went to England. As her stomach settled and her legs adjusted to solid ground, she looked around her. In Famagusta, the houses were small and whitewashed, with flower boxes on the windows – in England April had called them cottages – and the shops and cafes made a big square that led up to the church. In Varosha, the homes were bigger, some had two floors and a garden that wasn't taken up with animals and machines. The hotels rose high above them, new protectors of the sandy beaches. But here, the tiny buildings were made of stone. They were close to the ground, maybe six or seven of them in a half-circle. Nothing else. The road was a track and there were no colours; Elena checked, none at all. But it was cooler here, a breeze ruffled her new headscarf and dried the sweat on her neck.

She had no time to say anything, no time to dawdle. Elena, with Krista and Sofia ahead and Irini and Antony behind her, was hurried by an old man with thick black-rimmed glasses and a billowing white shirt into the first house, through one big, empty room, and into the yard. It looked like someone had tried to clean up the mess of tractor parts and bicycles, of stones and rubble, and someone else had pushed them to the sides. The messy piles made a corridor and there, those someones had laid a long table with meat and salad, the souvlaki roasting over a homemade fire at the far end. Elena suddenly felt sick again and was grateful that the elderly lady who had tied back her hair saw it and put a hand to her forehead.

'You are hot, child,' she said. 'Come, all of you, wash your hands and faces and then we will eat and give thanks.' She nodded towards a tin bath filled with water.

'In there?' Krista looked disbelieving. 'Where's the bathroom?'

'Krista...' Irini's voice held a note of warning and, muttering to herself, Krista curled up her top lip but obediently splashed her hands and face.

Elena, intending to do the same, stopped. She thought she might faint, but she didn't know how. Above the trough, pegged by its long legs to the string washing line, was a rag doll. It was Jemima, Sofia's toy that they had left behind in Varosha; she had cried and cried and Antony found her a cuddly lion instead. But this Jemima doll was dirty and her apron was flapping. Her head was hanging, almost chopped off. *I'm a dingle dangle scarecrow with a dingle dangle head...* Pictures flashed through Elena's head from left to right like signposts at a station when you were on a fast train: shiny Jemima, Irini with a handkerchief to her mouth, scarecrows in a field with their dingle dangle heads, torn, patchy overalls on washing lines, a whole row of washing lines then another then another then another...

42

Nicole is furious about something, that much is obvious by the way she separates herself from the rest of us as we leave Kantara behind, sitting silently in the car and smiling without humour at one of Kevin's absurd jokes. She was like this, a diluted version, that morning when we drove to Famagusta and snapped out of it of her own accord. I hope she'll do the same today because I've no idea when or how to approach her.

I concentrate on Yiannis' meticulous plan to travel on to Cape Apostolos Andreas ('The pointy finger, right?' Kevin confirms) tomorrow. For tonight, he says, Petros, in his capacity of hotelier, has found us a small guest house on the edge of the town.

'My choices were limited,' Petros himself cuts in. 'Dear friends, I did my best.'

'If you need to manage our expectations, it does not bode well,' Nicole mutters.

Grumpy she might be, she's also not wrong. The reason for its last-minute availability is obvious as we pull up outside: a whitewashed concrete roadhouse set back in a bare parking lot, there's a faded and indecipherable swinging sign above the front door and the windows are shrouded with net curtains.

Kevin starts whistling the theme tune to *Psycho*, hyping it up until Red gives him a very un-priestlike Chinese burn, causing the adopted Father Jake to offer a soulful and gentle shake of the head. Petros just grins and warns us not to judge totally by appearances. 'Although it is a former police station, I believe,' he adds. 'Shot at during the 1974 troubles and... er... repurposed. I admit it does look like a gallows should be hanging from that sign out there.' As he points us in the direction of our rooms, he catches my eye. 'Sorry, April, Nicole. It is definitely not what Thia Ana would approve.'

'Cypriot-April's taking it all in her stride,' I say.

'And I draw the line at bedbugs, that is all.'

I laugh and Nicole bares her teeth politely. Then, just as quickly, inexplicably, she brings me back into the fold.

She knocks on my door, dressed to hit the bright lights of Yeni Eerenköy town. 'May I come in?' she asks. 'The light is terrible in my room. What is Petros thinking?'

But this place is not the cause of the fury I see in her set lips and tense shoulders. Perhaps it's a row with Andreas? She's been on and off the phone half a dozen times, and her Greek still sounds raging to me, even when it's merely energetic.

'My rings,' she frets. 'If I do not wear them, speculation is both rife and audible. Andreas hates that.'

I bite back the words that Andreas is not here and nobody who is will think to tell him; somehow that sounds more clandestine.

She roots through her handbag for her engagement and wedding rings, which she forces over the knuckle of the fourth finger on her left hand. She picks her bag up from the flimsy dressing table. 'The microscope of small-town life.' She half shrugs, half smiles; the olive branch.

I only wish I knew why we need one. I want to explain about Red and me, at Kantara, but she brushes it aside, and anyway, she was out of sorts before that.

'Maybe I should buy myself a costume set of those, save a lot of trouble.' I indicate the rings, trying to lighten the atmosphere.

'Maybe you should have kept the ones you had—' Nicole puts her newly adorned hand to her mouth. 'I am sorry, April, that did not come out correctly. I mean, yes, you could have protected yourself from other stupid men. An investment.'

'Oh, I invested the originals alright,' I tell her. 'I sold them all and put the money towards a baby grand piano.'

Nicole laughs out loud, genuinely. 'I admire you, April Rose,' she says, 'I would probably have spent it all on a dozen Louboutins and a French manicure.'

'No you wouldn't,' I say. 'But if you did it you'd be doing it in Paris. That's true style.'

She steps behind me to fasten the zip I'm struggling with, and I smooth the skirt down over my hips. It's still strange wearing this dress, knowing that I won't be performing in it any more. Well, not in the musical sense anyway. I think that's why I brought it with me, old as it is, expensive as it was, to test it in another life. It's also the only thing I've not worn, night after night.

'Very English rose.' Nicole holds me at arm's length, the way Elena's mama would once have done. She squints at my hair. 'Do you ever wear your hair up, April?' she asks.

'You mean in a proper style, as opposed to sticking it in a scrunchie thing to get it out of the way of the music? Not often.' I remember something. 'Not since I was little. When Elena was there, I wanted long hair like she had. I tried to grow it and it took ages, but I remember her mama used to plait it for me. It was barely long enough and needed half a packet of hair grips but I loved it.'

'Sit down,' Nicole instructs, glancing at her watch. 'They can wait.'

'Oh, Nicole, there's no need.'

'Sit.'

It takes her only a couple of minutes to twist up the back into a sort of French roll and to smooth the sides and pin it all up.

'Classic,' she approves. 'The epitome of 1960s chic.'

I wish I'd thought to have this hairstyle all the other times I've worn the dress. I look less ordinary and more, more…

I'm not sure what the word is. Elegant, maybe. Poised. And if it's a little severe, it's only hours if not minutes till my hair starts to escape the sleek chignon and tickle my cheeks. It used to do it all the time when I was playing but after a while I never noticed.

Nicole herself checks the buttons on a knee-length cerise silk wrap-over dress. Her hair is loose, falling in neat waves. Now that, I think, is elegance, and I know she must have got us both right when Petros looks at us outside the restaurant. Where the glass door borrows light from the mock lanterns that jostle above the entrance, he just stops himself from giving us his charmer's smile. He recovers and grins naturally. 'Wow,' he says. 'Ladies, you make a very fine couple.'

Nicole laughs, her face so animated that the diners inside the doorway look up and smile. Flicking her mood switch again, she is kind, so kind tonight, at her most interesting and approachable.

'Andreas has finished your portrait,' she says, out of the blue, towards the end of the meal.

'He's *finished* it?' I know nothing about the procedure, but that seems like quick work even after his rapid 'arranging' and sketching. I expected him to toil over the finer colour mixes and line definition or whatever for weeks.

'He has worked day and night,' she points out. 'He does, when he has a piece of work in progress. It is done and I have seen it.'

'What's wrong with it?' I ask, triggered by her flat tone.

'There's nothing wrong with the painting,' she says. 'It is good. One of his best. It secures the best of you, April. Well, half of you, the April you show in public...' She pauses, giving me time to wonder what she means; I think of the two sides of Petros that Andreas captured in a couple of simple strokes. Especially when she continues, 'He is intent on a more abstract version too, but is less happy. It is too crude—'

'Oh, dear God, please tell me he's not planning a life-size, masturbating, defecating nude to enter for the Turner Prize?'

Wildly, I recall our conversation over the prized bottle of Maratheftiko, and imagine that hanging above Red's presbytery mantelpiece. 'Nicole?'

She's laughing again; too much, reassuringly, to answer. 'Of course he has not,' she manages to splutter, and then pulls herself together. 'Of course not. I told you it was not intrinsically bad. April, where did you get such, such a flight of fantasy?'

'But?' I prompt.

She shrugs. 'Andreas has grand plans. Oh, it is nothing terrible. Indeed, many would be delighted. But not you. I do not think you will like it. I told him so and we are fighting about it.'

Aha. One question answered, at least.

The other one isn't. Everyone around us is suddenly moving, and still smiling, as she ushers me outside, Nicole murmurs, 'I will explain later, April, about your painting.'

The consensus is that we return to what Kevin is calling the Bates Motel-elect for drinks and some music. Apparently, I will provide the music.

'What with, my air guitar?' I ask. 'I didn't see a Steinway next door to the luxury swimming pool. Or should Kevin and I do a selection of Irish hymns? It won't be the same without Jarlath and the priest costumes though.'

Once back, Jake clamps his beloved mobile phone to his ear and vanishes for a late-night heart-to-heart with Erica. Drinks poured, and settled in the comfortable enough if barren sitting room, everyone else appears to have had too long a day to want anything more. Except Kevin. He actually does produce – very smugly – a real guitar.

'Here's the deal,' he says. 'I'll clean off the cobwebs and scrape the woodwormy yokes and you teach me a tune. Look, I've got surgeon's hands.' He holds them up. 'I'm already a shoo-in for the chords.'

'Give it here.' I uncurl myself from the oversized, overstuffed armchair, balance my empty glass on the arm of it, and go and perch beside him. I haven't the heart to tell him I'll be making it up as I go along. 'Can you play anything?' I ask.

'Nope.'

'Me neither,' I mutter under my breath. But I can wing it. '"You Are My Sunshine",' I announce.

The ensuing racket means that, very soon, Petros has an urgent need to find a telephone and check Jarlath hasn't burned down or sold Verena Bay; Nicole decides we need coffee; Yiannis goes to consult his route maps for tomorrow.

It takes them all an uncommonly long time. Red, alone, braves it out. But Kevin appears to be having the time of his life.

'C to G.' I demonstrate. 'You need a smoother and faster transition, see?' I do it a few times, showing the motion of my fingers and moving slighter faster each time. I know I'm aiming too high but I hand back the instrument anyway. 'Try again, Kevin. You know you can do it.'

Ten minutes later, I'm throwing in the towel, Red is crying with laughter, and Kevin, undaunted, is making the kind of noise an enthusiastic toddler might.

'Please, don't,' I beg. 'I'm doubting myself as a teacher.'

'He lasted as long with Suzuki violin,' Red notes.

'You could have told me that before,' I say, and to Kevin, 'Maybe you should save your fingers for being a great surgeon.'

'Really?' Crestfallen doesn't come close. 'Fair dos, I suppose. But the stakes are lower with the guitar. I can't kill anyone...'

'True,' I say, to cheer him up. 'We can do this again for fun anytime. You don't have to be good to enjoy it, and you'll get better.'

Kevin looks up at Red. 'Why'd you let them get to you, bro? Why'd you do it? You could be after marrying a lovely girl like April here, and I could come over for music lessons every weekend. She'd be the best auntie.'

'She wouldn't be your aunt, she'd be your sister-in-law, you clot.' Red throws a cushion at him.

Kevin gives one last tear across the strings and I collapse against Red, one ear against his chest and my hand clapped to the other.

We're both still there, giggling, when Yiannis comes back with Petros, who is holding the door open behind them. Yiannis looks between Red and me, volubly saying nothing; Petros smirks. Nicole, right behind with a tray of coffee, is more forthcoming.

'Very cosy,' she comments.

Red and I sit up straight and take our coffees.

Chastened, I think is the word.

43

I have no precedent for quarrelling; voices were never raised in our house when I was growing up. Strained silences, perhaps, tight lips from my mother and worried frowns from my father, but excitement, as my father called anything above a moderate and controlled voice, scared them. Which meant it scared me. The first Saturday night I spent at Elena's house, I watched Krista and their mother, and was nearly sick with nerves.

I walked in to find Krista with a pair of shoes in one hand, cheap and showy flowery wedges that I coveted. Krista was pointing one at her mother, flapping it up and down like an offensive weapon and screeching in Greek. She'll have a sore throat tomorrow, I noted in my mum's voice. Their mama was just standing there with her hands behind her back. I waited for the inevitable outburst, Elena's subsequent embarrassment, probably tears, and I would be sent home... In fact, the only shouting Elena did was so that her mother would notice us hovering in the background. When she did, she came over with a beaming smile, hugged me, whipped the sandals out Krista's hands and put a pair of worn, flat pink ones down instead. Krista broke off in what appeared to be the middle of a sentence, turned round and looked at me appraisingly.

'Do *you* get to wear your mama's shoes?' she demanded, the first words she had ever directed properly at me.

'No, no...' An image of my mum's sensible black lace-ups floated in front of my eyes; I didn't like to say I wouldn't have wanted to and neither would Krista. I couldn't believe my mother would ever wear these flimsy tropical-pineapple-motif sandals that Elena's mama had confiscated.

Krista tossed her head, dismissed me and sat down on the floor to pull on the pink little-girl sandals. 'If I am laughed at, it will be all your fault,' she threatened her mother – in English, for my benefit.

'I accept that,' said Elena's mama, smiling. 'And when you are twenty-one and going to your first formal party, as I did, then you may wear those shoes, as I did.'

Krista got up and slammed her way out of the hall. 'I'll be dead before then if I have to live in this family any longer. I'll kill myself,' was her parting shot.

'You won't break your neck in my shoes, at least,' Mama called after her.

I gasped at this sacrilege, not sure who shocked me more. Then Krista came banging back through the door, yelling, '*Kalisperos*, Mama, *s'agapo*,' and she pushed me aside to give her mother a huge hug and a kiss.

I saw it a lot over the next few months, and while it opened up a new world of being, I wasn't ever comfortable. My own relationships – Jake, for example – lean more to sulking or silent treatment. Jake liked to talk through difficulties in a focus-group, care-and-share, academic way; not that we ever had much enough worth fighting about.

And now here I am, having an argument with Nicole. Not an out-and-out row; it can't be, because, once more, I'm not exactly sure how it's arisen or why.

'April, please come with me,' is all she says, as the evening draws to a close. 'One more drink, yes?'

I follow her into her room, beside mine, and she goes over to her suitcase.

'There is a bottle of ouzo in here,' she says, pushing her

hair impatiently behind her ears. 'Maybe you do not like ouzo? Try it again. Taste changes, you know.'

'What's wrong, Nicole?' I ask. 'What is it?'

'Ouch.' She's struggling with her pashmina, her red-orange nails like fire against it. She checks the snagged one, and it's rough at the edge.

'Nicole? Has something happened?'

'It is Elena. This fantasy of Elena. You are not chasing Elena,' Nicole bursts out from nowhere. She must see the confusion on my face and she stops. 'What?' she says. 'What did you expect me to say?'

I let out a breath I wasn't aware I was holding. 'I don't know. About Red, maybe. Or Jake?' I'm floundering. 'But not that.'

'Well, this I must say or explode,' she announces. 'April, you are chasing a dream, a memory you do not even have. The Elena you want, she does not exist.'

'I know that—'

'The Cyprus you want, it does not exist. The perfect, oh-so perfect family you want, that does not exist.'

'I know that too. I said—'

'You are not chasing Elena, you are chasing April.'

She won't let me get a word in, not even to agree with her: I know all of this, I've already accepted it. We've discussed it. 'Where has all of this come from?' I really am bewildered. 'Two, three days ago, you were interested in Elena. The tree houses—'

'I know what it is I said, and I meant it all. I do still. It is only that—'

'Only what? Nicole, *what*?' I'm circling an elephant in the room that I can't even see.

She sips the ouzo, pulls a face and picks up a bottle of water instead. 'When will you learn,' she says, 'that the April that you want to be – no, that you *think* you should be – she does not exist either?'

'What you say is true,' I tell her. 'Absolutely.' For a

second, I really think she might throw the water at me. 'So why are we fighting?'

At that she just looks at me in disbelief – and then laughs. 'Fighting? You would call this a fight? Oh, April…'

'Arguing then,' I amend. 'You're arguing with me because I'm trying to agree with you. And I'm confused. What have I done, exactly?'

Nicole laughs again. 'That is the problem, April Zarney. Nothing. Absolutely nothing. It's all me… I… It's all me, wishing that you would not… underestimate yourself.'

'Do I? I don't think I do.'

'Yes. Take the risks. If you want to find your Elena, say so, do not apologise and say it is not important. If you want to pursue Red, then tell him so. If you want to… oh, I don't know.'

'I took a big risk coming to Cyprus,' I say, stung. 'And I'd say that I'm taking a huge one searching for Elena – whether or not I find her, or anything about her.' The rest of her words catch up with me. 'As for Red, I don't want to pursue Red.' As I say it, I realise it's true. 'I like him. He likes me. You've seen that but you've also seen he's done his damnedest to stay away from me. He's not free and he doesn't want to be.' *So there*, I want to add and probably stamp my foot too, but I don't. 'So you see, I do take risks,' I amend, and for good measure pick up my untouched glass of ouzo and down it in one. Spluttering. 'That's horrible.'

Nicole says nothing. She looks deflated, the fight gone, but she's still on edge. With a flash of insight I think, *She's talking about herself, angry with herself, not me. She's using Elena and all this is a smokescreen for whatever it is she's not saying. Alright then.*

Heart beating hard – in case she flies off the handle altogether – I say quietly, 'Maybe you have things you want to do, risks you want to take. Maybe people need to listen to you.'

'Such as what?' She's not looking at me, but she sounds interested, not angry.

'I don't know.'

'Go on. Don't stop now that you've started, April Rose.'

The faint smile on her lips emboldens me, and I cast around in the outwardly charmed life that's Nicole's and pick on the obvious. 'You and Andreas? Your life is all tied up with him and his family...' I stop when she winces, knowing I've hit a nerve head-on.

Nicole slumps onto her bed. I sit down slowly beside her. 'Yes,' she says, and it's so calm it crosses my mind that she's been waiting for a way in. 'Andreas. Andreas and me. Precisely why you should not believe that your grass-is-greener images are anything better than your own muddle.'

'You're not happy?'

'We are not unhappy.' She taps the half-full water bottle on her knee. 'We get along perfectly well. We suit each other, for the moment.'

Fifteen years of marriage is more than a moment, I want to say, but settle for, 'Happy for now not happy ever after?' I read that somewhere, and have wondered ever since why the 'ever after' bit is such a goal.

'It was always an arranged marriage in the true old-fashioned sense of the term,' she says. 'Just maybe for different reasons for us than for the proud parents who brought us together and now wait in vain for their grandchildren.' She sighs. 'April, Andreas is... different. I do not know if there is a correct word for it but I have known him since he was a boy and he was the same then.'

'The artistic temperament?' I hazard, thinking, *I know this too*.

She shakes her head, impatient. 'That, yes, but more. He is... celibate. Asexual.'

I turn my intake of breath – I wasn't expecting this – into an, 'Oh,' but I don't think she notices.

'I am not sure how to say it. He was born this way and

he will die this way. He says it himself. He has always said it. To me. Only to me. We are a united front.' She turns away from me, briefly, looks back. 'And I have told nobody, ever. It is not my secret to tell.' Then she adds, 'You are not surprised, are you?'

'Not really.' I consider that. 'I mean, that scenario didn't occur to me...' Damaris' words echo in my mind: *I know, as a mother knows, that Andreas is not true to himself... a fiction is fine as long as I know it's a fiction...* 'But I suppose there was always something different or unsaid, I just put it down to Andreas being the artist he is.' *Wife, mother, sister, babysitter, muse,* I think. 'Nicole, I won't say anything.'

She smiles. 'That I don't doubt. I never met someone as inscrutable as you. It is okay. Perhaps your coming here and confronting your life has made me think. I discussed it with Andreas the night before we went with Damaris to Famagusta. He said I should do what makes me happy. I said that I am—'

'Not unhappy,' I finish for her. 'Snap!' Sitting forward, I hug her. She looks surprised for a second, then she puts her arms around me. Her cheek is cool against mine and she leaves it there for a few seconds before kissing me lightly on the forehead.

'You are correct,' she says, 'I am not angry with you, but with myself.'

'Something will happen, maybe something little, and it will make all the difference,' I tell her. 'Look at me. I saw a flight to Larnaca beside a flight to Berlin, and something just clicked. Not,' I add, grinning, 'that I know what's going to happen next.'

'We are going to sleep,' Nicole says. 'Tomorrow is a new day and change is in the air. Remember to close the shutters against the morning sun. *Kalispera. Kali nihta.*'

I wake during the night, clinging to the cloudy dream threads that leave me inexplicably elated. I am sidetracked though, by

Andreas' secret, Nicole's confession and, again, by how we got there. So many 'whys'. Legitimised by my half-comatose state, I wonder if they sleep in the same bed, have strange, perfected non-sex together. Whether he pulls her towards him and cradles her head so that they slumber peacefully, bodies and minds moulded except in the most fundamental of ways. Maybe Andreas consoles himself in his art but Nicole is such a tactile, voluptuous figure whom I can't imagine celibate. Lying wakeful, the pendulum swings until it's melancholy and loss I see in the moonlight, through the shutters that I left open after all.

By morning, it's a blast of Elena and the thirty-year-old heartache all over again:

Nicole has gone.

44

Troodos Mountains, Cyprus
August 1974

Elena knew she felt sorry for screaming, guilty that she wasn't being calm, but she knew she had to scream, she had to force out the pictures from her head. She did it methodically, one scream after another, but it wasn't strong enough. She knew she was kneeling down now on the sandy ground, leaning over the trough that was half full of dirty water and bits of hay. She leant too far and she saw her reflection all out of focus, her hair missing, her eyes wide and staring, her mouth open. She looked like a witch. She was a witch. The pictures flashed behind her, in front of her, and the words, *I can wave my arms like this, I can wave my legs like that,* echoed all around her.

Elena did the only thing she could do to make it all go away. She grasped the sides of the bath and banged her head on it. Over and over and over again. Her skin and bones made a dull thump against the blunt metal, the sweat stung her eyes and left a greasy mark behind.

Then Antony was prising her hands away and she bit him, and she was sorry she bit him and guilty. He was stronger than her and as he grabbed all of her and laid her down on the path she clamped her lips together so she wouldn't bite any more; dogs bit, not people. She opened her eyes and saw Aunt Irini there too, the old lady handing her a big bottle, but Elena's mouth was tight shut and she couldn't open it, she didn't dare open it for the medicine Irini wanted to give her.

'I'm sorry, darling, I'm so sorry,' Irini was saying, and Elena wondered if she was sorry for the scarecrows or for shouting at them or for not bringing them to Mama, but then she knew it was for none of those. It was for tipping Elena's head back and pouring something brown and burning into her nostrils, and pinching them tight shut as Elena gagged and bucked and coughed down the liquid that flowed over her throat and down to her chest. Elena knew Antony picked her up and carried her inside and laid her down somewhere but the flashing pictures started to get muddled and faint. Then suddenly there was a new one, a calm and focused image inside her head. She opened her eyes wide and asked for Krista.

'What's the matter with Elena? What is it?' Krista stayed standing by the door. 'Elena? What?'

Elena opened her mouth and said distinctly, 'I remember now.'

'What do you remember, my darling?' Irini's voice was as tight as the hand that gripped Elena's. 'What?'

'Tazos. It was Tazos. Will his bones be under the orange tree still?'

Elena smiled over at Krista and then up at Irini. Aunt Irini's face, getting blurry, was a mix of relief and concern. 'Elena, I don't…'

'It's alright, Aunt Irini,' Krista interrupted. 'She hasn't gone bonkers from bashing her head on the bath. Though she must have been a big bit bonkers to start bashing her head on the bath, mustn't she? She was talking about it in the jeep. I was going to make her guess. I wanted to sing.' Krista seemed to lose her train of thought. 'Could she go properly mad now, do you think? Will she get concussion? Or a brain tumour? If she does, can I—'

'Krista. Enough.'

Irini sounded severe and Krista surprised, wounded. 'I was just asking.'

'Well, just tell me who is Tazos? And what does she mean about bones?'

Krista was looking at her aunt as if it was obvious. Elena couldn't see it all, but she could hear it. It was like she was sitting outside herself, it was floaty and comfortable.

'The cat,' Krista said, and flounced out of the room.

Irini looked after her and shrugged. 'As long as it makes sense to them,' she murmured out loud. She turned back to Elena, whose eyes were closed again, and Irini made as if to tiptoe away, when Elena spoke.

'Aunt Irini?'

'Yes, darling? Are you feeling better? You should rest now.'

'I will,' Elena said sleepily, 'I will. But, Aunt Irini, scarecrows are dead things, aren't they?' she asked. 'They can't come back and hurt us?'

Irini hesitated, as if deciding how to answer, then softly she spoke. 'No, my darling. Scarecrows can't hurt us. Nothing will hurt us now.' Her voice went up slightly as if she had asked a question that she expected Elena to follow up. But Elena just nodded and sighed.

'I didn't think so,' she said. Then she turned over and fell asleep.

She slept on and off throughout the afternoon, vaguely aware of Irini and Antony swapping places to sit beside her in the shaded room. The shadows had grown very long when she awoke properly and sat up, suddenly hungry. Sofia was slumped on the end of the daybed, picking at a scab on her knee and lining up dead pieces of skin on her leg. Elena looked around the room. It was really half a room, separated from the rest by a shiny curtain, small and square with a low ceiling and whitewashed walls that had grown dirty and patterned with black cracks. There was a table covered with a flowery plastic cloth and two stools that didn't match; above them a shelf of old books, their titles in a foreign language. The same letters, Elena saw on a wall calendar that had been stuck up crookedly, its edges curling from damp. She couldn't read the words but she knew they were Turkish.

Elena's gaze wandered on to Sofia, who was flapping her hands crossly to gain attention.

'Is this home now?' It took Elena a minute to understand the signs, because Sofia still had her toy lion clamped tightly under her arm and seemed unwilling to move very far. She signed again. 'Elena, is this home now?'

But Elena couldn't answer. She knew what Aunt Irini had said that night but she'd been right to be suspicious because very bad things had happened. And she didn't know where home was any more. She wished April was there with her, not being scared. She wished Krista would pinch and kick and that Sofia would bounce again. Instead they were all slowly becoming flat like Fuzzy-Felt sticker people. That is, if there was a Fuzzy-Felt called In the War. There probably wasn't; there would have to be pictures of killing people, and killing people and stringing them up along the roadside like scarecrows was wrong.

45

It takes me a little while to realise that Nicole has disappeared. Despite the broken night, I wake early – the sun through the shutters – and thirsty. There's no water left in my room, so I throw on my sweatshirt over pyjamas and wander down to the kitchen. Yiannis and Red are just exiting the front door; on their way to Mass, they say in passing, telling me to help myself to breakfast. Petros calls this a guest house but it's really a self-catering place, and I find all the breakfast things are sitting in a big box next to the sink. Jake is already rooting through it.

'You're up early,' I say. 'Not going to Mass with the others?'

He gives a little sheepish shrug. 'Not sure all this churchy stuff is really my thing.'

Really? Jake's crazes usually last a bit longer. 'I thought you were building up a credible portfolio as a priest.' He can take that as he likes; I no longer have to humour him.

'And I thought April was all-think-and-no-say,' he hits back.

We both grin faintly at each other.

'Coffee?' I see the pot simmering on the stove, but he points to a cup of pink tea beside his mobile phone.

He sits down at the big table and says, 'I do sometimes get a bit carried away, don't I?'

'You could say that,' I agree. 'Although I never thought *you* actually would say that or see it.'

'It was Erica,' he admits. 'Last night and just now too.

She says I have notions. She says I need to be a man and get a proper job. Can you imagine she said that? Long distance. On a mobile phone. Maybe it's hormonal?'

'More like common sense.' I don't add that she probably wanted to slap him too; I never thought this Erica and I would have things in common.

'Oh.'

'Well, what were you talking about when she said it? Orchids?'

'Orchids? Why would we be talking about orchids?'

'Because that's what brought you here, wasn't it? Yiannis' orchid hunting.' And telling me about the baby, but no point going over it all again. I don't really know why I'm bothering now. That reminds me of something. 'By the way, what about that rare orchid you saw on the Troodos walk? I've forgotten its name, but was it one?'

'I don't know,' he says. 'Yiannis took the film in to be developed but there was something wrong with it, it came out blank. Shame.'

'Oh.' *Well played, Yiannis.*

Jake inspects his hands, all the better to avoid my gaze. 'We weren't talking about anything much, me and Erica.' He reverts to that. 'Chit-chat. I was making conversation about the trip. Meeting such an inspiring group of people and thinking about different lifestyle choices—'

'Lifestyle choices?' I can't help myself. 'Oh, Jake, let me interpret: you were talking about how great Red is, how he's a priest and how sexy he makes the Church. Da-di-da-di-da.'

'Christ, April. When did you get so harsh?' he complains. He looks up, ready to be hard done by, and is disconcerted that I'm smiling.

'I'm right.'

He pulls a face and then relents. 'Fair cop,' he admits. 'But it's all so interesting, April, isn't it? Life is so exciting, all these twists and turns. How can we do the same thing forever? I want to try out so many different things.'

This is Jake at his best, his enthusiasm is infectious, like watching an innocent three-year-old discover the world and its possibilities. This is what I fell for, but it doesn't always translate well to the real world. His son or daughter will adore him, rightfully, but God help Erica with two toddler brains on her hands.

'And Red,' he goes on, impervious. 'A bloke like that becomes a priest; it must mean that religion has something I've never seen before. Of course I'm curious. You are too, April, don't pretend.'

'He's an exceptional man.'

'Exceptional man,' he mimics.

I fiddle with the coffee maker.

Jake gives a low whistle. 'It's him, isn't it? Red. He's the one.' In my peripheral vision, I see him lean back in his seat and fold his arms. I say nothing. 'For God's sake, April, I knew it was one of them. Petros probably. Then, that day on the phone I realised Yiannis had got a look-in. I wasn't having that, I...' He's digging a hole and he knows it. I still say nothing. 'Red,' he blusters. 'The ultimate Mr Unavailable. No wonder I got the brush-off.'

He's goading me and I can't be bothered any more; Jake and I should be past bickering. 'You know, you're right.' That surprises us both. 'It could have been Red. But it isn't.'

'Same old April. Somebody will knock that invisible wall down one day.' He tries to look regretful that it won't be him. I let him waffle on; I suspect he'll get little enough opportunity in the future, and I busy myself with the breakfast box. When it's empty I go to stand it outside and find there's a note underneath. Two lines, from Nicole, saying that she's had to run away to do an errand but will phone later. Please carry on without her. *What?*

'Did you know about this?' I interrupt Jake, waving the piece of paper at him.

'Nicole? Yeah. Yiannis saw a taxi pick her up at some ungodly hour.'

'Is everyone else still here?'

'All present and correct, ma'am – I suppose.' Jake furrows his brow. 'Why? What's your problem? It's not an assignation, you know. Nicole's a happily married woman. You should try it some time.'

'Jake?'

He looks up enquiringly.

'Would you do me a favour and just. Fuck. Off.' I stomp away, leaving him open-mouthed.

In the bathroom, I squirt toothpaste and overshoot. Bloody *hell*. I can't stand the sticky texture of toothpaste on my fingers. Where the fuck has Nicole gone? And why? What kind of errand could have turned up in the millisecond between us going to bed and now? Muttering to myself, I don't really register the lukewarm shower trickle, and my wardrobe doesn't require any thought. Maybe she's gone home to confess her indiscretion to Andreas. Or he could have phoned her; yes, sent her to stalk his next victim. And that reminds me, I drag a brush through my hair, wincing at the knots, they still haven't told me what's the story with my stupid painting.

I wonder where the nearest piano is; if my hands and heart could pound through Prokofiev's 'War Sonatas' – my fail-safe stress-buster – it would stop it pounding through my head. It's angry and dissonant and fast but, never admitted in public, I always hear just a little bit of the *Keystone Cops* capering in it and it cheers me up no end. Even thinking about it helps. By the time I've thrown my meagre belongings into my suitcase and zipped it shut I've decided to see myself for the idiot I am. Nicole is a lovely, kind person who has gone off on a perfectly innocent quest for – something. Why shouldn't she go? Why should she tell me?

46

Troodos Mountains, Cyprus
September 1974

Dear April and Mrs Gale's class,

My mum is back! She is really. She arrived early in the morning today with the farmer who sometimes brings us milk. Aunt Irini woke us up, and there was my mum, climbing out of the trailer and running to us. She already had her arms open wide to hug us, all three, and she cried and said she should never have let us go. I dropped the milk jug and all the precious white liquid swam out into a messy puddle, but nobody even thought to scold me.

My mum is back and everything is going to be alright. I will see you soon, April. I will write another letter when I know which day my mum is bringing us back. I am sorry, Mrs Gale, I have missed the beginning of the term but I will work hard to make it up.

Love from, Elena Z
xxx

PS I didn't keep my promise to write one letter every week because I was a bit poorly. Some bad things happened and Aunt Irini said I should try to forget about them. I haven't forgotten them but now I am better.

She wondered how many times she had wished and wished that maybe this would be the day Mama came.

When dreams came true, you were supposed to be happy, Elena knew that. She knew it but it hadn't happened, and she felt ashamed. It was just like with the tree houses, she had wished and wished then and look what happened. She had thought everything would be fine when she saw Mama again, she really had. But already there were arguments in low voices filtering through the bedroom door. Mama was not back even a whole day. Elena put a glass against the wall like Krista had shown her and was interested that it worked. It was bottom-of-the-sea-ish but she could hear. She didn't care that it was not for her ears, a sin, because all around her everyone was doing much bigger sins and God hadn't struck them down.

'The whole of Southern Cyprus is a refugee camp.' Elena held her breath to hear what Mama was saying. 'There are no public buildings not heaving with bodies. There are families living in trees, for heaven's sake.'

'We can see that, can you see the overcrowding here? This is a tiny village, doubled, tripled in size, more than even when the summer tourists come. We are living three families in two rooms. What are we supposed to do?' Aunt Irini sounded tired.

'If we got the ID cards—' That was Antony but Mama cut him off straightaway.

'No,' she said, sharp like a needle. 'No. No paper trail, it is too dangerous for all of us. If they find you here, they find me and—'

'How? How? We do not know where you are. We know nothing.' Elena thought Aunt Irini was crying now. 'Meanwhile, the girls need food and warmth. The rain is here, the cold is coming and soon it will be winter. We need blankets. Do you know there is not one blanket in the whole village? We arrived here with nothing. No things. *Nothing.*'

Mama said, 'Where are my girls?' It sounded as if she

was getting up, the springs on the bed twanged. 'I need to see them, to tell them.'

'Tell them what?' Aunt Irini sounded unkind. 'That Stefan turned out to be more than a business arrangement after all? Or that this is a flying visit and you'll be gone again, puff, like the wind, as soon as darkness comes?'

The voices grew even quieter then and Elena thought about the happy and carefree chatting that had gone on in the sitting room above the chip shop in England. *Tell them what?* Please, *please,* St Mary the Theotokos, it would be about them going back to England. She moved quickly and silently away from the bedroom door and went outside before she could be shooed there.

Elena sat in the yard of the strangers' house, not doing very much except scratching her name on the stones with a stick. There were no chores to do. There were so many aunties staying in the half-moon of houses that they all squabbled over who would wipe the dishes and straighten the beds and sweep the yards. Although it was impossible to do any of those things anyway, as far as Elena could see; there were so many people that they lived in shifts. At any hour of the day or night there were half a dozen bodies eating or sleeping or sitting around outside. That Mama, Irini and Antony were alone in the bedroom showed how serious their conversation must be. *Tell them what?*

That word stuck in her head: refugee. Was that what they were, Elena and her sisters? She knew what it meant but she hadn't thought it was still a real thing that real people were, it belonged in history books. Anna from *When Hitler Stole Pink Rabbit* was a refugee. She rolled the word around her mouth. *Refugee.* They were refugees. People would read about them and feel sorry for them. April might read about them and Elena didn't want her to feel sorry.

The world was beginning to remind Elena of a book she had once read, where a girl travelled through a mirror and lived her life the same but back to front; after a while the girl couldn't remember which side of life was real. Elena knew exactly how the girl felt: up in the mountains the right things were in the wrong place but just as the sisters started to get used to them, everything shifted again.

47

It doesn't help that there's a weird air of anticipation throughout the morning, pre-Christmas or wedding-day vibes: the house phone ringing, low voices, closed doors and Yiannis procrastinating over Apostolos Andreas. Maybe it's about Nicole but maybe that's me projecting and I'm not ready to know anyway, so I pretend not to notice. They could be male-bonding over Kevin discovering Petros' worries about his prostate or something, except that there's no sense of concern.

It's Kevin who lets the exhausted penny drop. I've wandered out into the yard. The land around the house is so much prettier than the building itself, there is even a pool, and beyond the boundary grassy, rocky fields and skittish, hee-hawing donkeys in the distance. The back door slams open and I hear him calling for Red.

'OF? There you are,' Kevin's voice says. 'Petros says Nicole was just on the phone with the green light. He thinks you're the one who should tell your girlfriend. Where is she, by the way? Oops.'

He's seen me. The rest is too cryptic to guess.

Red catches me by the boundary wall.

'So what is it?' I ask as we walk. 'I take it you're some sort of spokesperson?'

'Yes.' Red's equanimity is incomparable. So is his honesty. 'That's what all the discreet and barely perceptible whispering was about. You wouldn't have noticed it.' His lips twitch. 'I'm supposed to kidnap you – subtly, obviously –and pretend we're going to buy groceries or something,' he says. 'And then whisk you off upcountry to meet Nicole. She has a surprise for you. I told them I was fairly sure you don't like surprises…'

I grin, but my heart is beating uncomfortably. 'You're taking me to meet Nicole? Just Nicole? Why?'

Red shrugs, clearly on the same page. 'I truly don't know.' He opens his palms in a sympathetic gesture.

'But what if…' I stop. Is this what last night was all about; what the preoccupation, the vanishing act, the *warning*, all point to? She's found something.

Red says it for me. 'What if she's found Elena? Of course it crossed my mind, all of our minds.' He looks out across the fields, then back at me. 'April, I don't know if she has. But I trust her, and she knows you trust her too. I think Nicole has much more tact and understanding than to haul in a stranger, trumpets blaring and flags waving.'

He's right. Of course he's right. But what if he's wrong?

'It's more likely she's found the tree houses,' Red suggests. 'Unless all of this is something random none of us has thought of.'

'Of course.' I take a deep breath which turns into a shiver. 'Of course that's it. The tree houses. I should have thought of that first.' Why is it only partial reassurance? Be careful what you wish for: thrown-away words flying back to me.

Red puts a hand on my shoulder. 'It's up to you, April. Do you want to take the chance? Shall I drive you? Or not. I can phone and say no, or you can phone and speak to Nicole instead.' He hesitates. 'You and I could go somewhere for a while, even. It doesn't have to be the community jolly to Apostolos Andreas. You *can* trust me.'

I sigh. 'I know I can. But I haven't any choice, Red. Neither have you.' We both know it. The Church is an anchor too heavy. And for me the past, or Nicole – I'm not sure which – is a pull too strong.

'True enough,' he says. 'Remember, keep an open mind, an open heart and... well, you gotta have faith, April.' He tilts my head back, looks at me and traces his thumb, the sign of the cross, across my forehead. 'God bless you, April,' he says. 'God bless both of us.'

But then, when he kisses me, it's as the man not the priest.

Red drops me off as instructed, further along the coast, and I go for a walk along the cliffs, feeling strangely like a bride being given away. Khachaturian thunders in my ears until I reach the closing bars, fade out, and there is nothing left but to put the truth together, like a jigsaw puzzle for which I've finally found a few more pieces.

Whoever said that thing about anticipation being better than arrival had a point. *Be careful what you wish for* – that one's on point too. *The past is a foreign country...* I could go on.

The truth is, here and now in Cyprus, having seen Famagusta and driven a contemporary approximation of the roads Elena and her family travelled – maybe – Elena just isn't here. My Elena is the English Elena, cosy and exotic together in the back room of the fish and chip shop, in our English tree house, in Mrs Gale's primary class. If I was to walk up a path and ring a doorbell it would be to see her there in those places, eternally ten years old. She's not a child who was dragged into the horrors of war, displaced and dispossessed. She's not a chambermaid in the Palm Beach Hotel, not the owner of a nightclub in Agia Napa, or a lawyer in Nicosia, a historian at Trooditissa. She's not a mother or a grown-up or forty years old – an older version of her mama when I knew them. I don't want her to be these things.

Nicole said I wasn't chasing Elena; I knew it then, I know it now. I'm chasing a time machine. I want my dream vindicated not destroyed and what I want is not an unknown, future – present – Elena but a symbolic one, a recreation of the warmth and fun of 1974. I only want Elena now if I can build her. My dream Elena.

So all the while we're facing reality, let's get this straight. I really only want to see Nicole. I don't want to see anyone, not even Elena – sorry, *sorry*, Elena – alongside her.

She should be here by now, Nicole. Standing on the headland, I can see the few and far between vehicles; service jeeps and tractors all of them. The open-top silver sports car comes into frame like an adman's dream. Absently, I admire the sleek lines of it as it slows, and purrs into the lay-by below me. *Tick that one off, Lucy Jordan.* That should be Nicole's car, I think: the elegant wrapping, the fury under the bonnet. I look again, and it is Nicole's car. Or at least, she's the person driving it.

And she's alone.

No passengers. No voluble Cypriot convoy.

She's tied a scarf round her hair, practical to keep the wind from whipping it into a frenzy and blinding her, but that and the sunglasses give her a fifties Hollywood aura, and the adman flaunts his face again. I watch her remove the grey silky material, attempt, in vain, to smooth it out and fold it, streaming in the wind, then secure it somewhere under the dashboard. She swings open the door but stays in the driver's seat to swap soft ballet pumps for something taller and spiky at the bottom of her white jeans. Even as I stand here, watching, I wonder if I'm really seeing all of this, or is it a trick of my mind? Am I simply seeing the beautiful advert; surely, she's too far away from me for such detail. Then she looks up, looks at me, and it is her, and she's really not that far away after all.

'April,' I think I hear her call, battling the wind. She waves, a big smile starts across her face. There's a split second of hesitation when the wave and the smile freeze, and then they are back, complete and determined.

It's then that I know. And it's so like nothing I've known before that I'm winded. Nothing like that strange familiar safety of meeting Red for the first time. Nothing like how I imagined reuniting with Elena. Nothing like anything. But it makes perfect sense.

The soundtrack is the Elgar cellos that everyone knows, no distraction, just beauty. A coup de foudre, the French call it, so obvious that I'm not sure why it's taken me this long. I suppose we only see what we want to see or are programmed to see. The reason I don't need to find Elena any more is simple: I've already found what I want. And I found her when I found Nicole.

We make our way towards each other, and I know there is a crease of trepidation mirrored on our faces. When we're close enough to speak, she goes first.

'I am sorry, April,' Nicole says. 'I am sorry I left without telling you, and with such poor timing, sorry for the grumpy cow I have been. It was partly the situation with Andreas and me, that is all true, but also I was so impatient, I wanted there to be a surprise and I wanted to make it.'

I shake my head to dismiss the apology, even as I say, 'What did you want to be a surprise?' I can hear the strangulated knot in my voice and she can too because she puts out her hands and waits for me to grasp them. Slowly, I do.

'Perhaps that is my second apology.' I've never seen her so uncertain, even in her anxiety over Damaris at the cathedral in Famagusta. There she was angry but firm. Here she's as nervous to tell as I am to hear. 'April,' she says, 'I have not found Elena. Yiannis' travelling circus might have led you to believe I did. It did not occur to me they would become so excited and imply that I have done so.'

I let out a carefully controlled sigh and give her a much more natural smile. 'Oh, Nicole, I didn't think you had,' I say. 'Well, maybe only for a second.' What a second. 'And only then because,' I grin and repeat her word, 'of Yiannis' circus back there.'

'Are you disappointed?' she asks.

'No, I'm not disappointed,' I say. 'Anyway, like you

said, none of it exists – no, don't argue, you were right. You are right.'

She looks at me for a long second, her brows faintly drawn, then shrugs acceptance. Her whole face lights up. 'But I have found something good, April. Something you will really like,' she says. 'You have guessed already?'

She's so delighted I'm glad I did guess, glad I've had my moment of doubt, glad I can please her now. I just want to make her happy. Feigning ignorance is no lie; I don't know for sure. Like Red said, maybe it's something else entirely.

Of course it's the tree houses. 'Go on…'

'I have found the tree houses, April. Elena's tree houses. I have found them.'

48

Troodos Mountains, Cyprus
Monday 16th September 1974

Elena was counting the days. When she got well, after the scarecrows, she had found a thick square calendar in the drawer of the cabinet beside the bed she was sharing with Krista, Sofia and, quite often, Aunt Irini. It had belonged to a boy called Derin, his name was still there on the top corner, faded and squint. The pages were tiny, with a motto that Elena couldn't read, and each day you ripped one off. Now she had a pile of thirty-two.

If they were still in England, they would be back at school now. Aunt Irini and one of the men from the tent camp nearby, who were teachers in their real lives, had wondered about doing some lessons with the children in the village and the camp, but was it worth it, they said to one another, when surely they'd be going home soon? Elena wouldn't mind some lessons. Even though there might be fifty children – nobody was exactly sure – in the village and in the tent camp on the plateau below them, somehow there was nobody else who was ten. Even Sofia had a friend, and everyone else was in a group: the old men huddled drinking coffee and fighting the war in their heads, the old women gossiped and looked for chores, and the young women went for walks and dreamed of the young men who weren't there.

Krista had joined a pack of older girls and was thrilled about it. Only Elena knew Krista had lied to get into their club: Krista had told them a long story about watching a hundred Turkish parachutists fall from the sky like a flock of human birds; she said that she, all alone, raised the alarm that evacuated Varosha. She had got the story from a smuggled newspaper in one of the villages and told it word for word. Elena had seen it too, and couldn't believe how the girls clustered around Krista's wilder and wilder tales. But as long as she kept quiet, Krista – and so the others – let Elena hang around on their edges; all she had to do was admire them. Elena didn't care about them but she couldn't be alone, so she pretended. She watched them now.

The bigger girls had just found three tins lined up in the shadow of the stone wall, half hidden by the trunk of a gnarled old tree. They were trying to screw off the lids, giggling and telling each other it was money that they would spend on lipstick and chocolate; there would be enough to bribe the soldiers at the camp to fetch it. Elena watched them dirty their nails and their knees and exclaim in horror when they found the cans full of dry grey earth and nothing else. A few minutes later, when they had disappeared to clean their hands and sponge their dresses, Elena put down her stick and went slowly over to the tins. Carefully, she stood the tins upright in a line and refilled them as best she could.

Krista, hovering between the girls' company and waiting for Mama, went over to Elena to frown and nudge her. 'What are you doing, daydream girl?' she said.

'Helping,' said Elena. Krista wouldn't understand. April would have, but not Krista.

She was doing it for Mamun, her friend at the tree houses. Long ago, before England, he had told her that when Turkish people left a place they filled a can with earth from that place and took it with them; it meant they took a little bit of home with them and would go back. That's what had happened here, Elena thought, but the treasure had been left behind. Perhaps the people from this village had had to leave in the middle of the night also, and had seen dreadful things on the road. Had the men come here too, with their loudhailers and their guns? She thought of Mamun's house opposite the tree houses. Was that what had been happening there on the day of the bonfire? Please God, he had time to fill his can. Perhaps if she put the earth back here, waiting in the cans, the magic would work anyway. For everybody.

Elena didn't say any of that to Krista. She just carried on working and Krista tossed her head, cross.

'Everyone is going mad,' she said. 'You are going maddest, Elena. You started it when you bashed your head on the bathtub. Now the only person madder than you is the mother of Maria Balis who cries for her washing machine. She is called Elena too, so maybe it is a mad person's name.'

Elena sighed, a copy of Aunt Irini, causing Krista to give her a hefty shove before stalking off to join her gang. Krista didn't understand one bit, thought Elena, and she wished for the millionth time that April was there – no, that they were both in April's tree house worrying about when Mrs Gale would let them be servers at lunchtime. She put the tins back where they came from, sitting down beside them and wishing she had brought a matchbox of earth or a stone or pressed flowers from April's garden.

Mama found her still there much later, when dusk was threatening and the shadows starting to twist and dance and Krista was still gone. What should she say about that? Mama sat down beside Elena on the hard stone, and Elena concentrated on being grateful that she was back, except... *tell them what?*

'My beautiful Elena, you understand that I cannot stay here with you, don't you?' she said. Then, more sternly, when Elena did not raise her eyes from the stick tracing shapes in the dust, 'Elena, look at me, please.'

Elena did as she was told, she even managed a small smile.

'Now that I know you are alright, I have to go and finish my work,' Mama said. 'And to find Stefan. We are going to have a baby, Elena. A new baby brother or sister for you all.' She patted her stomach which was hardly rounder than usual. 'Won't that be lovely?'

'Yes,' said Elena, but she whispered it. She wondered if Aunt Irini had told Mama about the scarecrows and that Elena wasn't really very alright at all. But good Elena never made a fuss.

'That's my good girl.' Mama hugged her. 'Soon this will be over, Elena. And we will live in Greece. There is a place I am dreaming of in the region called Peloponnese; safe and warm, a land of stories and legends.' Her voice was muffled, soaking into Elena's shoulder. 'We will make a new forever home, yes? All together.'

Greece; she'd never been to Greece. What about England? What about April? Elena's head swam. It swam for too long.

'What do you think, Elena?' Mama was asking. 'Elena?'

'I thought you were here to take us home,' she whispered finally.

'Home?' Mama sat back and chucked Elena under the chin, forcing their eyes to meet.

'I never said goodbye.' Elena's whisper turned into a croak. 'To April. She's my best friend, she will be waiting for me—'

'Oh, my darling.' Mama's voice was bright and brittle, a shade off impatient. 'England was never home, just a... a stopgap. April will have made new friends by now, and you must do the same. This is life, Elena. It moves on always, people move on to new things.'

Back in England, April's mum had a cuckoo clock. It had a man and a woman who popped out of a little door when the cuckoo called, but they never came out at the same time and when one appeared the other disappeared. Elena thought of it now because Mama was here and Krista was gone. That meant when Mama went away again, Krista would be back safe. It did. Elena didn't need to say that Krista was missing, because she was coming back.

'Elena?'

She heard her mama say her name again, louder.

'What is it, Elena? Tell me,' Mama was saying.

How could Elena tell her? That her world, already off-kilter, was pulling away from her, like soft sand under waves. That Mama, her rock, the one she trusted above all, the one who was always right, had just said something Elena knew was wrong, very wrong.

'Elena?'

Everything, Elena trusted, everything *would* turn out alright one day just as long as she never forgot about April and April never forgot about her.

49

Nicole stage-manages it perfectly. She stops the car beyond the curve of the bay and we walk, only for five minutes or so, then she stops and faces me again.

'This is your moment,' she says. 'Yours and Elena's. Say hello to her in the place you were always supposed to meet her.' She drops back slightly, motioning me forward, and then...

The tree houses. Right here.

Waiting.

Fanciful, I know. But oh, Elena. It's exactly as you described. Exactly what I've imagined all these years. I stand, looking and looking, drinking in the scene. In just a few hours the tree houses will be a different experience, mine and Nicole's, but right here and now, they are still yours, all yours. The only thing of yours that you and I have – finally – shared here; everything else is from England. I hadn't realised that mattered till now.

There's no music, Elena. No music. And the silence is right; it's so right that I don't notice it. Of course, the tree houses come from a time before I played any music and it surely proves that these eternal soundtracks in my mind are learned not innate... but stop. *Stop it.* That's for another time.

Thirty years disappear in this first view. *Tree house* is the perfect name for these ramshackle wooden lookout posts

– shacks, really, shacks on stilts with glassless windows looking over the sea. They stand in three irregular rows following the curl of the water, their brown staining faded and weather-beaten, resembling a robotic army, ragged in hasty retreat, toes almost dipping into the water and frozen by a last-minute command. Are they exactly as you remember them, I wonder. Or has the grown-up Elena seen them for herself once or a hundred times since 1974, even this year or last? Has she? Have you, Elena?

The beach itself is pebbled and stony, gritty sand and gorse-like grass poking through. I bend down beside a single and sparse clutch of yellow wildflowers, straggly but determined. I'm about to pick the bravest, tallest, when I hear footsteps behind me and look back. Nicole is in my shadow, as if she doesn't quite belong.

'Do you think these are orchids?' I ask her.

Nicole steps forward, leaning over me to look. 'I don't think so,' she says. 'I'm sure it's okay to pick them.'

'No,' I say, straightening up. 'They're better here. Yellow for friendship and happiness.'

'We can sleep here tonight, if you would like?' Nicole says. 'I met the owner this morning and told him – just enough. He lives over there.' She indicates the small whitewashed building, a guest house, just across the road, where a middle-aged man is hovering discreetly.

'Alan Keeble, formerly of Selly Oak, Birmingham,' he introduces himself to me. 'Like I told your friend, you're welcome to stay. Make your choice.' He waves us towards the tree houses. 'There's nobody else here. This is rustic living at best and too early in the season for all but the most diehard nature lovers.' Alan explains he bought the complex from a Turkish family, five years ago, when they headed inland for a more comfortable living. It was a rash decision, he says. He found the cabins quirky, thought it a great gimmick. 'Nothing's changed for forty years, just the basic upkeep and a lot of patching. It's a wonder they've lasted.'

But not for much longer, Elena. Occasionally the overspill from the turtle conservation project nearby camp here but most people ask for the guest house; travellers want the appearance of rustic rather than actual rustic. So that's what he's going to give them. A makeover.

Elena, it's the eleventh hour. Another few months, a couple of years at most and your tree houses will be a boutique hotel. Then again, you might well have longed for those facilities if you had to hide here at the height of the war. Nicole tells him a little more of your story – I'm silent, still looking – and Alan agrees.

'It's hearsay,' he says, 'but apparently refugees did pass through, staying for a night then disappearing into the next one until the Turkish army – or maybe the Greek, nobody seems too sure – moved in and commandeered the whole piece of land. I thought I might look into the archive, but there's nothing. Nothing either side will admit to. The tree houses are a piece of history nobody wants.'

'I do.' I come to, at last, and fishing in my bag, I show him your picture, Elena. The three of you all together, here. Alan peers at it and I can see he wants to give me a story – a solution – but he doesn't have one. He himself admits he had barely heard of Cyprus in the seventies.

'I've never thought of these rooms as tree houses,' he says. 'I'm certain nobody around here calls them that.'

As if to compensate, he walks with us, determined to find the actual tree house in the photo. The three of us stop in front of each one and Alan pours over the grainy print and eventually decides it is number three: front row in the middle. I agree, Nicole agrees, but more out of good manners and wishful thinking than reality.

'You could try asking Marco if he knows any more,' Alan offers. 'Over at the turtle place, SPOT.' He jerks his thumb over his shoulder. 'Marco's an environmentalist who knows this area inside out. He's been coming here for years, but I don't really know him. Oh, he's not unfriendly, but he doesn't say much. Make it quick though because I think he's away home tomorrow.'

'Okay.' We both nod.

'The important thing is that we've found the tree houses,' I say. I'm not convinced either he or Nicole believes I'm telling the truth.

Alan returns to his office and Nicole goes to fetch the car. As incongruent as it will be amidst the tree houses, all our belongings are inside. I sit down against the stilts of tree house number three and alternate my gaze between the photograph and the water.

With some more slow-burning recognition, I see something new in your picture, Elena. How could I have missed it? Maybe I needed to be here for the spell to work. It wasn't taken in the summer of 1974, was it? It couldn't have been because Krista's hair is long, very long, and she'd had it cut the week you vanished. How your Aunt Irini yelled! Do you remember? She knew your mama would hate it. I'm not sure Krista liked it that much, but she loved the effect it had. This photograph must have been taken the year before you came to England? It can't be more; apart from Krista's hair, you look as I remember you, although maybe Sofia is a bit shorter than when I knew her?

It's a blow, Elena. The photo is no less precious whenever it was taken, and you might say what does a year or so matter? It matters in war though, doesn't it? I've been banking on the fact that you all looked so happy, like children on holiday, and therefore why ever you ended up back in Cyprus, it was cheerful and fun. But maybe you were the refugees by then, the ones that stayed here overnight, rushed to a high-rise in Varosha, circling back and forth, no longer smiling, before finding your refuge – *please* – in the mountains or the remotest of inland villages—

'April? April, are you okay?' asks Nicole's voice.

I blink rapidly, dash away the tears, and look up over my shoulder, feeling the light touch of her hand. 'I'm fine.' I shuffle slightly – and pointlessly in this vast expanse of emptiness – on the sand so she can sit down beside me. 'I was composing an imaginary letter to Elena. I think,' I wince, 'it's called closure.'

'Closure? Then you believe this is the end? So sudden? The tree houses really are the finale of your search for Elena?' She brings her knees up and rests her chin on them, head tilted towards me.

'I don't know.' I consider what she says. 'It feels as if I've found something real at last. More real than Varosha, and... Oh, I really don't know. Maybe I've filled in a bit more of that big hole which started with Damaris and Famagusta and carried on with Soussana's stories. I'm not sure why it feels full circle, but it does. Even if...'

'If?'

I explain my thoughts about the timing of the photograph.

Nicole thinks it through before saying, 'April, you are a person who overanalyses much too much... Yes, you know I am right! Maybe it is most important to know only that your fairy-tale friend really did exist. People make such pilgrimages all the time.'

'Petros once said something similar.'

'Then how can you doubt two utterly self-confident Greeks?' She pushes her hands into the sand. 'And here is one more thing Petros and I would agree on: we need to eat. I have taken nothing since breakfast and I expect you are the same. Alan says there is a restaurant along the road that will cook for us. I am weak with hunger and whilst I would be happy to see the real Elena here in her tree houses, I do not wish her apparition brought on by faintness.'

'There's no apparition in the world that would dare appear to you,' I tell her. 'And there's nothing remotely eerie about this place. Look. Listen.'

The sun is setting quickly now, bleaching the colours monochrome, and soon we'll be enveloped in an inky, velvet darkness. There's no wind, and the water is still, at best it laps the shore with a languid touch.

'There's nothing to fear in this silence, Nicole,' I whisper.
'I believe you.' She is equally quiet. 'April?'
'Yes?'
'You were relieved when you saw I had not found Elena. You were brittle like... like dried leaves, and your eyes darted this way and that.'
'I'd no idea I was so transparent.' I shift uncomfortably, but there's no point denying it.
'Why, April?'

Because it is you I've been looking for, not Elena, and Red was a decoy, is what I want to say, but I hold back. For the second time. 'Nicole, I want to meet the ten-year-old Elena. She's the dream I've carried around.' I prevaricate with my earlier musings. 'Oh, God, I don't want to meet my... my middle-aged, jaded, cellulite-ridden, glasses-wearing contemporary – don't laugh – the woman who's bound to remember the past so differently. What if I met her and she didn't remember me? Or worse, was indifferent? I don't want to find that the treasure has disintegrated.'

'You want to feel important to someone?' Nicole asks slowly.

'Well, yes.' It's a left-sided question but I consider it. 'I suppose I do. I want to belong. Don't we all?'

Nicole digs her hand deep in the sand again, lifts it up and watches as the grains run through her fingers. When they have all disappeared, she asks: 'If someone, no, if *I* did find her, Elena – would you want to know?'

I try to access Nicole's train of thought. 'I'd want to know that you would tell me. I mean, you'd have to tell me, even if I didn't want to know.' I watch her pick through the maze to the meaning of that; she nods faintly. 'Too much of my life has been unspoken,' I say. 'Even with people the most important to me. I want that to stop.'

She nods again, more firmly this time. After a long while, she leans in close. 'April?'
'Yes?'

'Why are we whispering?'

'I don't know.' I raise my voice to normal. I cast out for surer ground. 'Come on, dinner it is. You are probably right, we need it.'

'Greeks are never wrong about food.' Her tone matches mine: forced heartiness. 'Elena's mama taught you that long before you knew me.'

'True. Tell me, are you always so confident, Nicole?' I'm joking, I think, still looking out to sea, and joking, but the quick retort I expect doesn't come. I turn to her and she looks unusually serious and slightly confused. I feel my muscles tense and I watch her without moving.

She stands up slowly, holding out a hand to pull me up too. 'I was.' She looks away. 'But now, not so much. And it is all to do with you, April Rose.'

It's the beginning of some kind of declaration, I know it is, but right now my ears are closed to it and I know that's the way she wants it too.

Not forever, just for now.

50

Lazily, and for want of a decent torch in a rapidly dwindling twilight, we drive the half a mile or so to the restaurant around the corner. The place is in darkness save for a low light on the porch that illuminates a handwritten sign: *Ring for food and drink*. We do, and the door is opened by a short, thin man who introduces himself as Salih.

'Welcome, welcome,' he says, painstaking in his English. 'My neighbour, Alan, he called me to expect you.' He clicks on the lights as we pass through a small reception area, a beige-tiled square room with plastic tables and chairs, which is obviously the main dining room, and into a conservatory with similar tables under the large windows. 'Choose.' He motions, expansive as if it's the Grill room at the Savoy. 'Beautiful views in daytime. You can imagine them. You see only each other tonight though. Sit. Sit.' He flaps at us. 'I will feed and water you with no delay.'

We sit in more or less silence, grinning at each other over the absurdity of it all. There is much banging and clattering from the kitchen, the occasional whoosh of something frying, and the intermittent hum of voices.

'I guess we eat what we are given,' Nicole says in a low tone. 'Why not when we are the only guests? It could be wonderful. Or not.'

I reply equally quietly. 'Remember, I'm the woman whose

previous dining extravaganzas have been at Georgios' tavern with Yiannis, the disappointed ex-priest, and Jake, the idiot father-to-be. There's no gold standard for food and no comparison for company.'

Whatever wise retort Nicole has is lost in a flurry of the kitchen door opening and Salih backing out, balancing a pile of dishes that all but hide his skinny torso. He serves with a flourish, reeling them off: 'Dolmades, shish kebab, *cacık*, *tahin*, *ahtapot*. And chips.'

We eat. We eat some more; octopus and chips isn't something you get every day.

By the time the savoury dishes are empty, cleared and replaced by sweet ones, the number of patrons has tripled – each couple appearing through the gloom exactly as we did – and hours have passed. To finish, Salih repeatedly sets fire to a cocktail he calls a 'Flaming Lamborghini'.

'A toast to your flashy, brazen and totally pretentious hire car,' I say.

'It is the only model they had,' she protests, 'without waiting for a delivery from Nicosia. This is the curse of the new marina being built on the other side of the island: new money, new expectations. But secretly, I—'

'You love it.'

'I really do. I love it,' she grins. 'Do not tell. I will deny, deny, deny.'

'To the car!'

We raise glasses and clink them; splutter, choke and go in for seconds. Salih tops them up delighted; he circles the room pouring effusively.

'I told Jake to fuck off this morning. In capitals.' My pride is fuelled with alcohol fumes.

'That is far more deserving of a toast. Whoops.' Nicole raises her glass, somewhat erratically, again. 'And, if I may say it, much overdue.' She stifles a hiccup. 'Excuse me. This drink is lethal. Why?'

'Why did I tell Jake to fuck off? Well... I can't remember

exactly what he did today, but I said it because he is a dick,' I explain. She's right about the drink; I feel assaulted by a hundred per cent proof.

'These are wise words. April, I am proud of you.'

'Thank you. I'm proud of myself. Thia Ana would be proud of me too; Cypriot-April saying what's on her mind. Let's drink to Ana.'

'I am proud of me too,' Nicole announces.

'Of course you are. You should be.' I nod. 'Why?'

'I gave up smoking. Yes, April, I did. You have not noticed.'

'No! Yes?' I try to think. 'Yes, Nicole. You're right.'

'Yes, I am.'

We drink to it. We drink to everyone: to Petros, to Damaris and Orestes, to Andreas, Jarlath and Kevin, to Yiannis. That's before we start on my parents, Elena and her family, and end on the Berlin Philharmonic orchestra. 'Without them, I might be on tour instead of here,' I explain. 'Imagine.'

'We have forgotten someone,' Nicole states. 'Who have we forgotten, April Rose?'

'We have forgotten someone,' I agree, through a fog. 'We have forgotten... We have forgotten – Red!'

'Red,' she repeats. 'To Red.'

'Poor Red,' I say. 'Poor Red, Nicole. We can't ever forget Red, because, Nicole, I love Red.'

'I know you do,' she replies.

She looks a bit sad, I think. I have to reassure her. 'I love Red, Nicole,' I say. 'But I love you too. Nicole, I love you more. In fact, I love you most.'

'Good,' says Nicole. 'Because I love you too.'

It could be a full stop or an opening paragraph but it's neither; we are both very pleased with ourselves and we are both very, very drunk.

There is a similar sense of bemused satiation emanating throughout the room. I doubt anyone who randomly knocks on the door here expects it; like finding a speakeasy in a Southern

Baptist church hall. Salih, on cue, counteracts it with a gallon of strong, strong coffee. This is what the Cypriot stuff was invented for.

At some ungodly hour with a sense of unreality and a high-intensity borrowed flashlight, we stumble outside into fresh air that barely penetrates; I feel like the Ready Brek kid from the adverts of my childhood, and check around my outline to see if I'm all aglow. I try to explain it to Nicole but I'm not sure she gets it. Arms linked, we ignore the car and stumble back to the tree houses on foot, blunder up the curiously endless ladder to number three, and collapse onto the thin mattress that all but fills the boxy room. Squinting, it's possible to see the pinprick stars out of the window and we vie to join the dots and make complicated pictures. When cross-eyed with that, we strain to hear the faint lapping of the sea on the sand. The world outside might have ended.

'There is no one but us, April,' Nicole states.

I ponder the profundity of the remark. 'No one but us,' I echo.

I'm not sure if she leans in to kiss me first, or whether I turn to her. Either way it feels like a very good thing, the only thing, to do. It's a short kiss, experimental. The second one is longer though. When it stops, I wait for the awkwardness.

'Why is this not strange?' Nicole voices it for me.

'I want to say because it is right. But it might be because we are drunk?'

'I suddenly feel very sober,' she says.

'Me too.'

'Then?'

'Then let us hold on to the magic at least for now.'

It is the perfect night.

The morning after the night before is less so. I don't have a hangover as such, not a pounding head or a desperate thirst – despite the fact that I so rarely drink – simply a sensation that my thoughts are wading around in treacle and need to be freed one by one before they can join a sentence.

If Nicole were Red… If Red were Nicole… Well, what? Where am I going with this? I try again: Red is a priest… too complicated. Nicole is a woman… so unexplored. Oh, Yiannis, bother you. Why couldn't you be more… just *more*.

It was just a kiss. A few kisses. A one-off. No, it wasn't *just* anything.

I turn over and see that Nicole is awake, watching me.

'You look as if you are having regrets,' she says.

'Only about the alcohol.'

'And the cold.' Nicole shivers theatrically through Alan's excessive provision of pillows and patchwork quilts.

'That too.' Fleetingly, I think how lovely to swim with the sun newly risen. Then I shiver too. Later in the season, maybe.

'We could walk along the shore,' Nicole offers, as if she reads my mind. 'Dress quickly and we will not notice the heavy dew. I do not think there is likely to be warm water in the shower—'

'I'll be the hero.' I grab for a fleecy layer, jeans and trainers, blessedly stored under the bed. I pull them over yesterday's summer clothes. The rest of our belongings are locked in the car abandoned at Salih's restaurant.

Nicole doesn't bother waiting, she follows me down into the bathroom, where we both shy away from the cool trickle of water that splashes and puddles on the concrete floor.

'Where do we go from here?' Nicole says as we follow the edge of the water.

'Literally or metaphorically?' I'm not sure about the first, the latter is a minefield.

'We should go along to the SPOT development and ask for Marco,' Nicole decides, taking, with my tacit approval, the easier path, the one to Elena. 'It is a – long shot? But why not? I was thinking also that when we collect the car and return Salih's flashlight, we may ask him about her. He is of an age to remember the war as a grown man.'

'Good ideas.' I might have said that stuff about closure, have a few misgivings about what I want to find, but it would be ridiculous to come this far without a little more chasing of Elena.

We walk until the sun is fully risen, and then sit for a few minutes on the sand, enjoying the watery warmth leaking from it. It occurs to me that this is probably the most romantic moment of my life; and I flush with – embarrassment?

'What is it?' Nicole asks, taking my hand.

'I don't know...'

Kissing on an intoxicating – intoxicated – moonlit night is a far cry from the cold light of day. Life might be simpler if the magic had disappeared.

It hasn't.

To hell with simplicity, I'm delighted. I know that she is too.

We return to where Alan has left a platter of olives, halloumi and bread, and a big flask of coffee on a picnic table outside the guest house. We sit side by side underneath a home-made canopy that bends and flexes in the breeze; the snapping sounds like gunfire in the stillness. I watch Nicole's hands curl around the tin utility mug. Her fingernails are painted pink, an orange-tinted pink that adds a statement to the casual girlishness. Even in vacation mode, she is stylish.

I think back a few weeks to my arrival in Cyprus; seeing the Verena Bay and Petros on home ground; that first day in Agia Napa meeting Nicole and Red, then Andreas and Yiannis. I marvel at how already the freshness is fading, the newness of it all gone forever and I will myself to enjoy the moment, appreciate the events that have brought me here to somewhere I'm starting to think I might belong. I catch my breath.

Nicole notices. 'What is it?' she asks, gentle.

'The power of chance. Of accident. Of coincidence.'

'The way in which you have come here?' she says. I nod and she adds, 'Call it what you will. It is life.'

'But how easily it mightn't have happened.' I find myself stupidly near to tears.

'If. If. If.' Nicole hands me a napkin to dab my eyes. 'If it had not been this it would have been something else. But I am glad it is this. And without the help of Ganesh or Caerus or any such talisman.'

One of us had to mention Andreas. It leads to a thought more prosaic. 'The portrait, Nicole. A lifetime ago you hinted that Andreas,' I swallow, 'intended something I might not like.'

'He wants to paint a second picture,' she says simply. 'A comparison piece, a study.'

'That's not so bad.' *If* he still wants to.

'He wants to paint it here, at the tree houses. He says your face, your whole demeanour, changed when you were sharing Georgios' photograph. That is what he wants.' She spreads her hands out on the table.

'What he "wants"?' I repeat. 'Will he still want that now? When he... if he...' I gesture vaguely between us.

'When,' Nicole says firmly. 'And, April, you could kidnap me, burn his studio down, force him to care for all of Damaris' pet cats, and Andreas would still want to paint you, yes.'

'Then tell him he can. It's, well, it's the least I can do.' I'm not sure how funny that really is but we both burst out laughing.

'He will be pleased,' Nicole says, after a minute. 'Less surprised than me too.' She hesitates. 'April, Andreas is a good man, a fair man—'

'I know he is.' I also know she's talking about a lot more than Andreas the artist. I clear my throat and push back my chair. 'Let's go and get the car and see Salih.'

Nicole nods quickly, and once more we make our way to the road and follow its contours, the water on our left. By daylight, it's a half-mile of empty scrubland and a badly surfaced road, benign rather than desolate. As the restaurant comes into sight, the car – the only vehicle in sight; I wonder if the other diners were less risk-averse, early risers or happened to be passing hikers – exactly as we left it. Nicole dangles the keys and stops.

'I suggest you speak with Salih alone,' she says. 'Who knows his political affiliations and personal loyalties? He may be less inclined to openness if a Greek-Cypriot is present. I do not wish to sound judgemental, I do not think I am that, but you have seen how sensitive people are and rightly so... Damaris, for instance; not everyone is an Orestes. Time does not always heal, sometimes it is only a veil.'

'Yes,' I say. 'Alright. What will you do? You could go and see Marco, the turtle man. Didn't Alan say he was leaving soon? I mean, only if you wanted to.'

Nicole looks amused. 'It is okay, April. I know you are not giving me orders. Maybe I would not mind anyway. Certainly, I will visit Marco-the-turtle-man.'

'I haven't time for your mocking.' I put my nose in the air. 'I've more important concerns. What about Elena's photograph? Why don't you take it because I can show it to Salih another time... What?'

'I have a copy,' she admits. 'I am so sorry, April, I should have told you. The time at home when you found me in your room? I photographed it and Andreas printed it out. Even before the picture from the tavern, I so wanted to find the tree houses and surprise you.'

Hers is an unlikely face of contrition. I have to laugh and I don't care anyway. 'It's fine. I'm glad you did. But hang on.' I can't believe I never thought to ask. 'How did you actually find the tree houses?'

'I can take little credit,' she says. 'As always, April, it is a case of contacts. In this case, Andreas' lawyers. I asked the intern in the legal office to follow it up. He has little enough work to do but is so very keen to impress. He located the magazine, the archive, the photography credits, everything.'

'And kept relaying it to you.' All those phone calls.

'Yes. Then he contacted me late that night in Yeni Erenköy and said he had identified the place and, of course, I rushed to check. His timing was perfect, mine maybe less so.' She smiles. 'Chance, accident, coincidence, whatever it was you said. April, you would have followed the same trail eventually.'

'But I didn't need to. You did it for me.' I hope she gets how heartfelt those words are.

'I wanted to,' she says, 'even though it caused us to disagree for a few minutes. April, *if* you are going to stay at Verena Bay, *if* that is ever to be your home, you will need to become more Cypriot-April in your arguing…'

'Go.' I wave her and her loaded comments away. 'Go, and bat your eyelashes at the turtle man.'

She blows me a kiss and roars off in her adopted car.

51

I turn to knock on Salih's front door. There is so much, or rather so many people, jostling for space in my mind, I close my eyes for a second. I try to banish Nicole, and the hovering Greek chorus of Andreas, Petros and Yiannis, and bring Elena back to the forefront. I wish Red, he of good sense, my soulmate-who-isn't, were here. I should phone him; he'll be wondering what's happening. I dwell for a minute on that earlier kiss – his kiss. I relive it and shiver. It was a great kiss; before now, I would have said the best. But it was also, definitely, a goodbye kiss, and a safe kiss, not an exciting, unknown one. And more, if I'm truly honest with myself, I quite like leaving it on the 'if only' note. I fish for my mobile phone, find his number and get his message service. I leave a quick sentence as Salih opens the door.

It turns out that trying to communicate with him is the best distraction of all. Salih has a lifetime's pent-up feelings about the Greek–Turkish dispute over Cyprus and needs only a safe receptacle to spill them into. Sitting at the same table in the conservatory – the daylight view as beautiful as he promised – I try to follow the political invective, peppered as it is with references to unknown characters and events and often in a language I don't speak a word of.

The flow is eventually interrupted by a short, very rotund

woman who might be made from two mounds of dough cut in the middle by her tightly tied apron. This is Salih's wife, Defne – he takes a moment out to introduce us – bearing hot coffee, sweet biscuits and an apparent tongue-lashing.

'She says to let you speak,' Salih reports with a sheepish grin. 'She says you must visit us with good reasons to want stories of war and of history. She says to also tell you that I, Salih, am a too-chatty, crazy old man. She says she would tell you this herself, if only she spoke English. But she does not.' He ends on a triumphant note, albeit enfeebled by the endearing honesty in his translation.

Defne herself smiles at me, and squeezes herself onto the narrow seat beside him. She pours the coffee and Salih takes a long drink.

I'll never have a better opening; I launch in. But this is no film or play or book reaching its denouement. Salih listens politely and he looks at Elena's picture. He shows it to Defne, and their gestures indicate that of course they recognise the neighbouring tree houses, but the three childish figures in front are, as ever, a mystery.

'We did not live here in that time,' Salih says. 'I told you that my son and grandson died. Boys, both of them. To us, just boys. I did not tell you, I wish not to insult your friend, that they were taken away and shot by Greek soldiers. Their home was taken first, the home Mr Alan has now, and their belongings burned. Ahmet and Mamun lived there fine, then they tried to help some Greek friends and the suspicious Greek army came and asked why? Why would you do this, help your enemy? The soldiers tied them up and took them away. Bang, bang. Dead.' His voice grows shrill, spit escaping from the corners of his mouth, a single diamond tear falling from his right eye. Defne squeezes his forearm and speaks rapidly, quietly to him.

I am horrified. Horrified at his story, and horrified at what I have done to him by invading his world, asking my questions in such a blasé manner. As I stammer apologies, I feel this morning's tears threatening me again. Again, I blink them back; to cry would be to take unforgivably from his grief, and from Defne's. But Defne sees, and her free hand reaches out to pat my knee. She shakes her head, as if to say, 'Don't worry, it's okay.' But of course it's not. It was her son and grandson too.

Salih sniffs and wipes the back of his hand across his mouth. 'It is right to feel the pain,' he says. 'I have no shame to cry and shout. A child should not die so. I say this, and yet today we still do this evil thing.'

I bite back the urge to blurt out Damaris' story; he sounds so like her. But why would the little boy Orestes saved be recompense for them? Calm again, Salih explains they took their daughter-in-law home to Turkey. Eventually, she remarried and ten years later Salih and Defne came here, back to their land to live where Ahmet and his young family had been so happy. They found their home had been titled and retitled and no longer belonged to them, something they were unwilling to fight, so they rebuilt an outhouse – here – and they opened their restaurant. They had, they *have*, found their peace.

I leave them a little later, with a sack of cookies for Nicole, another for Alan, and promises that we'll return this evening for another dinner and a – different – cocktail. Salih's story circles my mind as I wander along the empty road, and I imagine it too, in Elena's happy times, the holidays when she and Krista and Sofia played here, when it didn't matter that their neighbours were Turkish. I think about Ahmet and Mamun; parallel lives. It's as if I have a jigsaw with the frame complete, but more and more pictures to be mixed and matched inside. Both Nicole and Orestes said I would hear Elena's story in so many guises, that all would be different, all would be the same. It's the first time I've head-on faced the thought that Elena's story – or Krista's or Sofia's – might be another version of Salih's grandson's. They were only on opposite sides of the road, they could have played together... I suddenly stop walking. I never was very quick at jigsaws and it's in slow motion I slot another tentative piece into place; one I missed in the emotion of the moment. The little boy, Mamun. Surely there was a real possibility he had been Elena's friend, the one she talked about when my dad built the tree house in our garden. How many other Turkish children of the right age, with the right name, living in such proximity to the tree houses, could there be? Of course I can't be certain but the odds must be strong. I feel shaky for a second and sit down on the grass to think it through.

'Oh, Elena,' I say out loud. 'I think I might just have met Mamun's grandfather.'

Instinct is to run back and share the possibility with Salih and Defne, but sense tells me it's a personal epiphany. There's not much news for them in the fact that three unknown little girls in an old photo played with – *may* have played with – their grandson before the military came and killed him. Even that Elena's family, or people like them, who were helped by a heroic Ahmet, have real identities isn't much solace when I don't know what happened next.

The music is back in force; crashing chords and 'Siegfried's Funeral March'. On autopilot I hear a car and make to move further onto the verge. But the car slows alongside me, and it's Alan who hails me. It's the jolt out of maudlin I need.

'Jump in,' he calls. 'I saw your friend roaring by a couple of hours ago. I can't offer you the same luxury but I have an engine and it goes. Going back to camp?'

I get up and cross towards him, thinking. 'I was. But Nicole's gone to see if she can find the Marco you mentioned. If you can point me towards the turtle place, I might catch up with her there. Unless she's back already.'

'She isn't,' says Alan. 'Not that I keep tabs on my guests but it's hard not to notice when there are only two of you, and with a spanking-new silver convertible. I'll drop you at SPOT. No, don't argue, it's not out of the way. She might have had a wasted trip anyway, Marco was up at the other end of the beach early this morning.' Alan glances back out of his open window and pulls off, driving slowly.

'Not gone home, at least.'

'No, but he would have been doing a last checking of the nests, so he's probably on the way.'

'Where is his home?'

'Greece. The Peloponnese. But I couldn't be more specific; Marco is a loner. Comes here summer after summer, and a few times out of turtle season. He marshals a whole array of volunteers, tourists and turtles, but he comes and goes alone. Nobody really knows him.'

'Oh. What age is he?' I'm making small talk of the type I never attempt; I'm so poor at it, it sounds like a job interview rather than genuine get-to-know-you interest. Worse, the answers are irrelevant; anything to keep Alan from asking me what I was doing with Salih.

'You're asking the wrong person, there,' Alan says. 'Late twenties? Thirty-five? I don't know.' He takes his eyes off the road for a second. 'Right age, wrong gender to be the girl in your picture.'

'He'd have to be nearer forty for that to fit, anyway. But it doesn't matter. I've found the tree houses. I'm happy.'

'Right.'

Maybe I sound sharper than I mean to, as Alan leaves it at that. So do I, but we're only a couple of minutes away from a turn-off on to a sandy lane.

'It's probably quicker if you walk down from here.' He slows to snail's pace. 'I'd really need the Land Rover for this. You don't think your Nicole drove that swanky machine down here, do you?'

'Probably.' It makes me laugh. 'I hope so. That'll put it in its place. Here...' I root into the big bag Salih gave me and hand Alan his share of the cookies. 'Salih sent these. And thanks a lot for the lift, Alan.'

'You'll be staying tonight?'

'I think so. I promise to let you know soon.'

'Either way.' He shrugs. 'There are plenty of beds in the guest house too.'

I watch him, caution personified, drive off. Then I pick my way over the rutted, compacted sand, that bit calmer for the interlude. I've gone no distance when, in a clearing on my left, Nicole's hire car is parked neatly beside a sort of safari – or beach, I suppose – jeep with a faded drawing of a mutant turtle on the white paintwork. Behind them is a neglected outdoor area, which might once have earned the title garden or courtyard, complete with a couple of old bikes and several pieces of a barbecue. It leads into a small, squat concrete… I want to say bunker, except that it's above ground. When I was growing up, the Water Board had something similar on the edge of our town, all fenced off and out of bounds. It looks like a second cousin to the Verena Bay stable block and the perfect hideout for a loner called Marco.

The door's open, giving access to a large kitchen-office-living room, but even as I call out, it's evident there's nobody home. I retrace my steps and walk down to the beach, shielding my eyes as I squint right and left but there's nothing in the immense empty space. Perhaps Nicole has located the elusive Marco in some shady cove as he does whatever he does checking turtles' nests. Maybe she knows where to look; my lips twitch as I think of her playing Jake at his own game on the way to Trooditissa and spouting the turtle-Latin. I know no more about turtles than I do about orchids so have no idea which way to walk and I'm not inclined anyway. The wind has steadily picked up and sand is snapping round my ankles. I'll go and leave a note for Nicole in the car and head back to the tree houses.

I decide it's okay to enter and borrow pen and paper, both lying just inside on a canvas table beside the gas cooking stove. The existing scribbled notes, crossed off and ripped, show I'm not the first. I'm just leaning over to write when there's a loud knock on the door and I jump about a mile into the air, knock the tin kettle sitting on the nearest gas ring and send it crashing to the stone floor, before I whirl round and say, 'Oh. Thank goodness. I thought I was about to be apprehended for the theft of one Bic biro and a sheaf of Post-its.'

'Probably for the breakage of one kettle and one gas camping stove also.' Nicole comes in and helps me right the toppled gadgets. 'Sorry, I did not mean to knock so loudly. I thought I saw you from the beach but you vanished. Then I heard the movement here and thought you might be Marco.'

'I think I see what you mean. You haven't found him then? Marco?'

'No. And I have walked a hundred miles of the beach,' she complains. 'Wherever the turtles make their homes, they appear safe from natural and unnatural predators.'

'I was leaving a note for you,' I tell her. 'I'll leave one for him instead.'

Nicole says, 'If you do so, I will go and turn around the car. Perhaps it is as well that an environmentalist and turtle conservationist does not see that monster in his yard.'

I bite the pen. I don't want to scare him off with a personal essay. I settle on the line that I'm looking at some history of the area, and add that he can find us, if he wants to, at the tree houses next door.

I'm already in the purring car when I realise I should have called at the guest house next door.

Nicole cuts across the thought. 'I can see you have had more luck than I did. What did Salih tell you?'

As the afternoon draws on, we talk over Salih's stories. Nicole is sure the couple would like to know that I think Elena and her sisters were friends of their grandson. Put so simply, of course she's right. It's only a big deal for me because, with the tree houses, it's – possibly – a real link to Elena.

'It is also a safe link,' Nicole says.

'Safe?'

'Yes, safe. April, do not pretend you fail to understand me.' Nicole, propped up on the bed in tree house number three, is clearly torn between humour and exasperation. 'Yesterday, you admitted your feelings of ambivalence for finding the adult Elena. Here you have the perfect distant and unsubstantiated link. Elena remains the Elena you know and love. You have learned nothing, nothing at all, April, about Elena's return to Cyprus.'

I stay silent because she's right, again, and it's another thing that's actually okay.

'Let us have dinner once more at Salih's restaurant,' she suggests. 'You can tell him and his wife then. They are expecting us anyway, yes? You cannot make a grown man cry and then run away.'

'Nicole...'

She grins and holds up her hands. 'A joke! Just a joke, okay in bad taste. What is not a joke,' she goes on, 'is that we cannot stay here forever. Perhaps tonight, yes? Although – would you feel disloyal if we moved to the guest house?'

'It was bloody freezing.'

'Then Yiannis and the others can collect us here tomorrow on their way home from Apostolos Andreas.' She pauses.

This time I accept the cue. 'Home?'

'Yes, April. Home. Verena Bay. Agia Triada. Either of them. Both. What else are you going to do? Where else do you want to be right now?'

Nowhere, is the answer. Absolutely nowhere. Even with all the buts.

'What are we going to do? You and me? And that's the thing, isn't it? It's all so much bigger than you and me. I mean, I know you don't know—'

'No, I do not know, April. I have no idea. But I have to believe together we will work it out somehow.'

'Whatever "it" is.'

'Whatever it is.'

'I suppose we'll always have the tree houses.' I wince even as I misquote.

'I think that is what you English call "cheesy".' Nicole grins. 'Dare I say, it has an element of truth too.'

52

Troodos Mountains, Cyprus
September 1974

Dear April and Mrs Gale's class,

Dear April and Mrs Gale's class,

Dear April and Mrs Gale's class...

Elena looked down at the rumpled sheet of paper, messy with scribbles and crossings out. It was not good, not being able to think what to write. She who never had to worry about words in Greek or English; she who always pleased her teachers; she who had even learned some of Mamun-their-friend-at-the-tree-houses' Turkish language, though that was mostly forgotten now.

The point on Elena's yellow pencil was a stub, and the pencil sharpener long lost. She rolled the pencil slowly between her two palms, over and over and over and over and over and over, until it dropped onto her lap. Then she picked it up and pushed the blunt end into the fat bit at the bottom of her thumb. It left a little grey mark but it didn't hurt, it didn't hurt, didn't hurt... Ow.

All everyone talked about was what they had lost. They

were all Maria Balis' mother, crying for their washing machines or cars or televisions in their villages that were gone, taken by the Turks... 'Well, we've taken theirs,' Elena wanted to shout. 'Look around you, see all their things.' She wanted to shout that but she never, ever would. Surely everyone just wanted to go back home? But where – Elena stifled the next thought, snapped a lid on it and looked around her. When they were doing the moonlight flits, everything had been a samey blur, but there was so much time to notice things now.

It still smelled different. Not smelly but not familiar. The way the houses were built was different. There were nameless family photos stuffed at the back of the kitchen dresser and unknown hair clogged in the hole where the plug went in the sink. It was like living with ghosts everywhere and the shadows were all different too. Even her own shadow, Elena thought. And Sofia, who they dressed like a boy, though Elena didn't know if that was to hide her or because there was no girl clothes to fit. Sofia needed lots of clothes, she had started to wet herself like when she was a baby. Sharing a bed with her was not nice.

Somebody started shouting. It came from the road in front of the houses; men's voices. Elena stiffened and a wave of fear washed over her from her head to her toes. Mama, had they come for Mama...? For so long she had wanted her mother to be with them and to know why she always went away. Now she did. And it made Elena wish for the opposite. It made her so confused. Mama was in danger here, every single day that she stayed. She worked for the government, she had finally told Elena, but it was top secret and she could never tell, not even Krista, especially not Krista. 'It's a boring job. For the goodies, of course,' she'd said, trying to make Elena laugh. 'Not the baddies. And we know that good always wins, don't we? In the end.'

She saw the rear of Krista jostling her friends to be first through the house and on to the road and she hurried to tag on the edge of the group.

'What is it?' Elena tugged at Krista who was on her tiptoes, trying to peer over the gathering crowd. 'Can you see? Have the men come?'

'No,' said Krista eventually. 'No. It's nothing exciting.' Her face drooped. 'It's just those stupid brothers fighting again. Idiots.' Krista had no time for the Papadopoulos brothers who weren't young or handsome.

But they were important, Elena knew, because they had a truck and they took it in turns to go down to the neighbouring villages when there was news of a new delivery of food or milk or shoes. What had they brought this time?

'What is it?' Elena asked. She thought of the conversation overheard in the bedroom. 'Krista? Is it blankets?'

Krista looked at Elena as if she was crazy and didn't bother answering.

Slowly, the story trickled back to them. It was a glut of oranges outside the tent camp, free for the taking, but Tomas Papadopoulos had refused to let his brother collect even one of them.

'Never,' he was shouting now. 'In my village I have property. I have land. I have an orange plantation and I, myself, give away oranges to the poor. I will die before I take oranges from others. Do you hear me? I will die.' Tomas was kicking the tyres of his truck, Elena could hear the thump, thump; she could picture his fists clenched and the spittle at the corners of his mouth. Tomas was always shouting.

'Yes, you will die if your pride refuses to let you eat,' his brother replied much more quietly. 'You will die, my brother, and the rest of us will die with you. Have we not already died a little?'

Then Elena heard sobbing which frightened her far more than the shouting ever could. The men didn't cry. They just didn't. The knot of old men and clucking women surged forward to offer comfort or restraint.

Krista, her eyes gleaming, looked around her gang. Elena watched as one by one they listened and then shook their heads. Krista shrugged and finally turned to whisper in Elena's ear. 'Oranges, Elena. Sweet and juicy oranges. I'm going down to the camp to get some.'

'Krista, no—'

'It's not safe,' Krista mimicked. 'Not safe. Don't worry, daydream girl, I am not going to be one of the stupid girls who gets raped and murdered. The soldiers are nice, they will look after me if I scream.'

'Please. Please don't go.' Elena was desperate. Mama was just back, Krista couldn't go. Even if it was just for one day, Elena wanted to be a whole family again. *Tell them what?*

'Shh. Shut up. I'm going. And if you tell, I will sing the dingle dangle scarecrow song every night and I will make a scarecrow from all your clothes when you are dreaming nightmares about the dingle-dangling.' Krista pinched Elena's arm hard. 'But I will bring you the best and fattest orange,' she added.

Elena, paralysed, watched her sister disappear. Through the little crowd. Behind the truck. Towards the trees. Then Krista was gone.

When the brothers and their supporters all started to melt away, Elena forced her feet to follow; she crept back to the yard, to her seat on the stones. The stick was where she had left it and she started scratching her name again. She waited.

When Mama found her there, Elena knew it was to say goodbye. She didn't say it with her lips because *walls had ears* but it was in her blinking eyes and in her tight hugs. Elena had nothing to say – there was nothing, not even about the baby that wasn't even visible yet – and looked blankly at her scribbled-out letter.

'What's that? Mama asked. 'Are you writing a story?'

Elena shrugged then tried to smile. She didn't want her mother's last memory of her to be grumpy. 'It's my letter to April and Mrs Gale's class. But I can't think of anything to write.'

Mama's eyebrows drew together and she looked... not

puzzled or anxious exactly but somewhere in the middle. 'Have you written many letters?' she asked. 'How many?'

Elena nodded, counting in her head. 'Maybe ten?' she guessed. 'The first was in the airport. I meant to send one a week for News class. We could do that or keep a diary for summer homework. But I've failed.'

'You haven't failed,' her mother said briskly. 'You will never fail, my darling. You're a kind and clever and brave girl. Always remember that. Promise.'

Elena nodded again even though she wasn't sure; when Mama sounded fierce like that it just meant that she wanted the best for them. She always said it: 'I want the best for my girls.'

Then her tone changed though, when she added, 'Your letters. Who posted them, hmm? You?'

Elena was nervous suddenly, as if she was doing her spoken English tests at school, not talking to Mama, and had gone wrong somewhere. 'I gave them to Aunt Irini or to Antony so they could get the special stamps.'

Her mother's stiff shoulders dropped slightly and she smiled again. 'Shall I take this one for you?'

'No.' Elena held it out. 'There's nothing written. See.' And she screwed the paper into a ball and crammed it into her pocket.

53

'Marco never showed up. He's probably back in Greece now.' We wend our dark way, again, to Salih's place.

'Probably,' Nicole agrees. 'Do you mind?'

'I don't know. No. Not really. I mean, what could he have had to tell us?'

Salih greets us like old friends. Tonight the restaurant is slightly busier, it is later in the evening, and the conservatory is nearly half full. He sits beside us for a few minutes whilst I apologise for upsetting him and he tosses it aside. 'Forgotten, forgotten. It is not you, but them.'

I've learned enough not to follow up the identity of 'them' but I do show him Elena's picture again. 'I think it's possible that my friends knew your grandson,' I tell him. 'Elena told me about the little boy, Mamun, who lived at the tree houses. My father made us, me and Elena, a tree house in my garden and she said she wished Mamun could see it…' I'm battling the sudden melancholy that it's likely his short life was almost over by the time Elena said that. I feel the pressure of Nicole's hand on my arm; moral support gratefully received. Salih is clearly quite taken with the news, he turns the photograph over and over in his hands and then he interrupts Defne in her cooking to come and share in it. Nicole looks at me, then towards the picture.

'Shall I?' she murmurs. I nod. She gives Salih and Defne her copy.

Then it's back to the brisk business of dinner, a variation of the previous night's mezze and just as delicious. Defne has been baking today too, and Salih eventually brings us a platter of sweets and cakes to try.

'Cocktails?' he asks, nodding hopefully.

'Just one,' we say together, and he roars with disbelieving laughter.

'Help me, April. I mean it,' Nicole says, when he has chuckled off.

'I hear you. I felt unreal last night. Really not myself.'

'Or maybe more of yourself?'

Both phrases hang, the 'whatever it is' already back with a vengeance. Then: 'What do you mean?' I ask, at the same time as Nicole blurts out, 'You said you love... Red.'

In that infinitesimal pause, she takes the easier option and we both relax.

Another pause.

'Yes. Yes, I said that.' I crumble cake and choose my words. 'Nicole, if I could have any man in the world, I would have Red, but it would be as' – I wonder; even now brother doesn't go with that kiss – 'as a friend, a cousin, perhaps. And that's even if he came with Jarlath and Kevin attached.'

Nicole is looking, very faintly, sceptical. Or maybe that's me, projecting.

'Really, Nicole. The first time I saw him,' I think back to the monastery meeting, knowing I'll struggle to explain, 'there was this mutual connection between us. It was as if we'd always known each other.' I shake my head. 'I can't put it any better. But it's a non-starter. It's not the basis of a relationship. It was like the end of something not the beginning. Oh, I don't know.'

'What does he say?' she asks.

'The same, I think.' I hesitate. 'And... isn't there something in the Bible about Jesus being tempted in the wilderness? Maybe that was me for Red.'

'You are Red's wilderness?' Nicole's lips are twitching.

'No, not exactly. Oh, stop teasing, Nicole, you make it sound weird.'

'Perhaps you should ask Yiannis for theology lessons,' she says. 'More joking, April Rose. Is it really so simple?' She doesn't wait for a reply. 'You see, it was the reason, one of them, why Kevin came on this trip with us.'

'What?'

She leans over and picks at the cake crumbs I'm piling up. 'Kevin told me he was wondering about Red and you. I am not sure whether he was more worried something would happen or that it would not.'

'Well, it didn't. It won't. Nicole, it *can't*.' I say it with a whole new respect for Kevin though.

Nicole sighs.

'You don't believe me?'

'Actually, April Rose, I do believe you.' She inspects her nails, then transfers her gaze directly to me. 'It is all part of your quest for the perfect family, is it not? What am I going to be?' she challenges. 'Your sister?'

'I don't know that. I don't know what you and I have, Nicole. Neither do you, you said so. All I know is, it's important.' I hesitate. 'There's one thing, Nicole, that Red said...'

'Yes?'

'At Kantara Castle. He said you were jealous of me. You know, when you saw me and him?'

It takes a long time for her to answer but her eyes don't leave mine. 'He did not say I was jealous of *you*, April Rose. Did he?'

'What do you mean?' I think back, I trace it forwards. Realisation dawns. 'Oh.'

I watch her take a deep breath but the moment passes; Salih is on his way back with another guest, making straight for our table. I struggle to slow my heart rate and marshal my Elena thoughts.

It's not often that real people look exactly as you've imagined them, but I know straightaway this is Marco. He's fit-looking, tanned, his dark hair curly and unbrushed. He has the makings of a beard, and is wearing long shorts and espadrilles. He looks exactly the actor Universal Studios would cast as a turtle-conserving environmentalist.

Salih, pulling a chair across from a neighbouring table, does a vague three-way introduction to confirm our identities and gestures he will bring coffee. Marco shakes his head and Salih ignores him. I try to concentrate. Elena. Tree houses.

'I won't stay,' Marco says. 'I'm on my way to Larnaca tonight. I need to cross the border before it closes.'

He has the most perfect voice I have ever heard; like I told Red, I married my second husband for less. It's low, accent-less, and suggests a refinement that takes the stereotypical edge off his demeanour. I hope he speaks some Greek too, so I can ask Nicole if it's the same in another language.

'Thank you,' I say. 'I wasn't sure if you'd get the message in time—'

'You said you were next door at the tree houses, that's what made me come.' He says it with a definitive full stop; not a man of unnecessary words. The enquiring silence must be sufficient to appeal to his sense of manners though. Looking between Nicole and me, he goes on, as if with effort. 'The tree houses. I don't believe I have heard the cabins called that before, but somewhere it struck a chord.'

'It's the tree houses I, we, wanted to ask you about.'

'Oh?' There is a faintly discernible frown above his brows. This man has disconcerting eyes, they are fixed on me and do not stray. 'I'm not sure I can help you with that,' he says. 'It's more usually island topography or the turtle-hatching patterns visitors enquire about.'

'It's this picture.' I note how, in another life – next year, perhaps? – I'd like to learn about the turtles. I take the photo out of my bag and slide it across to him. 'I'm trying to identify it.'

I resist a full-on description of who, what, when, and just let him pick it up and glance over it.

'If you need confirmation these are the cabins here, I agree,' he says, placing it back on the table.

'You do not recognise the girls in it?' Catching my eye, Nicole speaks for the first time. Marco doesn't answer but he follows my gaze and when she repeats the question, he speaks.

'No. Is there a reason why I should?'

I'm distracted for a second; it's that voice, or rather the tone of it... I put it to one side. 'No.' I sigh. 'It's a long shot. The three of them, well, this one, really,' I jab at Elena, 'was a friend of mine, and I'm wondering what happened to her. Alan said you came here so often we should ask you.'

'It's an old photograph.' Then he appears to realise what he has implied and politely qualifies his remark. 'I've been working here for eight years, but this is long before that time.'

There's another silence.

'I'm sorry,' he offers. I watch him make an effort to show interest when all he wants to do is catch his plane home. Part of me wishes he wouldn't bother; now I just want to get back to the conversation with Nicole. And I'm dying for a pee.

'What was her name, your friend?' he asks.

'Elena. Her sisters were Krista and Sofia.'

'And her mother's?'

I look at him blankly. 'I don't know,' I say. 'I've never known. I only ever knew her as Mama or Mrs Zacharia. Her stepfather was Stefan.'

He picks up the photo again. 'Elena. This one, you said.' He points to her.

'Uh-huh.'

'And you knew her here, in Cyprus?'

'No.' I say. 'In the UK. We were ten.'

Marco shakes his head slowly. 'I'm sorry,' he repeats. After another silence, it seems almost unwillingly and certainly unnecessarily, that he adds, 'I know very little about my Greek-Cypriot family, other than that they lived somewhere here before fleeing to the Troodos region after the Turkish intervention. My mother was a minor political activist and she was killed. I was newborn, abandoned and passed around the community for a few months before my father found me and took me to his parents in Sweden. It's where I grew up.'

Nicole says something in Greek; Marco does not answer. He continues in English.

'My mother was Greek-Cypriot, my father Swedish. He never talks about her. Or about that time. I think he was here for a while, but he won't discuss it. I assume it was very traumatic. I,' Marco hesitates, 'I have upset him very much by working here. It began by chance but now I feel some connection...' He stops abruptly. 'I am sorry, this is not your business. I don't know why I brought it up.' He's already scraping back his chair to leave. I wonder how far to push it, knowing how I would hate a stranger grilling me, however delicately, about my parents and their lives and Polish ancestry.

'Wait.' Nicole puts one hand gently on his wrist. She smiles up at him and I see him weakening; I wonder if she knows the effect she has. 'You spoke because you remembered something, no?' She pauses, and I wonder. Then she goes on. 'It is unfair of us to accost you in this way, but please, April here, she is not unlike you, she knows nothing of her family. I can only imagine how this feels, and I would like to help her find news of her friend.'

Marco looks at me and gives a small smile, but he looks no less uncomfortable and even more intense. I guess his faultless English and pure accent are not effortless.

'So,' Nicole continues – watching him respond to her tightened grip, I realise what the Law Society has lost – 'may I ask you one more question?'

'Go ahead.' He inclines his head once more.

'You recognised the name Elena, did you not?'

Marco hesitates. 'No, not particularly.' He reverts to silence for another long minute.

'Not particularly, but?' Nicole prompts.

Marco gives in. 'It's nothing. Only that I have a feeling my mother had children already when she married my father. Something my grandmother said once, and was told to hush, about my ready-made sisters. Perhaps, just perhaps she mentioned the name Elena. But I can't verify it. It could have been Eleni or Magdalene or Helen. Or none of those.' He looks around, his eyes fix on the pot of rapidly cooling coffee and he pours a tiny cup and drinks it in one. 'She would probably have been this girl's age. I had not thought of this for a long time, and your picture, the name, reminded me. That's all.'

'Thank you,' Nicole says softly. She looks over at me, semaphoring that it's up to me now, what I want to do with this information, or non-information.

'Thank you, Marco,' I echo, and am about to continue when he says, somewhat unwillingly, 'My father's birth name is Erik-Stiven, but he has never to my knowledge used Stiven alone. Or any variation of it.'

Push hard enough and we'll make these tenuous links, I think. Enough. 'Thanks for stopping and talking to two strangers with vague questions, Marco.' I say. 'Maybe, we could learn more about the turtles another time instead?' I smile and he looks slightly bemused, as well he might.

'Of course, my pleasure.' He smiles faintly. 'I understand turtles.' He gets up and clears his throat. 'I must get to my plane. After Athens, I shall go to Sweden to see my father who is not well…' It's clearly his parting gift to us, a thank you for letting him go.

We smile and shake hands, and he turns to leave. Good manners, I'm sure, prevent him hurrying.

'Marco?' I raise my voice. The other diners look up, although my voice is not that loud.

'April,' says Nicole, 'What—'

'Ssh,' I hold up my hand, winking to take out the sting.

Marco doesn't stop. He continues out of the conservatory and into the dim dining room beyond.

'He's deaf,' I say, pouring cold coffee into my cup, just for something to do.

'What?'

'Or hearing-impaired, whatever it is. Maybe not much, or maybe he has those magic invisible hearing aids. I bet that's why he's known as quiet and someone who "keeps himself to himself". Did you see how closely he watched us speak? How even his own voice was? I thought it was just the language, then it clicked.'

Comprehension dawns on Nicole's face. 'Okay,' she agrees. 'But does it matter?'

'No.' I realise I've never told her. 'Except that Sofia, Elena's little sister, was deaf.' I drain the horrible coffee and pull a face. 'Coincidence, I'm sure, but an interesting one.'

'Along with maybe-Elena or Eleni and Erik-Stiven for Stefan?'

We look at each other. 'Do you know the phrase clutching at straws?' I say. It's my turn to push back my chair. 'Just going to the loo.'

In the bathroom, I rerun the conversation in my head, testing the vague similarities, and conclude they have no more foundation than Soussana's stories. Like the toilet cubicle, as someone comes knocking, it's all so flimsy.

54

I'm washing my hands, gazing through the partially frosted window, when I see Marco, Columbo-like, return. *This is it*, I think – but what is it? I've actually no idea what I think I think.

Still, I can't explain why I hold back: drying my hands thoroughly, running my fingers through my hair, scraping at a long-faded stain on my cuff. Only then I open the outer door to the corridor and turn slightly so I can just see the conservatory. Nicole, at our table, is looking up at Marco, who is leaning over her and writing something down. He looks over his shoulder – luckily towards the kitchen. She takes the paper and slips it into her bag. It looks secretive. I shrink back, vaguely ashamed of myself and still not exactly sure what I'm doing. When I'm certain he's gone, I head slowly back to Nicole.

She's staring into space. She looks more than beautiful, enigmatic; Andreas' ideal model. As I slip into the chair opposite her, she comes back to earth and gives me a beaming smile.

'Marco came back.'

I try not to heave a sigh of relief, or wriggle with guilt, but she notices.

'You thought he would? So, why did you leave?'

I look out of the viewless black window where all I can see are our reflections. She has to tell me. She promised she would. I'm so busy wishing, it takes a second to realise she *is* telling me.

'He offered to ask his father about the photograph.' She looks at me levelly. 'He said, if you would like him to do this, to send him a copy. He has an email address, I said you did too. He did not offer a telephone number or a postal address. I did not ask.'

The original photograph is still lying on the table. I indicate it. 'You didn't tell him to take this?'

'Of course not.'

I don't know what to say. She does.

'You were testing me.'

'Nicole, I'm sorry, I didn't mean—'

'Yes, you did. I will spell it out.' She's still speaking in such a neutral tone, I have no idea if she's furious or curious. 'Yesterday, you told me that if I found Elena, you would need to know that I would tell you. That, I believe now, is more important than me or anyone actually finding her. What you were really saying is that you wish me always to be honest with you. Have I passed the test?' she repeats.

'It was stupid. I don't know what I was thinking. I saw him come back and give you something and I thought you were hiding it.' I put my head in my hands. 'I don't know what I was thinking,' I say again.

'Too much,' she says. 'As ever, April Rose, you were thinking too much.'

And she smiles, and I smile and everything is okay.

'I put the scrap of paper away, only because Marco asked me to keep it to ourselves.'

'Oh. Okay.'

'Yes. It seems Salih has recently got a dial-up internet connection here and when Marco is not here, Salih already ties up the SPOT system sending him large files of the empty beach. He is "helping" keep watch over the turtles.' She reaches into her bag. 'Here—'

'You keep it.' I slide over the photograph. 'And this. If I want them, I'll ask you for them.'

'Are you sure?' she asks.

'Absolutely.' The photo goes too far and flutters to the floor. I bend down to pick it up.

'Oh – April.' Nicole suddenly sounds alarmed.

'Really.' Coming up, I knock my head on the side of the table. 'Ouch. I'm certain, Nicole.'

'No, it is not that. Look…'

Ah. Salih is shepherding more visitors through the door. Well, my heart plummets, not visitors but one visitor in particular, the last person I've the stomach to see. Salih points to us, Nicole waves as if it's a casual encounter and I shoot up straight then freeze: my fight-or-flight instinct in two minds.

'Andreas,' Nicole says as he looms over us. 'I wasn't expecting to see you tonight.'

'No,' he replies, looking at me. My gaze is level with his shirt pocket and there's the miniature Ganesh, just peeking out. His hand strays to it unconsciously. 'I could not wait any longer. I need to paint April again at those tree houses. As soon as there is daylight.' As he speaks, his eyes bore into me. 'You told her?' he says to Nicole.

'Yes—'

'And you will agree,' he says to me, somewhere between beseeching and a command. 'Without this I have an unfinished piece of work, yet Nicole said it was an invasion.' Now he sounds disbelieving. 'We argued.'

'You can paint me,' I manage to say, knowing I sound strangulated. 'Ah, if you want to.'

'I need to,' he corrects me, taking the elephant out of his pocket and tapping it three times. 'You, here, is the missing link.'

I don't know how Nicole is sitting here so coolly, as if we're three acquaintances discussing the weather. I can't semaphore *help* with my eyes as Andreas still hasn't taken his off mine. Then he does.

'Then I can relax,' he says. He pulls a chair across from

the neighbouring table and sits down, straightening the water jug, wine and glasses into a still life. 'So should you,' he says to me, in a different tone, and Andreas the artist morphs back into Andreas the man. 'What's for dinner? I did not delay to eat.' He hoovers up everything Salih brings out, saying suddenly, as if he's just noticed there are only two of us with him, 'Where are the others?'

'Apostolos Andreas,' Nicole says, giving him a precis of the last couple of days.

'Hmm. Cape Zafer – the Turkish. We are in the North now, remember.' He waves his fork at me. 'The Karpass Peninsula. You can see Syria from there. Did you not want to visit?'

'She wanted to come to the tree houses more,' Nicole says quietly.

'Yes. Of course.' He nods. 'The real thing. Powerful.'

This acute change of focus, one minute Marco was here, the next it's Andreas, with so much unknown, is like trying to sight-read a piece of music with no transition between movements and no dynamics.

Andreas looks as if he's waiting for my response. 'Very powerful.' I clear my throat. 'Er, you won't have seen them yet?'

'No.' He takes a large gulp of wine. 'I should. Shall we go?'

I wonder what Alan thinks of us, two become three, as we cluster on the doorstep of the guest house. All he says is, 'Beds for three? No problem. In the cabins – tree houses, as you call them – or here in the house?'

'I will take the tree house.' Andreas doesn't hesitate. 'Immersive art.'

'Not boyhood memories of camp?' asks Nicole.

'Why not both?' He shrugs.

'April? Nicole?' Alan says.

'I'd like another night in the tree houses too,' I decide. 'I've come all this way and it's probably my last chance.'

'I think you are both crazy. I will have a nice warm bedroom and inside bathroom, please, Alan.' Nicole gives a mock shiver.

'Right you are. Two cabins, numbers three and four,' Alan says, 'and a key for the first-floor guest room.' That he hands to Nicole and motions to the stairs. 'You go and warm up. I'll show these two across.'

'That is okay, April?' Nicole looks uncertainly at me.

'Fine,' I croak. 'Fine. Really. Goodnight, Nicole.'

'Goodnight. If you need my hot water for thawing out, I will save some.'

I lag a little behind Andreas and Alan, letting Alan do his hosting bit. Andreas seems engrossed by the physical tree houses, and I'm sure he's already planning colour, perspective, positioning, whatever. When I get to number three, I go to scuttle up the ladder, muttering goodnight.

Alan is striding back to the guest house when I hear Andreas, halfway up his own ladder, say my name. 'April?'

I pause. So does he.

'She told me all about you. How she feels,' he goes on easily, in that casual way people do introductions. 'Do not feel awkward. The difficulty is not you, it's us. There will be a way. There always is. Now, relax, sleep, and at first light, I will paint.'

55

Troodos Mountains, Cyprus
September 1974

Mama was behind the curtains that cut the sitting room in half and hid the extra bed, where she was packing her bag to go away again. She'd asked Aunt Irini to help her, but not Elena, though Elena couldn't see why it took more than a minute; her mother had a satchel the same size and colour – black – that she and April had chosen for school last year.

'She doesn't need a suitcase, stupid,' Krista said when Elena had marvelled at how light Mama travelled. 'Isn't all our stuff lost? Lost at the airport, then in villages, then in trucks and cars and on walking through the night.'

That was true, Elena considered. The village aunties had altered their clothes to make big pockets, inside and out, but still Antony carried a rucksack.

Before she could say this, Krista added, 'Anyway, she has a gun. She can just point it at someone and say, "Hands up or I'll shoot," and they'll give her anything.'

A gun? 'Why would Mama have a gun?' Elena knew this was another of Krista's stories, shared with the giggly friends she'd made. They all thought guns were cool, the long, thin hunting rifles the local men kept and the handguns that flashed from holsters. Again, Elena opened her mouth, but Krista didn't give her the chance.

'And, daydream girl,' her sister's eyes gleamed, 'what's the betting that our mama isn't pregnant at all? I think her bump is a big hollow cushion and that's where she keeps all her secret things.'

That was nonsense. Elena had seen the gentle swell of their mother's stomach. It hadn't grown much yet, at all, only as big as a person who had eaten too much birthday cake and drunk too much soda pop.

'You will see, when she comes back with no baby,' Krista went on. Then she lowered her voice and whispered, 'But I do know who *is* having a baby and is hiding it. Shall I tell you?'

All these thoughts running idly through Elena's head made her realise that Krista wasn't back yet and she was never so late. Up here in the mountains the nights were black, the darkness like a solid wall punctuated only by small fires in the distance or truck lights sweeping though. Nobody was supposed to be outside the village perimeter when the light went. Elena hesitated while the clock ticked on, trying to decide if the bad feeling lodged inside her was about Krista or mostly about Mama leaving. Should she tell that Krista was out, maybe missing? Or would Krista be back any minute, like the bad penny Mama always called her, and furious with Elena for telling tales?

Mama and Aunt Irini must have finished. Elena strained her ears as they tiptoed past and then clicked open the back door that had a lock like a gate. They were going to smoke a cigarette. Quietly, Elena got up to follow them. She pulled back the edge of the dividing curtain, ready to slip through, when she spied Mama's satchel leaning beside Aunt Irini's familiar one on the sagging couch. Krista's words echoed in Elena's head – 'she has a gun' – making her hesitate. It wasn't snooping, was it, if the bag was open and she just peeked in? Her feet took her that way before her brain made a decision, but as she reached out to push the straps aside, it was something in Aunt Irini's tapestry bag that caught her eye—

'Are you a thief, daydream girl?' The whisper right into Elena's ear almost made her squeal. She turned it into a squeak by clamping a shaking hand over her mouth. 'Because if so, you're a very bad one because, first, you did not hear me and, second, you've taken nothing,' Krista went on.

'Sshh!'

Krista looked taken aback as Elena hissed her shush, grabbed her arm and pulled her back behind the curtain to the girls' side of the room.

'What?' she complained. 'Stop. You'll make me drop your oranges.'

With part of her mind, Elena watched as her sister thrust out her larger-than-usual chest, fished inside her sweater and pulled out two fat, round oranges, warm and clammy from Krista's skin. 'Thank you,' Elena muttered, taking the fruit.

'What?' Krista said again, suddenly alert. 'What happened? What did you *find*? Was it the gun?' She dropped the other orange onto the small bureau, not even noticing it roll to the floor and get stuck beside one of the dusty castors.

'No.'

'Oh. Then *what*?'

Elena sat down heavily on the edge of the bed, the other end from Sofia's sleeping head. She was crushed. Not angry or sad or mad or hurt – or maybe all those things – but *crushed* so that she had no individual feelings left. Krista, though, was almost dancing with curiosity and excitement. Elena's thoughts whirled: her sister wouldn't understand or care but she did love an injustice.

'All my letters,' Elena said flatly. 'All of my letters I wrote to April and Mrs Gale's class are still in Aunt Irini's bag. I saw the rainbow colours and read the addresses. They promised to post them and they didn't…' She could see Krista's interest deflating. 'They promised,' Elena said as fiercely as was possible in a whisper. 'They lied. They cheated. Now April will think I don't care about her and, like Mama said, she'll have forgotten me and got a new best friend. And,' it was an important afterthought, 'when we get back Mrs Gale will give me zero merits for not doing my summer homework.'

'We're not going back to England, we're going to Greece, remember, when we escape this shit place.'

Krista looked scornful but backtracked when Elena glared at her and said, 'I don't care. I want April to get my letters.' She did care but that was for another day. 'And they promised and they lied and cheated. What will April be thinking about me?' Elena thought her sister even looked a little bit impressed at her temper.

'Why didn't they post the stupid letters?' Krista wondered.

'I don't know. I know they had to get stamps, but the airport letter had the right stamp.' Elena was trying to find a gap in the crushing feeling to get an answer. 'And they pretended they had posted them.'

'You could ask Mama to take them?'

Elena's tummy squirmed. The way their mother had reacted to the letters earlier today now seemed suspicious. *That word again.* 'She won't.'

'I know!' The light of battle shone in Krista's eyes and she swelled in importance. 'I'll post them for you. That will show them.'

'How?' Elena was sceptical. 'Even if you buy a stamp and find a postbox, they'll see the letters are gone and we'll get in trouble.'

'Durr. They can't say you stole the letters when the letters are not supposed to be here any more because they posted the letters. See?'

There was sense in that muddle. Elena felt the first stirrings of happiness again, but what about the rest of it? She needed to think fast before Krista got bored and changed her mind. 'I could write a new letter to April and explain—'

'No more writing. That's not showing them. You need to

send those letters,' Krista insisted, pointing in the direction of Aunt Irini's bag.

It was the fight Krista liked. She didn't care about April waiting in England for news that never arrived. She didn't care that April would be thinking her best friend had just vanished in the night. She didn't care how they had made so many plans to go to the tree houses together... and that wasn't going to happen now, Elena thought bleakly. 'What if I send the first letter?' she said after a minute. 'That has a stamp on it already. I know! It's a big envelope and a short letter. What if I open it and put one of the others inside it?'

'Alright.' Krista sounded grudging but then slowly a smile spread across her face. 'I have a brilliant idea, Elena. You keep on writing your silly old letters and Irini will keep stealing them and we'll steal them back and send one each time. I know how to trade for things.' She looked smug. 'And stamps are easy-peasy.'

Then she jumped up and yanked back the curtain. In two strides Krista crossed the room, slipped an all-too practised hand into Aunt Irini's bag and drew out the slim bundle of letters.

'Here.' She thrust them at Elena. 'You have two minutes, so no daydream girl. I shall go out there and ask for a cigarette and boast that I just got home. I am sacrificing myself for you. You will owe me a lot of favours forever. If I scream that a spider bit me, you know that your time is up.'

As Krista marched off to do her worst, Elena's shaking fingers plucked at the letter she'd written in Nicosia Airport, which seemed like in another life. She turned it over and checked how easy it was to open – very. The seal on the envelope tasted so bad, and Krista had told her, with relish, that everyone knew cockroaches laid eggs in the glue, she'd only sealed the pointy bit. She eased it open and hesitated, heart beating, ears listening for Krista's scream. Quickly she found the Varosha postcard, removed it, and then, after making sure the string holding the rest of the letters together was tightened, she went and put the letters back in Aunt Irini's bag.

There was no need for Krista to scream. By the time she sidled back into the room and winked at Elena in the light of the dim lamp, Elena had put the postcard into the envelope with the letter and, out of a thought, taken last year's photo of the three sisters at the tree houses from her exercise book and slipped that in too. She'd licked her finger and run it round the envelope seal, sticking it down properly and wiping her hands on the bedspread in case of insect eggs.

'Done,' she mouthed, and handed it over to Krista, who shoved the precious letter up her jumper and into her vest where the oranges had come from. 'How will you...'

'Do not even ask me,' Krista whispered grandly. 'I have contacts. I am owed favours. I know things.'

Elena was on the cusp of sleep when a thought slid in. If Aunt Irini and Antony weren't going to send the letters, why was Irini keeping them? They should have burned them, one by one, lighting a match, using the stove, fuelling a campfire. An image of Irini swam into her mind, saying, 'They meant so much... I just couldn't do it.' The stone of betrayal lodged in Elena's tummy shrank just a little but she still prayed and prayed that one day April would understand.

56

At first light Andreas paints.

I know it's time when his all-night snoring stops vibrating through the still air and a watery sun creeps up from behind the water. I've lain awake, not from cold but from surprise, confusion, *optimism*. I've thought it before and I think it again, maybe I'll never stop, but on this island nothing and nobody is as I expect.

Except for the instructions, exhortations and manhandling that model-me has learned is Andreas' method. Nicole feeds me flatbreads, halloumi and hot coffee as he tells me to 'act natural' and takes photo after photo on a cheap Polaroid camera. I assume he'll want me looking out of the tree house window, over the sea, the twin to my position in his studio. He doesn't though. This time I'm halfway up the ladder and looking backwards, over my shoulder. It's even more uncomfortable than before, especially with the *essential* bare feet.

But Andreas knows what he wants. I dig deep, hang on to the rungs, and by mid-afternoon when I'm sweating rather than freezing, he's finished. The first I know of it is when he comes up the ladder behind me, plucks me off it and swings me down to the ground. Then he presents me with a bag of Wine Gums. I feel like a ten-year-old; imagine Krista doing that to little Sofia as Elena looks on.

'You ate them last time,' he reminds me. 'And today, there

is no Maratheftiko to celebrate. I must drive straight home and begin the real work.'

Half an hour after that, he's gone. It's just me and Nicole again, standing watching his brake lights disappear around the bend of the coast road.

'Did I just dream all that?' I say.

Salih's restaurant has become a home from home. I count in Jake and Kevin first, then Yiannis, Petros and, finally, Red, watching their faces light up as they see us waiting. Expertly, Salih moves chairs and tables with the minimum of fuss, and in seconds we're all seated at the terrace end of the restaurant, and they are all speaking at once.

'... several messages. Ape... ril, they are called *mobile* phones for a reason...'

'... you found the feckin' tree houses. Fair play to yous...'

'... so Andreas gets his second painting: English-April meets Cypriot-April...' That's Petros, of course. 'And you will have much to tell us, I think,' he continues with his widest, most innocent look: his Aunt Ana's look.

Everyone is looking expectantly between Nicole and me.

'Clever Nicole found the tree houses.' I state the obvious.

'As we thought.' Yiannis nods. 'A very special end to our small trip.'

'What's her prize, OF?' Kevin pipes up. 'You promised the tree house finder a prize. And don't say feckin' eternal gratitude or something poxy like that.'

'Cake,' says Red. 'Lots of cake. *And* eternal gratitude.'

Nicole's eyes twinkle. 'The finding is the best prize, but I will take eternal cake.'

Salih interrupts the nonsense by bringing a pile of small dishes. He watches with approval as they're passed around, and immediately calls to an invisible Defne for more.

With the food, I offer round a clutch of Andreas' discarded Polaroids. They're blunt, often out of focus or from odd angles, and definitely I feature in too many, but they show the tree houses alright.

'Yes, yes, they're exactly as Elena said,' I hear Jake chime in as if he'd been there in 1974, but this time it doesn't irritate me – much. Luckily, he's sidetracked by Salih at his elbow with something large and meaty. Yiannis shrinks back, and Petros mediates. He sees me watching and winks very faintly. I think of something else then.

'Yiannis?' I sort through the messy photos for the couple I took. 'These flowers – what are they?' As I hand over the snaps, I look at Nicole. 'It would be a lovely touch if they were orchids, but they're not, are they?'

Yiannis studies them briefly. 'I'm afraid not. My best guess is *Lapsana*. Wild, pretty and endemic but not orchids. Appropriate though.' He nods encouragingly.

'Yellow, the colour of friendship and positivity,' says Nicole.

'And of new beginnings,' Petros adds. He looks casually from Nicole to me and back. 'So Thia Ana taught me.'

Nicole smiles at him, total innocence. 'Speaking of Ana and the matriarchs, I think I should call Damaris,' she says, pushing her chair back, 'and check Andrea returned safely.'

Red, sitting close beside me, nudges my arm with his. 'Are you alright?' he asks in an undertone. 'Sorry I couldn't stop the mass welcome-committee family dinner.'

'It's fine.' I smile back. 'Really it is. Er, sorry you had to kidnap me.'

He lowers his voice further. 'Your message was cryptic in the extreme.' But his look tells me it wasn't.

With Nicole at Elena's tree houses. I think I've found me. That's what I said.

'I won't claim certainty or anything near it,' I say. 'But for now – well, I'm going to stay here. At Verena Bay, I mean.' I glance at Petros as I say it, hoping he'll still be pleased. He'd better be – he's the one who always said Nicole and I would get on famously.

Red doesn't let me dwell on it. 'Good for you. And in more startling news,' he raises his voice slightly, 'so is Jarlath. Staying in Cyprus, eh, Petros?'

'When you know you know,' Petros says. 'And our young friend knows.' I'm sure he winks at me. Infuriatingly.

'Jake, Kevin and I are heading back at the end of the week,' Red goes on. 'Yiannis and I have broken the back of this thing, and I swear, April, I will never, ever attempt to write a book ever again.'

'Do you know, I've never even asked what it's about?'

'The comparative metaphysical and literal histories, interpretations and miracles of transubstantiation in the Greek Orthodox and Roman Catholic doctrines,' he reels off.

'Fabulous. Um, very complex…'

'Yep. It's as likely to go on your bookshelf as your portrait is over my mantelpiece.' Then he lowers his voice again, 'You really are alright, April? You and Nicole? You and me?'

'Yes, Red. Absolutely alright. All of it.' I smile at him, 'I think. Maybe.'

By the time Nicole returns to the table, the dishes are cleared, I've heard all about Apostolos Andreas (no confirmed orchid sightings but an excellent hike round the headland) and I'm improvising a health warning in advance of Salih's cocktails.

'How are they, Damaris and Orestes?' I ask. Then, after a beat, 'And Andreas?'

'They are all fine. With the luck of Ganesh and Caerus on his side, Andreas is already home and painting furiously.'

Jake's self-obsessed ears perk up. 'Now, an artist in action, that is something I'd really like to see,' he starts.

I mouth, 'Erica,' to him and he stops.

Nicole goes on, 'Damaris is now threatening her own trip here to see the tree houses.' She fans herself in mock horror. 'And Orestes is his usual gentle self, holding us all together. Are we only gone three days? It feels longer.'

'What about a toast?' Red suggests, when the cocktails

– a Girne Grenade tonight apparently – arrive. 'A toast to friendship and family.'

'Past and present.'

'Love and life.'

'To finding the right road at the crossroads.' I smile at Red.

The toasts come as thick and fast as the cocktails; Petros holds up his glass last, and waits for silence. 'To Verena Bay,' he proposes.

'Verena Bay,' we all join in.

Then Yiannis, his drink untouched, speaks. 'April, Nicole?' he says. 'Tell us more about your adventures here.' His hand sweeps around the table and out across the bay. 'I doubt Apostolos Andreas can compete.'

Nicole and I look at each other, and for a brief second, time rewinds.

Where do we start? Or stop?

57

Troodos Mountains, Cyprus
Every day 1974

Mama was gone again. And then, so was Krista. Elena said nothing. She helped Sofia get up and dressed and have her breakfast and then they played with Jemima Long-Legs in the dusty yard. As Sofia giggled, the sun rose higher and Elena checked on the half-hidden cans she'd filled with earth for all the Turkish people who hadn't had time to take a little bit of home with them when they left their village. Then, busy imagining how pleased and surprised April would be when Mrs Gale finally read the letter to them, Elena settled down to wait for Krista to come back. Then, later, she would start waiting for the return of Mama and their new baby. She was good at waiting, Elena realised, really good. Looking up at the blue sky, remembering the world far beyond the mountains on this little island, Elena held on to her dream that April was reading her letters, and one day, she would come too.

All they had to do was wait.

58

I'm back in my original bedroom at the Verena Bay Hotel. Petros has space again and it feels, I don't know, too close to home, to be in Nicole's guest room right now. I open the balcony doors and look out across the moonlit water. The horizon is hidden at this hour, so the sea is like an infinity pool, and all that space, all that calm and cool space helps my thoughts stop racing and my mind run free. Behind me, on the dressing table, I've got three images propped up: Orestes' painting of Varosha, Georgios' newspaper shot of the tree houses and, snug in the middle, the little black-and-white photo of Elena and her sisters. The missing link is provided by Andreas' painting of me at the tree houses, and I'm going to get a snap of that, somehow, and make up the four. Superimposing 1974 on the present is the only way I can keep my promise to Elena to meet her at the tree houses.

Elena, I think, as my eyes roam over the water. I don't know where you are. I still don't know.

I've found snippets of you in the lives of Damaris, of Soussana, of Salih and of Marco. There are distant glimpses in the landscape of Famagusta, Trooditissa, the tree houses; a sense of you in this makeshift Verena Bay family of mine. But you – the *you* I know – doesn't exist any more and, like it or not, I understand that now. It was the right decision to come here, and I think I'm reaching some sort of a finish line but, these days, I have to say it's Nicole and the others who I see, who I want, waiting for me. How permanent it is, this my love affair with all things Verena Bay, I don't know. My mum and dad are here forever. Perhaps the hotel, Ana's home, really will become my home. Perhaps I'll return here to the revamped tree houses. Perhaps I'll contact Marco again.

Perhaps Nicole really is the grown-up soulmate that you were aged ten.

I don't know how much you know about music, Elena, or about Latin for that matter, but there's a musical term called a caesura. In English, it's a grand pause, a brief and silent break when time is not counted. That's where I am now. In a solo, the musician decides herself when it is right to resume – and that's where I will be.

Oh, Elena, is it too much to hope that your return to Cyprus was your own grand pause?

It may be offbeat, and wishful thinking – 'the drink talking', as Kevin or Jarlath would say – but I like to think, I'm *going* to think, that you've had a hand in this. Not just bringing me here, but in all of it, right from Ana moving in next to my parents and introducing me to Petros: fate, predestination, whatever. For sure, I would never be where I am now without you. And if I never see you again, I'll still see you everywhere. As you did when we were children, you've brought the colour into my life.

Thank you, Elena Zacharia, wherever you are.

Acknowledgements

Whenever I think of Cyprus I have to remind myself that neither Verena Bay nor the people who live there are real. But my many adventures on the island have been, as are the old friends I travelled with and the new friends I discovered there. The geography of the island in the book is generally true to that of 1974 and 2004, although I may have taken minor liberties for the sake of the story. Thank you to everyone who has made *Letters From Elena* possible.

Do you want to read more from Anne Hamilton? Here is a sample from her debut novel, *The Almost Truth*.

I've found him, Ali. But...
But.
There was always going to be a but, and it was always going to be a big one. Alina wondered which of the big three Ds it was: dead, disordered or dispossessed? They were an irreverent trinity that fitted most of life's 'buts'.

I've found him, Ali. But... Yes, that was all Fin's text had said, all it had needed to say. Alina wasn't sure when he'd sent it. Her phone had emitted a brief flurry of beeps, and then nothing. He wouldn't have expected her to call back. Maybe he'd even timed the message to fit her journey limbo, an attempt to let her get used to the notion – right. Eight years hadn't been long enough to do that, let alone eight hours.

A cry went up from the waterside, and Alina felt the cumbersome launch jolt hard against the harbour wall. With a choking waft of cheap fuel, the engines rumbled and shuddered, causing a flurry of last-minute passengers to race towards the deck, where willing arms were held out to haul aboard their varied baggage: babies and chickens, apples and cauliflowers, even a giant TV.

Alina adjusted her orna to sit neatly round her shoulders instead of sweeping the floor, and got up from the plastic garden chair plonked outside her so-called VIP cabin on the third deck. She leaned over the rusted rail and watched the commotion below her, scanning the crowd for the dozen or so children who had crammed themselves into the tractor and trailer. A wall of sad faces, jostling for a final cuddle or handshake; they were always insistent on coming with her and Mizan to say goodbye. There! She caught a flash of bright blue shirts: three of the boys, halfway up a cluster of palm trees, leaning over to wave enthusiastically, it being impossible to make themselves heard above the din. They gave toothy matching grins as Alina mock-admonished them with a waggling finger and pointed down to their less adventurous friends below. Alina blew some overly exuberant kisses that made the girls – Khalya, as ever, their ringleader – giggle behind their hennaed hands and dry their tears. *They* had worn their best red and gold party dresses for her send-off, and were a splash of sunshine against the grimy grey riverbank.

Half a year here in remote Bangladesh, half a year there, crossing from Scotland to Ireland. Alina had lived in all three camps for over five years now, and while she was no longer starry-eyed nor scared witless by her journeys into the Bay of Bengal, her arrivals remained exciting and her departures came with a pang. Now, watching her Great Uncle Takdir – who paused to look up and salute her – shepherd the boys and girls back to the orphanage that inside its doors was never referred to as an orphanage, Alina stifled a bigger sigh than usual. For the first time, her Irish grandparents, Miriam and Patrick, wouldn't be waiting at the other end of her convoluted journey. Instead, something else, something life-changing – *I've found him, Ali. But...* – was going to be there.

'Alina?'

She was using the end of her scarf to blot her tears when Mizan appeared at the top of the iron staircase, and his face stifled her sob to a grin. Mizan's horror of tears from females over the age of ten was well-documented and widely played upon.

'Don't bolt,' she said. 'It's just the engine fumes or something making my eyes water.' Which was true enough.

The scent of moist cooking oil, dirty water and gutted fish, horrible but somehow addictive, was, for Alina, evocative of rural Bangladesh. She turned her back on the river. 'You really didn't have to come with me, you know,' she told Mizan. The words were pointless, but it was a rite of passage to have the conversation. 'Especially when there are no children needing to come to Dhaka.'

'I know. I like to come. I enjoy this alone time we have.' Mizan was taking out a packet of cigarettes from his trouser pocket and feeling for a lighter.

'Right...'

He had the grace to look shamefaced. 'Okay. Also, I like to smoke, and where can I do this now you have banned it in the boundary and my wife has done the same in our rooms?' He held up the hand with the lighter in it in mock surrender. 'Yes, it is better for my health, and a good example for the children.' Then he looked at her, a hint of challenge. 'Still, I like our time alone more.'

'So do I, Mizan, but—' Alina wouldn't bother to disagree. Their exchange was nothing more than harmless flirting, a nod to the past. Her smile faded, as she remembered another, more distant, past: *I've found him, Ali. But...*

'Alina?'

'What? Sorry. I'm hot. I'm going to get changed.'

'Are you okay?'

'Fine.' She knew she sounded abrupt. She just wasn't sure she wanted to share the text message with Mizan. For all his machismo he had a perceptive streak – or maybe he simply knew her too well. Either way, was she ready to discuss it?

'I will bring us tea,' she heard him call as she disappeared into the small, stuffy cabin. Smoke wafted in through the open window on the other side, and she let it. A deterrent to mosquitoes, at least. This was one of the oldest, slowest launches: no air-conditioning, just a noisy fan with tangled, loose wires above each of the single beds; the obligatory, if old-fashioned, television set high on a shelf. There was a suspect blanket on a chair and a hairy cake of soap in the attached, unplumbed bathroom. Alina wasn't complaining. It was a square of private space. She only had to go down to the open deck, where whole families spread across the ground for the overnight sailing, to be grateful. And years back, on one of her earliest visits, she'd come face to face with the biggest homemade rat trap she'd ever imagined, and by morning it had been filled with the biggest, angriest rat she'd ever seen. *This* was luxury.

Darkness came suddenly over the Bay of Bengal. In the few minutes it took Alina to step out of her yellow and orange salwar kameez and into loose-fitting jeans and a muted long-sleeve top, the sun had become a mirror to the water. She left her long, dark hair loose and, winding her orna back around her shoulders, opened the door back on to the deck. Mizan was sitting on one of the battered plastic chairs, his bare feet up on the boat rail. His silhouette stood out against the lengthening shadows, and beyond him, across the water, Alina saw yet again the inspiration for the Bangladeshi flag – the red sun sinking below the green horizon.

Mizan was holding his phone aloft. 'Signal is gone. We are in no-man's-land for eight hours minimum.' He must have heard the creak of the door behind her.

Time suspended. A faint whiff of the forbidden – of possibility – hung in the air. Oh, nostalgia had a lot to answer for. But Alina felt some of her tension ease. Mizan was right: they were uncontactable for tonight. *You're the queen of compartmentalising*, she told herself. Enjoy the journey. *Worry about Fin and what he's found when you get home.*

'Do you know if Takdir got the children home alright?' A retired District Commissioner her great uncle might be, but he was first to point out that staff under him unquestioningly followed orders; twelve overexcited children, all but two of them deaf, were less biddable. Alina settled herself in the second chair and looked up to see Mizan nod.

'He is fine. They are fine. Safe home. He is staying tonight, to play Grandfather, while you and I both are gone.'

'He's always the perfect dadu.'

'Yes.'

There were forty residents, spanning the ages of five to late teens, living at Sonali Homestay, only made possible by Takdir and his family trust. They were ably cared for by houseparents, but Takdir brought stories and games, and sweets and treats for all. A night of being spoiled always helped them forget Alina would be gone for the next six months. *If* it was six months this time. Following the too-close deaths of her English grandparents, Takdir and his wife, Husna, were Alina's nearest relatives, and Takdir had asked Alina outright to consider a permanent move over.

'Will you come back and live with us now?' Mizan might have read her thoughts. 'Here is your home, Alina. Your uncle. Khalya. The other children. And, of course, me.' He paused and raised his eyebrows. Then added, 'Why not?'

Why not, indeed, with her own mother and father also long gone; did that make her an (albeit aged, well-aged, at forty-three) orphan, like the children she left behind? Takdir certainly thought so, but it was still a huge decision to make. Would relocating to Bangladesh mean going home or running away from it? Alina winced; she'd done that once too often, even if it had ultimately worked out well. Now, Fin's message had moved the goalposts again, but by how much she wasn't yet sure. Dead, disordered, dispossessed – maybe it all depended on which one.

'My Great Aunt Husna doesn't like me,' she said. Prevarication, but true.

'She doesn't like anyone. Nobody likes her.'

Also probably true. Alina sighed. 'There's Fin…'

'Your son, he is a man now. He can visit any time.'

It was all black and white to Mizan. All of it. He was still the only person in the world to refer to Fin as her son. Technically, he was correct, of course, and Alina knew from personal experience that families were more acceptably fluid, anyway, in South Asia.

She was still deciding how much to say when the rattle of crockery heralded teatime. The boy, he looked about ten, put the cups of milky, sweet tea carefully in front of them, glancing at Alina as he did so. 'Very boiling water, apa,' he said. 'You no get sick.' She smiled and played along, the foreigner commenting on his good English. The boy grinned and spoke Bengali to Mizan. 'Is she your wife?'

Mizan shook his head. 'She's my boss.'

Alina busied herself clattering a teaspoon. Mizan was stretching a point for effect. They shared the job running the Sonali Homestay, though Mizan lived there full-time. The boy looked disbelieving, as if he were being teased. 'Apa, speak in Bangla,' he challenged Alina, and when she did, he roared with laughter. When Mizan winked and tossed him a couple of taka notes, he skipped off and arrived back in seconds with a packet of cardamom-studded biscuits that he handed to Alina with a flourish.

'You look beautiful,' Mizan said once the boy had gone.

'I look foreign.' Alina indicated her clothes. 'Even after all this time.'

'This is what I like.'

They both knew that sometimes clothes *did* maketh the woman. Once in Western dress she was assumed a foreigner and people were fall-over surprised when she responded in – passable, mostly – Bangla. Changing dress was another travel ritual. Once on the launch, the first stage of her long journey back to Scotland, Alina began a metamorphosis from her Bangladeshi self to her Irish-honorary-Scottish self. More than that, for a few hours she reverted, outwardly at least, to the Alina who Mizan had first met, what, fourteen, fifteen years ago? It probably wasn't very sensible of them, she thought now, but it was harmless.

After a while, the whine of the engine distanced itself into white noise, and the night grew quiet. The boat's searchlight swept hypnotically over the river, highlighting an odd rowboat, duos of napping fishermen, or the startled eyes of cows under transportation. When deckhands, seeking any available space to stretch out their mats for the night, peeped over at Alina and Mizan, it was their cue to move to Alina's cabin, where they sat on a single bed each, the door carefully propped open, their innocence broadcast to prying eyes. Probably nobody aboard cared who slept where and with whom, but, as directors of a charity, they couldn't risk a whiff of rumour making its way back to Bhola.

'What is on your mind, Alina?' Mizan asked eventually. 'You are too quiet. You do not even abuse your sworn enemies, the mosquitoes.' When she remained silent, he went through a list of her favourite worries. Finances. Accommodation. Not being a 'real' Bangladeshi. The lack of enough signing interpreters. Whether Khalya was truly her niece or the daughter of the maid. How to keep rampant adolescent hormones under control in a mixed home...

'Do you keep a spreadsheet? Stop it!' Alina begged him, finally laughing.

'That's better,' Mizan approved. 'So, which?'

'It's none of those. Well, of course, it's all of them,' Alina admitted. 'Khalya, especially. She's of the age when her mother will decide marriage is a good idea, and whatever our actual relationship, I've no control—'

'But Takdir Sir has. These days, the law has. And that woman is crazy. No person will force Khalya into a child marriage, this I promise you.' Mizan frowned. 'Do you not trust me?'

'Of course I do. Idiot.' And she meant it. 'It's not that.' *I've found him, Ali. But...* The words might well have been superscript, hovering in the silence. 'It's home. Scotland,' she said eventually. 'It's, well, Fin has found his birth father.' Her voice seemed to ring out an announcement. It was a relief to blurt it out.

'Good,' Mizan said. 'Every man needs to know his father.'

'Even if it's not good news?' Alina shifted awkwardly.

'Is it not?'

'I don't know.'

'What do you know?'

'I... Oh, read it.' They could go round in riddles all night. Alina fumbled with her phone and passed it across to him.

'"*I've found him, Ali. But...*"' Mizan read the words, tried to scroll down the screen, then looked over at her. 'This is all?'

Alina nodded. 'It's the *but* I'm worrying about.'

'Of course you are.'

'I don't think he's being deliberately cryptic.' She went on as if Mizan hadn't spoken. 'He's giving me an early warning, time to prepare myself for – well, whatever it is. So it must be something big. You see?'

'Of course,' Mizan repeated. He fished for his cigarettes and put one, unlit, to his lip. '*But...* he is dead? *But...* he is a villain? *But...* he is uninterested to know his son?'

Alina, who had been nodding along, was startled at that most obvious one – why hadn't it occurred to her? *Because you're too concerned about what this news means for you rather than Fin*, an ugly but truthful inner voice spelled out. Was she? It was fifty-fifty if she was honest. Tears threatened and she blinked them away, impatient with herself.

Mizan swung his feet to the floor and sat facing her. 'My promise to you, Alina – that day, you still remember? Hmm?' He paused, needlessly. Cryptic to outsiders, it made perfect sense to her. 'My promise, those conditions, both of them still stand. Yes?'

'Yes.' Alina barely whispered it.

'Remember that, always.' He reached over and, unusually, touched her. He squeezed her shoulder and she held her breath. 'I would hug you, *but...*' She let it out. The smile Mizan gave her was rueful; she wondered if it was the hug or that he realised what he'd said.

'I am going to smoke,' he said. 'Right now, it is the littlest of all possible sins.'

Follow Legend Press on Twitter
@legend_times_

Follow Legend Press on Instagram
@legend_times